4

SHOOTING
IN THE
DARK

Also by John Baker

The Sam Turner series
Poet In The Gutter
Death Minus Zero
King Of The Streets
Walking With Ghosts

Other novels
The Chinese Girl

Visit John Baker at:
www.johnbakeronline.co.uk

SHOOTING
IN THE
DARK

John Baker

ORION

For Anne

First published in Great Britain in 2001 by Orion
an imprint of The Orion Publishing Group
Orion House, 5 Upper St Martin's Lane, London WC2H 9EA

A CIP catalogue record for this book
is available from the British Library

ISBN (cased) 0 575 07172 9
ISBN (trade paperback) 0 575 07173 7

Typeset by Deltatype Ltd, Birkenhead, Merseyside
Printed and bound in Great Britain by
Clays Ltd, St Ives plc

The city and places in this novel owe as much to the imagination
as to the physical reality. The characters and institutions are all
fictitious, and any resemblance to real people, living or dead,
is purely coincidental.

The earth is strung with lover's pearls and all I
see are dark eyes.

Bob Dylan

And he, repulsed, a short tale to make,
Fell into a sadness, then into a fast,
Thence to a watch, thence into a weakness,
Thence to a lightness; and by this declension
Into the madness wherein now he raves,
And all we morn for.

Hamlet

Vision is the art of seeing things invisible.

Jonathan Swift

For their valuable and helpful criticism, comments and insights I would like to thank Anne Baker; Michael Rose, Diane Roworth of the York Blind & Partially Sighted Society; Elaine Sommerville and Simon Stevens. Any inaccuracies or offended sensibilities are the responsibility of the writer alone.

He died on 6 January so it is not surprising that my epiphany happened on the same date. As with any sudden spiritual manifestation, this epiphany happened without my conscious participation. I did not go in search of it, but while I was busy doing other things it discovered me.

Science has been my passion and my life. I have been a troubadour for reason and rationality, and yet it is only now that I am beginning to understand the relationship between reason and intuition.

For the record, this is what happened.

I was in the library and I picked up a copy of Pascal's *Pensées*. This is not my usual reading matter. I do not remember having looked at this book before and cannot even be sure that I was aware of its existence.

I opened it at random and read the following:

> Memory and joy are intuitive; and even mathematical propositions become so. For reason creates natural intuitions, and natural intuitions are erased by reason.

Later the same day I came across the two women at the matinée performance of *Titus Andronicus* at the Theatre Royal. This wasn't entirely coincidental. I had suspected they would be there. They make a habit of frequenting cultural events together and prefer the afternoons to the evening. But the play was shocking. Surely it is the bloodiest series of sketches to have dripped from Shakespeare's quill? The horror was too much for several members of the audience who had to leave before the final curtain.

According to the programme notes, Shakespeare wrote it under the influence of Thomas Kyd's *The Spanish Tragedy*, which was one of the first revenge tragedies of the English theatre.

Afterwards, in the theatre bar, I watched the two women. I wasn't close enough to hear what they said, but I assumed they were discussing the play. They didn't stay long. And it was then, when they were leaving, that the younger one suddenly glanced over her shoulder, directly at me. And with a perfectly innocent-looking Campari and bitter lemon clutched in my hand I was visited by a *je ne sais quoi*. An insight of grace. A certainty.

It came together in a lightning flash, the reason behind Pascal's intuition, the blood and gore of *Titus Andronicus*, the woman's knowing eyes. It was all enclosed in the moment. And in that moment all of our fortunes were raised up into the heavens like a flock of geese winging away from a frozen lake.

ONE

S am Turner had a glass of water on his desk. He took a drink
and tipped the glass sideways, playing with the level of the
liquid. Cool, clear water. His mind tumbled back to the
times he'd held a glass like that in the past. Times when the liquid
had been deep amber; or the washed out violet of meths. Times
when the glass could have contained anything other than water.
Better if you couldn't see through it. Better if it was thick and
opaque so you knew it'd coat your brain with mud. Dam up all
the images. Hide everything you found impossible to face.

There was a tapping sound, faint; not in the outer office, but
further off, somewhere else in the building, maybe on the stairs.
Something rhythmical about it, like the introduction to a song.
The image of a conductor's baton came to mind, then a drumstick
on a long dry bone.

Sam took another sip from the glass, felt the liquid roll down
his throat. Business had dried up during the summer. York had
been flooded with tourists, as always, and a good percentage of
them had been ripped off. A few had been mugged and robbed,
mistakenly believing that Saturday night was for having fun. A
Spanish girl had been raped and murdered in her hotel room in
late July. But the perpetrator turned out to be a tourist himself. An
Australian from Byron Bay. None of these misdemeanours came
the way of Sam Turner. He read about them in the *Evening Press*.
That summer in York there had been rain every day, but the
current account of the Sam Turner Detective Agency had almost
withered and died.

The cash held out, though. Just. Sam hadn't laid anybody off.

There was a trickle of jobs through local solicitors and insurance companies, repo work, false claims, warrants to be served. Bread and butter work. Plodding, mind-numbing fare. The kind of stuff you handed to Geordie or Marie and they jumped for joy, their lights shining like beacons, volunteered to work overtime without pay.

Tap-tap, tap-tap. Closer now. Not quite as musical. A hollow sound to it, empty and desolate. He shrugged. Lots of music was like that. Some of the best kind.

This last month the trickle of work had turned into a stream. They were working two missing-persons cases and an insurance scam involving the arson of a country estate. Last week they had wrapped up a political corruption scandal that everyone in town had known about for years. Everyone in town, that is, apart from the local boys in blue, who were either blind or involved in some of the pay-offs.

And that wasn't the end of it. Sam was sitting at his desk waiting for another couple of paying customers to appear. Ms Angeles Falco had made an appointment for herself and her sister, Isabel Reeves, at 9.15 this morning. The old firm was starting to earn again. Big time. Looked like they'd have to invest in a couple of barrows to get all the money over to the bank. Maybe buy some new socks as well, on his way home tonight.

The political case had ended with Sam getting his right hand smashed in a police car door. A careless moment for Sam; and for the police inspector involved, one of those instances when revenge is sweetened by the public ambiguity of the act. On the emergency ward, later, Sam reported the injury as a physical assault, but the police did not pursue it. The deputy chief constable wrote him a short note which described the event, after an initial inquiry, as an unfortunate accident.

Tap-tap. On the outer office door. Sam checked his watch – 9.27. He heard Celia walk to the outer door and open it. There was an exchange of words and then Celia's footsteps bringing someone towards his office.

Celia's head appeared around the door. She had dyed her hair red again, which took years off her. She was trim and could use make-up and wear threads and jewellery like a professional. If you didn't know she was older, you'd think she was on the rosy side of

4

sixty. Never guess she'd spent forty years of her life as an English teacher.

'Ms Angeles Falco,' she said. She opened the door wide to allow the visitor access. The woman was twenty-seven going on thirty-five. From where Sam was sitting there was no sure way of dating her. With a tree or a horse you can be fairly specific. We know the age of the earth and the solar system, the stars and the universe. With most things we can say how long they've been around. But this one belonged to that breed of women who are adept at hiding all the clues. And when they're good at it, they're really good.

Dark curls lightly gelled. Tanned skin with a hint of the Mediterranean, or perhaps it was South America. The suit was simple, modern, out-of-reach expensive. MaxMara or Escada. Sam had never been a fashion expert, but his nasal system reacted to the kind of dust activated by money.

She was wearing designer shades with a price-tag that would feed a private detective for a month.

It was only after you'd swallowed all that that you noticed the other thing, the thing that had caused the tapping. The long white stick with the silver handle. And suddenly a whole host of preconceptions winged their way around your consciousness, and you found yourself up and out of your seat and going to help the woman into a chair.

Celia gave him a look and left the room, closing the door behind her. Sam shook his visitor's hand and apologized for not using his right. He went back to his chair and looked across the desk at her, realizing that he hadn't a clue why she was here. She'd made an appointment, but she hadn't said what it was about. Sam waited for her to tell him, but she didn't speak. Maybe she was mute as well?

'I'm in the dark, here,' he said, trying to grab the words as they came out, stuff them back in his mouth.

Ms Angeles Falco smiled. She raised a hand to stifle any apology that Sam might be contemplating. She held her head at an angle and looked towards him, perhaps slightly to his left. When she spoke it was without a hint of an accent. 'Yes,' she said, a mischievous tone to her voice. 'We're two of a kind, Mr Turner.'

Sam sat back in his chair and watched her, tried to make out if she could see or not. She moved her head once, twice, as if

5

listening for something. But she was reading his mind. 'I have some residual sight,' she said. 'If the light is good I can see outlines. At the moment, because there is a window behind you – is it a window or a light? – you appear to me like a dark smudge. Shoulders and head. I would guess your hair is cut short, but I'm not entirely sure.'

Sam laughed. 'Yeah,' he said, 'I'm a dark smudge in the mornings. Start to brighten up and fill in the details after lunch. By early evening people start taking notice.'

'You mean women.'

'Do I?'

'Oh, yes, Mr Turner. I may be blind, but my other senses are intact. You can be kind, and sometimes violent. I'm sure one could say many things about you. But the portrait would not be complete if it didn't take into account that you are an attractive man with a powerful sensual spirit.' She smiled and folded her hands, placed them on the expensive material of her skirt. 'You attract women. You may not make them happy. But you certainly attract them.'

Sam picked up a pen and watched her some more. He wondered which of her four remaining senses had told her so much. There'd been a slight touch when he introduced himself; she couldn't have got much from that. And she hadn't tasted him, not even one tiny bite. Which left hearing and smell. He'd had a shower that morning, what, two hours ago. Surely he wasn't pushing pheromones out into the atmosphere already. Maybe all of his personality was encapsulated in his voice?

'It's good to be flattered,' he told her. 'I could sit and listen all day. But that's not why you're here.'

'No. I was supposed to meet my sister outside, but she hasn't turned up. She didn't ring you?'

Sam consulted his pad, knowing it only contained a thumbnail sketch of a dog. 'Mrs Reeves? No, Celia would have mentioned if she'd rung.'

'I'll try her mobile,' Angeles Falco said, fishing in her bag. Her body tensed. 'That's strange. My phone isn't here. I must have left it at work.'

'You can use this phone,' Sam said. 'Or we could start without her?'

'Yes, of course. It's just not like Isabel to be late.'

'We can re-schedule the appointment for another time,' Sam said. 'I'm happy to play this any way you want.'

Angeles Falco bit her bottom lip. 'It was Isabel's idea to come here, Mr Turner. Someone's been watching her, following her, for the last couple of months. We didn't think much about it at first, but now the same thing is happening to me.'

It was understandable. She was a beautiful woman. Sam could imagine himself following her around for a couple of months. Maybe even longer. 'Start at the beginning, Ms Falco. I need to know everything, all the facts, and your suspicions as well.'

'You know we're sisters. Myself and Isabel. She is two years younger than me. Daddy was Argentinian and Mummy English, but we lived here, close to York, up in the Howardian hills. My father was successful in the soft-drinks industry.' She hesitated momentarily, a dramatic pause, indicating a moment of import in her story.

'Mummy and Daddy were killed in a road accident five years ago. A pile-up on the M6. Isabel and I inherited the estate. We are major shareholders in the business. We are comfortable. No money problems. Then, a couple of months ago, Isabel noticed she was being watched. It cast a shadow over her life. She's happy, having a love affair, getting divorced from a man who has made her unhappy for years, and she's making plans to move in with her new lover.'

Sam cleared his throat. 'Does she know who is watching her?'

'No. That's what we want you to find out.'

'Description? Male or female?'

Angeles Falco shook her head. 'We don't know. Isabel hasn't actually seen anyone. It's more like a feeling.'

Sam put his pencil down. 'I see,' he said. 'And the one that's following *you*, is that more like a feeling as well?'

She shifted in her chair, unsettled now. Her head moved from side to side, as if she'd caught sight of something out of the corner of her eye. 'It must be the same person,' she said. 'They didn't believe us at the police station. Oh, they said they'd follow it up, make sure the man on the beat checked our doors at night. That kind of thing. But I could tell they thought we were neurotic.

'Even my doctor thinks I'm paranoid. I wouldn't mind, only I've known him all my life. I've never been ill, not like that. Childhood illnesses, the occasional bout of flu, but nothing mental. I'm not paranoid. Someone is watching me. If Isabel says someone is watching her, then someone is watching her. She wouldn't make it up. We're not like that, Mr Turner. I know someone has been watching me for the last month and I'm not imagining it.'

Her voice got a little shrill there, towards the end of her speech. The eyes, if he could have seen them, maybe beginning to bulge? You set up in business as a private eye; you're really setting yourself up for anything that comes along. She wouldn't be the first crazy to come in off the street. Sam had sometimes played with the idea of changing the sign outside the office, so it announced him as a psychoanalyst instead of a private detective. Same kind of work in many ways. You follow up a line of clues, hope you find a crock of gold at the end. You know 50 per cent of the time it'll be the other kind of crock, but the guy who hired you is the one paying the bills.

There were good policemen and bad policemen, everyone knew that. Sam Turner wasn't a bigot. Hell, Sam Turner knew there were good policemen and bad policemen even though he had never, in his entire life, met one of the good ones. Same goes for doctors. It was in their interest to make you feel secure, like they knew more about your body than you knew yourself. They couldn't afford to let it get out that there was a whole lot more they didn't know about disease, that when it came to matters of life and death, they were just as mortal and fallible as the rest of us.

If Angeles Falco was fighting against the police and her doctor, it seemed to Sam that she needed a helping hand. 'I don't think you're paranoid,' he told her. 'You don't seem like the obsessive type. I can't promise anything, but I'll take the case.'

Her shoulders relaxed, she leaned against the back of the chair. 'I brought a thousand pounds,' she said, drawing a long white envelope from inside her jacket. 'Will that be enough to get you started?'

Sam blinked, edged up to the line and was first off his mark.

He took her down the stairs and she asked what was wrong with his right hand.

'Got it caught in a car door,' he said. 'It's not a hundred per cent at the moment. I'm seeing a physio every other day.'

'Ah,' she said. Just that one word. A vague smile played around her mouth, as if she was waiting for him to catch up.

Sam looked down at his hand, hoping for a clue. But nothing came.

Except a faint whiff of whiskey. She'd tried to mask it with mint, maybe a mouthwash, but there're some things you can't hide.

He watched her tap her way across St Helen's Square. The stick was long, came up to her nose when she held it against her. She refused a taxi, said she had some shopping to do in the town. The crystals of frost that had covered the road earlier in the morning had now evaporated.

Back in the office, Sam gave Celia the money in the envelope and watched while she opened it up. 'Should keep us buoyant for a while,' he said.

'I'll put it in the safe,' she said, fanning the notes. 'There are criminals around. There were bells ringing in the bank this morning. The place surrounded by policemen.'

Sam shrugged. 'What do you think, Celia? Is it as criminal to rob a bank as it is to start one?'

'Usury used to be seen as a crime. Now they tell us it's the only way to run the world.' She slipped the money back into the envelope and walked over to the safe. 'When I was a girl, we believed the meek would inherit the earth. Everyone thought that. It was taken for granted. Now it's the exact opposite. The people who inherit the earth are the cruel and the callous. It seems to have fallen into the hands of people who have no feelings, no heart. Overbearing people.'

'Hey, what happened to my optimistic secretary?'

Celia smiled. 'I'm still here,' she said. 'This must be the only office in town where everybody believes in losers.' She put the money into the safe and closed the door.

'Will you give the sister a ring?' Sam said. 'Isabel Reeves. See if I can see her soon as possible. Better have the story from both of them.'

'I'll do it now.'

'And d'you have JD's number?' Sam asked.

9

'Yes, I'm the secretary, Sam. That's my job.'

'Give him a ring, will you? See if he's free for a few days. I'm gonna need someone to help with surveillance on these two, see if we can find who's watching them.'

JD Pears was a crime writer, a poker player and a drummer in a band, a voracious dope-smoker, who had come to Sam's detective agency to do research, and ended by getting himself employed from time to time. JD's head was full of American *noir* slang, so he sounded like a gangster in a Bogart film. Sam liked having him around.

'You don't think they're paranoid?' Celia asked.

Sam shook his head. 'I don't believe in paranoia.'

'Another medical fact goes out of the window.'

He smiled. 'Oh, people get frightened, start twitching. Doctors call it paranoia, like it's something inside you. But when you feel like that, you're just sensing the uneasiness that everybody else takes for granted.'

Celia walked back to her computer, moved the mouse to clear the screen-saver.

Sam said, 'D'you notice any kind of smell in here this morning?'

Celia sniffed at the air. 'Can't say I do. No.'

'I mean me,' he said. 'Can you smell anything different about me?'

She took a step towards him, her nostrils flaring. 'No, Sam. Are you feeling all right?'

'Yeah. It was the blind woman. I got the feeling she might've got a whiff of something.'

'Maybe she did. They say that if you're down one sense, the others come in to compensate. If that's true, she can probably smell things a mile away you wouldn't even notice.'

'Think I'll just pop out for a new toothbrush,' he said, shaking his head.

TWO

J D watched himself in the mirror over the bathroom sink. He wore glasses with heavy frames, the arms of which disappeared into a thick growth of wiry beard and hair. He was forty years old and wore a threadbare suit which he'd recently had cleaned and re-textured. Under the suit he had a sky-blue shirt which he'd washed and ironed. He glanced down at his sixteen-hole DMs, black and buffed to a high shine.

He shook his head and the image in the mirror joined in. He'd scrubbed himself clean this morning, as he did every morning. There was nothing wrong with his clothes, except the suit was hurtling back towards limp. You know you're OK, you're a guy who cares about his appearance, takes pains with it. And yet there's this other thing in the mirror that always looks like a scruff. It was as if they were twins, identical twins, except one of them had a flaw.

JD thought maybe he should get a mirror like they have in the chain-store changing rooms. Mirrors back-lit with a series of filters to make you look bright-eyed and bursting with health. You look at yourself trying on a new sweater, and you never looked better in your life. You could leave the sweater behind and go back to looking like shit, or you could give the sales assistant your last hundred quid. Even while you reach for your wallet you know you've been conned.

He knotted a string tie around his neck and pulled his fingers through his hair.

His mobile rang and he plucked it from the bathroom chair, hit the talk button.

'JD Pears.'

'JD? It's Celia.'

'Yeah. How you doing?'

'I'm fine. Listen, Sam was wondering if you could spare us some time.'

'I'm on the brink of a new novel. I suppose I could put it off a few more days. What'd I have to do?'

'Mainly surveillance, but you'll have to talk to Sam. We've got a blind woman and her sister who think they're being watched.'

'Watched? Followed? So I've got to watch them as well, see if I can find out who else is watching them?'

Celia laughed. 'Something like that. Can you come in to the office?'

'Pronto, my dear. Soon as I get myself together.'

He put the mobile down and looked at the messy guy in the mirror. He took his glasses off and the image took a step back into a mass of pixels. Looked better for it, too. Must tell Celia that we don't use the word 'blind' any more. Some people are 'partially sighted' these days.

JD closed his eyes, and the scruff disappeared altogether. Must be weird to be completely blind. He concentrated on keeping his eyes closed for a couple of minutes. Listened for sounds inside and outside the building, the sounds made by his own body. Felt the lip of the wash basin, the subtle texture of the porcelain, the low temperature it maintained. He ran the cold tap and scooped up water, drank from the palm of his hand. A few drops went into his beard, found their way to his cheeks and chin.

When he was younger, still at home with his brothers, they had argued about which sense they would rather lose. 'Would you rather be deaf or blind?' Jack would say. 'Come on, you have to choose.' JD had always thought deafness would be worse than blindness, but he wasn't sure any more. The novel he was about to write had an artist who was going blind as its central character. The half-blind man was an essential eye-witness to the murder of his wife. JD relished the thought of playing with the metaphor of blindness. He had been researching how expressionism developed out of naturalism, and how the naturalists were insistent on getting the object down on the canvas in complete clarity, while the expressionists were more interested in observing it with half-closed eyes.

12

There was a kind of faith in expressionism, a distrust of the obvious, of the objective. Expressionist artists and writers wanted to use distortion and exaggeration for emotional effect. Like Hammett. He would write an expressionist novel like Hammett.

When he opened his eyes and put his glasses on, he couldn't hold the world still. It danced away from him. While his eyes adjusted to the light, the scruff in the mirror could have been someone else entirely, some thing, an angel or a devil.

THREE

I'm going to be quiet and remain hidden, and remember the first rule of a policeman: 'Never forget to keep your eyes open.'
She is a silly woman. She has no eyes, but neither does she have insight. She begins to suspect that she is being watched. For the past week or so she has felt my eyes on her. But she has no idea that my eyes have been on her for almost all of her life. How could they not be? Where else would I look for satisfaction?

I am the watchman, the sentry. I have kept my vigil, and will remain at my post until the scales are balanced.

We have to learn how to value a human life. People don't care about this. They say that they care, and the people who run the organizations that prop up our society, they say the value of a human life is the most important thing in the world. Politicians and churchmen, especially, always have something to say on this point. But they are talkers, propagandists. They don't believe what they say. They don't have a tool with which to measure the value of a human life. They haven't taken the time to develop, to invent a tool that would do the job. That is how serious they are.

God makes those judgements every day. Two people are on a motorway. They hurtle towards each other in separate vehicles, each unaware of the other. When one of the vehicles crosses the central reservation there is a moment, before they plough into each other, when the eyes of each driver make contact. They have never seen each other before. As far as they are aware, they have nothing in common. And a second later one of them is dead. We don't know why. It isn't because of a lack of seat belts or SIPS or air-bags. In our materialistic way we pin all our hopes on the

14

mechanics of the situation, believing we can avoid future occurrences if we understand how metal and rubber and plastics react in relation to each other and to velocity and mental stress.

But the answer to why one human life is saved and another taken away lies in the mind of God. God can look down on the people in those vehicles hurtling towards each other, and He can say the one heading north is worth more than the one heading south, therefore He will save the one heading north.

God is the one in control. He is an artist. The rest of us are characters He has created. This world is God's fiction, and He has created each of us to provide the narrative and the drive and the interweaving plots that make up His final vision.

The church doesn't know this.

Neither does the government.

They both believe that God is dead.

But I am the watchman, and I know. I can value a human life.

For example, take Miriam. I go in this tourist-trap on Pavement most days, buy myself an all-day breakfast for a few quid. I get two sausages, egg, bacon, hash browns, fried bread and beans. When I've had that I have a cup of tea. And Miriam serves me. If one of the other girls tries to serve me I wave them away. Usually they don't try any more, because they know I want Miriam to do it. And they know that Miriam would rather serve me than anyone else. Miriam belongs to me. This is not entirely of my own making, this situation, this state of affairs. When I first went to that place one of the other girls served me. I think it was Debbie, the one with long hair in a pony-tail. But Debbie never looked at me. While she was working there, in the café, she was always somewhere else.

I noticed Miriam because I saw her watching me. She'd give me a glance as she walked past my table, another one when she was coming back with dirty pots. And it wasn't just a look she'd give me, what she'd give me was a look that said something.

I'll tell you this as well. There is no such thing as sexual morality. Sex is just sex. Sex is two people or two animals, birds, fishes, whatever, that are brought together by a chemical rush. There's no morality involved. Morality becomes involved in cases of life and death, in social and personal conduct. Two people having sex, that's something else. God is not a Victorian prude.

15

He doesn't judge someone who acts out of perfectly normal instinctual behaviour.

She isn't a glamour girl, Miriam. That first time I saw her I thought she was about twenty, but it turns out she's twenty-three. All the girls in that place wear white blouses, and it isn't until you see them together that you realize how many different kinds of white there are. Miriam never gets around to ironing her blouse, so it looks as though she's slept in it. Anyway, she had that on. I can't remember anything about the skirt, I think it was probably nondescript. Black? What was most striking about her was that she had no breasts. She does actually have a pair of small pigeons, but that morning, what with the wrinkled blouse and everything, she seemed to have the chest of a young boy. She has short hair, curly, but the greasy atmosphere of the café makes it shine. And she has this weird jaw: her bottom teeth and chin protrude.

She's not ugly. I know she sounds ugly from my description. But she isn't. I wouldn't say she was beautiful, either. She's pale, though. Without make-up, her eyes are small, and her lips are the same toneless shade as the rest of her face. That's what I noticed about her that first day.

We have to take notice. We have to be aware. We have to watch. That is why He gave us eyes. That is why the elect are never blind.

For two months after Marilyn Monroe's suicide in 1962 there were over three hundred more suicides than would have been expected during that period. I know things like this because my research was directly concerned with the association between the media and crime. What specifically interests me are the images of violence portrayed on television and in films and the relationship between those images and the violent behaviour that is endemic in our society.

Many of my colleagues insisted that there is no proven relationship between the images and the reality, but that does not explain why so many more people committed suicide in those two months following Marilyn's death. We also know that when a major heavyweight boxing match is televised, reported murders will tend to increase by 12 to 15 per cent over the following three days.

Not all scenarios are as simple as the one on the motorway. Life is a complicated business. Life and death are as complicated as

16

heaven and hell. This is because we have free choice. We can be good or we can be evil. It's up to each one of us to decide. We can watch a child die, or we can decide to sacrifice ourselves so that the child might live. We can make those kinds of decisions. God will stand back and watch us while we make those decisions. He will not interfere.

He will hope in His creative mind that the child who is saved is of more value than the one whose life is sacrificed for the child. We will all hope that. None of us would like to think that a good man has given his life so that an evil child can live and grow into an evil adult.

But suppose something like that happened, what would be the reaction of those in power on the earth, the rulers and the priests? Just suppose. And don't think for a moment that it hasn't happened, because in this world fact and fiction are completely interchangeable. To you it might well be fact, but to God it is all fiction. Everything stems from an idea He had.

Miriam didn't have a boyfriend, so she was glad to get me. She'd had a boyfriend for a year once, but he got depressed and all the fun went out of it. She'd had a couple of one-night stands since then, just for the sex, but that's no way to live your life. With me she gets it regularly, and I never get depressed. She wants us to get married, and I can't think of any reason not to do it. We'll have to wait, of course. I've still got other things to attend to.

This isn't simply an animal thing; Miriam and I are on the same wavelength. We are spiritual pilgrims. I am an emissary, and she is my handmaiden.

Listen. The rulers and the priests would do nothing. They never do anything. Their function is to invent platitudes, to make us forget our responsibilities. They want us to work and to create capital and to believe that our duty is to serve them, and not our maker.

Actually, they are insane. We are ruled over, both on the material and the spiritual planes, by lunatics.

That is why I have had no choice in my life but to become the watchman. That is why I have to watch the woman and her sister with no eyes.

And when I have watched enough. When I am absolutely certain.

Why, then, the hand of the Lord will be with me.

17

FOUR

Geordie was watching Janet watching the television with their baby daughter, Echo, on her lap. Echo had been changed and fed and she was burping and farting gently, talking to herself and the world in some primitive language nobody had ever bothered to translate. Janet was not looking at Echo. Her hands were running over the child, and Geordie thought there must be a kind of communication going on between them. But Janet's conscious mind was taken up with whatever was spewing out of the television.

Janet had had ten hours sleep through the night while Geordie carried Echo around the flat. As long as she was being carried, Echo slept. But every time Geordie laid her down on the couch or in her cradle, she'd open her eyes and her mouth and her lungs and scream until he picked her up again. The result was that Geordie hadn't shaved or got around to washing his face or teeth yet. The inside of his mouth felt like shit. Janet had had a shower and changed into fresh clothes and she looked wonderful, like one of those impossible women in the posh magazines.

How did it happen? That was what Geordie was forever trying to work out in his mind. One day, when he was still a child, his mother had run off with a guy and left Geordie alone, and from that point everything had been a downhill slide. They'd taken him into what they called 'care', carted him off to an orphanage. For a while Geordie thought his elder brother would come and rescue him from that place, but his brother had signed up on a boat and was somewhere in South America. After he escaped from the orphanage, there'd been a period on the streets, then a spell in

18

gaol. Finally he'd ended up in York and Sam had plucked him out of the gutter and found him somewhere to live and trained him up in detective work.

The downhill slide had ended there, and since Sam came along he'd been on an up. First Celia had become a friend, and then Marie and JD and Janet, and now there was Echo.

So how did it happen?

Geordie thought it was an important question. Because the answer was that Sam Turner came along and offered a helping hand. That's what happened that made the difference. Just that. Nothing else. It all depended on one man.

Geordie thought that if it was possible for one man to turn his life around, to stop him being kicked from pillar to post and starving to death, then it was probably the same with governments and countries. They should put it on the TV, and in magazines, videos, tell people that they could help each other out, not be fighting each other all the time. Cut out the way people are always competing with each other, shove a bit of co-operation in there instead.

When he said these things to people, even to Janet, they'd nod and shake their heads and say he was naïve. And Geordie would say, 'Well, what's wrong with that?'

Janet flicked the television off with the handset and put Echo over her shoulder. 'I'm gonna take her for a walk,' she said. 'You should get some sleep.'

'No, I'm going in to work,' he said. 'I talked to Celia on the phone. JD's coming in, there's a new case with a couple of sisters, one of them's blind. And Sam's not much good with only one hand.'

Janet shook her head. 'You'll be shattered.'

'I'm always shattered,' he said. 'Just like you. I'm getting used to it now.'

Geordie and Janet both had six months leave from their jobs, so they could get used to being a family with a baby, do all the bonding work. But they took it in turns to keep their hands in; Geordie at the Sam Turner Detective Agency, and Janet at the bookshop.

'D'you think we're workaholics?' Geordie asked.

'No. I think we like the work we do, that's number one. It's

19

good having Echo and I wouldn't want to live without her now she's arrived, but it's good to have a job to get away from her at least some of the time, that's number two.'

'Yeah,' Geordie agreed. 'Horrible thing to say, but it's the truth.'

Venus, Janet's black-and-white cat, nudged Geordie's leg with her nose. Her black sister, Orchid, watched from her perch on the windowsill.

They walked through the university grounds together, around the frozen lake. Echo was sleeping in her pram, not visible to passers-by or the ducks that skidded on the ice. Janet waited with him until his bus came, and then walked back again with her daughter. Barney, Geordie's dog, looked back once or twice, wondering why he couldn't do the bus ride.

Geordie blew on his fingernails and remembered dreaming that he'd turned up Salman Rushdie by mistake. He'd been on a case with Marie, which involved knocking on doors, looking for a witness to a miscarriage of justice. He'd come to a house with a large oak door and boarded-up windows.

'Go round the back,' he told Marie. 'He might skip out that way.'

But the guy didn't even try to escape. He came to the door in a dressing gown and a night-cap with a long tail and a pom-pom at the end. Round spectacles. His cheeks were red, as though they'd been scrubbed, but his grey-streaked beard looked greasy and unkempt. 'Is it time?' he asked Geordie.

'No,' Geordie told him. 'I thought you were somebody else.'

Salman did a bit of a twinkle. 'Yes,' he said. 'I am most of the time.'

Geordie couldn't make out when the dream had been. As far as he remembered, he hadn't slept for thirty hours. Maybe he'd dropped off while walking Echo round the sitting room.

He got off the bus at Clifford Street and cut through High Ousegate to Parliament Street. The pavements and roads were littered with shoppers, seemingly normal, healthy people who had suddenly been infected by the Christmas bug. The spending fever hadn't got to Geordie. It felt to him as though there were still several weeks to go.

As he drew level with Feasegate there was a prickling sensation

20

at the back of his neck, and he turned suddenly. A large woman with two parcels, one under each arm, collided with him, and Geordie and her packages clattered to the ground. 'Holy mother,' she said.

'Sorry,' Geordie said, scrambling to his feet. He retrieved her parcels and sent her on her way.

'Great clumsy oaf.'

'I'm sorry,' he said after her. 'I'm sorry, I'm sorry.'

What it was, that prickling sensation, it was the feeling you get when someone is watching you. It was one of those psychic things he'd talked to Celia about. There were these people who could talk to the dead, and others who could read your mind, and there were young people who could make glasses shatter if they got mad. All kinds of things. Phenomena, that lived in the world. Most of it couldn't be explained. It was just out there, like the wind or a shower of rain. It happened, and then it passed on, maybe visited somebody else.

Geordie hadn't felt threatened. There was nothing that was particularly weird or scary about it. He had thought that somebody he knew was behind him, and when he turned he'd expected that he'd see whoever it was.

But a large Catholic lady had ploughed him down.

FIVE

When Marie arrived at the office, they were all there. Sam was talking on the phone, and Geordie and JD were locked in some deep conversation about drugs that make you sleep. Celia was pouring steaming coffee into their mugs, humming to herself, an old Burt Bacharach/Hal David number, 'Twenty-four Hours from Tulsa'.

'Like your hair, Celia,' she said. 'Maybe I should do the same?'

'I wouldn't,' Celia said. 'Wait until the grey hairs start arriving. Then you can have it any colour you like.'

'Something happening?' Marie asked, glancing at the men around the room. She took her mug from the counter top.

'New job, dear,' said Celia. 'Ladies in peril.'

'More than one?'

Celia lifted an eyebrow. 'Well, one in particular.'

Marie smiled, glancing sideways at Sam, still engrossed in his phone conversation. 'As in, a young lady in peril.'

'Keep going. You're on the right track.'

Marie took a sip from her mug. 'Sam interviewed her this morning, right?'

'No more clues.'

'OK, we're talking about a gorgeous young lady in peril?'

'Right,' said Celia. 'But there's still something else. You're warm, but you're not burning your fingers.'

'Something else?' said Marie. 'A gorgeous young lady in peril. That would normally be enough to get his teeth into. What's missing? She would be ... vulnerable in some way. She's an unattached, gorgeous young lady?'

22

'Yes, but you're still not there. And whether they're attached or not hasn't made much difference in the past.'

Marie laughed. 'Are we talking extremes here, Celia? Like an unattached, gorgeous, and far-too-young lady in peril with a built-in tragedy. She's handicapped in some way. A one-legged gorgeous lady?'

'No, you're not going to get there,' said Celia. 'She's blind, and she's got an exotic name, and she wears clothes to die for, and she's rich as well, I wouldn't wonder. She's all the other things you said, as well. I think I liked her.'

'And is she a possible soul-mate for the chief detective?'

Celia smiled wryly. 'Well, dear, they're all possible.'

'Especially the young and the beautiful.'

Sam put the phone down and came over to collect his coffee. He picked up the mug with his left hand. 'You talking about me?'

'Is there anything else in here to stimulate a girl's imagination?' Marie asked.

We were speculating about your love life,' said Celia. 'Doesn't seem to be a lot happening on that front.'

'There's the physiotherapist at the hospital,' Sam said. 'Seems like a possible.'

Marie and Celia exchanged glances. They both smiled.

Sam eyed them both, Marie first, then he passed on to Celia. 'I'm not gonna fall for this,' he said. 'You two trying to set me up with someone?'

'We'd decided you don't need any help,' Marie said.

'That's right. I don't. If someone comes along, you'll be the first to know. In fact, if past form is anything to go by, you two'll probably know before I do.'

Marie looked at Celia, and they both fell on each other, peels of falsetto laughter filling the office.

While Sam, sitting on the corner of a desk nursing his right hand, told them about his interview with Angeles Falco, the others grouped themselves around him. Celia maintained her position by the coffee pot, Geordie sprawled in a chair, his long thin legs spread wide apart. JD had moved towards Marie, but had pulled up short before he reached her. It was as if he sensed an invisible barrier which he was not to cross.

There had been a time, when they first met, that Marie had

23

fallen for JD in a big way. But he came with too many problems for her to handle. Marie's counsellor, and Celia, most of her friends, all said she was too fussy, that the perfect man never happened. JD wasn't that bad, he was kind and he kept himself clean, didn't overdo the booze. Most women in her position would've settled for him. But Marie wouldn't settle for anything. JD was fine, she could work with him; if it came to it, they could spend time together after office hours, but she didn't want to find herself sharing the same bed with the guy. No, please.

Unfortunately, JD still thought there was a chance for him. Marie had told him several times that he had passed out of her sexual landscape, but he couldn't grasp the concept. For a writer, the guy seemed to have a distinct difficulty with the language.

'You mean you don't want to screw me,' he'd say.

'Absolutely not. The only thing on offer here is friendship. Talking. Full stop. For physical contact to happen your life would have to be in danger.'

'But we could have a meal together?'

'Not with candles. And not in the evening. No dinner. We could have lunch together.'

He'd sigh. 'What about movies? Do we have to see movies in the afternoon?'

'Yeah, and on the front row.'

'You could have a word with the manager, maybe he'd arrange to leave the house lights on.'

'I want everything to be straight,' she'd say. 'There's never going to be anything sexual about this relationship.'

'You might change, Marie. After a while things could seem different.'

'No.'

'Why d'you have to be so rigid?'

He couldn't take it in. By making sex a no-go area, she was aware that it became a more attractive proposition to him. Forbidden fruit. If she made her body available to him, he'd probably be sniffing around other women, especially the groupies who followed his band. But that wasn't the answer for Marie. And, anyway she was already sharing her bed with a new boyfriend. David Styles, Steiner school teacher, probably the hairiest man on the planet. All she could do was keep JD at arm's length until someone came forward to claim him.

'The first thing is to cover Angeles Falco,' Sam said. 'I've yet to see her house, but I'm assuming it's secure, or we can make it secure without much trouble. So we won't have to watch her at night. But, at least for the first couple of days, I want her under surveillance all the time. That'll mean two of us doing, say, six-hour shifts.'

'Watching for someone who's watching her,' said JD.

'Yeah. We'll split that between us. You take the first shift, JD, then I'll relieve you, and Marie can follow me.'

'What about me?' said Geordie.

'Thought you was on leave?'

'I am on leave. That doesn't mean I can't help out. Especially with you having the bad hand. Me and Janet've agreed on that. That Echo's the best thing that ever happened to us, but we've gotta be able to get away from her some time. Sam, babies drive you crazy. They turn people into vegetables. What she is, she's kind of like a machine, and you stuff milk in one end, and before you can say Michael Owen, you've got liquid shit spurting out the other end. That's like 25 per cent of the time. Seventy-five per cent of the time she's in some kind of pain. It's either she's got wind from converting the milk into shit, and you have to find exactly where the wind is, and push it out of her; or it's because you haven't given her enough milk and cereals and stuff, and she's stopped digesting for a few minutes. And that gives her so much gyp you think she'll scream her lungs out. Then there's the other, say, 15 per cent of the time when she smiles and laughs and smells like she's had a bath, probably because she has had a bath, and you love her mostly because of that 15 per cent. See what I mean? You have to watch yourself or you lose the will to live.'

'That's 115 per cent!' said Celia. 'Impossible.'

'This's what I'm saying,' said Geordie. 'You gotta get away from her some of the time. You lose the power to add up.'

'So, you wanna work?' said Sam.

Geordie smiled. 'Not every day. We can't plan anything. But when I can, I wanna work. I got this idea I might stay sane if I work for you.'

'I'm assuming that these sisters aren't crazy,' Sam said. 'I wanna proceed on the assumption that they are being watched.'

'Have you talked to the other one yet?' JD asked. 'Isabel?'

'Isabel Reeves,' Sam said. 'No, Celia's been trying to get her on the phone, but she's not available. Her husband says she went out this morning. He doesn't know where and he'll give her the message when he sees her.'

'We don't really have the manpower to cover them both,' said Marie.

'No. What I'd like is for Isabel to move in with her sister for a while, then it'd be easier to keep tabs on them both.'

'Her husband will appreciate that,' said JD.

'The word is she's ready to leave him, anyway.'

'You think maybe someone's got a grudge against the family?' asked Marie.

Sam nodded. 'Could be. The parents were killed in a road accident. Or it might be something far less insidious. But either way we're gonna have to find out something about the family. We should interview anyone who knows them, and especially people who are close. Like Isabel's boyfriend. I want to know if they've got enemies. That means talking to neighbours. Maybe start with the people who live around Isabel's house.'

JD said, 'And while we're doing that we might end up talking to the guy who's following them. Tip him off that we're after him.'

'That's possible,' said Sam. 'We have to take the chance.'

Geordie snorted and his head fell to one side. Marie and the others looked at him. His eyes were closed and his mouth had fallen open.

Sam smiled. 'This is the guy who wants to work,' he said.

'Maybe he'll be able to put the odd hour in,' said Marie.

'I'm listening to all this,' said Geordie without opening his eyes. 'I don't have to have my eyes open to stay awake. And you know something else about babies? This milk, that the mother makes, it's designed especially for that one baby on that particular day that the baby gets it. It's designer milk, you know that? Like a mother rabbit, when she starts producing milk, she puts so much protein in it that the baby rabbits double their weight in the first week. That's why you shouldn't drink cow's milk, 'less you're a calf.'

26

SIX

Angeles was writing an article about retinitis pigmentosa when the detective arrived. She left the computer and opened the door to let him in. He had a firm handshake with his left hand, large bones. She guessed he was almost a head taller than her. He projected his voice, enunciated each syllable clearly so there was no doubt about his intentions. But he didn't shout, which was a relief. Angeles would have sacked him and gone looking for another detective if he'd shouted at her.

What was it with sighted people? So many of them thought if you were blind you must be deaf as well. A good percentage of them thought you were stupid, too. Since losing the battle with retinitis pigmentosa when she was seventeen, Angeles had made a study of the way the sighted world used the enigma of blindness, in its stereotypes, its metaphors and its prejudices. Much of her energy was now devoted to initiating the sighted into an experience of the world that most of them could not imagine.

He followed in her footsteps until they reached the large sitting room where she felt him veer off towards her computer. The screen-saver must have kicked in because it was playing a John Fogerty song, so low it was barely a rustle.

'That Credence?' he asked.

'No, later.'

'Yeah,' he said ambiguously, difficult to know if he had recognized the period, or if he would've been amazed at anyone playing John Fogerty. 'I'll borrow that sometime, take it home and play it real loud.' He spoke with a smile in his voice.

'Would you like something to drink?' she asked.

He began to protest, but she cut him short. 'It's really no bother. I keep coffee here, in a flask.' She showed him the large stainless-steel thermos, loosened the top and poured some of the steaming liquid into a cup.

'I'd love some,' he said. 'I didn't mean . . .'

'People think we'll burn ourselves in the kitchen. Either that, or we'll make the coffee with salt or scouring powder.'

'Sorry,' he said. 'This's new ground to me.' He turned his head away from her, touched the desk. 'Is this a Braille keyboard?'

'Yes, I was working.' She poured a little milk into his coffee and carried it over to him. 'I'm involved with an organization, a pressure group. We campaign against discrimination, work on rights issues.'

'You produce a magazine?'

'Not me. I write for it, but I'm not the editor.'

'People who work for pressure groups sometimes make enemies,' he said. His voice was deep with a barely discernible vibrato which set up a wandering echo within her, caused a momentary constriction in her throat.

'We have disagreements,' she told him. 'Some blind people don't want to rock the boat, they accept whatever crumbs the sighted world deems fit to leave at the table. We discuss such things, we argue about attitudes.'

'But you're not militant?'

'Militant.' She thought about the word. It was not one she would normally associate with herself. It conjured up an image of a woman with a Kalashnikov. 'No,' she said. 'We aren't militarists.'

'But not pacifists, either?' he said.

'We're reformers, Mr Turner. We're not violent. The blind have made certain gains in the last few years. If you're very determined, it's possible to be blind and independent. The organization I belong to defends the rights we have won and does what it can to improve our lot. Not long ago, the destiny of a blind person was to sell matches on a street corner. We are not prepared to go back to that. We are not Uncle Toms, but neither are we terrorists. If we leave out armed combat, I suppose you could describe us as a militant reformist organization. What are you getting at?'

'Have you heard anything from Isabel?'

28

'No. It's not like her to go away without telling me.'

'Are you worried?'

'Yes, but I think she'll get in touch today.'

'I hope so,' said Sam. 'Listen, you tell me that someone is watching you. I need to know if anyone has a motive to harm you. If you've upset someone. From what I hear, you belong to a bunch who don't believe in keeping their light hidden under a bushel.'

'You think I'm being followed by a blind man?'

'I didn't say that. I'm looking for motives.'

'Because it may've escaped your attention, Mr Turner, but it wouldn't be easy for someone without sight to follow me around. Unless, of course, this is one of the fabled blind men who, when he went blind, immediately found his other senses gained superhuman proportions. His hearing is so sensitive he can hear the fleas on his dog, and he can sniff out a drop of Rochas Tocade behind a girl's ear from the other side of the street.

'OK, I might well have upset someone in the blind community. It's just possible that I could have upset someone with a psychopathic personality. A dormant, sleepy blind man, who has now been roused into murderous insanity by my militant reformism. But I don't see how he's going to have much luck stalking me.'

Sam Turner was quiet. He walked over to the nest of tables where she kept the liquor bottles. There was the rustle of cloth as he bent to inspect them: whiskey, vodka, Spanish brandy. Then he said, 'Do you ever listen, lady?'

Usually she would have asked him to leave at that point, but she held back. The man was uncouth and insensitive. A typical sighted male, the kind of man who grabbed you and pushed you across the road whether you wanted to go or not. Someone who suddenly discovered he could do a good deed and leave you stranded and disoriented in the middle of town. 'I'm listening, Mr Turner,' she said, and caught the after-taste of that superior tone that had lurked around her vocal cords most of her life, returning time after time, no matter how often she thought she had banished it for good.

'That's the first thing,' he said. 'Nobody calls me Mr Turner. The name's Sam, take it or leave it. And seeing we're hitting it off so good, I don't suppose you'll mind me calling you Angeles, though I might be tempted to shorten it from time to time.

'The second thing is, I never met anybody who was blind before, and I'm lost on the protocol. I'm gonna say the wrong thing every so often, and you're just gonna have to swallow it. I try to take people at face value, and give them as much rope as I can. Don't like it when people stereotype me, and so I try not to do it back. If I fall for the blind stereotypes, you can pick me up on it, and I'll learn where I can go and where I can't. And if you read me wrongly, I'll sure as hell come down on you like a ton of bricks.

'You know more about blind people than me, you know what it feels like to be blind, and I can only guess at it. But I know more about my own game than you do. I know that if someone is following someone else around, then they usually have a good motive for it, and it's my job to discover what that motive is.

'I wasn't suggesting that a blind man was stalking you. But you might have upset a blind man and his friend who has perfectly good eyesight. Whatever. I don't have answers at the moment. At this stage we have to take all possibilities into consideration. Then we start eliminating them until there's only one left. You wanna play or not?'

While he had been talking Angeles had moved back to the table and poured herself more coffee. Now she held the thermos out to him, and he came to her and took it. She listened as he trickled coffee into his cup. 'Is there enough?' she asked.

'I think you know exactly how much there is.'

'I was being polite.'

'You wanna play or not?'

'What if I call you Mr T?'

'That kind of thing makes me militant.'

'Sam, then. But my name is Angeles. If you shorten it, I'll spit.'

'Deal.'

She didn't answer. She felt him move away from her, back to the desk where the computer was still humming away to itself. He was fascinated and frightened by Braille. He knew it was saying something, but he'd never know what it was.

'Oh, yeah,' he said. 'A couple of other things. You drink spirits during the day, you're gonna end up in trouble. And don't feel like you have to apologize. I'm used to people insulting me.'

Nice house. Everything neat in there. Nothing out of place. Sam made a pot of tea in the kitchen. Checked to see he'd put everything back exactly where he found it. Went outside to have a look at the swimming pool, wondered if it was heated. *You kidding? This is England.* Remembered to lock the back door again when he came inside.

Upstairs was the same. Everything in its place. There was nothing thrown on the floor. Not one single object.

The carpets didn't show it, but it felt as though there should have been tracks worn into them, along the regular routes she took. If she hadn't been blind and lived in that place, you would have thought she was obsessive. But maybe she was obsessive, could be that was what blindness did to you.

He stopped himself there.

OK, leave aside the stereotyping. Blind people are just people who're blind. Some of them'll be obsessives, but there'll be scatterbrains among them as well. Some blind people probably live in houses where they can't find anything, their clothes are all over the floor, every time they get out of the chair they fall over and break a bone. When they go outside they get lamp-posts running into them, post-boxes; and dogs and cats and street kids get tangled in their legs.

And some of them'll drink.

This is a woman who looks good. She makes no secret of the fact that she finds him attractive. Ignore the deep irony there; just let it go past. She's into some kind of militant wing of freedom and independence for the world's unsighted, tinged with feminism. She is completely blind at night, and during the day she can see shadows in a blinding snowstorm. She's capable of losing her cool and spitting like a snake. She wears high-fashion gear, expensive threads, which would suggest taste as well as money, except this afternoon she is wearing a bra with false nipples. How is he supposed to read that?

There is someone following her, watching her. Someone unknown. And now her sister has gone missing.

Could be a madman, someone burning with passion. The flames of his rage fed by a storehouse of frustrated love.

She was trying to figure out how to program her new mobile when he came back from his tour of the house and garden. He looked

31

over her shoulder, listening to the digital voice that explained which buttons to push for redial, how to store numbers. 'This specially designed for the blind?'

'Yes. It's new. I think my other one must've been stolen.'

'From the house?'

She shook her head. 'I was jostled in the street,' she said. 'The day before yesterday. The man must've taken it out of my bag. Anyway, it's gone.'

'Is this an occupational hazard?'

'Quite the opposite,' she said. 'Most people are over-solicitous.'

He was quiet for a moment. 'You work out?' he asked.

'I keep fit,' she told him. 'I don't use a gym.'

'You go walking? Jogging?'

'Why do you ask?'

'I'm interested,' he said. 'Your calf muscles are hard, well developed, and your neck is strong. Most of the time you're working in an office, you sit in front of a computer, so I wonder how you keep yourself trim.'

'Trim,' she said, feeling the word's contours, letting it spill from the tip of her tongue. She gave it back to him. 'Trim?'

'Something wrong with that?'

'Am I under observation?'

'Hell, no,' he said. 'I was just looking, I didn't mean . . .'

'It's all right,' she told him. 'I'm not offended. Suddenly we're talking about my body. I was . . . surprised.'

He blew a long stream of breath between his teeth.

'Really,' she said. 'I'm not offended. I've got the pool. I use a public baths to swim lengths; I ride a horse and a bicycle. I've got an aerobics step and a small trampoline upstairs. I do all those things, and I've got a sauna.'

He didn't respond immediately. She listened to the silence between them, his shallow breathing.

'Yeah,' he said. 'That explains it, why you're so trim.'

There it was again.

'And you?' she said. 'When did you stop smoking?'

'Some years back,' he said. He didn't ask her how she knew he'd been a smoker, if she'd heard it in his breathing, the damage to his vocal cords. 'I would've thought riding a bike was dangerous if you can't see where you're going.'

'I don't ride in traffic,' she said. 'And I need a sighted guide. But it's good fun, one of my favourite things.'

'You mean like a tandem?' he asked.

'No, I've got my own bike. I need to put my hand on a sighted rider's shoulder. It's like walking, only faster, and there's more of a thrill to it.'

'I've got a bike,' he said.

She waited, but he didn't take it further.

'Is that an offer?' she asked.

'Yeah, some time. Whenever you want.'

'Thanks. I'll bear it in mind.'

'Is there anything you don't do? You don't drive a fast car, anything like that?'

There was humour in his voice. Restrained, but it was there. 'Roller skating,' she said. 'I like that, but it's not really a fast car.'

'Skiing?'

'I've tried it,' she said. 'In Italy, but I never got off the beginners' slopes.'

'Sounds better than me,' he said. 'I never got off my ass.'

She laughed with him.

'What else is there?' he said. 'Ice skating?'

A tremor went through her.

'I've done it again,' he said. 'What'd I say?'

She fought to control her breathing, mastered it quickly, but could only speak in short sentences. 'Nothing. It's all right.'

'C'mon. What'd I say?'

'Ice skating,' she said quietly. 'It's the one thing I can't face.'

'No big deal,' he said. 'You do the things you like, the rest you leave to the other guys.'

She went inside herself. She didn't tell him about the couple of times she'd been on the ice. How she'd sat there and screamed until they'd carried her back to dry land.

SEVEN

Sam had never been to Skewsby, so he drove out to Malton first. Put a few extra miles on the clock, but the Montego had already done 50,000, so it was past complaining. There were still leaves on some trees, but most of them were skeletal now. The sun had been strong enough to chase the early morning frost away, but had spent itself and was pale, hanging low in the sky.

He stopped briefly in Malton, parked by the railway station, took ten minutes to walk around the market place. He'd done it before, three or four times, fascinated by the lack of identifiable life forms. A red-nosed toff dressed from head to foot in checks came out of the Green Man. Sam shot him dead, but the guy didn't notice, went on to his next drink with a neat hole between his eyes, tiny trickle of blood running into his eyebrows. Next time Sam felt like dying, it wouldn't be a problem: he'd come here. Wouldn't take long.

But compared to the tiny village of Skewsby, Malton was like Belgrade on a Saturday night.

There was a sharp hill for a couple of miles before the declamatory landscape flattened out for long enough to build a main street and a few houses. If there was a shop there, it wasn't drawing attention to itself. The place looked as though it had never recovered from Dutch elm disease.

Sam found the house where Angeles' sister, Isabel, lived with her husband. A reconstituted building, parts of it looking like authentic Elizabethan, but the bulk of it composed of twentieth-century materials. It wasn't a big place; Sam guessed three or four bedrooms, a couple of baths. The front door was stained oak, and there was a fake bell-pull, which chimed electronically.

Quintin Reeves looked like a young cabinet minister. He was soft and overweight, and came with a prepacked facial kit of twinkling eyes, pink complexion and silky hair gone silver grey at the temples. He smiled broadly and extended his hand, stood aside so that Sam could come inside the house, get out of the cold morning air.

Sam sighed. He'd been here before, with this kind of guy, really difficult to pin down. Quintin Reeves was the type, he'd ask you to give him a tenner for two fives; and you'd give him the tenner and look at the two fives, examine them minutely. They'd have the little strip of metal in them, and there'd be the watermark. They'd look and smell and feel like genuine fives. You'd bet your life on them being kosher. But at the same time you'd never shake the feeling that the guy was ripping you off. You wouldn't know how he'd done it, but you'd have lost something in the transaction and he'd have made a killing.

He was wearing a white shirt with those expandable bracelets that keep the sleeves from falling down, midnight-blue trousers with creases to cut bread with and a silver-grey tie with a knot that looked like a machine had tied it. It was time for an epiphany and something akin to bells ringing occurred in Sam's consciousness. He knew suddenly and certainly that the guy never appeared anywhere without a tie. You wanted to catch this man without a necktie, you'd have to sleep with him. Quintin and his ilk were one of the main reasons Sam Turner believed in bloody revolution.

In the living room the carpet was white and the pile came up to Sam's armpits. Could've drowned in it if he wasn't a survivor.

'Sam Turner, isn't it?' the man said. 'Quintin Reeves. I spoke to you on the phone.'

'Yeah. Good of you to see me.'

'How could I refuse when you're retained not only by my wife, but by my sister-in-law as well?' A thin and begrudging smile creased his features. The smile wasn't frequently resorted to by this man. Sam guessed he allowed himself one a month, sometimes two.

'I have a confession to make,' Reeves said. 'I promised I'd answer your questions, and I will. I'm a man of my word. But I wanted to meet you face to face because I'm worried about Angeles.'

35

'But not about Isabel, your wife?'

'Isabel too, but in a different way.'

'Yeah, Angeles's under some pressure.'

'Precisely, Mr Turner. You must be aware that she's letting her imagination run away with her?'

Sam shook his head. He hadn't got that impression. He'd talked to a woman who was facing up to it. She was looking for help along the way, but she wasn't cracking.

Reeves folded his hands and leaned forward in his chair conspiratorially. 'You haven't known her long, Mr Turner. Angeles isn't as strong as she'd have you believe. Oh, I don't think she's going to crack up. I certainly hope not. She's had delusions before, and I'm sure she'll have them again. What I'm concerned about is that she isn't taken advantage of. What are your fees, Mr Turner?'

'You think I'm charging her over the odds?'

'Not intentionally, no. But anything my sister-in-law pays for an investigation into something she's imagined would be over the top.'

'If I'd've thought that was true, I wouldn't have taken the case.'

Reeves clapped his hands together, but not with enough enthusiasm to make a sound. 'You're a moral man, Mr Turner. I don't want to take this any further. I only needed to tell you what was on my mind, to share it with you. I've got one more thing to say on the subject. After a few days, a week maybe, you will no longer be so sceptical about my comments. When that time comes, I hope you'll see that to prolong your investigation will not be to Angeles' benefit. That her general health will be improved if her fantasies are not given free rein.'

'If I arrive at that decision,' Sam said, 'I'll tell my client how I feel.'

'That's all I ask,' said Reeves. 'And I'll see to it that you aren't out of pocket. I and my wife are the only family that Angeles has, Mr Turner. She would have you think otherwise, but she does need looking after a little.'

Sam eyed the guy squarely. 'My business is with Ms Falco. Not with you or anyone else, Mr Reeves. If I end up out of pocket, I'll chase her for it or take the loss.'

Reeves nodded. 'Of course. Forgive me. I'm something of a

clodhopper. When you're touched by tragedy, you sometimes become his student.'

'Tragedy. You refer to Isabel?'

'Yes, Isabel, my wife.'

'Do you know where she is, Mr Reeves?'

'No, but I've a good idea what she'll be doing. It'll be a young man with a big dick and a surfeit of energy.'

'You knew she was having an affair?'

Reeves laughed ironically. 'I don't remember a time when she wasn't.'

'But I understood that her present affair was serious. That she was in the process of leaving you.'

'All of Isabel's affairs are serious. But not so serious that she'll get around to leaving me. She needs the illusion of being in love. She flits from lover to lover in the same way that a bee flits from flower to flower. She takes what she wants, and moves on. I accepted the situation long ago. Had affairs of my own from time to time. Ours is a modern marriage, Mr Turner. We are both errant, but we know which side our bread is buttered on.'

'And her boyfriend, the present one, is no different to the others?'

Reeves shook his head. 'They're going through the making-plans stage, swearing undying devotion to each other. But they haven't got to the point where she has to make the actual decision. Once that time arrives, Isabel will back out. If she hasn't already.'

'D'you know why she's gone away?'

'She thinks she's going blind. It may well be true. There's this wretched disease they have. Retinitis pigmentosa. Hereditary. She's seen what it's done to Angeles, and she can't face the same thing happening to her. I think it's been playing on her mind, she'll have gone away with her boyfriend.'

'Does she think she's being watched?'

'If she does, she hasn't said so. I think if Isabel was being stalked in any way, she would have mentioned it to me. We don't live in each other's pockets, as I've said. But we are married.'

Time to go. Sam got to his feet and said goodbye. He blazed a trail through the carpeting to the front door. It was true and he'd always known it: the chain of wedlock is so heavy that it takes two to carry it, sometimes three.

When he left the house, Sam passed a pond in the garden, its surface frozen hard. Someone had broken the ice with an iron bar that leaned against the fence, but it had frozen over again. Now the surface was ridged, the fresh ice welded around chunks of the old, forming peaks and an opaque natural patchwork which hid everything beneath it.

It triggered a memory which took time to surface, and Sam hesitated, watching the crystal patterning to give it time. Angeles' response to his question about ice skating. Other physical activities she'd been open about, glad of the chance to show that she was fit and able, but as soon as he mentioned ice skating she'd clammed up.

Sam turned towards the house, thinking to ask Reeves why she would do that. But he stopped and made his way back to the car. He'd had enough of the guy for one day. So the lady didn't like ice. People are allowed to have their little phobias. Even private detectives have no-go areas, subjects they'd prefer not to talk about.

It wouldn't leave him alone, though. There was a frozen pond in his mind, and the picture of the lady sucking in her breath when he mentioned ice skating. Had to shake his head real hard to get it out of there.

But Quintin Reeves' last words carried on working in Sam's head as he drove back to York. Sam had had more partners than his own sense of credibility allowed. It's always possible to make a fundamental mistake in the choice of a woman, and with more or less average luck at this point in history, you could get it wrong twice. But Sam Turner, if he had the space and thought really hard about it, had set himself up with almost as many partners as the fingers on his hands.

Some of them were dead, and others had walked off into the distance. A couple of them he'd abandoned for what seemed like good reasons at the time. And there were two – or was it three? – he couldn't immediately remember their names.

Not a good record. But one he couldn't do much to change. Usually he'd lie about it. If it came up in conversation, he'd make reference to 'my first partner' or 'my second partner', but he never got around to talking about his 'eighth partner'. Christ, people would think he was Bluebeard.

He felt better about it at the moment, because he hadn't been involved with a woman for nearly twelve months. Since Dora died. A pragmatist, Sam had dealt with the problem of his emotional life in the same way he had dealt with his alcoholism. Abstention.

The blind woman had picked up on it. He couldn't remember her exact words, something about doubting if he made his women happy. What was it with her, anyway? Was she some kind of seer? No one had ever before suggested that Sam might have a fundamental flaw. Except Sam himself, who'd always suspected it.

There was always the chance, of course, that Reeves was right, that she imagined things. Sam didn't think so, but there had been times in his own life when he had lived with visions stoked by booze.

He liked thinking about Angeles Falco. Putting her image together inside his head. It was warm and comforting and exciting at the same time. He liked the ambiguity of her vulnerability and fierce independence. He'd once or twice fallen for weak women, kittens who needed constant attention, and known suddenly, just after it was too late, that he would never manage to carry them.

But that wouldn't happen again. Next time he'd . . . refuse the drink. Find a good book. Eat an apple.

'You ever read Descartes?' JD said, when Sam had climbed into the passenger seat of his van.

'*Cogito ergo sum*?'

'That's the guy, yeah.'

'What about him?'

JD's van was in the middle of the parking lot outside the Haxby Road offices of Falco's soft-drinks factory. He had a camera with a large zoom, a pair of binoculars, two A4 notepads and a selection of different coloured pens. 'I was thinking,' he said. 'That business about "I think therefore I am", it must've made people insecure.'

'They wanted to burn him at the stake,' Sam said. 'Guy must've got up their noses.'

'Theologians. Sensitive crowd at the best of times. They'd have had him as well, if he hadn't escaped to Sweden.'

'Dunno,' said Sam. 'I know about *cogito ergo sum*, and that he wasn't the flavour of the month, but I don't understand why.'

39

'We're talking seventeenth, eighteenth century here. Everybody assumed that they lived in an ontologically consistent universe. There were problems of life and death, people died with horrendous diseases and sometimes starved, but they all felt good about themselves. They knew who they were, and they didn't have any doubts about their place in the world. About being. They were absolutely secure: God was in the heavens, the king was in his castle, and the poor man was at the gate. There were squabbles occasionally, know what I mean? But there wasn't any really serious angst, not concerning the self. Psychoanalysis hadn't been invented yet, because there was no need for it. The only people who were in real mental anguish were lunatics, heretics: a tiny minority of the population.

'Then Descartes comes along and lays this "I think therefore I am" thing on them, and there appears a tiny crack in the known universe. Suddenly, just for a moment, there is the possibility of an evil genius running the world, and we catch a glimpse of this monster through the chink made by those two words "I think".'

'You're losing me,' said Sam.

'No, hang in there. What happened was that people ceased to be people. A man stopped being a man, and became instead the thing that thinks. Everyone was reduced. They weren't men and women any more; they were things that think. And that allowed all kinds of doubts and uncertainties to gain dominance over us.

'So now we have people saying, Christians, for example, who say, "Do I believe in God, or do I just think I believe in God?" They don't know any more, not really.'

'Is that right, JD?'

'Yeah, and it's all down to old Descartes.'

'So what are you actually telling me here?'

'Nothing you don't already know. We live in a shithole universe. God's dead, and we're all replicants with pre-programmed memories and emotions. All we can do to escape it is to fly off into a fantasy world, but then we have to wonder if the fantasy world isn't the real world, and all the horrors we thought were the real world are just thought patterns that the devil torments us with.'

'You want us to stop thinking, right?'

'No, we can't do that anyway. And if I could, I wouldn't go that way. It's just a great adventure to me. I really like it here in hell.'

'And what you like best about it is describing how we got here.'

'Yeah, you're reading my mind.'

'So, perhaps you could tell me how we got to be sitting in your van in the middle of a car park outside a lemonade factory.'

'That's easy.' JD smiled. 'I followed a blind woman here. A car picked her up from her house around ten-thirty this morning, delivered her here with a briefcase, and she disappeared through the swing doors. She looked gorgeous, little black suit with a short skirt, made me feel like I've been asleep for a hundred years. She hasn't been out since. One or two shady-looking characters have gone in (I got photographs of them), but they've all come out again. None of them seemed in a hurry, no bloodstains on their clothes, far as I could see.

'The lady's up on the third floor, second window from the right. Sometimes comes to the window, as though she's having a look at the world. Leans on the windowsill. She's in the room by herself, or at least I haven't seen anyone else at the window, and she doesn't seem to be talking to anyone.

'Oh, and she promotes libidinal urges within me.'

'Does she do that?' asked Sam. 'Or do you just think she does that, but in fact those libidinal urges are entirely your own, and not related to her in any way whatsoever?'

'Now that's an interesting topic you're raising there,' JD said. 'There is in fact a school of thought which declares that all sexual activity is masturbatory. It doesn't really make any difference if you do it with your hand or a man or a woman or a goat or an organic vegetable. The sexual partner is wholly imagined, a sexual fantasy. A sexual partner is never a woman or a man in the whole kernel of his or her being. You don't get the other person, you get what you imagine the other person is.'

'Yeah,' said Sam.

'Yeah, what?'

'I know you don't get the other person. I've known that all my life. The real problem is when you don't get anything at all, you don't get reality and you can't catch the illusion either. What d'you do then?'

'Easy,' said JD. 'You write a book.'

41

EIGHT

Marie Dickens didn't sleep well that night. Dreams littered with erotic, sometimes horrific images left her in a misty, lemurian landscape from which there seemed to be no escape. A cup of hot chocolate at three o'clock seemed to help, but when she went back to sleep a warm dream involving her new boyfriend turned into the sadistic gang-rape of a blind child between two goalposts. More hot chocolate, watching the clock grind its way from a quarter after four to the croak of dawn. Then, as inexplicably as before, two-and-a-half hours of deep, uninterrupted sleep.

When she'd finished breakfast she put the cereal bowl in the sink and took her coffee over to the window alcove, looked out at the river. She picked up the phone and dialled Sam's home number. He answered on the seventh ring.

'Did I interrupt something?' she asked.

'Yeah. I was in the shower.'

'Alone?'

'That's how I seem to do it these days, Marie. I'm still dripping here. Something I can help you with before the carpet rots?'

'Yes, I thought I'd talk to Isabel's boyfriend, Russell Harvey, but I wanted to check if she'd turned up yet.'

'No sign of her. I talked with Angeles about half an hour ago. She'd already rung the husband, Reeves.'

'Quintin?'

'Quintin Reeves, yeah. You find that funny?'

Marie laughed. 'You know how words give rise to images, especially names? There's something decidedly porcine about Quintin.'

'When're you thinking of seeing him, the boyfriend?'

'I'll give him a ring now. See if I can go this morning. Maybe Isabel's there?'

'Hope so,' Sam said. 'I've got a bad feeling about her. If she doesn't turn up soon, I'm gonna tell Angeles to bring the police in.'

Russell Harvey didn't answer his telephone. Marie tried five times in the next forty minutes and each time she got the engaged signal. If Isabel had decided to leave her husband and set up house with the boyfriend, that would explain why the guy didn't answer his phone. They wouldn't want Quintin Reeves ringing in, looking for his wife, and maybe they were playing at being the only people in the world. Living together on sex and French bread and sex and booze and sex and whatever it was that turned them on.

When Marie drove out to Russell Harvey's house in Fulford and knocked on the door she fully expected it to be opened by Mrs Isabel Reeves clad in little more than an apron.

What she got, however, was something quite different. First, the sound of an uncurling chain, and then what might have been a grizzly bear hitting the other side of the door, followed by a rattling series of snarls and barks. She took a step back as the invisible, but seemingly huge canine presence on the inside of the door tried to break its way through to her.

The rumpus was momentarily quelled and superseded by a high-pitched, but masculine voice. 'Emperor, shut the fuck up. Get back in this basket. NOW.'

The scratching at the door continued, and the hound let go with a howl of rage and frustration that would have scattered a colony of ghouls. There was a loud slapping sound, like the crack of a whip, and the human voice came through the door again. 'Emperor. Basket. Now.'

The canine sounds were muted. Small whimpers receding from the door, the links of a chain dragging over a paved area. Finally the door was opened two or three inches, and from the gloom inside the house there appeared a thin, chiselled, unshaven face. 'What's up?' the man said.

Marie took a hesitant step forward. 'My name's Marie Dickens,' she said. 'I'm looking for Isabel Reeves.'

The man opened the door wider and motioned her to follow

him. Marie stepped inside, closed the door behind her and followed his hunched form down the narrow corridor. A leather strap hung from his right hand, longer than a belt, more like something one might use to keep a trunk fastened. With each step the odour of old dog grew in strength. Harvey turned into a large Victorian kitchen, the main feature of which was a solid-fuel range which was pumping out more heat than the space could handle. Within seconds of entering the room Marie was aware of a thin film of sweat on her forehead and upper lip.

Emperor was a cross between a black Alsatian and a wire-haired terrier. A runt of a dog with tiny black eyes and chiselled features, not unlike his master. His chain had been hooked short to a metal peg on the wall so he couldn't lie down. He avoided eye contact and gazed off into the middle distance, never betraying his optimism, the certainty that his day would come.

'What d'you know about Isabel?' Russell Harvey asked.

His gaunt features and slack posture made him seem old, but he could not have been more than thirty-five. He had a wild crop of black hair on his head, and a day's growth of beard. His eyes were quick and active, flashing as they measured Marie's legs, her breasts and hair.

'I was hoping to find her here,' Marie said. 'Or that you'd tell me where she is.'

Russell Harvey was sitting on the edge of a pine chair. His body was wasted like that of a Muslim fakir or someone suffering from anorexia. His large, grubby trainers seemed grotesque in relation to his stringy muscles.

'She was supposed to come yesterday,' he said. He stared at the dog for a moment. 'Thought you was her till Emperor started.' He looked directly at Marie as if trying to penetrate behind her eyes. 'Has something happened?'

Marie shook her head. 'We don't know. She went out the day before yesterday, and she hasn't been seen since.'

'She would've come here if something was wrong.'

'You haven't seen her?'

'No.'

'Or heard from her?'

He looked towards the windowsill, where the phone was unconnected. He plugged it into the socket and replaced the handset in its cradle. Then he put his head against the glass and closed his eyes. Marie moved closer to him, instinctively at first, perhaps to put an arm around him, offer some kind of comfort. But the angularity of the man, the odour that surrounded him, the sheer size of his despair all conspired to keep her at arm's length. 'We don't know that anything's happened to her,' she said. 'She's under pressure. Maybe she's gone away for a few days? To rest, to think, to get some perspective on her life?'

Harvey turned to face her. He looked at and seemed to speak to her breasts. 'We were in love,' he said. 'That's not pressure. We were going to live together. Everything was settled.'

'For you, maybe,' Marie told him. She refused to join him in his use of the past tense. It was as if Isabel Reeves was already dead and buried. 'But Isabel still has to make the break with her husband. Whatever their relationship, that's not an easy thing to do.'

Harvey shook his scrawny head. 'She wouldn't've gone away without saying something to me. If she's missing, he's done her in. That's what's happened, mark my words. At the end of the day you'll find he's done for her.'

'Who do you mean? Who's done for her?'

'Reeves, the husband, who do you think? He'd never let her go. He told her that.'

Marie looked back at the man. His eyes were black holes. There was a quiver to his lips, the only sign of emotion in his face. But his arms were held out like a supplicant, arms that were thin and stick-like, closed at the ends by white-knuckled fists.

You can only use your nose, Marie thought as she settled herself behind the wheel of the car. Some people can lie so convincingly that it's impossible to tell. Lying is a talent. You either have it or you don't. Russell Harvey was plausible; there was no denying that. But was he honest?

It was not impossible that Isabel Reeves was locked in one of the upper rooms of that house. Maybe dead, which would account for his insistence on the past tense.

She turned the key in the ignition and checked the wing mirror as she moved out into traffic.

And another thing. What would a woman like Isabel Reeves see

45

in a man like Russell Harvey? The guy was a stick insect. He didn't shave, didn't bother much with soap and water, and his house was a shithole. He looked at you, watched you with those sex-hungry eyes, so intently that his stare was almost tangible.

Men did look at women, and women looked at men, too. Except there was a difference in the way they looked. A woman couldn't look at men like Harvey had looked at her, because if she did, the man would interpret the look as a come-on. Men didn't understand about being looked at, being watched. It took a long time to get used to it. Women, most women, they learned early to take it in their stride. But even then, there would always come along some guy who could make you squirm.

And Russell Harvey was one of them.

Marie's nose told her that he was honest as well, at least in relation to his involvement with Isabel Reeves. But there were no certainties in the job or in life. Sometimes the nose was a good indicator and other times it was completely wrong. The only safe way was to keep an open mind until all the leg-work was over.

NINE

It was around midday that Dave Taylor and his new girlfriend, Amber Hill, strayed from the well-beaten track of the Cleveland Way a mile or two to the north of Cold Kirby on the edge of the North Yorkshire Moors. The sun was bright and apart from a few low clouds over to the west, the sky was clear.

They'd been warned about straying from the path, and knew they were in danger of losing their way if visibility suddenly became difficult. But Dave had been getting more and more randy throughout the morning, and had joked about his erection for more than an hour and a half before Amber admitted to herself that she wanted it just as much as him.

They climbed down a hill and crossed an ice-cold stream, picking up a sheep-run, maybe eighteen inches wide, which led into an area of thick heathers and a scattering of blueberries. Dave unzipped his sleeping bag and threw himself down on it, holding his arms out for Amber. 'Come here,' he said. 'Jesus, just come here.'

Amber flashed him a smile, but some movement caught her attention further down the hill. 'I think there's someone over there,' she said.

'Christ.' Dave got to his feet. 'It'll be a sheep. There's no people up here. I thought we was gonna screw.'

'I want to check it out, Dave. You can hang on a bit longer.'

'This is torture.' He took her by the hand and they walked towards the spot where Amber had seen movement. Within about fifty yards a large ewe leapt out of the heather and made off up the hill. 'What did I tell you?' Dave said. 'There's only sheep and rabbits up here, maybe some grouse, wild birds, whatever they call 'em.'

'Still needed to check it out, though,' Amber said. 'I don't want some shepherd or gamekeeper walking in on us when we're getting at it.'

Dave smiled. No point in upsetting her. He took her hand in both of his and brought it to his lips. 'I know where there's a really warm sleeping bag,' he said. 'And it's in the middle of nowhere, with no people, except me and you and a hard-on that feels like its gonna break off.'

'You shouldda been a salesman,' she said. 'The way you talk.'

'I am a salesman, Amber,' Dave told her. 'What do you think I do in the sports shop all day?'

But Amber wasn't listening. He felt her shake and when he followed the line of her sight something began to shake inside Dave as well.

The body was in a sitting position only a couple of metres above the path. A mound of earth supported the woman's back. It was as if she was looking out over the moor. She was wearing a black suit and flat shoes and one of her eyes had been pecked out of its socket. The eye was still there, hanging by the remains of a vein and some threads of tissue, resting on the lower part of her cheek. Her face was criss-crossed by the dark footmarks of birds that had clung to the flesh, and her suit was speckled with the lime from their droppings.

Her arms were stretched out and the open palms were scarred, as if someone had tried to gouge holes in them with pieces of flint. Her feet, which were crossed one over the other, were similarly scarred.

Most of the exposed flesh was black, but at the neck of the suit and the cuffs of the jacket it was a creamy colour. There was an odour of decay and putrefaction.

Amber retched and vomited, going down on her knees. She wiped her mouth with the back of her hand and returned her gaze to the body of the woman. 'That's horrible,' she said. 'Really horrible.'

Dave wanted to tell her not to look, but he couldn't stop looking himself. He stared abstractedly, remembering the time he'd gone with some mates to a girlie show. There was the same confusion over how to interpret the image. The thought that there was a conventional response which somehow didn't connect with his feelings. The result was paralysis, an inability to opt for either alternative. He couldn't help wondering what was behind the closed lid of the woman's other eye. If she were suddenly reanimated, would the wink reveal an empty socket?

'We'd better tell somebody,' Amber said.

'Yeah.' Dave followed her back up the hill. 'No point hanging round here.' Somehow he couldn't keep up with Amber's pace. When they found the track of the Cleveland Way, she went even further ahead, well out of earshot. 'This's a real ball-breaker,' Dave said to himself.

Sam got to Angeles' house a few minutes after receiving her message. He'd been to see the physiotherapist at the hospital, and arrived at the office an hour late. His hand was healing slowly, he seemed to be able to do more with it every day.

She was wearing a dark shirt and a striped Breton jumper. There must be some way she could tell what looked good when she dressed in the morning, but he couldn't imagine what it was. It isn't possible to feel colours, yet she never wore combinations that clashed. Always looked as though she'd been personally dressed by one of those couturier guys.

She was calm and collected but the tension in her facial muscles betrayed the effort involved in maintaining the mask. 'I want you to drive me,' she said. 'I have to identify the body, that's number one, then I want you to find out who killed her.'

'Shall we take it a step at a time?' Sam said. 'It might not be Isabel.'

'We'll soon know,' she said. 'Can we go now?'

'Yeah. The car's outside. What about her husband? Shouldn't he be involved in this?'

'Quintin's not here,' Angeles said. 'He went on a business trip last night. The police are trying to contact him, but he's not due back until tomorrow.' She pulled a beanie hat down on her head and slipped into an ankle length, fitted coat. She did it nonchalantly, without thinking, but in a way that made Sam want to share his life and prejudices with her.

He followed her through the door. 'So he doesn't know about the body being found?'

'No.' She took his arm and let him lead her to the car. He opened the passenger door and waited until she'd settled herself inside. He watched her smooth out the wrinkles in her skirt. As he walked round to the driver's door he wondered if there was anything else in the world apart from sex. No, he mused, not a lot, apart from birth and death. Music? The politics of power came into the equation somewhere. And starvation was always good. Homelessness? OK, the world was a complicated place, full of joys and disappointments, an infinite variety of emotions and experiences. It was just that sex was the best.

She'd been at the bottle. There was the minted mask which only drew attention to her breath. There was the careful walk, the conscious placing of one foot in front of the other. And there was the slight tremor of the hand. Sam couldn't leave it alone.

'I'm an alcoholic,' he said.

She didn't respond, her eyes seemed as though they were following the road.

'Booze isn't going to help,' he said. 'It might seem like it will, but at the end of the day you have to get yourself through this.'

'I had a stiff drink,' she said. 'There's nothing wrong with that.'

He drove the car, nodding inwardly. She'd had at least three. Big ones. But the real danger sign was that she could hold it.

What it looked like, apparently, if you were a policeman, was that Isabel Reeves drove up to the moors, parked her car, took an overdose of sleeping tablets, and wandered off into the bracken.

'Part of her face had been eaten,' Angeles said. 'Birds had pecked out her eye. It was the only time in my life that I was glad I couldn't see.'

'Could you identify the body?' Sam asked.

'Yes.'

'How did you do that?'

Angeles sighed. 'She was my sister. I know her body, her hands, her jewellery. There is a birthmark on her thigh. There's no doubt. It was Isabel.'

'They can't have held a PM already. There'll have to be an inquest.'

Angeles put her hands forward and rested them on the dashboard. She jumped when a huge truck with airbrakes went into a sneezing fit beside them.

'They said the preliminary results show she died from the combined effects of the sleeping pills and the exposure. Temazepam. They think she committed suicide.'

'But you don't?'

'No, I don't. If she did that herself, then someone drove her to it. The skin on her palms was broken. It felt as though someone had tried to gouge a hole through her hands.' Angeles swiped a tear away from her cheek. 'How can they think she'd do that to herself? She was happy. She was in love. For the first time in years she had something to live for. So why did she kill herself? If she killed herself.'

'You told them about being watched? That someone was following you and Isabel?'

Angeles nodded. A tear slipped out of the corner of her eye and splashed on to her cheek. She brushed it away impatiently. 'They said there was no evidence to link anyone else to her death. They've had a forensic team up on the moor, but they haven't found anything suspicious.'

'So they've already solved it?'

'Sounded like it. They said their inquiries would continue, but I didn't get the impression they were going to put much effort into it.'

'Maybe we're looking at a vendetta,' Sam said to Marie when he got back to the office.

'Why do you say that?' asked Marie. 'My money would be on the boyfriend, Russell Harvey. He was seriously weird.'

'There was something strange about the husband, too,' Sam said. 'But we're still left with sister number two, and we have to assume that the guy who was watching Isabel is the same one watching Angeles.'

'You think Angeles is in danger?'

'We can't rule it out.'

Marie shook her head. 'No, we can't rule it out. It's just that there is a motive for Isabel's husband. And the boyfriend seems like he could be seriously disturbed. They both might have had a reason to kill Isabel, but neither of them has any reason to kill Angeles.'

'As far as we know,' said Sam.

'OK, I see what you're saying. I'm getting stuck here; I should be looking at the bigger picture. But even if I do that, I don't arrive at a vendetta. The closest I can get is a stalker who goes too far. Some guy who stops stalking and starts getting physical.'

'No, I don't think so. With stalking, the motive is random or peripheral. The stalker sees someone and makes an association. But this seems more systematic, as if the perpetrator is working to some programme. I'm assuming that Isabel was killed or somehow driven to take her own life. And now the same guy is left with sister number two. If that's what happened, we're looking at some deep-seated resentment on the part of the killer.'

'Someone with a grudge against the Falco family?' asked Marie.

Sam nodded. 'Yeah,' he said. 'A grudge. A grievance. We could be looking for someone who cringes when he hears their names. Someone who has identified them with evil.'

Angeles rang the next morning. 'The police were here,' she said. 'They've changed their minds about Isabel.'

'Tell me,' said Sam. He put his aching hand on the table, balling it into a fist until the nerves screamed.

The line was silent for a moment. 'It wasn't Temazepam,' Angeles said. 'It was some kind of veterinary drug, injected. Apparently it's not available here. Someone must have imported it. They're going to search her house as soon as Quintin gets back, but I told them they wouldn't find anything. Isabel hated injections, she'd never do that to herself.'

The clink of a glass came down the wire. He didn't hear it, but he imagined the glugging sound as the liquor came out of the bottle. 'They're treating it as a murder case now?'

'Oh, yes,' she said. 'The drug wasn't the only thing.'

Sam waited until she steadied her voice. When she found the words they came in a rush. 'Her back was broken,' she said.

TEN

'It's like being trapped inside the covers of a book,' said the blind hero in the opening sentence of the opening chapter of JD's novel. It was a good start. Now all he had to do was follow it with another hundred thousand relevant words.

The hero was going to be half-blind, a man with failing sight, eyes that could not be trusted to tell the truth. But in working surveillance on Angeles Falco, JD had begun to think of his hero as totally blind. The book wouldn't work that way, because the plot involved the hero witnessing a murder, but JD's mind was already tinkering with the plot.

Sight was a spatial dimension, whereas hearing worked in the realm of time. Most people feared losing their sight more than their hearing because they imagined that their spatial universe would recede and disappear, that they would lose contact with the world of things. But the physical universe exists in space *and* time, and to be condemned to experience it without full access to one or the other is perhaps an equal disability.

Not a disability that was impossible to overcome, JD reminded himself. Angeles Falco functioned in the world as well as many sighted people and in some areas better than most.

She was not a helpless stereotype, stumbling around in a black cellar with her arms outstretched. She was an independent, rounded character, someone who embraced the world and responded individually to whatever stimuli it put in her path. She would be a real-life model for JD's fictional hero.

And the fact that she was in trouble, that she was being watched by some hidden presence, well . . . JD smiled. That was

53

the lot of all fictional characters. As soon as a writer created a character and put him or her into a book, the character became the focus for the reader of the book. The character's every move was seen and noted. The inflexions of speech, the inner thoughts, the dreams, fears, aspirations. The being of the character, existentially, the fact, the survival of the character was dependent on him or her being continually observed. Being watched.

Without a constant flow of readers, the fictional character was, in reality, trapped inside the covers of a book. And perhaps that was the reason why the best fictional characters tried to take on a life of their own, tried to charm, to captivate the reader. They wanted to insert themselves into the consciousness of the reader, so that he would carry them off inside his head when he came to the last sentence and closed the book. Then the fictional character would go on living, vicariously, it is true. But there are many among us who live by proxy, through another's joy or sorrow, and yet still experience their lives as real, valid.

JD did a word count, saved his work and shut down the computer. Time to go back to reality, watching the blind woman, try to keep her safe from whoever it was killed her sister. He pulled on his coat and closed the door behind him. Ten words. It was a start, a beginning. He'd have to expand on it a little. Couldn't really claim it was a novel yet.

ELEVEN

When Echo was born Geordie couldn't imagine what she saw when she gazed at him. Celia had quoted William James' 'blooming, buzzing confusion', but Geordie hadn't wanted to believe that his daughter didn't hold him in some kind of focus. She imitated him, didn't she? Mimicked his facial expressions. But more than that, it seemed to Geordie that the transactions that took place between Echo and himself were rich in emotion and understanding.

JD reckoned that babies were almost blind. That they negotiated with the world by means of touch and hearing and their vocal cords, but that they didn't actually see very much. Not until they were around two months old. He'd read a book about it.

'Why is it,' Janet asked, 'that people like Celia and JD, who've never had babies themselves, are always the ones who know everything about them? Echo sees me just as clearly as I see her and she has done since the moment she was born.'

'Yeah,' Geordie agreed. 'It's because they're intellectuals.'

Janet held Echo close to her body. 'Silly people,' she said to the child, using her own version of mother-talk. 'She's got beautiful eyes.'

'You know what's beautiful to me?' Geordie asked rhetorically. 'Things that're mysterious. Everything that's mysterious.'

'Echo's the most beautiful thing in the whole world,' Janet said, but she wasn't answering Geordie so much as talking to her child.

'Yeah,' Geordie said. 'You and her are the most beautiful things in the world. But that's because you're mysterious.'

'There's nothing mysterious about us,' Janet told him. 'We're living in the world like everybody else, trying to get by, doing the best we can.'

Venus and Orchid, Janet's two cats, slunk into the sitting room. They'd been hanging round the koi pond at number thirty-eight, but they didn't appear to have had much luck. Venus was heavily pregnant, her stomach almost grazing the floor as she walked.

Geordie thought about what Janet had said while he put his coat on, and he thought about it some more when he got down on his haunches to say goodbye to Barney. The dog licked his face, eyes, nose and ears, and would have gone on for much longer if Geordie hadn't pushed him away.

He got to his feet and kissed Echo on the forehead and Janet on the lips. 'You're all a mystery to me,' he said. 'Everybody I know is a mystery.'

The sky was overcast. There was an oppressive feeling to the grounds of the university. The students had gone down and apart from the ducks there was only a gang of gardeners cutting and clearing timber. The hollow sound of their axes followed him, and when he stopped to talk to the statue of the Buddha, they were still there, in the distance. Chop-chop, chop-chop, a sound echoing with nostalgia, though there were no trees in Geordie's childhood or anywhere in his memory.

He missed the bus and decided to walk into town. The rain had held off so far, and he hoped it would give him another twenty minutes. Besides, there was something he wanted to think about, something on the tip of his brain. He couldn't formulate what it was, and hoped the walk would give him the peace to root it out. For the last couple of days it had been there in his head, like an itch.

When he passed the Barbican he thought of calling in, see if Sam was working out in the gym, trying to get his hand to work again. But Sam would be with Angeles at this time, either with her or keeping an eye on her.

Nevertheless, when he'd crossed over the road, he found himself looking back, somehow expecting Sam to come out of the Barbican entrance. There was no one there, though. No one in sight, only the feeling that he was being observed.

What it was, it was probably lack of sleep. He wasn't getting enough rest so his mind was playing tricks with him. You had to have enough REM sleep – rapid eye movement sleep – otherwise you didn't dream, and then you couldn't concentrate on the day. Geordie wasn't sure if he'd got that right, but he could ask Marie later, she knew about that kind of thing, in fact it was her who told him about it in the first place.

Cutting through Dixon Lane to Piccadilly the feeling was still with him. He glanced behind a couple of times, but there was no one there. A few spots of rain hit the road and dried up immediately. The sky was in two different moods, couldn't decide what to do.

He deliberately hallucinated footsteps. The feeling of being watched was so strong, so real, that he wanted to give whoever it was observing him a physical form. There were eyes on him, pinned on him. That was not an hallucination. It was exactly like it had been the other day in Parliament Street, that prickling sensation at the back of the neck.

A big truck went past, and the guy behind the wheel eyeballed Geordie, gave him a real stare. Registration number HUD something, couldn't get the numbers. There was a moment there when Geordie thought the guy might've been contemplating running into him, just checking to see he'd got the right man first.

Maybe you're going mad? Geordie thought. Losing it? This business of Angeles being watched had somehow got lodged in his mind, and that, combined with the lack of sleep, was rotting his brain. Jesus, and it would have to be now, he thought, when he'd got Janet and Echo and his life seemed to be sorting itself out. That was just the kind of trick the mad genius who ran the universe got up to. Give a guy everything he ever wanted, then turn his brain into mushroom soup.

He didn't go mad when his mother ran off with the landlord or when they put him in the council home. He didn't go mad when he was homeless, flogging himself to perverts and begging on the streets. Oh, no, he came through all that. He didn't go mad when he started working with Sam and that crazy woman shot him in the back. He had to wait until now, until he had Janet and Echo and everything was coming up roses.

Maybe if he ignored it, Geordie thought, if he pretended there wasn't anybody watching him, then it would go away.

Because you know what happens? Soon as you start telling

people you're having hallucinations, they cart you off to the mad house. They don't try reasoning with you, because if you're having hallucinations, it's fairly obvious that you're past the reasoning stage.

So, keep mum about it. That's the way. Look as if you're happy and normal, and listen to what people say, so you can have the right response. If you hear footsteps coming up behind you, whistle a tune, so you can't hear them any more. Even if you're in a dark alley, and you hear footsteps, and maybe some thug shouting his mouth off about what he's gonna do to you, rip your head off your shoulders and shove it up your ass. Just whistle something, like from an Elton John album, or Madonna. Anything'll do. *Like a Ve-er-er-er-gin.*

Geordie stopped, froze to the spot. The HUD truck was stationary outside the Banana Warehouse and the driver was climbing down from his cab, his eyes fixed on Geordie. The guy was as wide as he was tall; shoulders on him like a goalmouth.

He dropped to the pavement, his legs spread apart. He wore a blue T-shirt a couple of sizes too small for him and each of his rippling arms was adorned with tattoos, identical serpents wound around long-bladed daggers. He had long curly hair parted down the middle, and two of his front teeth were missing. He fixed his beam on Geordie and rolled towards him with a gait like a sailor.

Geordie looked around for some means of escape. He didn't know whether to believe this was happening to him. He'd thought someone was watching him, but he'd never been *sure*. Somewhere, he'd almost convinced himself that it was an illusion. On balance he'd thought he'd rather have the illusion, especially when he took in the sheer size of the guy who was bearing down on him. Geordie was probably as tall as the trucker, but only half his weight. And in terms of meanness there was no contest. The trucker would get the gold for meanness every time, even if he hadn't lost his teeth. Geordie wouldn't be able to read the entry form.

By the time he managed to animate himself it was too late, the guy already had him by the shoulders. There was a powerful sense of oil and truck and stale sweat, and there was that old dizzy sensation that accompanies terror.

Geordie was shaking right up to the point where the guy spoke.

There was reassurance in the tone of the man's voice. It wasn't what he said, because Geordie didn't hear what he said. It was something else, something more basic and instinctual than language. It was the quality that is in the keening of the bereaved or the sigh of satisfaction or of wonder of a mother who has seen her infant child for the first time. It was a quality of soul, carried on the breath and embedded in the sound that the man produced.

There was compulsion in his voice. He said, 'Geordie? What's the matter with you, man? Don't you know who I am?'

And there was tenderness there in the words and the way they were spoken. There was concern, anxiety, heart. Geordie looked up into the man's eyes. He shook his head and said, 'No, I don't know who you are.'

But while he was speaking the words a picture began forming in his head. The picture of two young boys, way back in Sunderland, shortly after their mother had run off with the landlord. Geordie was twelve years old, and his brother, Ralph, was almost sixteen. Geordie was absolutely certain that it was all a mistake, and that their mother would return once she realized what she'd done.

He was screaming at Ralph. He could see the arched posture in the picture forming in his head. He was like a bow, tense and ready for battle. And Ralph was silent, shaking his head. 'She's not coming home, Geordie,' he was saying. 'This's the end of us, man.'

In the picture Geordie's mouth was open wide. His eyes were bulging. He was reminded of those horror films, where the moon comes up and the hero begins the howl that will transform him from man to beast.

Their mother had never returned.

Ralph had got himself a job as a cabin boy on a tramp and sailed off into the distance. He hadn't told Geordie he was going, but he'd left him a note, worded almost the same as the one from their mother. *Dear Geordie, I know this'll come as something of a shock . . .*

Geordie had lived alone, then, in the house, until all the food had gone. It was when he was caught leaving the local supermarket with two cans of baked beans and a bottle of sherry up his jumper that the local authority became involved.

All the other kids in that place were orphans. Their mothers were dead. 'But I've got a mother,' Geordie tried to explain to the staff. 'I'm not an orphan. There's been a mistake. If I'm in here, nobody'll know where I am. When my mother comes home she won't know what's happened. And what about Ralph? When he comes home from sea?'

But nobody was listening. They were carers, these people. They were paid to care not to listen.

The rough stubble on Ralph's cheek was nothing to do with the brother that Geordie remembered. The large, ugly face with the missing front teeth, the coarse accent, the way the man had his arms around Geordie's back, half lifting him off his feet; none of these things struck a match in Geordie's memory.

But the salt did. The tears. If he'd stopped to think about it, Geordie wouldn't have known if the tears belonged to him or to Ralph. What he knew beyond any doubt was that the tears that were smeared over both their faces were the same tears that had been smeared over their faces when they found themselves alone in that house in Sunderland ten years earlier.

People change and remain the same. The young Ralph, with whom he'd shared the news of their abandonment, was still there, in glimpses, peeking out from behind the brawn of the trucker. He'd always be there, always abandoned, never fully able to hide.

They broke apart, still holding on to each other's shoulders; Geordie gazed into his brother's face, and Ralph looked back with the same glint of wonder.

'How'd you find me?' Geordie asked.

'I've been following you for days,' Ralph replied. 'I didn't know if it was you or not. I still didn't know, not really, until I got hold of you.'

Ralph laughed. Threw his head back and roared out a laugh that came from way down in his belly.

Then there was another sound which Geordie couldn't identify at first, until he realized that it came from himself. He was laughing. The two of them, standing together outside the Banana Warehouse, laughing like a couple of loonies.

People passing by on their way to work, or to do their shopping, watching these two men laughing their heads off, wondering what the joke was. Geordie wanted to tell them there was no joke. There wasn't anything funny. Just an ocean of relief.

TWELVE

When Celia arrived Angeles came to the door with red eyes, a mess of wet tissues clutched in her hand.

'Come in,' she said, moving aside. 'I'm sorry. I must look awful.'

'You look as though you're giving yourself a hard time, m'dear,' Celia said. 'But that's only to be expected. Take me to the kitchen and I'll get the kettle going.'

She followed Angeles into the kind of kitchen she'd only visited in dreams. She couldn't imagine preparing food in there, scrubbing vegetables or grilling fish. Everything was immaculate, each separate item of equipment gleamed.

'I'll do it,' Angeles said. 'You don't know where anything is.'

'You sit down, m'dear. I'll find everything I need. Tell me how you're coping.'

Celia kicked her shoes off and stood on the quarry-tiled floor. She knew the tea would be somewhere near the kettle but still had to hunt it down. She found it on a small shelf just above eye-level: a beige metal caddy with the word TEA stencilled on its side. She smiled, firstly because she'd taken her shoes off and was standing in her stocking-feet, and secondly because the caddy was labelled with a name that Angeles couldn't see.

'I keep forgetting she's dead,' Angeles said. She'd taken a stool from under the table and sat on it, her knees together. 'Then it comes back at me like a tidal wave. I don't know what to do. I went to work today and that was fine, kept my mind off it. But as soon as I got back here I started howling.'

'I'm not sure you should be alone,' Celia said. 'Isn't there someone who could stay?'

'I'm used to being alone, Celia. I don't want anyone else here.'

'It's all right to cry, love. In fact it's the best thing you can do. Howl as much as you like.' Celia poured boiling water into the teapot. She glanced over at Angeles with a smile on her face. She knew the girl couldn't see it, but hoped the feel of it was in her words.

'I could've loved her more,' Angeles said.

'You couldn't m'dear. Not while she was alive. It's only after they've gone that we believe that. I said exactly the same thing when my mother died. But really it was because I wanted to beat myself. Punish myself.'

'And all the petty things,' Angeles said. 'How I was jealous of her because she could still see. Jealous of her boyfriends, jealous of her marriage. God, I wouldn't have had Quintin Reeves in the house, let alone marry the man.'

Celia let her talk. She found cups and saucers, a carton of milk in the fridge. She poured the tea and took it over to the table, pulled out a stool for herself.

'Mummy had another child,' Angeles said quietly. 'Between me and Isabel. A boy called Simon, but he only stayed for three days.' She pushed her hands down between her thighs and looked up at the ceiling. Her eyes were running with tears but she didn't make a sound. Celia watched the river of salt-water course along her cheeks and down her neck. After several minutes Angeles spoke again.

'I wonder how it would have been different if he'd lived. If he'd been there to stand between us. Isabel and I were almost the same person. I knew her so well that there were times I couldn't tell where she ended and I began.'

Celia reached out and took her hand.

'You know what they say when someone dies?' Angeles was shaking her head from side to side as she spoke. 'When someone dies the soul can get stuck for some reason. It goes into limbo and can't travel on to wherever it's supposed to go. That's because it can't leave the earth behind. It still has business here.'

The tears came again, then. Angeles gave herself over to them, made no attempt to damn them up with words.

'Isabel is like that,' she continued eventually. 'Stuck in limbo. Because there's a part of her that's me and part of me that's her, and the one can't go on without the other.'

She began to shake. The sounds that came from her lips were dragged up from way below the belt. Celia got to her feet, afraid that Angeles would fall off the stool. She went to her and took Angeles' head and pressed it to her breast and gently rocked her back and forth, letting her own body absorb the violent spasms that threatened to turn the younger woman inside out.

'There,' she said. 'There, m'dear. Let it come.' There were no words of wisdom within her. The rocking and the rhythmical way she used her voice was the most she could bring. Angeles would have to work her way through her own pain, face up to her own demons.

It was another one of the amazing things about life. That we seemed to arrive here with no experience at all and had to learn to cope with everything that the world threw at us. Angeles Falco would manage. She didn't quite believe it just now. But she'd come out the other end, with scars, of course, but also with a lust for life.

THIRTEEN

Miriam said I'm as crazy as a two-bob watch.
It was a joke.
She said it three days ago, and it keeps coming back to me.

This was because I said that people who worked for money were a waste of time and in contravention of God's dream for us.

Miriam: 'Why would I work for anything else? I spend eight hours a day in that place and I hate every minute of it. If there was no money involved, I wouldn't go in.'

In a conflict situation like this Miriam is defensive, she takes on an aggrieved tone, and when she's finished speaking, or between sentences, while she's thinking about what to say next, she grinds her front teeth. She doesn't look at me, either. She hangs her head. In the midst of her arrogance and pride there is humility.

I wear a voice-activated cassette recorder. The microphone is tiny and clips behind the lapel of my jacket and the cassette recorder itself sits snugly in my shirt pocket. It is a sensitive machine. As I listen to it now I can hear Miriam's teeth grinding together.

'I'm not against people making a living,' I told her. 'It's when it goes beyond that that the devil gets involved. When money-grubbing becomes a way of life. We've got politicians lining their pockets, chiefs of industry and commerce cheating and lying and cooking the books. Churchmen who know what is going on, but remain silent, refuse to bear witness, because they benefit from the proceeds.

'This is the kind of society we live in. Everything is valued in terms of money. People, technical or social achievement, and works of art, they all have a price. And people are blinded by money. Once it gets in their eyes they can't see anything else. We're led to believe that the best films are the ones with the biggest budgets, the best books the ones that have earned the largest advance. Most people, if they meet a millionaire, they don't ask where his millions came from, they just admire him.

'The devil uses money to shove us around. But he can only do that if we continue to make money the centre of our lives.'

Miriam shook her head. 'My boss,' she said, 'the one who owns the café; he drives a maroon Jag. Inga went in it once and he put his hand up her skirt, but she said it was worth it. She liked the smell of the leather.'

'When I hear things like that,' I told her, 'there's an Old Testament prophet rises up inside me who'd like to strike both of them dead.'

It was then that she said I was as crazy as a two-bob watch. She was quiet for a moment, and then she shook her head and said it with a laugh.

I didn't think it was funny. I still don't.

I looked it up in the dictionary. Australian slang, apparently. Harking back to the days before decimalization, when a bob was a shilling. So a two-bob watch would be a watch that you bought for about ten pence. Something cheap, something totally useless.

I explained to Miriam why I thought chastisement was in order, and she agreed with me. It could have taken many forms, but in the end we thought that physical punishment was the way forward.

She lay over the end of the bed and I gave her ten good wallops with the hairbrush.

Afterwards we had sex.

I am not a two-bob watch.

I am a watcher. I am the watchman.

There is only one of the two sisters left. The blind one. And I do believe she has got herself a minder. But that's all right. I've always been a fair man. As a blind woman she has, of course, a built-in disadvantage. She is handicapped in relation to me. But if she has a minder, then her handicap is nullified. We are equal. She has herself and her riches and her minder, and I have my fortitude and my God.

This has been my life. I have remained awake for the purpose of devotion; through long years I have kept my vigil. There was a period when it seemed that my vigil was in vain. But I kept the faith, and now it is beginning to pay off.

I am not by nature a violent man. I am a watchman, and by virtue of my watch I am drawn to strike the balance. A good man was lost, and should I stand idly by while others profit from his death?

Last night I told Miriam how I used to pray as a child and about crying myself to sleep at night. I didn't mention the bed-wetting. I told her how my mother was worried because she thought I was left-handed. My teacher, too; they all thought I was left-handed. If I'd been left-handed, there would have been something wrong with me. I would have been different to the rest.

That was the first time I remember witnessing joy in the eyes of other people, when they finally decided that I was ambidextrous. If they'd thought I was normal, right-handed, and then discovered that I was ambidextrous, it wouldn't have been such a joyful occasion. Just something to remark about. But because they'd thought I was handicapped, and then discovered that I was super-human, they thought it was a miracle.

And maybe it was.

Suxamethonium. The name of the drug I used. A pleasant sounding word, don't you think? Suxamethonium.

Isabel was by far the more predictable of the two sisters. I calculated how she would react when I turned up on her doorstep. A long training as a student of psychology helped, but my observations of her over the past months had convinced me that she would go along with my little scheme.

'Good morning,' I said. 'Mrs Reeves, isn't it? I've abducted your sister, Angeles Falco, and I'm here to discuss the terms of her release.' I smiled at her. I watched her mouth fall open and the dawning realization that one of her worst nightmares was taking place.

I stepped forward, over the threshold, and the woman moved to one side to accommodate me. Someone else would have slammed the door in my face and immediately rung the police. But not Isabel Reeves. Shock had the effect of paralysing her.

When she'd recovered a little, she wanted to ring her sister to make sure I wasn't lying. I let her do that. She dialled the number and started when her sister's mobile began ringing in my pocket. I took it out and pushed the talk button. 'I'm sorry,' I said into the mouthpiece, 'Angeles Falco can't come to the phone just now.' Isabel Reeves put her own mobile down on the sideboard and looked at me with vacant eyes. She was in a no-win situation.

She was pale; her hand kept flitting to her mouth and then fluttering by her side. She was perspiring and from time to time she would shake her head as though to clear her vision. I told her I wanted ten thousand pounds and she said she would have to have a glass of water. She drank the liquid and wept for a moment. She said she couldn't give me money just like that, she'd need some kind of proof that her sister was alive.

I had predicted this as well. It was as if the woman was a puppet, someone without free will. I made a suggestion and she responded to it precisely as I expected.

'We'll use your car,' I told her. 'You drive. You don't have to get the money until you've seen the proof.'

She was anxious. Her skin was cold and clammy. But what could she do? I was holding all the cards.

I directed her up to the moors and we travelled a high, narrow road that was populated by sheep and only the occasional car. It was not a short journey and from time to time she would turn and ask if I was sure that this was the right way.

I was sure.

Following my directions, she parked in a lay-by which led to a public footpath. I told her to follow the path, walking close behind her. When the road was out of sight we turned off the path on to one of the sheep-runs. She did as I directed for about a hundred metres before she rebelled.

'Angeles isn't here,' she said. 'I'm going back. I don't know what you're up to, but this isn't right. She can't be here.'

She pushed past me and ran along the narrow sheep-run. I took off after her and pushed her into the heather. I straddled her and flicked the cover off the syringe, pushing the needle into the top of her chest.

It was remarkable how quickly the Suxamethonium took effect. Within seconds she was still, unable to move, her eyes staring with fear.

I hadn't thought through what to do next. I suppose I could have given her more of the drug but I wasn't sure that would satisfy me. At first I thought I might strangle her, but in the end I turned her on to her face and knelt on the small of her back. I took her by the shoulders and pulled until her spine cracked.

I don't mind admitting it: I felt and still feel that this killing was beneath me. Don't get me wrong; I'm glad she's out of the way, that she's dead. But I want the disposal of the next sister to be a more creative act.

When people hear that I worked in forensic psychology they want to know about offender profiling. This is because offender profiling is the new sexy specialism of the profession, and there are many of us, professionals and ex-professionals, who wish it wasn't so. It is a technique (though the word itself adds dignity to what might turn out to be mere romance) that is as yet unproven, and is certainly unscientific. The profiler prepares a biographical sketch of the offender, the ingredients of which are gathered from information taken at the scene of a crime and from the personal habits and history of the victim.

And there have been successes, some of them startling. Nevertheless, offender characteristics are extremely complex, and there is no reason to get excited just because one or two early results were positive. Research and slow, painstaking work are what adds to our knowledge base. At the present stage of its development offender profiling is irrelevant in the detection of crime. You would be better off tossing a coin.

Catharsis is much more interesting, though not as sexy. Freud's concept was that the existence of drama allowed the spectator to vicariously discharge his aggressive drives. There have been various research projects built around the idea of catharsis, but, as yet, no one has come up with a definitive result. Some studies show that the depiction of violence leads to more violence, while others seem to suggest that catharsis is at work and acting as a safety valve.

My own research involved a field study. I had access to a group of boys in a young offenders' unit a few miles to the north of the city. What I intended to do was feed half of them on a diet of violent television, video nasties, slasher movies, etc., while the other half would be submitted to pastoral, seasonal and calming filmic images. I needed permission to run this experiment for ten weeks, during which the behaviour of the boys would have been constantly observed and measured.

I was the observer. I. The watchman.

Yesterday Miriam came home from work in a foul mood. She stripped off her apron and her blouse which were stained with tomato sauce. They'd been serving spaghetti bolognese in the café. She marched around the flat like a soldier. Her hair was greasy and lank and there was pallor to her skin. Her eyes flashed danger.

'Don't anybody say anything,' she said, although I was the only other person present, and I hadn't breathed a word.

'One word, just one word, and I'll scream. I'll bring the fucking roof down.'

This is the love of my life.

She is so skinny her ribs are visible, protruding like those pictures from the concentration camps. She was wearing a patterned bra, red roses washed out to pink, sweat stains under her arms. She has two more like that, bought at the same time in a sale, before we met. Her pigeons are several sizes too small for a bra. Surrealist images come to mind: a nipple in a marquee.

She goose-stepped into the bathroom and slammed the door behind her so hard that it came open again. I could see part of her as she sat on the bowl: one leg and the lower half of her arm, and I could hear her stools splashing into the water.

I gave her an hour, an hour and a half. If necessary I can be patient.

We have a tall chair in the kitchen. It is too tall for the table. When you sit on it you have to lean down to reach the cornflakes. Miriam was sitting on it. She had a woollen cardigan over her shoulders, fastened with one button. Her arms were bare.

I took a breath and she looked towards me.

'Bad day?' I asked.

She nodded. 'You could say that.'

'I don't think I contributed towards it,' I said. 'But you're making me suffer.'

'Yeah,' she said. 'If I have a bad day, everybody else should as well.' She smiled quickly. She went to the bathroom and returned almost immediately. 'You're as crazy as a two-bob watch,' she said, handing me the hairbrush.

FOURTEEN

Sam's late wife had left him a house with five bedrooms. He had plans for it; he'd had plans for it ever since Dora died. But his ideas about the house never materialized. The first thing he'd thought of doing was moving out and giving the place to a housing charity – Shelter, one of those. Because what did he want with a great rambling place like that? And Dora's ghost was forever there.

Next, he was going to take in homeless people, fill the place with life, give it a reason to exist. There must be lots of other kids like Geordie, who needed a helping hand, somewhere they could get a little shelter. People needed a base, somewhere they could begin to be whoever it was they were supposed to be.

The latest thing was that he'd advertise the rooms, let them off to whoever wanted them. People who wouldn't be dependent on him. People whom he wouldn't have to bail out on a Saturday night, and whom he wouldn't have to hassle to clean up the kitchen.

But now he'd come round full circle, and was thinking of moving out again. The place was an emotional burden. He felt guilty about taking up so much space. Should have moved out in the summer when he wasn't busy, instead of laying about in the long grass in the garden and watching the tourists littering the medieval streets, wondering when he was going to slip and buy some hooch.

Saturday today. Most of the day off. His surveillance stint didn't start until five o'clock. He'd been to a midday AA meeting at the Friends Meeting House and walked into town, have a look at the people. It was cold, but he bought a packet of fish and chips in Petergate and took them to a bench in King's Square. The fish was hot, and when he broke through the crust of batter he burnt his fingers on the white flesh. There were a dozen or so others in the square, mainly tourists. Two Norwegians, a lone Japanese woman, and a young American family, most of them tasting real fish and chips for the first time in their lives and some wondering why they'd bothered.

Sam wasn't drinking at the moment, hadn't touched a drop since Dora died. He didn't want a drink today, and if that changed as the day turned towards evening, it wouldn't make any difference. He'd ignore the craving, talk to Max, his AA sponsor. If Max wasn't around, he'd talk himself through it. He was working, and there was the woman called Angeles. There were reasons to stay sober. If you looked hard enough, there were always reasons. The gospel of a hopeful cynic.

There'd been a blind woman at the AA meeting, Sally Stone. She'd said that her blindness and her alcoholism were the same. The only way to live with either was to accept it as a fact. Her alcoholism meant staying away from booze. If she didn't, her life fell apart. And her blindness meant that she had to use a cane or a dog to get around safely. 'As soon as I begin to ignore the fact that I'm blind,' she said, 'then I get hurt or in trouble.'

Yeah, there it was, coming out of somebody else's mouth, somebody else's experience. You have to take the treatment, and treatment primarily involves not taking a drink.

Pigeons strutted about the square, quick to pounce on any scraps the people left behind. Every couple of minutes one of the American kids would rush them, and the square would erupt into a flutter of rushing feathers. The birds flew up, out of range of the children, and immediately alighted again in another part of the square. The pickings were rich, fatty and stuffed with protein.

The Japanese woman finished her fish and dropped the paper with the remains of her chips into a waste bin. She wandered off, round the corner into Church Street.

As if on cue a madman stalked out of Goodramgate, his mouth full of strange oaths and curses. He was tall and thin with a stoop, but his body was animated, his long arms waving around, seemingly out of control. His face was strangely elongated, unshaven for three or four days, and the light covering of hair on his head was long and unkempt.

He stood in his army greatcoat, which had no buttons, and addressed all four points of the compass, muttering incomprehensibly. He was like a mystic at prayer, Sam thought. But the guy wasn't praying. He was hallucinating. Maybe talking to the ghosts of some of those ancient Romans who used to live here. Constantine the Great? Maybe he was Constantine? The American kids moved in close to their parents.

The guy went straight to the waste bin and came up with the discarded chips. He sat on a low stone wall and opened the packet. His eyes shone. He paid no heed to anyone else in the square, just downed the chips one after the other in quick succession. Sam wondered if they'd retained any heat. Probably not.

The madman screwed up the empty paper and threw it across the square. Then he was back in the waste bin. There were more chips there, and the heel of a fish, all of which he put away within a few seconds.

Sam glanced down at what remained of his own dinner, wondered how he could pass it over to the guy without seeming to patronize him. He could give him money instead, let the guy go buy himself a packet of fresh. Except the guy wouldn't buy food, he'd already eaten. He'd buy booze, something to help him forget he was a prince with the world at his feet.

Sam's musings took only a few seconds, but when he looked up again the guy had gone. It was a busy life, harvesting the streets. You couldn't hang around one spot too long.

The tourists on the other side of the square were becoming animated again now that the perceived threat had disappeared. The American couple were whispering comfortable lies to their children. They and the Norwegians were up on their feet, ready to move on to the next museum or heritage site. It was a busy life treading these historical pathways. You couldn't hang around one spot too long.

Sam tossed a cold chip to the pigeons and they tore it apart in seconds. The city was a place of contrasts, but the dissimilarities were modified, intensified by their relationships to each other. The homeless and the tourists were all displaced. Difference was the homeless followed a route that the world didn't recognize, while the tourists were on a circular trip, return tickets in their back pockets.

The biting wind intensified and by the time he arrived home Sam's ears and nose were glowing pink. His lips were blue in the bathroom mirror. He'd picked up a paperback on the psychology of perception, hoping it'd give him some insight into Angeles Falco, but it was too technical. He thumbed through it for half an hour, but there wasn't much he could use. He read that our perceptions of the world were always delayed because of the speed of light, and because of the time taken to get messages to the brain; that our perception of the sun is over eight minutes late. What this adds up to is that we can never perceive the present: we always sense the past. Knew that already though, before he'd bought the book.

What he also knew subliminally, but which he needed the book to spell out for him, was that light was only a small proportion of the total electromagnetic spectrum. The difference between colours is simply in the frequency of light, but outside that frequency range there are other wavelengths that we do not see: radio waves, ultra-violet, infra-red and X-rays are just some of them. When you take into account the narrow band of frequencies that actually stimulate the eye and allow us to see, you could say that humans as a group are almost blind.

Geordie arrived with Echo in her pram and Barney on a new tartan leash. Echo was sleeping so Geordie left her in the pram in the garden. After he'd licked Sam's face, Barney took up position as guard-dog.

'Imagine if somebody kidnapped her,' said Geordie. 'I'd go out of my skull. Plus Janet'd kill me for being so careless.' He looked out of the window, make sure the pram was still there. 'Before you have kids,' he said, 'you don't think like that. You're just free. You don't have to think about things at all, let your mind drift. Know what I mean?'

Sam nodded. 'Not sure if I agree with you, though. People who don't have kids have their worries.'

'Tell me about it,' said Geordie. 'Before I started worrying about Echo I was worrying about Janet. Before Janet it was

Barney. There's plenty of times I was worried about you. I've been worried all my life. Hell, I worried about Ralph for years. Even when I wasn't thinking about him, there was a part of me that was worrying away in the dark.'

'Who's Ralph?'

'Ralph's my brother. He's come back.' Geordie told Sam about Ralph, about how Ralph had been watching him, making sure that Geordie was Geordie. He told about their meeting outside the Banana Warehouse.

'That's great,' Sam said. 'Where's he living?'

'He's at our place at the moment,' Geordie said. 'Until he gets somewhere of his own.'

'Is that a good idea?'

'What could I do, Sam? Turn away my brother? I couldn't let him sleep in his cab.'

'What does Janet think?'

'She's glad for me. It'll be fine, Sam. Ralph isn't gonna stay for ever. Just a few days.'

'Yeah.' Sam picked up a CD case with a picture of Dean Martin on the front, Borsalino on his head. He walked towards the stereo stack. 'So you're only marginally worried about it?' he said.

Geordie laughed. 'You think you know me, Sam. You think you can read me like a book. But there's parts of me you'll never reach. I worry because I've got an active imagination, that's what Janet says. And Janet should know, she's there even when I'm asleep, talking in my sleep, in dreams. There was this time before Echo was born, and I saw that *Alien* movie on the TV and I thought Echo might be born like that. I didn't really believe it, but when you think it, and then you start to build it up, you get to thinking it could happen. It just could. Like there's me and the midwife and Janet all waiting for something to happen, waters to break or whatever. And suddenly there's this cracking sound and Echo comes bursting out of Janet's chest.'

'You tell Janet about this, when she was pregnant?'

'What d'you think I am, stupid? I mean, if I'd told her about it, she'd've gone up the wall. Probably had a miscarriage or something. No, I only told her about it a couple of days ago. And I only told her about it then because I knew that she was ready to hear it. That's another thing about being a nuclear family. You get

74

to know when you can say things, even things that you can't normally say. You feel how the other person's gonna react even before you say the thing that normally they'd react differently to.'

'You been reading those psychology books again?'

'No, but I've been to pre-natal classes, and the ones on breast-feeding and ante-natal and how they respond to the spoken word. Natural Childbirth Trust, all those. You got any questions on that stuff, just ask.'

Sam pushed Lou Reed's *New York* into the CD deck and nodded to himself as the first strains of 'Romeo and Juliet' came through the speakers.

'I need to go into town,' Geordie said. 'Wondered if I could leave Echo here for a while?'

'Tell you what,' Sam said. 'You go do your errands and I'll walk her back to your place. Is Janet in?'

'Yeah, and Ralph.'

'Kill three birds with one stone, then. I'll meet your brother, get to see Janet, whom I haven't seen for weeks, and me and Echo'll start to get acquainted. She'll need to know who I am, get to know my little ways.'

Geordie did a double-take. 'You mean you're gonna push her in the pram?'

'No,' Sam said. 'I thought I'd take her on the bike, give her a croggy, leave the pram in the garden shed.'

Opera North had brought their production of *Carmen* to town and Angeles Falco would be going to that evening's performance. When Sam tried to buy a ticket, the woman in the booking office told him it'd be easier to get knighted.

He asked her to repeat it, and she said the same thing again, which was a change.

At five o'clock he relieved JD and sat in the Montego fifty metres down the road from Angeles' house. His injured hand was playing up this evening. He flexed his fingers repeatedly, but couldn't stop them cramping up.

There it was again, that irrational effect of a strange woman walking into his life. You could probably narrow it down to a physical effect, the result of mixing a few chemicals and hormones together. The attraction of opposites. Sexual tension. But some-where deep down Sam believed in miracles. He strung days together into weeks, and the weeks became months and there was no sign of a woman. There were always females around, other people's women or friends or colleagues; but after a while you forgot the absurd effect of being knocked sideways, ceased to believe in it as a possibility.

Then she walks into your office. You're the oldest and the greyest guy in town; you've been celibate so long you're beginning to philosophize. You're so sad you don't bother brushing the dandruff off your collar any more. You slap at it but it's building up, beginning to make you stoop. You watch her, you listen and smell, and the feel of her when your hands touched lingers on. You feel foolish and you like it. You remember worlds you inhabited which were crazy, and the world you're living in now suddenly seems unstable.

It was quiet. At 5.12 a new BMW arrived at the large white house two doors down from the Falco residence. One of the Stepford wives got out and carried her shopping into the house. At 5.17 a maroon Daimler with white-walled tyres juddered to a stop outside a substantial, gabled mansion, and a stereotypical drunken lord rolled out of it. He wove his way up the path to his front door, leaving the motor almost parked.

5.48: Canary-yellow Peugeot 306 Cabriolet playing a Björk CD louder than the tone of the neighbourhood dictated. Drove at speed, the engine booming, into the garage of a bungalow called 'Home'. Rustling of white bond paper as the other residents of the street prepared to write letters of complaint.

A minute or two before six, Sam walked down to Angeles Falco's house. Before he turned into the gate he noted that the street was deserted apart from a paper-girl with a green mountain bike who was delivering the *Evening Press*. She used the bike like a scooter, with one foot on a pedal, and at every stop she let it fall to the ground with a crash.

Sam rang the doorbell and waited for Angeles to let him in. She'd been to the hairdresser during the afternoon and her dark curls were stiff from the tension. She wore a thin housecoat over a three-quarter-length silk slip. Bare legs with fine hairs on the shins, silvered in the lamplight.

He followed her to the lounge and let himself sink into the luxury of the sofa. There was a game of Scrabble set out on the table, Braille version. A cut-glass tumbler with two rocks of ice swimming in Laphroaig. But Angeles was more interesting. You could watch her all the time. It didn't matter. She wasn't aware she was being watched, or if she was she didn't find anything wrong with that. Maybe blind people didn't know that it wasn't socially acceptable to stare? Why should they know that? Or even think about it? It wasn't their problem.

'I'm getting dressed,' she said, heading for the stairs. 'You can come up if you like, help me choose.'

'This is not the kind of offer I get every day,' Sam said, as he followed her up to her bedroom. 'There's usually a little more work involved before I get into a lady's boudoir.'

'Bedroom, not boudoir,' she said.

'Poetic licence?'

'A boudoir is a small room, somewhere a girl can sit and sulk. My bedroom is rather large.'

The bedroom was enormous, taking up three-quarters of the upper floor of the house. The wall opposite the windows was lined with cupboards from floor to ceiling. Two walk-in wardrobes were open and Sam followed Angeles into one of them.

'This could be a boudoir,' she said. 'If it wasn't a wardrobe.'

'I don't think you need a boudoir,' Sam told her. 'Can't imagine you sulking.'

'Oh, I don't know,' she said, waving her arm histrionically. 'It's not unknown for me to have a long face. When I was small I had fits of pique.'

There was no indication that she couldn't 'see' her surroundings. She must have penetrated this room, this house, with her fingers, with every living sense in her body. She inhabited it completely, in a way that a sighted person rarely could.

She took down a hanger with a full-length skirt and jacket in black silk. She loosened the skirt, which had a Turkish feel to it, from the hanger, and held both garments against her. 'Dior?' she asked rhetorically. Sam didn't bother answering. She wasn't going to wear it.

'This one's fun,' she said. It was a mini dress with a feather boa at the hem and a white lace jacket. 'But not for the theatre. Difficult to sit in.'

'How can you remember what these clothes look like?' Sam

asked. There was a line of twenty, twenty-five outfits on the rack. But every time she reached for one she knew exactly what it was.

'They're special labels,' she said. 'I can tell by touch what each outfit looks like. More important is what it feels like to wear. I can usually remember that. Or when I get it out of the wardrobe it comes back to me.'

Sam got into helping her. No, he didn't like the yellow one. Yeah, maybe the midnight-blue cocktail dress wouldn't be suitable. Pity, though. She settled for a wool crêpe creation with satin ribbons hanging from the waist. There was a naïve part of Sam Turner that believed he was going to watch her slip into the thing. A few seconds ticked away when he didn't know if he'd manage to stop himself chewing a hole in the Persian rug.

She didn't ask him to leave the room. At least he didn't hear her. But she stopped talking, stopped moving, and she raised her eyebrows. It was a signal passing aircraft might've picked up with these modern instruments they have, and it got to Sam as well, only a few seconds later, because he didn't have the technology.

'Right,' he said, reality catching at the back of his throat. 'You get yourself dressed. I'll wait downstairs.'

He couldn't read her face. Didn't know if it was relief or disappointment.

Neat trick, the thing about Braille labels on her clothes. Obvious when you knew, but before then it seemed like magic. There must be other things going on with her that he didn't see. Little tricks she was using to find her way through the world, but that were hidden from him because he could only think with his eyes.

Did she know what he looked like, for example? Once or twice he'd wondered if he should offer up his face to her fingers, but he couldn't find the courage. He wasn't sure she'd want to feel his face, anyway. Felt like too intimate an act for the current state of their relationship. Maybe later?

He sank into the sofa and closed his eyes, used the tips of fingers to feel around his forehead, his eyes and nose, the line of his lips. There was the rough edge of stubble as four hours' growth of beard pushed its way through. The flesh was cool and puffy, sagging a little round the jowls. If the woman ever got her hands on it, she'd think she'd run up against a monster. He'd have to try

78

and explain it to her beforehand, somehow hint that he didn't look a lot unlike Gene Hackman.

She'd understand about the whole being greater than the sum of the parts, she was an intelligent woman. The nose on its own, hey, laughable, you know what I mean? The ears without any context, just stuck on each side of the head. The eyes, the chin, the lips, all these parts don't mean anything by themselves. But when they are seen as a whole there takes place a transformation, a metamorphosis. Something magical happens, what could have been a disaster turns out to be, well, not compelling exactly, maybe the right word is intriguing.

He listened as she left the bedroom and came to the head of the stairs. He opened his eyes, expecting to see her descend. But she didn't appear.

'Sam?'

She spoke quietly, trepidation in her voice. He got up from the sofa and crossed over to the foot of the stairs. 'What is it?' he asked.

'There's someone in the garden.'

'Go back to the bedroom,' he said. 'Lock the door.'

Sam stood in the shadow of the back porch and cocked his ears. He scanned the garden. It was dark with a light breeze; clouds almost obscured the moon. There was a grey slate paved area, flat and recently constructed, and there was the oblong patch that represented the swimming pool. Then the land began to rise. A path of limestone slabs led a winding way through shrubs and ferns towards a stone wall and a quaint shed with a shingle roof. In the foreground there were three mature trees, a sumach, an ash and a stunted beech. Between the beech and the swimming pool there was a long, low bench which could have been carved from a single stone. Nothing moved. There was no sound.

The stars, the constellations in the sky winked and fluttered in a silent void.

Sam waited for two, three minutes, all his senses straining before taking one step forward and down on to the paved area. Immediately there was the sound of an intake of breath and the silhouette of a figure appeared from behind the ash. Sam moved quickly, but the man was already in full flight, legging it along the limestone path. He stepped up on to a pile of bricks and was over the wall and out of sight before Sam was half-way along the path. By the time Sam got over the wall and ran along the back passage round to the street, the man was already disappearing around the corner on a bicycle.

There was the possibility of getting the car and giving chase, but Sam thought he should check on Angeles, make sure there wasn't an accomplice walking up the stairs to her bedroom.

He tapped on her door and she asked, 'Did you get him?'

'No.' He wanted her to open the bedroom door, wanted to engage with her eyes. Wanted to see her face framed in that wreath of dark hair. Talking through a closed door, you couldn't see what she was thinking, assess her reactions.

'Did you see him?'

'Yeah, but it's dark out there. I got some idea of him, his height, build, age, but I wouldn't be able to pick him out of a line-up.'

'I would,' she said quietly. He heard her move away from the door. The next time she spoke her words came from the other side of the room: 'I'll be down in a minute.'

He went downstairs and found a perch by the kitchen table. The guy had been six feet tall, slim and fast, no more than thirty years old. He'd been playing cat and mouse with Sam in the garden, hiding behind that tree. Maybe had some kind of military training, to remain quiet and hidden for that long. You couldn't be sure, though, some people simply had a talent for concealing themselves.

The bike was a stroke of genius. No number plates, nothing to distinguish it from other bicycles. Except it was a mountain bike. Blue? Green? Hard to tell in the dark. In the dark you were blind.

Not a lot to go on, then. More than before, but it was all as vague as the mayor's morals.

He heard her bedroom door close and listened to her steps on the upper landing.

When she came down she was wearing a rainbow-striped shiver of a dress, which was not one of the ones she'd shown him upstairs. It was so simple and fitted so well you could've cried.

'Changed my mind,' she said, as if there was a way to explain it.

When Angeles was at the opera and Sam was in the bar outside not drinking alcohol, Quintin Reeves stood up in his living room and switched off the television after watching an episode of *EastEnders*.

The news of Isabel's death had not really penetrated his consciousness. He knew she was dead, but the plethora of causes and effects, the multiplicity of the event as it ricocheted around his settled life had not been given space enough to alter his routine.

He kept it at bay, instinctively knowing that once he gave it credence and began to accept its implications, he would be swamped by it.

His body, however, coped with the shock and horror of Isabel's death in its own chaotic way. The ability to see with his left eye disappeared. He blinked several times and it returned. But a few moments later he lost it again. A thrombus formed in one of the large arteries in his neck and was sent spinning along in the white-water river of his bloodstream.

As he pressed the off button on the remote control the thrombus hit his brain at the speed of a very fast car. The impact took out the mechanisms whereby his brain communicated with the motor nerves on one side of his body.

It was a stroke which was to leave his right arm and leg paralysed and force him into a premature retirement from the world of high finance.

FIFTEEN

Marie had been at Russell Harvey's house for a few minutes when the police arrived. She'd got past Emperor, the old dog, and settled herself in a high-backed chair in front of the solid-fuel stove. Isabel Reeves' boyfriend was much the same as the last time they'd met, except his eyes were red and puffy from a constant stream of tears.

'I can't believe it,' he'd said. 'I can't take it in. I know she's dead, that I'm never gonna see her again. I tell myself, "It's just you, Russell, you and the dog. That's all there is from here on." And then I hear her coming through the front door. I hear her voice when I'm lying in bed, when I wake up in the morning. It's like she's haunting me. I get a whiff of her perfume. There's no reason for it. I'm sitting here thinking, wondering if I should kill myself, and suddenly I'll smell it, sweet and real strong, like she's sitting there next to me.'

'You're not allowed to kill yourself,' Marie told him. 'It seems like there's nothing to live for at the moment, but there will be later. When you've passed the grieving stage. Isabel would've wanted you to carry on. She'd have wanted you to live out your life.' Her words sounded hollow, even to herself. Looking at Russell Harvey and his dog, at the poverty of his life in this greasy hell-hole of a house, she could understand that suicide was a real option for him. Still, you had to try. Attempt to bring some comfort even when you could see that there was no place the comfort could get lodged.

That was when the knock on the door happened. It was a policeman's knock. It would have been recognized all over the world. Elsewhere it might have been the KGB, the Stasi or the Securitate. But whatever it was called, it meant the same thing. It meant that your life was going to take a turn for the worse. That whatever control you thought you had was going to need a radical reassessment.

Russell Harvey looked at Marie for a moment. His eyes searched the room as if there might be a way out.

'Shall I answer it?' she asked.

When she opened the door, it was to two plain-clothes officers (there was a uniform standing by the car on the road), Detective Superintendent Rossiter and his female assistant, Detective Sergeant Hardwicke. Rossiter was the youngest detective superintendent in the country, and probably the most conceited. Marie had come across him on previous cases, but he never showed an inkling of recognition, merely flared his nostrils and steamed on to the object of his quest.

The WDS, Hardwicke, was fresh out of uniform, intent on impressing her governor, and had her eyes set, ultimately, on the Police Staff College in Bramshill.

'You been thinking of taking a holiday in the Mediterranean?' Rossiter asked Russell Harvey as soon as he entered the kitchen.

Harvey looked past the policeman, at Marie. He was shaking from head to foot. Marie didn't know if he'd heard Rossiter, but he couldn't answer.

WDS Hardwicke waved a piece of paper in Russell's direction. 'We have a warrant to search the premises,' she said. 'There's a squad of officers on their way, be here in a couple of minutes.'

'Why?' was the only syllable that Russell Harvey had.

'I want you to come down to the station with us,' Rossiter told him. 'We've got a car outside.'

Russell opened his mouth, but nothing more came out.

'Go with them,' Marie said. 'I'll get you a solicitor.'

Hardwicke took Russell by the arm and led him out of the house. The uniform opened the rear door of the car for them.

Rossiter looked quickly around the room. 'Absolutely stinks in here,' he said. As he left the house a police van with a group of six men in coveralls arrived.

'She's wearing this dress, I've never seen anything like it, and the guy who picks her up in the taxi is blind.'

'The taxi driver?' asked Celia.

'No, not the taxi driver, the escort, the guy she's going to the opera with.'

Marie let them carry on talking. Once Sam and Celia got going it was usually worth listening to. She sat at her desk and doodled with a 4B pencil, watched as a caricature of Russell Harvey appeared. A guy with hopelessness stamped all the way through him.

Celia laughed. 'Goodness,' she said. 'A blind taxi driver. Whatever will I think of next?' She shook her red hair. 'What was he like? The escort?'

'Short guy, thick-set, middle-aged. Nothing to write home about. But the point I'm getting at, he's blind. She's dressed to take your breath away, and she's going out with a guy who can't see her.'

'But she can't see him either,' said Celia.

'So what? Who wants to see him? The guy's nothing. If he walked past the window, you wouldn't notice. But her! Jesus, she's like a jewel. You get an eyeful of her and you don't know if it's night or day. You're reeling around, feels like you've got your shoes on the wrong feet.'

Celia exchanged a glance with Marie, then snapped back to Sam. 'She rang this morning.'

'Is she all right? Does she want me to ring back?'

'She didn't mention you.'

He looked disappointed, like he'd been robbed of a dimension. Then he took in the sly smile on Celia's face. He turned to Marie and saw that she, too, was not going into a depression.

'Oh, you two,' he said. 'Christ, you say guys are all clammed up and they don't know how to relate to their emotions. You want us to hang loose and not get so uptight about everything, then as soon as we relax you start taking the piss.'

'Thing is,' said Marie, 'what you have to be able to do is to hang loose and let all your emotions spill out, but you have to be able to laugh as well.'

'And do the washing,' said Celia. 'Clean the lavatory.'

'That'll come later,' Sam said. 'At the moment I'm in my stunned period.'

'As in,' Celia said, 'you were stunned by Angeles Falco, or you were stunned by my cruel joke?'

'Christ, I was talking about a dress,' Sam said. 'I mean, she's got walk-in wardrobes. Clothes, shoes, you know what I mean, threads with labels, Armani, all that stuff.'

'Ah, threads,' said Marie.

'Yeah, threads.'

'Dresses. You were talking about dresses.'

'Screw you,' he said. 'Screw both of you.' Which, for some reason, started them cackling like a flock of geese.

'Russell Harvey's been arrested,' Marie told them when Celia had made coffee and Sam had finished licking his wounds. 'Rossiter picked him up this morning, took him to the Fulford Road nick. They're searching his house.'

'You think he's in the clear?' Sam asked.

Marie nodded. 'He didn't do it. The man's shredded. Isabel was the only decent thing in his life.'

'The guy I chased last night was a different build,' Sam said. 'Must've been six foot tall, slim and fast.'

'That's not Russell,' said Marie. 'He's like the guys you see in photographs of internment camps, someone who hasn't seen a decent meal for months. He couldn't move fast. I can't imagine him running, he'd fall over.'

'So what's Rossiter up to?'

'Going through the motions. Maybe they want a fall-guy, in which case Russell Harvey was made for the job. The state he was in, he'll tell them whatever they want to hear.'

'In the meantime,' Sam said, 'I want Angeles Falco out of her house. We can't cover the back and front at the same time, and the guy who was in her garden last night will be making a return visit.'

'Where are you thinking of putting her?' asked Marie.

Sam shrugged, ran his hand over his chin, producing the bristle sound.

'I've got a spare room at my place,' said Celia.

'On second thoughts,' he said, 'maybe it would be better if someone moved in with her.'

'I wonder who that's gonna be?' said Marie.

SIXTEEN

When Geordie woke up in the morning his eyes were stuck together with testosterone. Janet was sitting with her back against the pillow, playing with Echo between her legs. He put his chin on Janet's thigh and made faces at his daughter. 'I'm sleeping badly at the moment,' he said. 'And I know I'm sleeping badly because when I'm sleeping I still have the feeling that I'm asleep. But when somebody's really asleep they don't feel like they're asleep. They only know that they've been asleep when they wake up.'

Janet laughed. 'You're the only person I've ever met who could wake up and say something like that. You're a fugitive from the law of averages.'

'That's because I grapple with life,' Geordie said without a hint of irony. 'Most people accept what happens, but I think about things. I can't help it. You do too. It's a feature in this family.'

'And these are the things that occupy you today, as soon as you open your eyes: doubt and the nature of sleep?'

'Yeah. And Echo as well. I'm always thinking about her, because she's in front of me all the time. Every time I look at her something's changed. Like it's teething at the moment, and you know how it's giving her gyp. I wondered if we should slip her a tot of vodka. You know what I mean, mix it with honey. Knock her out till the morning. What d'you think?'

'Jesus, Geordie. You can't do that. You'll turn her into an alcoholic. Trudie knows this herbalist woman, I was going to ask her for something.'

'Maybe that's what happened to Sam?' Geordie said. 'His mother gave him whiskey when he was a baby.'

'We're not going to do that to Echo, though,' said Janet, talking to the child. 'Are we my darling?'

Geordie shook his head. He rolled over and sat on the edge of the bed. 'Yeah. That's not the way to go. Just a brown thought.'

Venus had laid five kittens during the night. She'd dropped them into the padded basket that Janet had prepared for her and they were suckling noisily when Geordie went down to make breakfast. He watched them rooting away, finding the nipples by smell and touch, as yet unable to see. He tried to think of people who might want a kitten but couldn't think of anyone. 'Five,' he said to Venus. 'Christ, what're we gonna do with that lot? You'll have to farm them out among your relatives. They can't stay here.'

Ralph came in the front door, pushing it back on its hinges so it smashed against the wall. All of the kittens stopped sucking and Venus wrapped herself around them protectively.

'What's that?' Janet shouted down the stairs, concern in her voice.

'It's OK, it's only Ralph,' Geordie shouted back. And then to Ralph, 'I thought you was bringing a bus in, man. What's all the banging for?'

'I just got the sack,' Ralph said. 'I took the truck back and the guy'd got out of bed the wrong side. He's giving me, "Where've you been with the truck, I called the cops; thought you'd stolen it," all that shit. I told him, "Fuck are you giving me all this for, this time in the morning. I've brought it back, haven't I? Only a couple of days late."

'But he can't stop and he's giving me all this mouth about how he's losing money and the truck's so filthy he can't put it on the road. In the end I told him to go fuck his mother and he's got my cards ready, the bastard. So I'm out of work. What's to eat? My belly thinks my throat's cut. And don't even mention that muesli stuff, I'm not a bleedin' bird.'

When Janet and Echo came down Ralph was adding a tin of tomatoes to the eggs and sausages in the frying pan. 'Here's the ladies,' Ralph said, making his eyes as big as they'd go. 'You want some of this,' he said to Janet, pointing at the pan. 'Build you up so you can feed the nipper.'

Janet shook her head. Geordie knew she'd got the sausages for tonight's dinner and she was pissed off because she'd have to go and get them all over again. 'It's all right,' he told her. 'I've got to go to the shops.'

Echo got restless and hungry before breakfast was over and Janet had to start feeding her while she was still eating her muesli. Geordie got up from the table and made coffee for Ralph and himself and mint tea for Janet. He brought the cups to the table and was about to sit down again when the whole thing blew up. Janet got to her feet, pulling Echo off her breast and letting her T-shirt fall back down. Echo screamed. Janet stormed out of the room and up the stairs shouting about how she couldn't feed her own child in her own house without being ogled by some filthy bastard.

In the kitchen it was so quiet Geordie could hear himself breathing. He looked over the table at Ralph and Ralph lifted his shoulders and made a face, as if to say, 'What happened there, then?'

'Did you say something?' Geordie asked.

'Not a dicky-bird.'

'I'd better see what's up.' He left his chair and made for the stairs.

'It'll be hormones,' Ralph said. 'Even money.'

In the bedroom Janet was trying to get Echo to feed again but the child was too distressed. Janet's face was streaked with tears. Geordie sat next to her on the bed. 'What happened?' he asked. 'What's the matter?'

'It's Ralph,' she said. 'I can't feed Echo down there while he's trying to cop a look all the time. It's impossible.'

'Look at what?'

'Jesus, Geordie, my tits. What d'you think he's looking at? Sitting there eating everybody's dinner and watching me feed Echo with his mouth open, drooling tomato juice.'

'I'll get some more sausages. I already said that.'

'Why should you get them? Why can't he get them?'

'He's lost his job. I don't know if he's got any money.'

'So we have to keep him as well?'

'You think he was ogling you, Janet?'

'I'm telling you. He's a sleaze. When I'm feeding Echo I want to be natural and relaxed. That's the only way it works. If I get tense the milk doesn't flow, you know that. If it carries on like this, I'll dry up and we'll have to start bottle feeding.'

'I'll talk to Ralph,' Geordie said. 'See if I can sort it out.'

Ralph was in the sitting room in front of the television. He was sitting on the base of his spine with his legs spread out in front of him. Geordie told him what Janet had said. 'I was watching her, yes,' he said. 'But it wasn't ogling, there wasn't any sex in it. Jesus, Geordie, she's my brother's wife. What d'you take me for?'

'It upsets her if you watch her like that.'

'Yeah, OK, that's cool. I can understand that. I was watching Echo, really, seeing how she was feeding, but I won't do it. I'll look the other way.'

Geordie went to the shop for the sausages. If you have to believe your wife or your brother, who d'you believe? No contest, he said to himself, you believe Janet. On the other hand you don't want to call your brother a liar, get him all pissed off as well. And you specially don't want to do that if you've been separated from your brother for most of your life, been dreaming about meeting up with him again. When you've finally got him back and there's so much stuff to catch up on, the last thing you want is for him to disappear again. Get on a ship and sail away.

He got the sausages but instead of taking them home he went round to Sam's house, see if the great man's brain could come up with a solution. 'All I know,' Sam said, 'it's almost impossible to live in a family when someone else comes in from outside. It happens sometimes, can work real nice, but usually it's a disaster.'

'Thanks a heap.'

'I'm just telling you what I think. What d'you think?'

'Dunno.'

'What does that mean?'

'It means I don't know what'll happen. Ralph could be here for ever, or he could disappear again. I doubt he'll go away, but that's all I can say about it. The only reality is doubt. Who said that? That the only thing you need never doubt is doubt itself? You can worry about God and your family, your friends, whether the world's round, if you're gonna get cancer and die before you're thirty. All those things are up for grabs, but doubt is a constant; you need never doubt it. Who was it? Who said it?'

'Must've been a philosopher,' said Sam. 'Descartes? Sound anything like him?'

'Day cart? Leave it out, Sam.'

SEVENTEEN

Janet felt like one of those figures in a Lowry landscape. Pushing Echo's pram into the wind, her slim body at a forty-degree angle, she didn't know where she was going. Geordie was out playing detectives with Sam. His brother Ralph had been watching her ever since Geordie left the house.

When he'd begun his surveillance of her, and his innuendo, the day after his arrival in the house, Janet had laughed and told him to go away. But his answer had been to step up the action into a higher gear. 'Man needs woman,' he'd said this morning. 'It's as simple as that. Like the poet said, man needs woman.'

He eyed the line of her rump, the outline of her breasts, and edged up closer as she bent to stuff Echo's clothes into the washing machine.

She closed the door of the washing machine, put Echo in the pram and left the house. She went back for a coat and slammed the front door so hard the glass in the top panel shattered into hard rain.

After Echo's birth, when they'd been discharged from the hospital, Janet had thought everything in her life would settle down to normality at last. With Geordie and Echo she'd found the family that had always been missing, and the kind of togetherness that she'd longed for seemed to be turning into a reality.

But now Ralph had turned up. There was always a Ralph waiting just around the corner. Someone who'd never give you a second look in other circumstances, but when you least wanted him he'd be there with his tongue hanging out.

She didn't know how to handle the situation. Geordie was so

overwhelmed by the fact that his brother had found him. So happy to have discovered a link to the past. If she told Geordie that Ralph was angling to get her into bed after he'd been in the house less than fifteen hours, what would happen?

They'd fight, that's what would happen.

It didn't matter who won or lost, Geordie would be hurt. He'd re-learn all over again that there was nothing to insulate him against the pain of existence. Just when you think that things are taking a turn for the better, you find that the devil's got you by the tail. Geordie would learn the lesson well enough, because he already knew it. He'd withdraw a little more into the thin shell that shielded him against the world. There'd be one more thing that he wouldn't want to talk about.

Janet was the only person in the world who knew Geordie. Lots of people thought they knew him: Sam, Celia, Marie, JD. Ralph thought he knew Geordie even though they hadn't met for more than a decade. But Geordie wasn't as easy as he appeared. He made himself into a clown to disguise his disappointment with the world. He pretended to be stupid, because it disarmed people.

But he was no more vulnerable than anyone else. He had spent several years on the street after the children's home, and he'd survived. He'd lived with people who had frozen to death in shop doorways, with others who had been raped and sodomized. He'd seen friends die with AIDS-related illnesses while they were still in their teens. The thing about Geordie that no one recognized was that he was not vulnerable. He was one of the strongest people she had met in her life. He was too strong for his own good.

He'd softened up since they'd met, and he'd softened up considerably more since Echo had been born. Now Ralph was in danger of undoing all that, of sending the more human Geordie scurrying back to the crustaceous existence he knew so well.

Janet's first thought was to visit Margaret and Trudy, a pair of working girls who had always been good friends. But Margaret would tell her again what shits men were and that she should let Geordie do his own worrying. Janet wasn't in the mood for that message this morning. She wanted to get away from Ralph, to leave reality behind for a while.

After walking for half an hour she found herself close to the street where Angeles Falco lived. She'd been thinking what it must

91

be like to be blind since the case had come up, and she'd wondered if Angeles had had much contact with babies, how she would be with Echo.

Geordie had said that Angeles was heavy with people who treated blindness in a sentimental way, that she'd torn a strip off Sam for patronizing her. If Geordie hadn't said that, Janet would've rung earlier in the week and made an arrangement to go see her. She couldn't help feeling that the woman must be in need of company since her sister had been murdered. Angeles was a virtual prisoner, under constant surveillance.

Rich, though. The real-estate value of the street with its individually designed houses would've kicked a hole in the capital of a Colombian drugs cartel. In the first drive was a new Ford Testosteroni bulging with technological gimmicks; the pear-shaped man gazing at it from his window bristled with an air of received pronunciation and right-wing ideologies.

There was a brass bell by the side of the front door. One of those bells you pull. It set up a tinkling sound inside the house. When the chimes faded away Janet thought she heard a sound from the other side of the door. The blind woman clearing her throat? Then nothing.

She made to pull the bell again, but as she did so there was the same sound. It was not someone clearing her throat.

Janet tried the door. It was locked.

She moved back to look at the upper windows of the house, but found nothing there. When she returned to the front door the sound had stopped. She had a vague memory, something she had read in a newspaper, about a woman who got an electric shock in her kitchen and went into a convulsion, ended up having a heart attack.

EIGHTEEN

As she worked at the computer the Toreador's song was in her mind, and she'd find herself humming it stridently, moving her shoulders with the rhythm. She wrote an e-mail to Felix, her escort of last night, thanking him for taking her to the opera. Felix was a piano tuner, gay with a permanent partner, and an old comrade in the arena of blind rights. He was also a musical connoisseur, and one who loved to share his knowledge and experience with Angeles. An arrangement which benefited them both.

After an hour's work she went to the kitchen and found some peanuts for the birds. She opened the french window and took down the wire bird-feeder that hung from the guttering of the patio. It was almost empty. She placed it on the garden table and filled it to the brim.

There could be another freeze soon. She should empty the pool and put the covers on.

There was a strong wind blowing, whistling through the trees and around the eaves of the house, but it was not loud enough to obscure the movement of a loose brick. Angeles' first thought was that the prowler from last night had returned, but she remembered that it was mid-morning now, daylight. A man would not risk climbing over her wall at this time of day. A cat, then?

There was a neighbour with a neglected Persian, Tilly, who came looking for titbits from time to time. Angeles knelt on the tiles and extended a hand, rubbing finger and thumb in the direction from which the sound had come. 'Here, Tilly,' she said. 'Here, girl.' She pursed her lips and made a series of small kisses at the air.

She strained to hear. No cat approached. Slowly, Angeles got up from her kneeling position. Cats had very well-developed sense organs: ears, eyes, whiskers and noses. They would sit and watch their prey in utter stillness and silence, and pounce without mercy. They could leap a great distance, their mouths open, their claws extended. The victim stood little chance of escape.

'Here, Tilly, Tilly.' But there was no cat there. No sound.

She returned to the garden table, suddenly self-conscious, wondering what kind of figure she cut. A blind woman with the dust of the tiles on her knees. When she had been younger men had wanted to be close to her, she had felt their breath in trains and buses, and she had sensed how they turned to look at her on the street. People still turned to look at her on the street now, but it was because she was blind. Before it had been because she was a young woman.

She shook her head, moved the thoughts away from her. Why the self-consciousness? Because she may or may not have been observed by a cat?

There was an intake of breath from the direction of the nearest tree. Angeles turned her head towards the sound. It was not a cat, it was head-high. Animals don't hold their breath, suddenly have to refill their lungs.

But all was quiet again. Her heart was pounding; her chest like a drum. Angeles tried not to make any swift or jerky movements. She took the wire bird-feeder and hung it on its peg. She turned again towards the sound and called quietly: 'Tilly, is that you? Here, girl; here, Tilly.'

But there was no further sound. No maniac running across the garden to send her sprawling to the ground. And there was no Tilly.

She found herself hurrying towards the french window, stumbling in her haste. She stepped inside the house and closed the door behind her, reaching to turn the key in the lock. Her heart was beating thunderously now, her breathing was short, staccato, and a thin line of sweat had appeared at her hairline.

Panic signs, she thought. The whole idea of the prowler, the thought that she was being watched, what had happened to her sister, Isabel. All of these events had conspired to undermine her confidence. Even her laugh, when she saw herself panicking over a cat in the garden, was tinged with hysteria.

The french window opened by itself while she still had her hand on the key.

Angeles parted her lips to scream but two strong hands drove into her chest, pushing her over backwards, knocking the breath from her lungs. Her head struck the leg of the table and when she tried to claw her way upright a sense of nausea and a series of convulsions overcame her.

For a short period she may have lapsed into unconsciousness, but her will was reactivated by the sense of the man's hands at her throat. She squirmed away from his touch and he grabbed the front of her blouse. She heard and felt it rip and wondered briefly if there was a possibility of reasoning with him.

But the man was standing astride her now, his hands with their long fingers striving for a grip around her throat. He made no sound. He was here with one, single, fanatical purpose.

Angeles kicked out. If she was going to die, and there was no doubt that that was what he had in mind for her, then she was going to inflict as much damage as possible on her attacker. She heard him gasp as her foot connected with his groin. He knelt astride her now, and she managed to pull his fingers towards her mouth. It felt like a thumb between her teeth. She bit down, hard, hoping to sever it from his hand, but he pulled it free.

She had found blood, though; the tang of it was in her mouth. She reached up to where she thought his face must be, clawing with her fingers, hoping to take out his eyes, to even up the stakes a little. She continued for as long as she could, while his grip around her throat deprived her body of the oxygen it needed to function.

She stuck two of her fingers up his nostrils, hoping to yank his nose off his face, but before she found the strength something inside her relaxed, gave up the struggle. I'm dead, she thought. I've been killed by someone and I don't even know who he is. There was a far-away sound of knocking and a high-pitched female voice, like something in a dream or an opera. One of her last thoughts was of the birds. Glad she'd got around to filling their feeder. Then there was the death-rattle, way down in her throat, below the relentless grip of the hands that cut off her life.

NINETEEN

J D watched the house from his car. The street was quiet and he had his notebook on the steering wheel. He wished he'd brought the current chapter of his novel to edit, but that was sitting on his desk at home.

He'd come across an odd couple in the post office yesterday and, while watching the blind woman's house, he was keen to get them down on paper. They were around forty, she in a wheelchair, obese, her hair uncombed; he was skinny, unshaven for two or three days and he wore cross-trainers, one of which had a sole that gaped like a slack mouth.

The woman held the telephone while her mate fed cash into the box and dialled. JD noticed that their faces were encrusted with dirt. When the woman put the telephone to her ear she exposed layers of sweat-rings under her arm. The material looked brittle, as though someone had been painting it.

He moved closer, hoping to overhear the conversation. He took an application for Income Bonds from a container on the wall and posed as an investor. This is what you had to do if you were a writer, spy on people, watch them and record the way they looked, how they interacted with each other and the world. They thought they were safe, their privacy intact: but they were wrong.

'Your dad sends his love,' the woman said into the mouthpiece. The man nodded his head in approval. 'He's all right. He's gonna mend the fence later. Maybe tomorrow.' The man shuffled his feet.

'When d'you think you'll get through again?' She listened to a long explanation at the other end of the line, nodding from time to time.

'That's all right,' she said. 'I hear what you're saying. We'll see you when we see you.' The man shook his head. He pursed his lips and frowned.

'The bloody neighbours have been at it again,' said the woman. 'Why, complaining about the smell. First it was the house, they said the house was stinking. Now they say it's us, our personal hygiene. Cheeky buggers. Somebody's coming down from the council, see if it's right, if we smell. We're going to Woolly's after this, get some perfume. Just in case.'

They'd talked a couple of minutes more, until they had nothing left to say. Language had dried up like rain under a hot sun. The woman handed the telephone to the man, who hung it up. Then, without a word passing between them, he'd turned the wheelchair around and pushed her out into the street. JD waited for nearly half a minute before he took in a deep breath of air, and it was still redolent with their spoor.

He didn't have a specific use for these characters. He collected anything and everything he saw. It was a habit now, something he did without thinking. The woman in the wheelchair and her skinny mate would not be used in his current novel. They may never be used at all. They were an insurance policy. One day he might need them, and if they weren't immortalized on paper, he'd carry them as vague ghosts in his mind. What captured the woman for him were the layers of sweat-rings under her arm. The smell was important, but it was something else. He hadn't described the smell in his notes because it could have been anything – sour, sweet, musk or a mixture of aromas. But the sweat-rings were exact; they encapsulated the woman's character.

He saw a woman with a pram enter the street, but he didn't see that it was Janet. In the order of his universe Janet was not in his mind. Deep within his unconscious, or subconscious, Janet was at home with Geordie and their baby.

He checked his watch and noted the time. He was about to write that a woman with a pram had entered the street, but an inner man prompted him to look at her again.

Janet crossed over the street to Angeles Falco's house. She walked up the drive and rang the front doorbell. She waited for half a minute before knocking on the door. JD couldn't think why Janet would be calling on the blind woman. Did they know each other? He couldn't imagine that they were friends. Two women from different sides of the tracks.

Janet backed away from the door and peered at the bedroom windows. Then she moved forward again and banged on the door with both fists. She seemed to be calling through the letterbox. She stood back and raised her arms as if she was waving. Then she grabbed Echo's pram and shoved it ahead of her down the side of the house and around to the rear entrance.

JD wondered if he should follow her. But it would mean breaking his cover.

She pushed the pram around the side of the house. There was a wooden gate but it wasn't locked. When she got to the rear of the house there was a movement in the garden, but it must have been a cat or bird, something disappearing at the level of the garden wall.

The back door was locked, but a patio door stood wide open. She stuck her head inside and called out a friendly 'hello'.

No reply.

Spooky feeling. The silence stretched itself into a taught line. Felt like it would snap.

She put the brake on the pram and stepped inside. Stood for a moment and listened intently. There was a ticking sound in another room, through towards the front of the house. Not a clock, something else. Heating controls or some kind of alarm system? Apart from that the house was silent.

Janet took another step inside. There was a small occasional table, which had been overturned. A heavy plant pot was broken; peat and the remains of a Christmas rose were spilled on the carpet.

There were three chairs but Angeles Falco's inert body was spread-eagled behind the sofa. Janet fell to her knees by the side of her. She felt her own body go into a convulsion, heard again the same sounds she had heard at the front door, only this time they were coming from her own throat.

Janet thought there must be something she could do but she was overwhelmed by a plethora of images, one piled on top of the others. Resuscitation. The movement at the back wall, it wasn't a cat. Ralph doing the moon-walk. Two sisters, both killed. The terrible silence that death leaves behind.

Another movement. The patio door being opened further and the dark figure of a man silhouetted against the glass. He looked from side to side and moved across the room towards them at speed. Janet tried to scream as he reached out for her, scrambled back against the wall and scurried forward on her hands and knees, must get to her child, must look to Echo and keep her safe.

'Get an ambulance.'

She stopped at the patio door. She looked back towards the voice. JD was leaning over the quiet body of the blind woman. He had tilted back her head and was giving her mouth-to-mouth, blowing the contents of his lungs into her. He paused momentarily, glanced over at Janet.

'Get an ambulance. Use the phone.' He'd taken over. He was giving orders.

He placed both of his hands on Angeles' chest and pushed down, once, twice. He kept going. The mouth, the chest, the mouth, the chest. Janet rushed through to the hall and dialled for an ambulance. Then she called Sam.

'Is she dead or alive?' Sam asked down the wire.

'I don't know,' she said. 'I thought she was dead, but JD's working on her.'

TWENTY

There are currently 110,000 men living in England who have been convicted of sexual offences against children. This is not a generally known fact. The Home Office knows it, because it was one of their studies that threw up the figures. And I know it, of course, because I am a psychologist and informed about such things. That I am a currently unemployed psychologist doesn't alter the truth. I qualified and I have clinical and field experience.

My ex-colleagues, of course, know that my employers felt it just to remove me from my post to avert a scandal. What is not generally known is that my research project was actually producing original and valuable data. And if I was so wrong in my treatment of the boys, why was I given such a huge sum of money to resign?

Your question is this: will these sex offenders commit more crimes against the innocent? I don't want to lie to you. The answer is that many of them will. Because although they have been convicted of sexual offences against children, and although many of them have served terms of imprisonment, they have not been cured.

Which brings me, neatly, to one of my pet subjects: is there such a thing as 'cure' for offenders like these? And the answer is no, at least not in the conventional sense. There is though, even in my liberal profession, a growing consensus that these people can be 'cured' in a number of different ways. We are beginning to look again at a range of tertiary preventions, including selective incapacitation, the use of boot camps, and keeping high-rate serious and chronic offenders out of circulation altogether.

Psychology is the art of observation, and observation is about watching people. All psychologists watch people, but not all psychologists see. Let me rephrase the last part of that sentence. Psychologists, like people in other professions, actually see what they expect to see.

This is best illustrated by the experience of eye-witness testimony. Because eye-witnesses can be 100 per cent sure about what they have seen and at the same time 100 per cent wrong. There was an experiment carried out on television in the eighties where viewers were shown a film of a mugging, and then asked to pick the offender from an identity parade of six men. Remember that they had just seen the offender commit the crime in front of their eyes. A couple of thousand people responded, but only 14 per cent of them picked the right man. With six possibilities to choose from, a random guess would produce a correct result by 16.67 per cent. So in this example eye-witness testimony produced a result which was worse than a random guess.

There has been an enormous amount of research on eye-witness testimony, and it all tends to show that people remember faces poorly and that they don't recall details from memory, but from stereotypes of what they think criminals look like.

There is so much that should be obvious, but few people actually see it. Why do we insist that perception and memory are like data stored on a hard disk? Why do we think of them as akin to a copying process or a photographic image? Nothing could be further from the truth. Perception is a process which interprets an event in the outside world, and memory is always either deteriorating or reconstructing, attempting to fit images and interpretations into a scheme which *feels* right.

Many of my colleagues did not understand this. They believe that crime can be controlled by means of education, or that it will respond to some form of psychotherapy or counselling. I fought them for all of my professional life.

I would be a good eye-witness, because I have trained myself to be observant.

I am the watchman.

The woman fought like a tiger. When I got home I hardly

101

recognized myself. My face was scratched and bleeding, the skin torn in vertical lines by her manicured nails. Her teeth had almost severed my right thumb; she had bitten down to the bone just above the knuckle and I had to swab it with iodine and wrap it in swathes of bandage to stop the flow of blood. A kick in the balls is never good news, but she had been particularly vicious and they had swollen up like tennis balls. I crept into bed, my head aching, and let myself drift into a numbing sleep.

Miriam was not well pleased when she came home from work and discovered the state of me. What could I say? My injuries had obviously been inflicted by a woman.

Her eyes flickered as she focused on the bandaged thumb then travelled back to my disfigured face. 'What happened?' she asked, her voice quietly controlled.

'Accident,' I said weakly, knowing I had no hope of getting away with it.

Miriam said nothing. She turned away from me and walked out of the bedroom. I waited but she did not return.

Eventually I got myself out of bed and hobbled through to the kitchen, where she was sitting on the high chair. 'I'm sorry, Miriam.'

She made me wait a full minute before she opened her arms and took my head against her scrawny breasts.

'I didn't want to hurt you,' I said.

'Who was she?'

I shrugged my shoulders. 'Nobody. Someone I met in a bar.'

Miriam knows how to be silent. She understands the power it gives her. When I looked up there was not a hint of amusement or forgiveness in her face. Her jaw and bottom lip were, if anything, pushed even further forward than usual. Her eyes were like the points of black pins when she looked at me.

'I'm really going to make you suffer,' she said.

I nodded. I knew she would.

Miriam has been silent since then. She wants the punishment to fit the crime. She needs time to think. When she's ready she'll tell me what she wants to do, and I'll submit to it. We have a democratic relationship. We are a modern couple.

In the meantime I nurse my injuries and crouch in that delicious space of doubt and uncertainty created by the silence of my vengeful woman.

102

I choked the life out of the blind woman.

I played back the tape and heard her death-rattle. She expired beneath me like a balloon being let down.

This has been my prayer: Father, if thou be willing, remove this cup from me. Because the truth of the matter is, I really didn't want this job. It was not my choice; I was mission-oriented. Later, if it all comes out, if the monsters who run the media get their hands on it, they'll label me psychotic.

I really don't want that to happen. I want truth to happen. I want light to happen. I want justice.

A crime is a social or political concept. It is nothing more than that. A crime in Pakistan is not necessarily a crime in England. The people who do the ruling want us to believe that crime is more than that. That crime is something defined by the Divine. But it isn't. It is man-made, and often only a tool that the power brokers use to maintain the status quo.

I didn't want to kill again. That is what my prayer was about. But my God did not take the cup away. It was mine to drink.

Another thing. They'll bring into dispute the level of my intelligence, maybe suggest that I am sexually inhibited. They'll question my early life, how I was disciplined as a child, the order of my birth. The psychologists, my friends and colleagues, will gather around like vultures.

I find this prospect disturbing. Psychology, for many of them, is a guessing game. What they will never understand is that I am of good intelligence, a skilled professional. I am not a random killer. I watch and I wait. I plan.

Also, they'll suggest that I am socially immature, when the contrary is the truth. I do not live alone, Miriam and I are an emotional unit. I am socially competent, from a good home. My father's work was stable, and, had he lived, he would have been recognized as a hero.

He was a hero.

They don't understand. That is the first point. The second is that they don't want to understand these things. They, the press, the media, are mere propagandists for the ruling élite. They uphold the laws of the land, and their job is to undermine anything that threatens those laws. I carry a divine truth within me and therefore I am anathema to them. They will tear me limb from limb.

Oh, I can hear them already . . . *a failure of empathic bonding and attachment . . . resulted in the child becoming emotionally detached . . .*

I want one thing to be quite clear. I was not abused as a child. There was no question of anything like that in my background. My father was a good man who served the community. I will do anything to preserve his memory.

I don't mind if they say I'm suffering from some kind of mental illness. I know why they have to say that. Because if they say I'm sane, and they believe that they are sane also, then there is something that they have to share with me. In some respects, they reason, we are alike, and if we are alike, then they might also be led to take life.

But the mental illness theory doesn't hold water. Why do they say that people with mental illnesses commit murder, when everyone knows that people suffering mental illness are much more likely to harm themselves?

Look at the thing objectively. Frederick and Rosemary West were responsible for the murder and torture of at least twelve young women. The Wests were evil people. I fail to see how anyone can compare the acts that they committed with what happens between me and Miriam. OK, so the new studded belt is a tad more savage (let's not mince words) than the hairbrush was, but this is something that happens between consenting adults in the privacy of their own home.

What we do could be identified as one of the paraphilias, because it involves a degree of physical suffering. And it is certainly sexually exciting. But it doesn't involve necrophilia or zoophilia or paedophilia.

And, this just for the record, I have never buggered Miriam. I don't have an anal fixation or incestuous desires.

TWENTY-ONE

S am arrived at the house minutes before the police or the ambulance. Janet was standing by a table in the garden, hugging Echo to her chest. There was a broken syringe on the path outside the patio.

'Where?' he asked, and Janet nodded towards the patio door.

JD was kneeling by the body of Angeles, which he had placed in the recovery position. The front of her blouse had been torn away in the struggle and one of the buttons had rolled under a chair. Sam moved quickly to her side.

'I think she'll be OK,' JD said. 'She's breathing now and she's got a strong pulse.'

Sam looked at him, saw the sweat streaking his face and neck. 'Has she said anything?'

JD shook his head. 'She's been out of it all the time. Could be drugged.'

Angeles had the imprint of the attacker's hands around her neck. The bruising was extensive, beginning under her chin and spreading out in dark waves over her shoulders and down the front of her chest. The fingers of her right hand bore traces of blood, and Sam wished beyond hope that she'd marked the bastard for life.

At least she won't be able to see what he's done to her, Sam thought, conscious that he was seeking a palliative. The drone of an approaching ambulance whirled into the spaces of the room. He remembered, as a boy, looking at his distorted reflection in the back of a spoon. And the pane of glass in his bedroom window which had carried a flaw. Angeles had never experienced these things. Never played games with the visual world. And she would not have seen her attacker.

When she recovered she would describe to them the way he felt, how he smelt. Maybe, with some luck, the sound of his voice. But no, he wouldn't have given that away. She'd have some sense of what his breathing sounded like, maybe even the taste of the man.

We live in different worlds, he thought. She is confined to a feminine universe of sound, while I am equally trapped in a masculine world of vision. Seeing is like having a gun with a powerful scope. You look down the barrel and focus on the part of the world that you want to isolate. But hearing is the opposite of that. The ear doesn't go out into the world like the eye, it is more fluid and responsive. It can take its time; doesn't mind waiting.

Sam and JD stood back while the paramedics took over. As they watched, the police arrived in the form of Superintendent Rossiter and his sidekick, Detective Sergeant Hardwicke.

'What happened?' Rossiter asked.

'Looks like somebody tried to strangle her,' said the chief paramedic. He helped his colleague lift Angeles on to a stretcher, leaning over to arrange the blanket around her.

Rossiter looked at Sam. 'You're never far away when there's trouble in this town,' he said.

Sam looked at JD, but he didn't say anything.

Rossiter raised his voice. 'I'm talking to you, Turner. I think you've got some explaining to do. What happened here?'

The paramedics pushed the stretcher out through the patio door, and Sam followed them.

'Hey, where the fuck do you think you're going?' said Rossiter, grabbing Sam by the shoulder.

Sam shook him off. He looked back for a moment, flexing the fingers of both hands.

'He wasn't here,' said JD. 'He's only just arrived.'

Janet appeared in the empty doorway after Sam had followed the paramedics down the side path. 'I found her,' she said. 'Then I rang Sam and called for the ambulance. He can't tell you any more than we can.'

But Rossiter wasn't listening. He turned towards Hardwicke. 'Go after them,' he said. 'If Turner tries to get in that ambulance, arrest him.'

'Yes, gov,' she said, a smile on her face as if something funny had happened.

Sam, sitting in the ambulance, could see the bruises deepening around the throat of Angeles Falco. He could hear an authoritarian voice, female, on the periphery of his consciousness. The voice was insistent, addressing a part of him, threatening him with arrest if he refused to step down.

The paramedic touched his shoulder. 'I think it'd be better if you stepped out of the ambulance, sir,' he said.

Sam looked past the man. Hardwicke was standing on the road, preventing the paramedic from closing the door of the ambulance. 'I'm only going to say this once more,' she said. 'Step down on to the road and return to the house. Detective Superintendent Rossiter has some questions for you.'

He looked at her. Navy power suit, slim skirt and flared jacket buttoned up to the chin, dark tights, highly polished shoes. A small face framed by a thick growth of auburn hair, chopped short. Sam spoke quietly. 'This woman is seriously ill,' he said, indicating the prostrate form of Angeles. 'Get away from the door so we can take her to the hospital.'

Hardwicke began climbing into the ambulance, her face set. Sam raised his voice. 'You're making a mistake, here,' he said. He stood to meet her and recognized the hesitation in her eyes. He quickly turned her around and marched her back on to the road, pushing her gently but firmly towards the house. Then he was back inside the ambulance, pulling the rear doors closed behind him. 'Go,' he said to the driver.

Before they turned the corner, he was aware of Hardwicke jumping around in the middle of the road, shaking her fists in anger and frustration. Couldn't hear her at all, only imagine the expletives. He'd only known Angeles Falco for a short time, but she'd already made him realize that you didn't hear *things*, only the sounds connected with their actions. You didn't, for example, hear angry policemen or women. You only heard them stamping or warning or barking.

TWENTY-TWO

WDS Hardwicke was spitting mad when she returned to the house. JD was reminded of Tinkerbell or Prospero's Ariel, a silly spirit whose purpose has been crossed.

'Where's Turner?' Rossiter asked, the incredulity in his voice as tangible as fudge.

Hardwicke passed the back of her hand over her mouth. 'He assaulted me,' she said. 'He fucking *pushed* me.'

'Where is he?' Rossiter repeated.

'He went in the ambulance,' Hardwicke said. 'He pushed me on to the road. He'll be at the hospital.'

'Have him picked up,' the detective superintendent said. 'Put him in the cells and let him stew there. I'll talk to him later.'

'It'll be a pleasure,' Hardwicke said. She brushed past JD as she made for the door. 'You'll be OK here on your own, sir?'

Rossiter looked at Janet and JD. 'I'll need someone to take statements,' he said. 'Send one of the constables in. Someone who knows how to write.'

A SOCO team arrived with their white plastic tape, their notices and their sterility. There was a police photographer and a couple of white-overalled forensic scientists, both women, who were pissed off because they had missed the body. They cheered up considerably when they found the broken syringe. They commenced to circle around it as if echoing some tribal dance; a rite of fertility in which the syringe was transformed into a sacred and untouchable object.

JD and Janet were ushered into the front hall by the SOCOS, but when Echo began crying Janet ducked the tape and walked back through the crime room to collect her. 'Jesus,' said the man in charge of the SOCOS, 'This job's impossible.'

Janet sat on the bottom step of the staircase, jigging Echo up and down on her lap. She looked at the young officer who was trying to take her statement. 'She's hungry,' she said. 'I'm going to have to feed her.'

'This's not going to take much longer,' the constable said.

Janet shrugged. 'She doesn't understand "much longer". She's a baby.' Janet lifted her jumper and guided a brown nipple between Echo's lips. She looked at the young constable and raised her eyebrows. 'Otherwise she's gonna howl.'

The policeman began writing at speed. 'You said you heard something when you approached the front door?' hc said.

Janet fussed with her child, taking care to see that both of them were comfortable. When she was ready she returned her eyes to the policeman. 'Sorry,' she said. 'Would you mind repeating the question?'

JD walked over to the front door and looked into the street. It was then that he noticed the slip of paper in the letterbox. The PC guarding the door had a moustache that wanted to emulate Emiliano Zapata's, but was severely hampered by police regulations. He gave JD a cop stare for a full minute, weighing up the possibilities of JD doing a runner. JD moved his weight from one foot to the other and then back again several times. He nodded at the PC, even attempted a smile, but the cop was having none of it. When he looked away, surveying the rest of his domain, JD concentrated on getting on to his blind side, using his body to block the cop's view of the letterbox. Slowly, he eased the slip of paper out and put it into the inside pocket of his jacket. Might be nothing, of course. But then again, as Sam would say, you never know when the breaks are coming.

There were two scenes of crime in this house. One was official and high profile and surrounded itself with science and team-work. And the other was unofficial and surreptitious and good at keeping its eyes open and looking for the main chance.

'Don't leave town.' That's what Detective Superintendent Rossiter told them when they'd finished giving their statements. 'Don't leave town.' He said it without a hint of irony, three flat syllables delivered in that standard officious manner that seems to affect all CID officers.

'Where does he think we're gonna go?' Janet asked when they were on the street. 'I've got a baby here, a husband back home. All my friends are here. I'm not likely to go on a runner to Brazil, wherever it is criminals are supposed to go.'

JD's laugh was whipped away by the wind. 'We're under house arrest,' he said. 'I expect we're the main suspects.' He reached his finger towards Echo's hand in the pram, and she grasped it for a moment. 'But I can't stay in York. Saturday I'm out of here.'

Janet stopped and looked at him. 'Where are you going? They'll arrest you if you do that.'

'Can't be helped,' he said. 'I don't have a choice about it. Leeds are at home to West Ham.'

Janet gave him her natural born killer look. 'Jesus, JD, what's that? A joke? That woman in there might've been killed. She's stuck in the hospital, Sam's got himself arrested, the police've been using both of us like doormats, and you're telling football jokes.'

'Sorry,' he said. 'I've got this pathologically persisting adolescence. It's a joke I was going to put in the new novel. I wanted to hear what it sounds like.'

'A book.' There was real anger sparking away inside her. Her eyes were like black gems, the flash of them capable of cutting deep. 'I just don't find it funny in the circumstances. You can go past Go, collect your two hundred pounds on the way, but don't come with no more funnies.'

Nothing was more calculated to undermine JD's confidence than a woman's wrath. His failures with the female sex were legendary and they were all recalled instantly, *en bloc*. Dozens of them descended on him, their voices trilling, their rounded bodies vibrating with confused anger. Then the vision died in a wheeze. 'I found this in the letterbox,' he said, handing her the slip of paper.

Janet took it from him. 'What letterbox?'

'Back at the house, Angeles Falco's letterbox. I stole it.'

Janet read aloud: 'To the Householder. On Tuesday evening my bicycle was stolen while I was delivering newspapers in this street. If it turns up, or anyone can help with evidence, please contact me at the following address.' The note was signed Christine Moxey,

110

and an address was given on Bishopthorpe Road. 'That's last night, when Sam saw someone in her garden.'

'Yes, and the guy made his getaway on a bike.'

Janet went to the hospital to enquire about Angeles, and to see if she could help Sam not get himself arrested. JD drove to the address on Bishopthorpe road and found himself at the door of a badly neglected house with fraying curtains and waist-high nettles in the front garden. The roof gutters thought they were window boxes and sported a screen of wispy plants. A long time ago a window in one of the bedrooms had been broken and covered with a sheet of plywood. The plywood had now buckled with exposure to the weather and some accidental chemical exchange had coloured it various shades of blue.

A thin-faced young man in a black leather jacket and designer T-shirt opened the door. His accent was born out of Liverpool. 'You've just come to stare, have you?' he said to JD.

JD shook his head. 'No, sorry,' he said. 'You remind me of someone I know.'

'D'you want me to guess who it is?'

'If . . . if you like,' JD told him, slightly taken aback, but disarmed by the guy's boyish smile.

'Brad Pitt.' He held the smile and nodded his head in complete agreement with himself. 'In *Seven*,' he said. 'You saw that?'

JD shook his head. As far as he could remember Brad Pitt was a blonde.

'Because if you saw him in that Robert Redford movie, *A River Runs Through It*, you won't think he looks like me.'

'I didn't see that either,' JD told him. 'It wasn't Brad Pitt I was thinking of. It was somebody else, a writer.'

The guy's face fell. 'Oh,' he said, all interest in the conversation lost. 'I thought you was talking someone famous.' He glanced over his shoulder, back into the gloom of the house, as though there was something fascinating there which he was being denied. Something or someone that couldn't manage without him. 'What d'you want, then?'

JD pulled the slip of paper from his pocket. 'I came to see Christine,' he said. 'About her bike.'

The guy glanced at his deep-sea diver's watch. 'Come in and wait if you like. She won't be long. I'm Clive, by the way.'

JD followed the man into the darkened interior of the house, which exuded a strong mixed aroma of body odours and stale socks. But that was OK. As a writer JD was a practical existentialist prepared to experience every situation that came his way. Every time he got into a lift he wondered if this was the time it would get stuck between floors. He didn't want to get stuck between floors, but there was something in him which thought he should.

'I've got some tea in the pot,' Clive said. 'Made about five, ten minutes ago. I could warm it up.'

JD shook his head. 'I'll pass,' he said. 'Thanks for the offer.'

'Have you seen *any* of Brad's movies?' Clive said. There was a tremor in his voice, as though he didn't want to face the possibility that there was someone in the world who wasn't a Brad Pitt fan.

JD didn't want to be the one to disillusion him. 'Hey, I don't really know, to tell you the truth. I'm not sure I'd recognize him if I saw him. I know the name, but I can't honestly put a face to it. Tom Cruise. Di Caprio, I know them. Robert Carlisle and Sean Penn, but Brad's a little more obscure. What was he in?'

'*Fight Club*? *Meet Jo Black*? *Interview with the Vampire*, you might've seen him in that. Or *Thelma and Louise*, about a couple of women who go away for a weekend and end up getting killed?'

'I've heard of *Thelma and Louise*,' JD said. 'But I didn't catch it.'

'Jesus. What about *True Romance*, *Seven Years in Tibet*, or *Johnny Suede*?'

'I don't go to the movies a lot,' JD admitted. 'Last film I saw was *Looking for Richard*, Al Pacino movie. D'you see that? Great film.'

Clive shook his head. 'That's really sad, you know, we're talking about a guy who's got everything. He's a brilliant actor, he's a sex machine, multi-millionaire. You name it, and Brad's got it; he's a guy who is known all over the world, you know, in Japan, anywhere you wanna mention, they've heard of him. They go to see his movies, and you don't even know what he looks like.'

'I'll try to catch up with him,' JD said. 'Next movie, it'll be one of his. I'll make a point of it.'

'He was a choirboy in Missouri,' Clive said. 'Brought up a

Baptist, so he has morals, too. Heart-throbs are a dime a dozen, but with Brad we're talking real class.'

'No, I mean it,' JD told him. 'You've convinced me, no need to say any more. I'm gonna keep my eyes peeled for the next film he does. I've missed enough good things for one lifetime. Hell, *Thelma and Louise* was a real mistake. How could I've missed that?'

'You know Robin Givens?' Clive asked.

JD shook his head. 'Can't say the name rings a bell, no.'

'She was married to Mike Tyson. She was one of Brad's girls. And Gwyneth Paltrow, she was another one. They were engaged. Jennifer Aniston, you know who she is? Women can't resist him. Even lesbians.'

'I dunno where I've been,' said JD.

When Christine Moxey arrived home JD was pushed back into a corner of an ancient sofa, half-buried by several hundred colour photographs and posters of Brad Pitt in various stages of undress. 'This's JD Pears,' Clive said. 'He's found your bike.'

Christine Moxey was maybe fifteen years old. She wore white pancake make-up with a landslide of eye-shadow and mascara. Her lips were glossed with a dark purple sheen. Large black plastic hoops dangled from her ears. In spite of the icy wind she had apparently been out without a coat, wearing only a skimpy sleeveless blouse and a mini-skirt. The blouse was too short to reach the waist of the skirt, and left a band of pimply flesh adorned with a navel ring.

'Have you brought it back?' she asked.

'The bike? I haven't actually found it,' JD said. 'That's a misunderstanding. I wanted to talk to you about it.'

Christine looked at Clive and did a double-take. Her imagination couldn't crack the code. 'D'you want a cup of tea?' she asked.

'Yeah, sounds good.'

'How d'you take it? Builders or lesbians?'

JD didn't blink. 'Bit of a mix,' he said. He watched her fill the kettle and put four spoons of tea into the pot. It wasn't just that she was young, there was a subtext to her phraseology that had been developed through generations of psychological layering. Most of the young men you meet, he thought, they want to get you into bed. But he wanted to get her down on a page.

113

'I work for a private-detective agency,' JD said. 'We're investigating a break-in that took place about the time your bike was stolen. We wondered if you saw who took it.'

'What've you got all these pictures out for, Clive?' She brushed some of the cheesecake posters aside and sat down next to JD. 'I'm sure the detective isn't interested in Brad Pitt.'

It was a question. JD and Clive looked at each other, and each of them waited for the other to answer.

'You can find guys as good-looking as him on the street,' Christine said. 'People think he's the best because of all the exposure he gets. It's the same with pop music, the promoters think they know their audience, and what they think is what we get.'

'That's all true,' Clive said. 'Except Brad is the goods.' He looked from Christine to JD. 'I was educating him. He doesn't do movies.'

'It's all right,' JD said. 'I've been learning.'

'You've heard of bird-watchers?' Christine said. 'Clive's a Brad Pitt watcher. He knows everything about him, every move he's ever made. Mum said he's got so much Brad Pitt in his eye that he's blind to everything else.'

Clive smiled modestly. 'I'm pretty sure there's a lot of things about Brad that I don't know.'

'Mum said . . .'

Clive's complexion changed. 'That's twice. Don't mention that woman's name in this house,' he said.

'If you'd've been half as concerned about her as you are with Brad Pitt, she'd still be here,' Christine said.

Clive raised his voice. 'She was bloody sex mad.'

JD coughed. He asked: 'Are you brother and sister?'

Christine crossed the room and took Clive's arm. 'No,' she said. 'Clive's my stepfather. Or he would be if he'd married my mother before she ran off with his mate, Eddie, the Australian sheep-shagger.'

'This is beginning to get complicated,' JD said. He wanted to know the details, though. You can't be a writer if you don't follow up on the leads. There was a human situation here, something he could turn into metaphor.

'It was an everyday story of love and lust on the Bishopthorpe

114

Road,' Christine said. 'The winners hitched up together and split, carved out a life for themselves in New South Wales. And me and Clive were the ones left behind to lick each other's wounds.'

'It was the least I could do,' Clive explained. He didn't say it, but you could see it there in his eyes: faced with the same situation, it's exactly what Brad would have done.

They fell silent, contemplating an ocean of submerged feelings; reefs of only half-glimpsed crustacean life forms. They need diving-gear, JD thought, something to enable them to get a clear view of their situation. There was colour there, somewhere, colour and movement and possibilities that were obliterated from the vantage point they were allowing themselves.

'So what do you want to know?' Christine asked.

JD was intrigued by the idea of the Australian sheep-shagger, but he stuck to the point. 'Did you see who took the bike?' he asked.

'No,' she said. 'It wasn't even that good a bike. Mum bought it second-hand before she . . . you know, did a bunk. I thought people only stole good bikes.'

'Where did you leave it?'

'There's an alley behind the houses. I always leave it there when I do that part of the street. Saves me lugging it along, 'cause I've got to come back the same way. There's old Mrs Hamson down at the bottom what gives me a drink and a biscuit, and I sat with her for a few minutes. When I got back it was gone.'

'Can you give me a description of the bike?'

'Yeah, it was a wreck,' said Clive, which was funny enough to double him up.

'It was a green Raleigh,' said Christine, ignoring him. 'Mountain bike . . .'

'Hybrid,' said Clive.

'. . . battered and dirty,' continued Christine. 'It had a Mickey Mouse bell, and the chain was rusty, and there was fifteen gears but you could only get five. And Mum had gouged my initials in the saddle, CAM. Christine Annabelle Moxey. I told the police all this when I reported it. They gave me a crime number so I could get insurance if we were insured.'

JD jotted it down in his notebook. 'I'll keep my eyes open for it,' he said. He handed her his business card, the one with Sam

Turner Investigations on it. He scribbled his own address and telephone number on the back. 'But do me a favour, will you? If the police find it, or if you get it back some other way, will you give me a ring? It might help us catch the guy we're looking for.'

'You gonna pay me for info?'

JD gave her a twenty. 'There could be more,' he said. 'If you ever find out who stole it.'

Christine showed him to the door. In the background Clive was still talking about his hero. 'Brad never played a private eye. He was a cop in *Seven*, but he never played a private eye. You know why that is?'

Christine came with a wide smile and closed the door. JD turned and walked along the street. He might never discover why Brad had not played a private eye. 'More sleepless nights,' he said to himself, 'worrying about that one.'

TWENTY-THREE

Russell Harvey was shivering. Since Isabel had died the temperature had dropped. Before Isabel the world had been a cold place for Russell, but now she was dead it was frozen.

That was the one thing. The temperature.

The other thing was his dog, Emperor. Russell didn't know how long he'd been in the police cell at Fulford; maybe two days? Whatever, it was far too long to leave Emperor unattended. He'd spoken to the policeman about the dog, the policeman who asked him the same questions over and over again – Superintendent Rossiter – but he couldn't get a satisfactory answer. What it seemed like to Russell was that if he signed a form saying he'd killed Isabel, then Rossiter would see to the dog.

The other one, Hardwicke, the sergeant, she thought that kind of behaviour was all right. She smiled whenever her boss spoke. It didn't matter how cruel he was. Confusing, really, the woman. Crossing and uncrossing her legs all the time. Her face was beautiful until she smiled.

Isabel had been the opposite of that. Isabel's face was not really beautiful at all. But when she smiled it lit up. When Isabel glowed like a spiritual fire she was more beautiful than anything Russell had seen.

It was like the text-cards that he got at Sunday school when he was a small boy. They had pictures of Jesus or Mary and the angels, and the figures were all suffused with that same warm glow. Made you feel good. Made you feel beyond yourself, out of the mire of schoolteachers and policemen and the street. What they did, those text-cards, they made you realize that there was a whole different world somewhere else, where possibilities abounded. A place where it was never cold and you didn't have to worry about where the next meal was coming from. The thought of money or fags wasn't part of the equation. You were free, you were free of everything that hung you up here.

The cell was blue, blue walls and ceiling, and there was a smell of paint, as though it had been done recently. Must've been, he thought, because there was no graffiti on the walls. They could have had it painted especially for him, but he doubted it. They wouldn't go to all that trouble.

The policemen walked like heroes. That was because of the uniform. When people put uniforms on it gives them a false dignity, makes them strut. Somehow the covering of the uniform envelops them in a self-importance that puffs up their chests and endows them with a bragging gait. Gives them ultimate authority, a moral superiority that is represented by their physical bearing and stature.

Isabel was in that other place now. Out of it, away from the screaming reality. No one could touch her up there: her sister, her husband, not even Russell himself. She was free of the physical world.

He shivered. The physical body had always seemed a kind of tyranny to him. It was so huge, so dense and material that it was difficult to imagine how the soul managed to live in it. When you took into account the bones and the blood and the lymph and the layers of muscle and fat, there were very few spaces left for anything else. Being a soul must be a squashed existence.

Once, when he was a young man, Russell had come out with this argument in a pub and after closing time the three guys he'd been talking to had taken him round the back and kicked the shit out of him.

Broke three ribs and left him permanently deaf in one ear.

This was the chaos that politicians called society, civilization.

TWENTY-FOUR

She had never been in love. Being in love meant turning your back on the world, meant closing down all possibilities except one. Angeles could not envisage a time when she would want to make her world smaller, when she would willingly whittle away the storehouse of life's possibilities. There had been men who had tried to insert themselves into her life, but none had penetrated further than the dark cave of her vagina.

She was aware of him sitting beside her, his large hand covering one of hers. When she moved her thumb she could feel the stiff hairs on the sides of his fingers. The mattress was firm and the air was etherealized cleaning fluid and urine. An alarm was activated and hurrying feet moved to answer it. Some way off the whirring of a floor-polishing machine confirmed that she was not dead, that she had arrived in a hospital ward.

When she spoke her throat ran with fire. The torn gossamer tissue of her vocal cords screamed in protest as hundreds of millions of incandescent cells reacted to the vibration of a single syllable.

His grip tightened. 'How're you doing?' he asked. That rich tone, concern enunciated in each word. And yet a maintained sense of irony and detachment was at work, lest the depth of his disquiet panic her.

'What do I look like?' she asked. Her voice was a whisper, a croak.

'Bruised. Vulnerable.'

'Tell me. I want to know.'

'You look like shit,' he said. 'But you'll mend.'

She smiled. If she had to wake up in a hospital bed looking like shit, she couldn't think of anyone she'd rather find holding her hand. 'Shouldn't you be out chasing whoever did it?'

'I'm going in a minute,' he said. 'I wanted to see you were all right. And I think you should move into my place when you get out of here. We can't protect you in your own house.'

'I'd rather take the chance and be in my own place, Sam.'

He shook his head. 'It wasn't a question. If you make me a list I'll collect the things you need.'

'What's going on, Sam? He tried to kill me.'

The detective shook his head. 'We don't know why. Not yet.'

Her body juddered. She relived the attack again but compressed into a single instant. Her breeding had taught her to put a brave face on things and that is what she did, but inside she was trembling with fear. Since the death of her sister, no even before that, her relationship with the world had altered. There was a malevolent force out there, someone was watching her, stalking her, waiting for a moment of vulnerability. She remembered calling to her neighbour's Persian, *Tilly, here Tilly, here girl*, and all the while there was no Tilly there. Only a man, a silent presence, watching, waiting to strike.

What kind of man was that? Someone who lived in the shadows, who moved in silence. Even while he was squeezing the life out of her he hadn't spoken. Not one word. When she bit deep into the flesh of his thumb he didn't wince.

Angeles lived in a middle-class world, a world where words were the primary method of communication. She had never come across people who didn't speak, who didn't declare their intentions. Peasants, they say, don't speak much, and nor do fishermen. But she was not being stalked by someone from another age. She was being stalked by someone from today's world who wanted her dead.

It had to be a mistake. He thought she was someone else, someone who had done him wrong. And yet he had taken Isabel as well. Surely he hadn't mistaken both of them?

'I haven't done anything,' she said to Sam. 'Why does he want to kill me? I haven't done anything.'

Sam stroked her brow with his free hand. He didn't answer. What could he say? Still, it calmed her. She felt herself stretching beneath the covers. The fear was still close by, but it was as if she had rolled it into a ball and put it to one side.

When he made to withdraw his hand she clasped it tighter. It was an involuntary movement, something she had not intended to do, but she felt him relax into it. Disturbing. This was not something she had wished for. She could only disappoint him. They were never going to enjoy a film together, or wander hand in hand around a picture gallery. But there were those small charges in their fingers. The quickening of her breath, the delicious fluttering of her pulse, and the heat emanating from her shoulders and the back of her neck.

If it didn't cost freedom, that closing down of possibilities, she'd opt for love with this man. It was obvious to her that he'd be pleased to close down possibilities in his own life to make room for her. That he'd be only too ready to put all of his eggs in her basket.

'I'm going to tell you something,' she said.

'I don't want to hear it.'

'I'm going to tell you anyway, Sam.'

'You don't have to tell me anything.'

She gripped his hand hard, felt her nails digging into the flesh around his palm. 'When I was young,' she said, 'I was a victim, or I experienced myself as a victim, because I was blind, because I wasn't like the other girls I knew. But there came a time when I realized that in many ways I had more possibilities than they did. I discovered that, for me, the world was a place of adventure and that I liked it like that. That I was an adventurer. Do you understand what I'm saying?'

Sam nodded. 'I knew before you told me.'

'The thing is, Sam, that I want it to remain like that. To become more like that. I need more possibilities, not less. If I give up what I have spent my life becoming, then I'll be nothing.'

'I spent most of my life becoming an alcoholic,' he told her. 'When I gave it up I was swamped by possibilities. If you make a space in your life, then other things can happen. But if you fill it to the brim, you don't leave space for anything else.'

She hesitated. 'You gave up something negative, Sam. If you give up something negative, of course it makes room for positive things. But I'm worried about giving up everything I've won.'

121

He didn't answer. She felt him loosen his grip, and this time she let him do it. She wanted to tell him that it was as much in his interest as hers. That if she let herself fall in love with Sam Turner, she'd break his heart.

After a couple of minutes he said, 'You're too young for me anyway.'

'Jesus, it's like Fort Knox trying to get in here.' It was the voice of Sam's assistant, Geordie. 'There's cops everywhere.'

'Keep your voice down,' Sam said. 'Ms Falco's not feeling on top of the world.'

'Sorry,' Geordie said. 'You have to turn the volume up with cops or they don't understand what you say.'

'We better go,' Sam said. 'I'll call back and see you later.'

'Thanks,' she told him. Meaning it.

'But I came to tell you about Russell Harvey,' Geordie said. 'Ms Falco'll want to hear it as well.'

Russell Harvey, Isabel's boyfriend. Angeles had never met him; all she knew about the man was what she had heard from Isabel and from Sam. Now she was going to learn something else.

'He's dead,' Geordie said. 'Topped himself in the cells. Tore up his shirt to make a noose. They found him this lunchtime.'

'No,' Angeles said. She felt tears escaping from her eyes and running down her cheeks. Tears for someone she had never known. For a minute she couldn't stop the flow and she didn't know why. Eventually it dawned on her that the tears were not for Russell Harvey alone, they were for her sister Isabel and for herself, and they were for Sam and the pity of it all. A terror had entered her life and she knew that that terror would be the end of her if she had to face it alone. All that stood between the terror and her death was Sam Turner, the man she had just told to keep his distance.

'Sam,' she said. She felt him approach the bed, but at the same time two sets of footsteps entered the room. Heavy footsteps, walking in unison. The kind of footsteps that one associates with authority.

'Sam Turner?' The voice was masculine, a voice that lived in a barrel chest. It gave rise to a vision of a shave that was unnaturally close.

122

'Jesus Christ,' Geordie said.

'There's no need for this,' Sam said. But his comment was followed by a crash, the sound of some item of National Health Service equipment coming to the end of a long life.

Geordie again, his voice incredulous: 'What the fuck are you doing?'

'Go and stand by the wall, and be quiet,' said the voice from the barrel chest. 'Mr Turner, if you continue to resist, you'll leave me no alternative . . .'

Angeles heard herself scream at the top of her voice as the two policemen frog-marched Sam Turner along the corridor and out through the swing doors.

Her scream hung in the air for some time. She convinced herself that she could hear it vibrating long after it had disappeared. Every sound made her heart beat faster.

She was alone again. *Under observation*, they would say when people enquired.

TWENTY-FIVE

George Forester did all the talking. Marie listened, but occasionally she couldn't hold back and forced herself into the picture. The policemen at the various stations they had visited were, without exception, rude and patronizing.

Forester was the first solicitor to have retained Sam when he began making a name for himself. At first glance he was not someone you would associate with Sam Turner; he couldn't hang loose, always looked as though he was suppressing a fart.

He wore a dogtooth Burberry overcoat, knee-length, with striped trousers and shoes that shone like mirrors. If his hair had been cut any shorter, his barber would have to qualify as a brain surgeon.

The desk sergeant said: 'Turner?' He ran his finger down a list of admissions. 'Nope. Sorry, nobody name of Turner.'

'Look again, would you, officer?' said George Forester. 'We were told by the desk sergeant at Fulford that he was brought here.'

The policeman took his time. His finger traced the list again, stopping every now and then at the long names, the ones with more than two syllables. When he'd finished he looked at them both and shook his head. 'Where did you say he was arrested?'

'He wasn't arrested,' said Forester, 'he was forcibly *taken* from the District Hospital.'

'Wouldn't've come here, then. If he were arrested at the District, they'd've taken him to Fulford. Who was the arresting officer?'

'We don't know. There were two uniformed officers, both of

whom are going to be charged with the use of excessive force.' Forester glanced at Marie and took a breath. His voice was high-pitched and carried camp overtones but there was no doubting its authority. 'Listen, sergeant, I have been given the run-around by you and your colleagues for nearly five hours. I am warning you now that I have had enough. If I am not given access to Sam Turner in the next fifteen minutes, I'm going to make it my business to see you personally bounced around the courts.'

The officer looked him square in the eyes, and found not a grain of compassion. The man swallowed and his Adam's apple squirmed under the slack skin of his throat. He forced a fleeting smile across his face. 'Tell you what,' he said. 'I'll give Fulford a ring, see if we can sort this one out for you. It's not my job to go upsetting the public.'

Forester glanced at his watch. 'Fourteen minutes,' he said. He led Marie towards a bench seat by the wall, and they sat there together. Forester took his watch from his wrist and balanced it on his crossed knee.

Marie was ill at ease in a police station. It always brought back the experience when Gus, her late husband and Sam's first partner, was killed. The police had suspected Marie of the murder, though she was working at the time on the other side of town. It had taken her a long time to recognize that she was bereaved and at the same time suspected of being the author of that bereavement.

She had come to terms with it largely due to the comfort and friendship of Sam, and for that she would always be grateful. Sam was impetuous and landed himself in trouble because he followed his instincts rather than his, usually, good sense. That was one of his problems. Another was that he could never deal adequately with officialdom, with authority figures, or with people in uniform. He didn't seem to understand that people apply for a job that involves wearing a uniform when they have a low opinion of themselves. And that the only way to deal with them is to massage their egos. One to one with normal men, women or children Sam could give and take, and would emerge from the encounter with some kudos. But whenever he came up against someone who assumed an air of superiority, he'd want to fight.

And, Marie thought, being a bloody stupid man, he would

fight. He'd never give in. That survival mechanism that allowed most people, after a period of pain or humiliation, to bow their heads and compromise, just didn't have a place in the make-up of Sam Turner. They could do what they liked with him down below in the cells: nail him to the wall or flay the skin off his back. He wouldn't move an inch, call them all fools.

Which was another reason to get him out of there quickly. While he was still breathing and in one piece.

'Time,' said George Forester next to her. He spoke the word under his breath, almost to himself. She watched him rise from the wooden bench and move across the floor to where the desk sergeant was speaking into the phone. Forester repeatedly tapped his fingers on the counter.

'Found him,' said the desk sergeant as he put down the phone. He made an attempt at a smile but it foundered on the stony response of the solicitor.

'Where is he?'

'Clifton, sir. The lads who were bringing him in had a bit of an accident. Their car was involved in a collision. They couldn't get it moving again, had to sit tight until we could get a tow truck out there. Anyway, it ended up with your friend being taken to Clifton. If you go down there, you'll be able to see him.'

'I hope you aren't trying to work another flanker on me, sergeant.' Forester fixed the desk sergeant with a stare and held it for several seconds, but the guy didn't flinch. Either he was a good liar or he thought he was telling the truth.

Marie went out into the wind with Forester and followed him to his new white Rover; she sunk into the soft leather seat. 'I'm getting worried,' she said. 'It's been too long.'

'He's at Clifton,' Forester said. 'It's OK, they can't keep us running around all night. This is the last stop.'

The police station at Clifton was an older building. They were met at the door by a uniformed chief inspector with a nose like a light bulb. Fate had tried to conceal him by naming him Smith. He had been briefed and knew who they were and the nature of their business.

'Mr Turner is with the doctor at the moment,' he told them. 'Just routine, no need to worry. We need to be sure he's OK before releasing him.'

126

'Chief Inspector,' Forester said. 'My client has been missing for more than five hours. I'm going to make sure there's a full-scale inquiry into this whole shebang.'

'You must do as you see fit, sir. But I can assure you there has been nothing sinister happening. A small motor accident and a series of misunderstandings, that's all.'

'We shall see.'

Marie went outside to use her mobile. She rang Celia and JD to tell them that they'd found Sam and would be bringing him home soon.

As she approached the steps to the front entrance of the police station, Chief Inspector Smith pushed the door open. George Forester, supporting Sam on his arm, was ushered out. The left side of Sam's face was dark, his eye puffy and closed, crisp and brittle as a meringue. His right hand, the one already damaged by the police car door, was hanging uselessly by his side.

'I hope you'll be feeling better by the morning, sir,' said Chief Inspector Smith.

Sam twisted his head back to the man. 'Go fuck yourself,' he said.

'Quite,' replied the policeman, slipping back into the artificial warmth of his station.

Marie went forward to help support Sam on his other side. 'Are you all right?' she asked. 'Can you walk?'

Sam grimaced. 'Yeah, I'll manage. They've done something to my knee.' He hobbled towards Forester's Rover and got in the back seat. Marie walked around to the other side and sat next to him.

'What happened?' Forester asked when he'd started up the car and was back on the road.

'What you'd expect,' Sam said.

'So, there was no car accident?'

Sam laughed hollowly. 'Yeah, there was a little bump. They hit a bollard and smashed the windscreen. Driver cut his head, but that was the extent of it.'

'Right,' said Forester. 'I want you to see a doctor first thing in the morning, and I'm going to bring in a photographer. They can't expect to get away with this kind of behaviour.'

'Yeah, yeah,' Sam said, laying his head back on the leather

upholstery, closing his eyes. 'But make it last thing in the morning, not first. I might wanna lay behind the clock a few minutes.'

Marie leaned over to touch his hand, but he drew in his breath sharply and pulled away.

'Bit tender just there, darlin',' he said. 'I must've stamped on it by mistake.'

'Why, Sam?' Marie said. 'Why did they do it?'

'Dunno,' he said. She watched his shoulders rise in a shrug. 'I only told a few bad jokes.'

When they arrived at Sam's house, Celia was waiting by the gate. George Forester said he'd leave them to it, but he'd be back the next morning. All three of them stood and watched him drive away.

'He's a good man, George,' Sam said. 'Good to have him on our side.'

'Yes,' said Celia. 'Look at the state of you. They've made a right mess this time. I'm going to stay the night, make sure everything's all right.'

'There's no need for that, Celia.'

'And it doesn't matter what you say or think,' she said. 'I wouldn't be able to sleep if I went home now, wondering if you were OK. I can curl up in the spare room.'

Sam began to protest, but Marie cut in. 'It's better if someone's here,' she said. 'If you send Celia home, you'll still have to lose me.'

Sam looked from Celia to Marie and then back to Celia. 'OK,' he said, 'have it your own way, but I don't want any fussing.'

When they reached the front door, they turned again at the sound of footsteps running along the street. Geordie jogged up to the fence and stopped, winded, letting his upper body flop over the top of the gate.

'Just came to see you were all right,' he said. 'Jesus, I ran all the way. I'm totally fit.' He was breathless, fitting in gulps of air between each word. 'That's what happens when you have a baby. You feel really shagged, because you're up half the night with changing nappies and feedings and all the things you have to think about, and your eyes are half-closed all the time. But really it keeps you fit.'

'There must be easier ways,' Marie said. 'I think I'd rather go to the gym.'

'That's just a substitute,' Geordie told her.

Sam walked back along the path towards Geordie. 'Thanks for coming,' he said. 'You can't stay the night, I'm afraid, we don't have any beds left.'

Geordie watched him struggling along the path. 'Jesus, Sam,' he said. 'You're walking with a pimp-limp. You can't be a PI and walk like that. People won't take you serious.'

Sam made it down the path and stood in front of Geordie, one of them on either side of the gate. They looked into each other's face. It was a relationship that was usually understated, kept at bay by a continuing banter of jokes and one-liners. But when the superficialities failed and the power of the thing stood forth, it felt as though sinews of blood and muscle tied them together.

Marie glanced at Celia, and Celia gave her a tight smile.

'Hell, Sam,' Geordie said quietly, looking at the dark bruise of his face. 'The bastards really did a job on you.'

Sam shrugged and drew in his breath with the effort. 'You know me,' he said. 'In for a penny, in for a pounding.'

TWENTY-SIX

FMS. False Memory Syndrome. During the last ten years or so I have watched my illustrious colleagues discuss the pros and cons of this phenomenon. The earnest professionals on the one hand and the sensationalist press and media on the other. They've loved every minute of it. The righteous amongst them have been truly outraged, while the shallow and uncaring have wallowed in a hot scented bath of titillation.

Those of us who have worked with vulnerable and often exploited young people have long known that the mind, and especially the memory, is fragile and easily influenced. Left to itself, if that were possible, memory is an affair of construction rather than one of mere reproduction. But when meddled with by a True Believer in the guise of a psychotherapist, it can be twisted into a million different shapes.

Propaganda is not a new concept; the brokers of power have practised it for hundreds of years. Historically, every time a new ruling élite comes to the fore, they bring with them hoards of propagandists, 'educators' and media types practised in the dissemination of selective information.

The other thing that we professionals know is a very simple fact. When something horrible happens in childhood, the child does not suppress it. He or she usually remembers every detail. The lives of these people are marked by a desire and a wish to forget those details, but, try as they might, they will have to live with them for ever.

Whenever I meet someone who claims that a therapist has helped 'awaken' them to a memory of childhood sexual abuse, I find myself looking around for a therapist who is passionately, no, hysterically, concerned with an agenda that has nothing at all to do with the client.

If I had been given another minute, if the woman with the pram had not come to the door, the blind woman's life would be over. My mission would be completed and I would now be settling down to a normal life divided between my work and Miriam. A pleasant dream.

I had to ask myself if the arrival of the woman with the pram at that particular moment was a sign. This is a fair question. There are legends as old as time itself which recognize the intervention of fate at the moment of execution. The neck of a hanged man is not broken. The soldiers drag him back to the scaffold, but at the second attempt the trapdoor does not open. The crowd become restless, their eyes cast towards heaven. They have been transported to the realm of magic. A moment before they thirsted for blood, but now they feel that the creator is focused upon the same scene, and that He wants this condemned man to live. If there is a third hitch in the hanging, the man will be pardoned.

It does not necessarily mean that the man is innocent of the crime for which he has been condemned, only that God has another purpose in mind for him. The man may be released and go on to provide comfort and succour for the poor and disadvantaged. Or he may be released only to face degradation and suffering, a fate worse than death.

In the case at hand the blind woman's life was saved, I believe, not by fate, but by an accident. The woman with the pram was in the wrong place at the wrong time. I don't know what brought her to the door at that particular moment, when I already had the victim by the throat. This is something we can never know. We can speculate, say, that the child woke earlier than usual, that the mother, stressed by her responsibilities, left the confines of her home and walked, by chance, to the blind woman's house.

Why didn't she walk in the opposite direction, find herself knocking at someone else's door? Are we to believe that some divine finger pointed her towards the house of the blind woman? That the same heavenly presence dictated the speed at which she travelled, timing her arrival at the precise moment when I was squeezing the last breath of life from Angeles Falco?

This would not be a scientific conclusion. All the evidence points to an act of chance. Should the same thing happen again, however, the data would have to be re-examined. And, certainly, if my third attempt at retribution were frustrated, I would have to take a long look at the arguments that have brought me to this pass.

In the meantime I shall remain steadfast. I am not in doubt. I know what I have to do.

Crucifixion was not designed for Jesus Christ. People tend to forget this. Crucifixion was designed for rogues and robbers and murderers. It was one of the methods used to rid the world of those who no longer deserved to live.

I walked through her ward in the hospital today. Visiting hour. The other patients had their loved ones around them, but she was alone. As I drew level with her bed I slowed to get a good look at her and she stirred in expectation, raised herself up on an elbow. I touched the rail at the end of her bed, just tapped it as I went past. Her face, which a moment before had been full of expectation, turned into a study in fear. In the time it takes to snap my fingers her features became a parody of the mother in Picasso's *Guernica*.

Looking back at her as I left the ward, I realized that I could torture her for ever. In many ways that would be a better solution for me. There would be enjoyment in it. Perhaps it would be possible to reduce her to a shaking wreck? To undermine her totally, so that she becomes the agent of her own death.

But no, I want her life. She owes me that much.

The scratches on my face were not as bad as I feared. They are healing nicely. The thumb will take a little longer. There is no doubt that the woman intended to bite it off. I have had a tetanus injection and, for the sake of my neighbours, invented a dog. I have been in the wars, but I shall come through.

Miriam wanted me to suffer for being unfaithful to her. It is strange to be thought unfaithful, because I would never dream of betraying her. But it is better this way; I cannot tell her the truth. She read about the punishment in a national newspaper. She bought a small cellophane packet of hardened steel nails from B&Q and handed them to me. She led me over to my work bench, which I keep in an alcove of the kitchen. She took the packet of nails from me and placed them on the bench. Then she took a hammer out of the tool box and placed it next to the nails.

I looked at her enquiringly and she nodded. She didn't smile. 'Is this it?' I asked.

She went into the bedroom and returned with a packet of tampons and a reel of surgical tape. I tried to imagine what was going to happen. 'Will it be bad?' I asked, but she wasn't going to say anything.

She undid my belt and let my trousers fall around my ankles and she tugged at my underpants until they were around my knees. I felt ridiculous standing there in a T-shirt, but humiliation is an essential ingredient in a meaningful relationship.

She asked me to open my mouth wide and then pushed one of the tampons inside. I now know the meaning of the word 'absorbent'.

'Now close it,' she said. 'Tight.'

I brought my lips together and Miriam took the reel of surgical tape, tore a strip off and placed it over my mouth. The beginnings of an erection stirred between my legs.

Miriam took hold of my penis and placed it on the work bench. It didn't lie exactly where she wanted it, so she tugged at it, making me shuffle forward a few inches. I could feel one of the cross beams of the bench against my shins.

I watched carefully while she opened the packet of nails and shook them out on to the wooden surface. I wanted to scream but the tampon had absorbed all the saliva I'd produced. She selected six of the nails and placed three on each side of my member.

When she picked up the hammer and began joining me to the bench I closed my eyes.

I went to the café this morning and Miriam's boss was there, his maroon Jag parked outside. He's younger than I expected, probably still in his twenties, but with a small tummy that would seem more suitable on a middle-aged man. He has nice manners and nice clothes and he smiles when he speaks to the girls, and the clever ones smile back at him, their faces lighting up as if by some internal illumination. He is in no way a hunk, his body is spidery and his face is close to a skull, with almost no soft tissue, the skin pulled tightly over sharp features.

His manners and his clothes act as a mask to hide other attributes – like his brains – which are singularly lacking. But Miriam was smiling brightly along with the other girls. People are impressed by power, and within the confines of that café all the power resides in the man with the Jag.

In the midst of all this I caught Miriam's eye and she saw that I had seen what was going on. She looked away for a moment and then came back and locked on to me again. She gave me a look that no one else on the planet would be able to interpret. It was a look that said, *OK, so I'm using my sexuality to impress my boss. Why not? He's the man who pays my wages. He can make my life better or worse. He's powerful.* But underneath the look there was another statement: *You've caught me. I'm going to be punished. Later, after work, I'll submit myself to you. I'll take whatever you mete out. Because you're powerful too.*

And I looked back at her. I didn't move my lips or my eyes. I didn't nod or make any external signs. But I could see by her reaction that she understood every nuance of our silent dialogue.

She wiped down my table and said, 'What can I get you, sir?'

'The all-day breakfast.'

She scribbled on her pad, touched her chin with the end of the pencil and walked over to the kitchen. A few minutes later she delivered the breakfast, together with a knife and fork wrapped in a paper napkin. 'Can I get you anything to drink?'

I shook my head.

I was aware of her on the periphery of my vision, flitting from table to table, delivering toast and chips and beans and fried tomatoes to the other customers.

When I'd finished my breakfast I counted out the right amount of change, added a twenty-pence piece, and left the café.

I keep my eye on Miriam, just as I keep my eye on the blind woman. I am the watchman. I am a reliable witness. I can testify to the crimes and misdemeanours of those I watch, just as I can confirm their righteous acts.

And I am a witness, also, to the power of faith. Throughout my conscious life, faith, and faith alone, has kept me fixed to the path of my destiny. I have seen where I must go, and nothing has stood in my way. In our time commitment is not a fashionable virtue. As a culture we are committed only to throw-away ephemera and momentary desires. And because of that our lives lead inexorably to depression, to insanity, and to death.

I know one thing for sure. My faith will lead me elsewhere. It will lead me away from this vale of sorrow. I shall be reunited with the greatest love of all.

The man from Neighbourhood Watch is supposed to check the garages and doors around midnight. Last night I saw him enter someone's house. He turned the door handle and hesitated before pushing it open. He looked around, made sure no one was watching, then went through and closed the door behind him. The woman who lives in that house is divorced. The kids on the street call her Sexy Sadie. She hooks scarlet underwear to her washing line, like bait.

These characters form the landscape of my life. I watch them because we can never be sure that the people we meet are real. People begin life with a genetic potential, a temperament, and an environment (including their parents) which is going to somehow modify their behaviour. As they grow, their genetic inheritance usually comes into the foreground, and by the time they have come through the chaos of their teens, they are more or less formed. They have become whatever it is that they were supposed to become.

But most of them are not satisfied. They look around and find the world populated by people more interesting than themselves. They see intelligent people, or beautiful people, they see people who are strong, or wilful, or talented. And the response is to begin a process of re-inventing themselves. They dream up an exotic past, stories of lost fortunes or family tragedies, historical links to the great and the good.

Binjamin Wilkomirski, the author of the book *Fragments*, describes his experiences as a three-year-old who was separated from his family in Riga and taken to the concentration camp at Majdanek. In the camp he witnessed and survived a series of harrowing ordeals, and ended up, after the war, in a Swiss orphanage. He was taken from the orphanage by a Swiss couple who showed no understanding of his experience, and who forced him to suppress all of his earlier memories.

135

Fragments is an interesting book. It has won awards and its child's-eye-view narrative has ensured an important place on the Holocaust circuit for its author.

But in the late nineties it was alleged that Wilkomirski is not from Latvia. He was never near a Polish death camp. He is not even Jewish. Instead he was born Bruno Grosjean in 1941 in Biel; in 1945 he was adopted by a wealthy Swiss couple from Zurich, who, when they died in 1986, left him a large inheritance.

Why is it so fascinating that someone should decide to invent a new identity for himself? Was Bruno Grosjean's real life so totally devoid of meaning that he could do nothing but dump it?

We don't know the answer, because Bruno Grosjean, in spite of the body of evidence against him, still maintains that he is Binjamin Wilkomirski.

In my profession and in the medical profession this phenomenon is well known. There is even a name for it. When delusions surface in physical symptoms, the condition is called Munchausen's syndrome. And patients with Munchausen's syndrome are so convinced and so convincing that they will repeatedly seek out and endure surgery for medical conditions that do not exist.

Some of us do not have the space or the time in our lives for delusions of any kind. We are different. Fate or circumstances has given us the lonely role of modifying the behaviour of others. In my case I have to bring the life of at least one more person to an end.

TWENTY-SEVEN

There was a knocking sound coming from the engine of the Montego, like the little guy who lived in there had certain knowledge of an impending disaster and wanted to get out. Sam thought about dropping the car off at the garage and collecting Angeles in a taxi. But the single tenner in his wallet convinced him he had to coax the car along for a few more miles.

Rosie, one of his old flames, had told him that machinery was always surrounded by invisible elemental beings, like imps and goblins, who weren't very bright. If you looked after the machine, made sure it was oiled and in good condition, then these little guys were happy to play about among themselves. But if you neglected the thing, let it get rusty and corroded, they were likely to start messing around. They'd trickle rust into the petrol tank, guide the tyres towards slivers of glass on the road, and they'd alter the fuel ratios until internal combustion failed completely. Any mischief they could cause, they'd go for it.

Come to think of it, that banging from under the bonnet could easily be those guys dismantling the car while it was travelling along the road. A pixie wrecking crew out of their skulls on exhaust fumes.

Rosie got religion really bad in the end. Seemed to spend the whole day on her knees. She lived on clichés and meditations and moved away to a New Age commune. Sam tried to think about Rosie but he couldn't remember her face or why they were attracted. He couldn't recall the sound of her voice. Just the weird things she said.

Angeles was sitting on her bed in a side ward on the top floor of the District Hospital. She wore stone-washed jeans with a navy, fitted jacket, and a charcoal-grey blouse. She was pale, her features drawn, as if someone had her skin in a tourniquet at the back of her head. 'Sam,' she said as he entered the room, a smile animating her face.

'You ready to get out of this place?'

'I think so, yes.' She was on her feet now. She handed him a sheaf of paperwork. 'Discharge papers. I still have to see one of the nurses. Then we can go.'

Sam collected her suitcase and stood close to her so she could take his arm. His hand was swathed in bandages but she didn't seem to notice. He walked her out of the room and along the corridor to the nurses' station. As they approached, a small nurse with her hair highlighted in different shades of maroon detached herself from the table. 'Ms Falco,' she said, 'here's your medication.' She held out a small paper bag, then remembered that Angeles couldn't see it. 'I'll give it to your friend, here.'

Sam had Angeles in one hand and her suitcase in the other. He grinned at the nurse and held the suitcase wide so she could slip the tablets into his jacket pocket.

'Any goodies in there?' Sam asked. 'If I should need a new way of looking at the world.'

The nurse shook her head. She didn't say anything. She'd heard it all before.

Sam got Angeles installed in the passenger seat of the Montego and walked around to the driver's door. She seemed to be having some trouble with the seat belt. He waited, not wanting to seem over-solicitous. There's something wrong with the woman's sight; she's not a cripple. If she needs help, she'll ask for it.

'This's broken,' she said.

'It's just awkward,' Sam said. 'I could show you?'

'It's broken,' Angeles said. 'I could show *you*.'

He turned in his seat and pulled the belt around her. There was that hospital smell, and then the scent of the woman muffled behind it. He slotted the male connector into the female receptor and listened for the click.

Angeles pulled on the belt to show him that the connection didn't hold.

'Yeah,' he said. 'It's supposed to click.'

She shrugged. 'It's broken,' she told him. 'It's never going to click again.'

He made the connection once more, held it with both hands so she couldn't pull it apart. She ran her fingers lightly over his hands and smiled. 'Are you going to drive like that?' she asked. 'You want me to take the steering wheel?'

'There's something wrong with the engine, as well,' Sam told her. 'Kind of knocking noise. The thing's falling apart.'

'It's nice to know I've hired a company that isn't over-capitalized.'

Sam looked across at her. She'd put on a poker face to make things as difficult as possible. All those old sexist notions started invading his consciousness. You listen to Celia and Marie and Janet and you take it all on board and change the way your mind works, alter your whole genetic make-up, then a woman like this comes along. 'Temporary problem,' he said. 'The old bucket'll last long enough to get you home.'

'You'll have to look out for a new one,' she said. She said it like someone who had a bank account. Sam counted to ten.

'OK,' he said. 'When I start the engine you'll hear the knocking sound. When I pull away from the curb it'll feel like she's listing over to the left. These are not things to worry about. The other thing is, the safety belt, as you mentioned, is in fact broken, so you're not strapped in. But you don't have to worry about that either, because I'm gonna drive real careful.'

He started the engine and pulled into the stream of traffic. He glanced across at her. She was facing forwards, a trace of a smile on her lips.

'I don't think it's terminal,' he told her quietly. 'I'll book it into the garage. They can usually fix these things.'

She was quiet for a long time. Sam concentrated on getting through the traffic without using the breaks.

'You're a realist, then?' she said eventually. Sam had just turned into his street. He cruised up to the gate and parked. She was looking straight ahead. The ghost of a smile was the only thing that gave her away.

'Yeah,' he said, beginning a laugh that took up all the spaces in the car. 'Me an' old King Canute.'

She took his arm and let him lead her along the path to the front door of his house, where she hesitated. 'I'm not entirely sure about this,' she said.

'The way round it,' he said, 'is for me to move into *your* house. But I can't be there all the time and the guy who attacked you is gonna try again.'

He could see her listening. She was standing on the threshold with her head cocked to one side, leaning into the house. 'You think you can hear something?' he asked. 'There's no one there. Nothing moving.'

She followed him into the house. 'I know that,' she said. 'I was listening to the silence. I'm used to the silences that I create around myself. Sam Turner's silences are altogether different. Something I'm going to have to get used to.'

'I've got CDs,' he said. 'A radio. There's a television some- where. You can make as much noise as you like here. There's no one gonna complain.'

'I don't believe you're that insensitive,' she told him. 'You think it's manly to be indifferent to the finer nuances. But it just makes you callous.'

'Social conditioning,' he said. 'I was brought up to pull the heads off flowers.'

'Well, don't do it when I'm around.' She let him guide her hand to a chair, which she explored quickly and efficiently. She pulled it around to the right and sat down. 'Just be still and quiet.'

Sam did as he was told. He closed his eyes and listened. There was nothing to hear. A great ballooning emptiness. From the kitchen a tiny whine, the fridge motor, occasionally giving a cough. And upstairs somewhere a window must be open, setting a door banging against its frame. Rhythmical sound, two beats to the bar, common time.

'What do you hear?'

He told her about the fridge motor, said it was probably going the same way as the car engine. 'All the motors and engines in my life,' he said. 'They're getting ready to crack up. The chain on my bike broke yesterday.'

She held her hands to her ears, made her look like one of the three wise monkeys. 'And something else,' he said. 'I can hear Dora.'

'Your wife?' she asked. 'The one who died?'

'Yeah. It was her house. Before I came on the scene. She lived here with her first husband, her kids. Died in the front bedroom.'

'What do you mean, you can hear her? Like a ghost?'

'Kind of. I suppose that's what people mean when they talk about ghosts. She had a way of being. She was a strong woman before she got sick, had an effect on the physical world. The house feels more like her house than it'll ever feel like mine. She's been dead eleven, nearly twelve months, but it's still her place.'

When Angeles spoke it was as if her voice came from far off. 'That's what I heard when you first opened the door,' she said. 'It felt hostile, but maybe it was just testing me, being defensive.'

Sam shook his head. 'I'm shaking my head,' he told her. 'Dora didn't need to be defensive when she was alive. She certainly doesn't need to now. She's not here any longer. If you can hear her, like I can hear her from time to time, it's because I want her to be here. What you hear is not Dora, or Dora's ghost. It's just some inadequacy in me, my idea of what it would be like if she was still around. If some part of her was still around. That's all. Nothing real.'

'Like the knocking in the engine,' she said.

'What about you? What does my house sound like to you?'

She smiled. 'Mildew,' she said. 'Damp. It sounds as though it's been loved at one time, filled with children's voices. But now there's just a private detective rattling around rooms that are far too big for him. There's neglect here, Sam. The house carries the sound of weeping. You ought to do something about it.'

'I know,' he said. 'I keep thinking I should give it away, some kind of homeless charity. Childhope or Shelter? One time we thought of moving the office here. It needs more than I can give it.'

'I'll stay for a while,' she said. 'As long as I can. Maybe the two of us together can bring some life back to the place?'

'Hope so,' he said. 'The alternative's got an altogether too final ring about it.'

'You know, there's something else I've learnt today.'

'What's that?'

'I don't want to sound patronizing, but it's good to know that you can think.'

'That's not patronizing,' he said. 'That's downright superior.

141

But you've got to think, Angeles, that's the only thing that separates us from the lentils.'

He slumped in the big armchair and listened to her exploring her room upstairs. Heard her opening and closing drawers, putting her clothes away in the ancient wardrobe, stumbling on the frayed carpet. He knew what it was behind all the other sounds in the house. That dull murmur was always there if you really tried to listen. It was all the times that had been, and were here no longer. It was all the times that had gone.

Celia rang the doorbell and Sam showed her through to his sitting room. 'I was going to make coffee,' he said.

She sighed and sank into a chair. 'It would save my life, Sam. I promise I won't stay long. There's a couple of things for you to sign, then I'm going home for an early night.'

Sam took a step towards the kitchen. 'Take it easy for a few minutes. I'll put the kettle on.'

Sam's business would have been impossible without Celia. What he brought to the job was all dogged inspiration. He knew people and what they were capable of and he could sniff out a lie at the stage where it was still being contemplated. But Celia could organize people, money, and filing systems. She was good at protocol and knew how to design a letterhead and keep accounts. Celia knew the difference between an invoice and a statement, and she could explain it to Sam in a way that made him wonder why he hadn't twigged it years before.

When they'd first met Celia had been a retired Quaker schoolteacher, kind and twinkly-eyed but as dry as a biscuit. Sam had been an alcoholic chancer desperate to drown himself in the arms of a million women. By all the laws of social convention they should never have met, but despite their difference they had each inspired the other to expand their individual horizons.

Celia had soon forgotten that she was almost seventy and she had delved into kitsch in a big way. Her neck and wrists were festooned with bangles and beads. Tonight she was wearing a purple cape over a beige mid-length dress with tassels. And she wore a gold anklet above a pair of shoes that wouldn't have looked out of place doing the tango.

Sam sometimes fell off the wagon, but usually he was dry. He fell off the wagon whenever he gave way to the heartbreaking obsession that he was in control. Sometimes he thought it was getting easier to deal with. And often he knew it wasn't. The craving never went away: over the years he'd evolved a way of hiding from it. You hid from the craving by ignoring everything that had happened yesterday and paying no attention to anything that might happen tomorrow.

Yesterday was gone and nothing would bring it back. It was in the realm of accomplishments and failures. Yesterday's word had been spoken, and old Khayyám was right, all the piety and wit in the world would not erase a jot of it.

Tomorrow: she's always unborn. She'll arrive with burdens, there's no doubt about that, and there's even a chance that parts of her will be splendid. But until she arrives we can only be certain that we have no knowledge of her.

Which leaves a perfect hiding place. Today. And any man can fight the battles of just one day. Any day you like, be it as bright as the sun or as black as Hell, Sam Turner can get up at dawn and take anything you care to throw at him. He'll keep going until nightfall. It's only twenty-four hours.

Today has no possibility of madness or disillusionment. Today you can get through without taking a drink. And it sure beats sitting in a cell.

He dampened the coffee beans and took in the aroma. He waited a few moments for the water to go off the boil before pouring it into the filter. When it was ready he transferred the coffee into bright red mugs and put them on the tray with milk in a small jug. Celia was used to things being presented properly. She would never criticize, no matter how things were served, but in her silent expectation she managed to raise the standard for everyone.

'Is she here?'

'Yeah,' said Sam. 'I collected her a couple of hours ago. She keeps walking into things. She knocked the radio off the kitchen shelf; went into the garden and couldn't find her way back. It's not gonna be easy for her. She's upstairs feeling her way around.'

'Nice,' Celia said, sipping from her cup. 'This house needs a woman.'

'If I say things like that, everyone jumps on me for being sexist.'

'That's because it would be if you said it,' Celia told him. She sipped from her cup, her face wreathed with steam.

'And another thing,' Sam said. 'When you say the house needs a woman, what you really mean is that I need a woman. That it's time I settled down, all that stuff.'

'Well, it is time you settled down, Sam. You can't go through life on one-night stands. It's not good for your health.'

How does she know that, Sam thought. As far as he was aware Celia had never had a sexual encounter in her life. She'd never alluded to one, anyway. Until the last five or six years her life had been devoted to literature and religion and taking care of an invalid mother. Still, it could've happened and she'd just decided to keep shtoom about it. Ships did pass in the night, presumably anybody's night.

'You like her, don't you?' Celia asked.

'Yeah, she's fine. Bit uppity sometimes, but I like her. We're not setting up house together, Celia. I like her well enough, but she's a client, and somebody's trying to do for her. I think she's safer living here for the moment. But that's as far as it goes.'

Celia looked at him with a pair of eyes that had once belonged to an owl. She blinked them slowly. She dipped into her bag and came out with a sheaf of papers, which she passed over to Sam.

He glanced at them and patted his top pocket. When he looked up Celia was handing him a pen. He took it from her extended hand and signed the letters: one to the bank manager explaining why last month's payment on the overdraft hadn't materialized, and another one, almost identical wording, to the landlord.

'We must owe these guys a fortune,' he said.

'They can afford it, Sam. They know you'll pay up in the end.'

'It's criminal, though, taking that much cash off a guy for doing nothing.'

'That's how they make their money.'

'Interest and rent,' he said. 'Villains have used the same tactics since time began.'

'Is this going to get political?'

'No,' he said. 'I'll stop. I don't make it political. It's the other guys hassling for money all the time. The middle classes. All criminals are middleclass.'

'Seems like a sweeping statement, Sam.'

144

'But it's not. Under the veneer of respectability we're ruled by a middle-class Mafia. We choose not to see it most of the time because it's too hard to live with. But that doesn't mean it's not there. I've never met a member of the middle classes who wasn't a criminal either in fact or by aspiration.'

'Long live the revolution?'

'Too right.'

'I'm middle class, Sam. What are you going to do about me?'

'You're not middle class, Celia. You just talk posh and read books. Anyway, we're gonna build in special dispensations for people like you. We'll stop your pension and make you take in washing. It'll be hard at first but you'll get used to it.'

'Similar to the present government?' she said.

Sam often thought that Celia was the sharpest tool in the box. Nothing much went past her. Maybe that's how you got if you spent your life reading books?

'It must feel good, though,' she said. 'To have Angeles living in the same house.'

Tell them anything, he thought, remembering a maxim from his misspent youth. 'Celia,' he said, 'it's bloody marvellous.'

In the night Sam peered up through the darkness towards the ceiling of his room. Through the wall he listened to the occasional creak as Angeles Falco adjusted herself to the vagaries of a new bed. Somewhere around them, perhaps close at hand, was the man who had killed Isabel Reeves, Angeles' sister. The man who had attacked Angeles and who wanted her dead. He eased himself out of the bed and walked over to the window, looked down at the garden in the moonlight, the spreading branches of the ancient pear tree almost touching the glass in front of his face.

Something moved over by the hedge. Not a maniac killer, nothing as human as that. Something small and quick, a rat or stoat. There'd been reports in the press about escaped mink in the area.

If death was close by tonight, he was wearing different shoes. An Italian moccasin, maybe, fashioned from soft leather, whereas at their last encounter he'd worn hobnailed boots.

He checked the windows and doors downstairs, beginning at the front of the house and working his way towards the back.

Everything was secure; nothing had been tampered with. If the killer were still intent on Angeles' life, he'd have to come here for her. He'd have to get past Sam Turner.

There was a good possibility that the man didn't know she was here. Unless he was able to spend all his time watching the hospital, he wouldn't know she'd been discharged.

Assume he doesn't know she's here, Sam thought, because he wanted life to get back to normal. But then he felt his face crinkle into a smile. Assume nothing, he said to himself. You're dealing with someone who is in the grip of an obsession.

He unlocked the back door and stepped out into the night. Half a dozen steps took him under the shelter of the pear tree. The combination of moonlight and branches put a dappled pattern on his forearms, a natural camouflage, giving him a degree of invisibility.

He watched the house and let his mind go back to the time he'd seen the shadowy figure in Angeles' garden. The guy, whoever he was, was also blind in a way. He couldn't see the obvious: that the death of Angeles wouldn't actually solve his problems.

Over to the west, high in the sky, a surveillance satellite blinked as it photographed suspect installations and beamed them back down to its controllers. The collective sum of military paranoia was increased minute by minute with each click of the shutter of its high-powered camera. In the old days men used to stand on the earth and watch the stars, perhaps wonder if the stars were watching us. Now there is no doubt about it. We are under observation.

This was a tough case. One of the most complicated Sam had undertaken. Why would anyone want to kill a couple of sisters, one of them blind? Neither of them had any links to organized crime, they weren't running drugs or girls. As far as he knew, they didn't have reason to fear anyone. Yet there was a man out there who had already killed one of them and had a good attempt on the life of the other.

Why?

For some reason Sam's mind kept wandering towards a symbolic or mythological solution. Maybe it was connected to Angeles' blindness? The only figure he could think of who was blind was Samson, after Delilah had cut his hair. And thinking

146

about Samson and Delilah didn't get him anywhere. Maybe there were other mythological figures who would throw up a connection. He'd talk to Celia about it, and JD. JD would be better.

Except mythological solutions only happened in detective books and American movies. In the real world no one got killed because of a mythological story. People got killed because of money or power or jealousy or revenge.

Angeles was jerked awake from another dream in which the blood from the man's thumb had congealed in her mouth. She listened to the night. He was there, somewhere. Not in the house but somewhere close by. He was not going to leave her alone.

She fought the image of him standing at the end of her bed. He was not there. This was Sam's house, and Sam was there to protect her. The man who was stalking her had insinuated himself into her head, so that she carried him with her wherever she went. But he was an illusion most of the time. The trick was to learn when he was illusion and harmless, and when he was reality and dangerous.

She put her earphones on and listened to the audiotape of Le Carré's *The Naïve and Sentimental Lover*. But it was too creepy and made the fact of being watched only more obvious.

But I'm not going to let this undermine me, she thought. I'm going to go on living my life. Even as she thought it, she wasn't sure if she meant it or not, if she would be strong enough to overcome the more or less constant fear that rolled her innards into a tight fist.

A stair creaked and she held her breath. Nothing. An imagination. But there it was again, closer now, and she heard herself shouting out Sam's name without thinking about it.

The door to her room opened immediately and she was already scrambling back against the pillows, trying to force herself through the headboard before she realized that the voice belonged to Sam Turner.

He strode across the room and sat on the edge of the bed. She let him put his arm around her and listened to the soothing tones of his voice as he stroked her back. The hollow thumping in her chest racked her body and her breathing was similar to an asthmatic attack for several minutes.

He'd been out to check the windows and doors. Everything was all right. There was nobody else in the house. She was safe. Perfectly safe.

He stayed for half an hour, until she was almost asleep. She felt him release his hand and move away from the bed, and she let him go, feigning sleep. She listened to him close her door and heard his soft footsteps make their way to his own room.

Angeles determined to control herself. An active imagination was not always a blessing. Tomorrow she would be more careful. Make sure that she knew what was happening.

Someone walked past the house. Angeles tensed as the footsteps became louder, and she took a long breath as they paused for a moment below her window. After a couple of beats they continued along the road, eventually disappearing altogether.

But what was the pause about, she wondered, as a throbbing sensation filled the spaces behind her eyes.

TWENTY-EIGHT

Janet baked two apple cakes that morning: a large one which she and Geordie and Ralph would demolish after dinner and a small one to take to Angeles. She hid the large one in the cupboard so the cats wouldn't get to it and the smaller one she put in a round biscuit tin together with a vial of arnica tablets.

She dressed Echo in a red and white babygro and fed her while sitting in the nursing chair next to her bed. She started with her left breast this time, making sure she didn't push Echo into a left or right bias because of her feeding routine.

The child gurgled softly on the bed while Janet dressed herself in a pair of cotton trousers and a halter-necked top in a lighter shade of blue. It was interesting and gratifying to have developed breasts at last, something worthy of the name. Adolescence had been a nightmare, watching all the other girls shopping for brassières and bursting out of their school uniforms. And then, later, taking the jibes of her mother and the boys who roamed the neighbourhood in search of a handful.

It had been like a miracle towards the end of her pregnancy when those two large nipples had developed a bed of plump flesh for themselves. And an even greater miracle when Janet discovered that they actually worked, that Echo lusted after them with every fibre of her being and was never less than stunningly satisfied with what they provided.

And, of course, Geordie, who had always protested that he loved her exactly as she was before the miracle – *hey, flat chests are sexy these days, it's fashionable* – was now delirious.

She smiled at her reflection in the mirror, still the same round face. Some things change, but others remain the same.

She carried Echo downstairs and showed her the kittens while Venus looked on suspiciously. She put her in the pram, packed the biscuit tin in the carrier and, after propping a note for Geordie on the kitchen table, set off for Sam Turner's house.

Angeles opened the door almost as soon as Janet rang the bell. 'I thought you weren't supposed to answer the door until you knew who was calling?' Janet said.

Angeles waved her stick impatiently; so long it almost touched her chin. It had a silver handle, small and rounded, abstract but maybe representing an animal's head. 'Rules,' she said, giving an amused snort. 'I knew it would be you. Have you brought the baby?'

'Yeah, she's asleep in her pram. I'm gonna wheel her into the hall.'

Angeles stepped back and waited until Janet had manoeuvred the pram over the threshold. 'I can smell baby,' she said, 'everything sweet and quiet.'

'Not all the time, believe me,' Janet told her. 'Echo can smell fairly rank sometimes, and she's got a voice to beat the band.' She took the biscuit tin out of the carrier and offered it to Angeles. 'I baked an apple cake. We could have some with our tea. Is that a black eye?'

'Yes, I walked into a door. But I know where it is now.'

Angeles seemed to have mastered the layout of Sam's house in the few days since she'd been installed. Janet watched her cross the kitchen, tapping knowingly as she went. She filled the kettle and set the water to boil. But she looked drawn and tired, as if she hadn't slept well.

'You saved my life,' she said.

Janet flushed. 'I don't know about that. I was there at the right time.'

'Sam said you saved my life. If you hadn't arrived when you did, the man would have strangled me.'

Janet shrugged. 'I'm glad I was there.'

'I'd like to give you a hug,' Angeles said, opening her arms.

Janet walked towards her and let herself be embraced. She put her own arms around Angeles' waist and held on tightly for a minute. Angeles was a full head taller and had real female curves. She was slim, though, unlike Marie, who was the only other woman that Janet had regular physical contact with. The head of the cane wasn't in the shape of an animal's head; it was a small sphere. Angeles' breath smelled strongly of spirit.

'Thank you,' Angeles said. 'I've been wanting to meet you since I was in the hospital. Talking on the phone is OK, but it's not a substitute for the real thing.'

They moved apart and Angeles retrieved the biscuit tin from where she'd placed it on the table. 'Oh, it smells gorgeous,' she said. 'But there's something else in here.' She rattled the bottle. 'Sounds like tablets.'

'It's arnica,' said Janet. 'For shock.'

'Homoeopathic?'

'Yes. Do you know about it?'

'Not much. My sister swore by homoeopathic medicine. I'm sure she mentioned arnica to me. I'm over my shock by now.'

'Just take one,' Janet said. 'The body heals slowly, and it needs all the help it can get.'

Angeles unscrewed the cap and put one of the tablets on her tongue. 'There,' she said, 'it's done.' She proceeded to make the tea while Janet cut two generous portions of apple cake. When everything was ready Janet followed Angeles into Sam's sitting room, where they sat on either side of a low mahogany table. There was a moment after they entered the room when Angeles scooped up a tumbler and tried to hide it behind a stereo speaker.

'It feels different in here,' Janet said.

Angeles laughed. 'I've had to get rid of a few things. I was black and blue after the first day, falling over chairs, piles of newspapers, CDs. When you can't see it's important to have clear pathways. Sam has put some furniture in the garage, and he's learning not to leave shoes around the place or throw his jacket on the floor.'

'But you like him,' Janet said. It wasn't a question.

'Yes. I miss my own house, but it's OK living with Sam.'

'Just OK?'

Angeles smiled. 'It's nice living with Sam. Is he dishy?'

Janet laughed. 'I'd never describe him as dishy.'

'I only know his voice,' Angeles said. 'His hands sometimes, when he's helping me get my bearings. I love his voice, but it's frustrating not knowing what he looks like.'

151

'He's definitely not dishy,' Janet said. 'Sam's face, well, maybe he was good looking when he was young. I didn't know him then. But now his face is kind of broken. He looks interesting, though.'

'Not much like Gene Hackman.'

'Is that what he told you?'

'Mmm. Yes.'

'Let me put it this way,' Janet said. 'I don't think Gene Hackman would like the comparison.'

'So, I'm living in the house of a man who looks interesting? Not dishy or attractive. Just interesting.'

'I didn't say he wasn't attractive,' Janet said. 'He doesn't spend a lot of time by himself.'

'Thanks. I've got an idea of him. I'm trying to build a picture in my head. It's not easy to do when you're blind. I'd like to be able to picture us walking along the street, see what other people see.'

'Oh, you look great,' Janet said. 'The two of you together, that's something else.'

'Me with a black eye and him with a broken face?'

'A broken face on a man; what's wrong with that? And your black eye isn't gonna last for ever. You seem to know your way around the house OK.'

'It's still something of an obstacle course for me.'

'Living with men,' Janet said. 'Never easy. I've got two of them in the house at the moment.'

'Geordie I've met,' said Angeles. 'He was at the hospital. He seemed nice. I liked him.'

'Oh, Geordie's great on his own,' Janet said. 'The real problem is Ralph, his brother.'

'The one who turned up out of the blue? I thought Geordie was over the moon about that.'

'They were separated when they were children,' Janet said. 'I don't know, maybe they were similar then, but life has taken them in different directions. Geordie's a bit of a softy; his whole life revolves around me and Echo. But Ralph's the opposite; he's on the look-out for the main chance. I just know Geordie's gonna end up being disillusioned with him.'

'Has he tried anything with you?'

Janet sighed. 'The guy's got more hands than a watch factory.'

'And you can't tell Geordie because . . .'

'. . . He's finally found the brother who he thought was lost for ever.'

'Oh, dear,' said Angeles inadequately. 'It's all going to blow up, isn't it?'

'Sooner or later, yes.' Janet pushed a small piece of apple cake around her plate. 'I keep hoping that Ralph will disappear, go back to wherever it was he came from. But everything's really cushy here for him. Geordie would do anything, and he's living free.'

'Can't Sam do anything?'

'I haven't talked to anyone else about this. I didn't intend to talk to you about it. I'd appreciate it if you'd keep it to yourself for now.'

'Of course, I won't say anything. But if you think I could help, I'd be glad to do whatever you think. What if we offered him a couple of hundred pounds to disappear?'

'He'd take the cash and come back for more. Besides, there's no need for you to get involved. You've got enough on your plate for now, you don't need another dirty piece of work messing up your life.'

'So do you have a plan?' Angeles asked.

Janet shrugged her shoulders. 'I'm just gonna see what happens,' she said. 'Play it from day to day. But let's talk about something else. What about you? Geordie said your father was from Argentina? It sounds so romantic.'

Angeles smiled wistfully. 'I never thought of him as Argentinian,' she said. 'Still now, when I think back, there is no nationality attached to him. He hated nationalism. He was my father. He was always around when we wanted him, he'd turn himself inside out for his children. He'd compromise all of his principles to make sure we were happy. Mummy said he spoiled us, and that he didn't have much choice about it. He saw himself as a provider and if it was in his power to provide, then he wouldn't see us go without. That was his nature. And he was exactly the same with Mother.'

'Material things?' Janet asked. 'Clothes? Holidays? Did you go to Argentina?'

'I wasn't thinking about material things,' Angeles said. 'He was always there for us. He was a physical person; he'd sit Isabel and me on his knee together. When we were very young he always seemed to be sprawled on the carpet, and we'd crawl all over him. When I think about him I have a picture of both of us girls hanging off him; Isabel on his back and me with my arms and legs wrapped around his waist.

'Yes, he bought us clothes and we went away to Spain and France, all over Europe. But not to South America. He wasn't allowed to go to Argentina and said he couldn't bear to be on the same continent and not visit his relatives.'

'So, do you have relatives in Argentina? People you've never met?'

'I suppose so, yes. Daddy had a brother, and when he married there were children. I have cousins, but I don't suppose we'll ever meet. We wouldn't know each other.'

'I couldn't bear that,' said Janet. 'It sounds so sad.'

Angeles smiled warmly. 'It doesn't feel sad to me. My father wasn't close to his family. His brother was in the army and happy with the political situation, but Daddy was a rebel when he was young, caused a lot of trouble for the generals. If he hadn't got out when he did, he'd have rotted in one of their prisons. If he hadn't been proscribed, he'd never have come to England, never have met my mother, and Isabel and I wouldn't have been born.'

Echo turned in her pram and called out in her sleep. Both women tensed, expecting her to wake, but she slumbered on.

'False alarm?' said Angeles.

'Mnm,' Janet replied. 'She'll wake soon. When she does that Geordie says she knows it's time to get up but the world's too big and unpredictable, so she takes a big breath and dives down into sleep for another half an hour.'

'He was in an orphanage, wasn't he?' asked Angeles. 'And living on the street? Geordie has seen a lot of things in his life.'

'Yeah,' Janet agreed. 'But everyone connected with Sam has seen more life than they bargained for. It's one of the qualifications for the job.'

'Living on the edge?'

'Going right over the edge to the other side, clinging on with your fingertips, then, somehow, coming back.'

'I can't imagine that,' said Angeles.

Janet came with a tiny laugh. 'Living with the damage, you

mean? You're going through it now. Your sister has been killed, and someone is out there looking to destroy you. You don't have to imagine it, Angeles, you're never going to be the same again.'

'It's true,' she said. 'I feel as though I'm under observation all the time. But I don't want this maniac to dumb me down. It's important for me to carry on living my life like everyone else. I agreed to come here for a few days, until I feel stronger. But I want to go back to my own house, live my own life.' For a few moments Angeles gazed into the future with her blind eyes. 'I get flashbacks of my parents' deaths.'

'A road accident?'

'Yes. The M6.'

'Could that have been connected with your father's politics?'

'No, there were too many people involved. They were in a pile-up with ninety other vehicles.'

'D'you know what happened?'

'A lorry travelling in the opposite direction jack-knifed and crossed the central reservation. They said my parents wouldn't have known what happened. They hit the car in front and then they were hit by a baker's delivery van. They sat tight and were overcome by smoke fumes.'

'Couldn't they get out?'

'They were probably stunned by the impact. Their doors were jammed, but the passenger door – that was my mother's side – could have been opened with a little force.' She shook her head from side to side. It looked to Janet as though she was in the car with them, that she was reliving a constant nightmare. 'The petrol tank exploded,' Angeles continued. 'They were burned to death.'

'I'm sorry,' said Janet. 'I shouldn't have revived the memory for you. I only thought there might be a connection with your father's exile.'

'They were travelling back from Bristol. They'd been away for a break. Four days together.' Angeles held out her hands, palm upwards. Janet moved around the table and sat next to her on the couch. She put her arms around Angeles and felt the other woman's response. They held each other in a silent hug for the best part of a minute.

Finally Janet drew away, and Angeles sighed and said, 'Thanks, I needed that. People tend not to touch blind people very often, we don't get as many hugs as sighted folk.'

'We think we'll frighten you,' Janet said. 'If we suddenly touch you. Make you jump.'

Angeles smiled. 'I think there's something deeper at work,' she said.

Echo yelled from her pram and Janet walked quickly through the house to collect her. Echo's face opened like a flower when her mother appeared.

'I need to change her,' she said to Angeles in the kitchen. 'Then we should be getting back.'

'I'm glad you came,' Angeles said. 'I feel we've got to know each other a little. I think we have more to talk about.'

Janet rolled up the used paper nappy and tucked it inside her bag. She cleaned Echo's bottom quickly and easily, as if she'd been doing it all her life. 'I'm fairly busy at the moment,' she said. 'Two men in the house as well as Echo doesn't leave me a lot of time. But I'll come when I can. It's been a real treat.'

'Maybe I could get to know Echo as well?'

'Sure,' said Janet, finishing the change of nappy. 'D'you want to hold her?'

Angeles held out her arms to receive the child. She sat on a high-backed kitchen chair at the table, and Echo gazed silently into her face.

Angeles explored the child with her fingers. There was nothing obvious or intrusive about the act. It was almost surreptitious. Supporting Echo's back with her left hand, she gave her a finger to clasp, at the same time stroking the chubby fist of the child with her thumb. When Echo released her finger she ran her hand the length of the tiny legs, unable to stop herself smiling at the wonder of them.

She didn't touch Echo's face with her hands; she ran the palm of one hand over the top of Echo's head, taking in the growth of soft downy hair and the still open fontanelle; then she brought the child up close to her face so that their cheeks touched. Echo's nose and mouth briefly came into contact with Angeles' cheek, and then she brought her back to her lap and gazed down at her as if she could see each tiny feature.

Echo blew a note through her lips, something that might have come from a tuba, and Angeles picked it up and blew one back.

'She likes you well enough,' Janet said.

Angeles laughed. 'We play in the same band.'

Janet returned Echo to her pram and Angeles held the door for them. 'There's mail on the floor,' Janet said.

'It'll be for Sam. Put it on the side.'

'Oh, dear.'

'What's the matter?'

'It isn't for Sam. It's for you.'

'Me. But no one knows I'm here.'

'It's addressed to Miss Angeles Falco. But it's not written, the letters have been cut out of a magazine and stuck on with Sellotape.'

While Janet watched, a shudder ran down the other woman's body. Angeles began trembling, first her hands, then her lips, and she tottered backwards up against the wall. She turned and took a step forward and to the side, her hands out in front of her. She turned again, and again, almost spinning, until she was so disoriented Janet thought she would fall over.

TWENTY-NINE

One of JD's many talents was as a drummer in a country rock group, and it was while practising his solo for 'When I'm Drinking I am Nobody's Friend' that he began cogitating on Sam's hypothesis about a mythological solution to the case. There were other mythical figures, apart from Samson, who were blind; Oedipus blinded himself before he went into exile. Athena blinded the young Tiresias by covering his eyes with her hands when he surprised her naked. Odysseus blinded the Cyclops, Polyphemus. The only blind heroine he could think of was Fortuna, the blind goddess of fate; though he remembered that the Little Mermaid was dumb.

None of them really fit the bill. JD couldn't make a connection between any of them and the case of Angeles Falco. And yet, he thought, there are none so blind as those who will not see.

Watching Angeles and using her as a study for the blind character in his novel, JD had confirmed something that he had suspected for a long time. As a musician, and especially as a drummer, he had always known that sound is almost indistinguishable from touch. When he played his drums he could feel the vibrations through his feet, and the group's violinist, Eddie Jones, had shown him how to tell a high note from a low one just by touching the instrument while it was sounding.

What this meant, of course, was that, while blindness was a kind of absolute, deafness was not. There was another route, touch, which led into the world of sound, whereas the visual world, the world of light, was isolated among the senses.

'Where are you going with this?' Sam asked him. 'This's only gonna be useful if it can catch the killer.'

158

'I don't know yet,' JD said. 'It's just an idea. The thing about a mythological solution doesn't work.'

'I knew that as soon as I thought it.'

'So we have to find something else to work with. I think the fact that Angeles is blind could be a factor.'

'Maybe,' said Sam.

'What d'you mean, "maybe"? You started this thing.'

'I mean "maybe", JD. I'm not discounting it. It seems likely at the moment.'

'All right. We've got light and sound. These are two phenomena with different qualities. Light travels in a straight line.'

'And it's fast,' added Sam.

'Yeah, fast. Sound, on the other hand, doesn't necessarily travel in a straight line. It's slower, and it can get blown off course.'

'Yeah,' said Sam.

'But something else,' said JD. 'When the band are playing we get complaints from the neighbourhood. Y'know why?'

'Crap band?'

JD let a wry smile invade his face. 'Because sound can travel through walls. It's much stronger than light. It can even go round corners.'

'It plays tricks, though,' said Sam.

'Yeah, and so does light. Magicians and illusionists use it all the time.'

'The other thing about sound,' said Sam. 'It gets reflected off the surfaces of things.'

'Echoes. And how many times d'you mistake somebody's voice? But the interesting thing is, you never get magicians and illusionists who work with sound. They always give us optical illusions because they are the kind that unsettle us. We believe in what we see much more than in what we hear. The things we see, or think we see, affect our sense of how things fit together in space.'

'That's right,' said Sam. 'We see things, but we don't hear them. I remember when that woman was jumping up and down in the road, after I pushed her out of the ambulance. I didn't hear a woman or a cop, I only heard the ranting.'

'That's right,' said JD. 'Sound gives us qualities. We never actually see light; we only see the things that are illuminated by it.

But we actually hear pure sound, not something that is in the sound, but the thing itself.'

'I suppose this all goes back to your man Descartes?' said Sam.

'Him and all the others who came before him, and the rest who followed him as well. It's a philosophical perennial.'

'Hasn't cracked the case, though, has it?'

'Maybe it helps us understand Angeles Falco a little better, and that in turn might help us to see the guy who's watching her?'

'Let's hope so,' said Sam. 'All this philosophy is going on her bill.'

'You have to take the opposites into account, as well,' said JD.

'Darkness and silence?'

'The dark impedes light. It stops you seeing things that are there. The wardrobe, the psycho in the doorway. But silence doesn't actually impede anything. It is silence in itself. It denotes the absence of sound. Emptiness.'

'People go mad with sound,' Sam said. 'They hear voices. Go insane.'

'Maybe that's the guy we're looking for?' said JD. 'Someone with voices in his head?'

'Something else,' said JD, 'which you'll say is completely irrelevant. If this was a novel or a Brad Pitt movie, there'd be a scene where the good guys get together and hatch a plot to make the villain show himself.'

'Like using the heroine as bait?' said Sam.

'Could be, yeah. That'd give it some tension. The one who was in love with her would argue against it at first. "You can't send that defenceless creature out into the dark night." But eventually the other guy'd win him round. They'd take care of every eventuality they could think of, then send her out there. And she'd want to go. She'd be sure that they'd look after her.'

'If this is a roundabout way of saying you want Angeles back in her own house . . .'

'It's not,' said JD. 'I'm just playing around with concepts here.'

'. . . I'm not gonna fall for it. She's staying in my house, and out of the way until we find some way of nailing the guy.'

'What I was coming round to,' JD continued patiently, 'was the Heisenberg Principle.'

160

Sam shook his head. 'JD, with you on the case it never gets dull. But it never gets brought to a conclusion, either.' He threw his hands up. 'OK, Heisenberg, German Jew, I suppose? Nineteenth century?'

'No, later than that, I think. And I don't know squat about his origins. But I remember the principle: when you measure a system you disrupt it. So those guys who did the experiments with rats, they discovered that rats often fulfil the aspirations of the watcher. If you believe a rat in a cage will take a certain path to its food, there will be a tendency for the majority of rats to take that route.'

'I'm getting a headache.'

'Private eyes don't get headaches. They get their hands smashed and they end up walking with a pimp-limp, but they don't get headaches. The watcher, before we got involved, he was in a closed system. There was just him and Angeles, right?'

'What about Isabel?'

'Keep it simple. There was him and the object of his obsession.'

'OK.'

'But now we've arrived on the scene. We're disrupting the system. We're becoming part of it. We know we've changed it, and he knows we've changed it. What we have to work out is how we can change it so that he shows himself to us without knowing that he's doing it.'

'I knew you were gonna end up here. You want us to use her as bait.'

'I want bait, yeah, but it doesn't have to be Angeles.'

'You suggesting we use somebody else? Janet, for instance? I can really see Geordie going for that. Or Marie?'

'They'd have a great advantage, Sam. They can see.'

THIRTY

Russell Harvey was in a box about two metres long. The undertaker had done a good job on him, so he appeared cleaner in death, altogether more healthy than when he had been drawing breath. A close shave and a touch of rouge to the cheek bones had removed the illusion of sleaze, transformed it into mere roguish charm. The bluish tinge high on the neck had not been obliterated by the black art of cosmetics and still bore faint witness to a death administered by his own hands.

Not entirely self-inflicted, though, Marie reflected. Russell Harvey had not been independent of the world. While it was true that he was a victim of his own personality, life had equipped him with a pack containing a fairly hefty wedge of bad cards.

It was late evening. She had let the day grow old and the shadows lengthen before making her way here. Putting off the inevitable.

'No one else has been. You're the first.' The undertaker's apprentice had confirmed what she already knew. She'd had to come and sit with Russell's corpse, because if she didn't do it, who else would?

She inspected the box; not for the quality of the work, the dovetailing of the joints, the depth of surface sheen, but for some obvious flaw that would mark it out as a factory reject. She didn't find anything and was surprised that Russell should be given something that would hold its own, not fail him at the last moment. Perhaps it was true, then, that death was a great equalizer? She shrugged, decided to ignore the quality of the boards and the fittings. Not teak or oak or African mahogany, but

162

some altogether softer, unrecognizable timber, perhaps a composition of sawdust and glue; and for its handles, only gilded pig iron, no silver or brass.

There's always more than one casualty to a murder, Marie reasoned. At the trial they spend a lot of words proving that the perpetrator has wasted a life. But there are other lives, in the wings so to speak, equally broken. The lives of the loved ones.

Russell Harvey was Isabel Reeves' loved one and when she was snatched away the rest of his life stretched out before him like a bed of cinders.

Marie Dickens, as an ex-nurse, had seen many lifeless bodies, the first well before she was out of her teens. It was part of the initiation into the profession to be able to deal with a patient whose essential systems had closed down. Most student nurses, by the end of their first year, have first-hand experience of the tasks involved. But for Marie that lingering sense of a soul departed, the shell-like emptiness of the still, carnal body, never failed in the poignancy of its moment. It had been there with every patient lost in the night, it had been there with her mother and her father, and it was here again with Russell Harvey. What had been human, with all its flaws, its spiritual or physical lesions, had come to an end. Packed up and skipped town.

You could choose to ignore it. Like one of those extremely efficient people who reach for a roll of string and a cork. But that was running away. A death, any death, is a full stop; it is a mark of punctuation that demands that you take a breath. And it is in the space of that breath, when the old sentence is buried and before the new one is begun, that a different language is spoken. You can call it grief if you like, grief or mourning or, simply, shock. In truth it doesn't have a name.

It is the space in which the only possible response is prayer. In the old world, when the line between humanity and the gods was clearly defined, our ancestors knew instinctively what to do. They didn't have to fall to their knees and lift their voices to the heavens. A silent utterance was just as effective; a ghost moving over the lips for the ghost of the one who has been taken.

Marie shook her head. Big problem in the twenty-first century. We've forgotten how to pray. The space where the prayer took place remains, but it is an empty place. The dead body before us is like a mirror. We see emptiness where there was life, and we know in that moment that there is the same emptiness inside ourselves. We can try to ignore it or we can fill it with rubbish, but it will remain there nevertheless, always empty, until our time comes round.

A trick of light passed over the coffin and Marie shifted uneasily on her chair. For a moment she thought the body of Russell Harvey had moved. He'd blinked, perhaps, or unselfconsciously wrinkled up his nose. But nothing had happened, his make-up was still intact, his lungs and heart and the synapses in his brain had closed for business. The shutters were down. The proprietor had gone away.

It was here, in this very room, that she had come to find the body of Gus and contemplate the end of her marriage. At the time it had seemed like the end of her life. It was, she reasoned, the end of the life she had led up to the moment that Gus looked into the gunman's eyes. Her first act had been to leave the hospital and take up Gus's place as Sam's partner. A role in which she excelled, and for which she had no regrets.

What had proved altogether more difficult was to plug the hole in her emotional life. There had been a more or less constant trickle of men and from time to time one of them seemed like he'd been designed for the job. Only use and familiarity would reveal a series of tiny errors or omissions that made life on a day-to-day basis impossible. An inability to change his socks, perhaps, or the gift of walking through a room and laying it to waste. There had been Clancy, she remembered, who could not, even for one night, lie from the head to the foot of the bed, but would shuffle around until his body was across it, and her. He had additional failings too, dear man.

Other men, usually the ones who seemed eminently possible at first, had more serious drawbacks, like wives and families. God knows, Gus, her philandering, now long-dead husband, had not approached perfection, but he had been like a prince compared to the fare she had been offered since he'd gone.

'Is it just luck?' she asked him in the coffin, there, thinking he looked strangely different and then realizing that it wasn't Gus at all she was keeping company tonight, but Russell Harvey.

'Is it just luck, Russell?' she asked. 'Did you meet a selection of slimy ladies before you found your Isabel?'

With more selective lighting, a candle, say, Russell might have made a sign. But there were no shadows in the room apart from the corpse himself. And Gus, of course, somewhere indistinct, rather as he had been as a husband.

Deep breath. Sit up straight. Get your act together, girl. Dwell not on the bloody past.

The current man was David Styles, Steiner school teacher, very hairy. Gentle. He was away for three days at a conference in Forest Row.

He'd been married once, briefly, to a mistake. No children. He was tall but not gangly, which was nice. Had hair on his head as well as everywhere else, which was also nice. He was a thinker, but not an intellectual. Read philosophy and was able to reinterpret it into everyday language. Of course, he was a teacher.

The best thing about him was his sense of humour, which was always present. He could make her laugh, and did so frequently, sometimes so much that she'd clutch her belly and beg him to stop.

The other thing, of course, the thing that clinched it for Marie, was his lack of materialism. He wasn't interested in the things that money could buy. Didn't own a car.

If there was a questionnaire, something you could fill in to describe your ideal mate, Marie would end up with something very similar to David Styles. He'd look more or less the same, but be broader across the shoulders. He'd have the same sense of humour and the same contempt for the world that puts things before people.

Only he'd be rougher. More like Sam. Not Sam himself, of course, that'd never work. He'd probably be a lorry driver rather than a Steiner school teacher. She didn't know why, couldn't work it out. David Styles, in some inexplicable way, was not man enough for her. He was too much like Marie herself. Her soft, rounded body yearned for hardness in a man. She wanted someone who had an oily rag hanging out of his pocket and calluses on his hands. Someone who went out in the morning and messed with the sharp end of life.

'God help me, Russell,' she said. 'Even when they're perfect they don't match up to requirements.'

Marie wanted Gus back, even after all these years. She wanted

Gus or someone so like him that it made no difference. And the search took her out in the morning and kept her at it until the stars came out. The result was an emotional desert with the occasional watering hole.

'The difference between you and me, Russell, apart from the obvious, of course, is that it didn't work for you. In the love department we both managed on fairly frugal diets. But yours killed you, whereas mine nourishes me. Only just, but I get by.'

Sitting up all night with the body of a man she hardly knew. She was keeping a vigil. It had to be done. Russell Harvey had spent his life alone, but for this night he would have company.

It was a wake, she decided, after the pale light of the dawn had crept over the surfaces in the room. She kissed the tips of her fingers and put them to his cheek. Outside the air was sharp, the streets beginning to stir with people making their way from bed to work. Marie headed for home and the warmth and comfort of her single duvet.

THIRTY-ONE

'Is Sam rich?'

'It's a simple enough question,' said Ralph. 'You don't have to repeat it back to me.'

'Is Sam rich?' said Geordie. 'How can you think he's rich? He's a private eye. Sometimes he doesn't have enough to pay us our wages.'

'That's exploitation,' Ralph told him. 'You could sue him for that.'

It was two o'clock in the afternoon and they were playing snooker in the Stonebow. Ralph had come up tops on a dog the night before, and when he got out of bed around 11.30 he'd taken Geordie out for breakfast. Geordie had already had breakfast with Janet and Echo four hours earlier, but he didn't mention that, not wanting to hurt Ralph's feelings.

They'd had the works, egg and bacon, hash browns, sausage, beans, mushrooms, tomatoes, chips and two mugs of dark brown tea. Ralph had tried to get his teeth round the waitress, a tall girl with a moustache and a black bra showing through a transparent blouse. He'd arranged to meet her in the Museum Gardens when she got off at three, so the snooker was to fill in time until then.

Barney, Geordie's dog, had crept under the snooker table. He'd been withdrawn and quiet since Ralph had arrived on the scene, but more so when Ralph was drinking. Occasionally the dog's nose and eyes would appear and he'd give Geordie a dirty look.

'What's the matter with you?' Geordie asked defensively.

Ralph was rolling when he came back to the table with another two foaming glasses of lager. It was their fifth pint in an hour and a half, and didn't look as though it was going to be the last. Geordie tried to think back to when he had drunk so much before, but he couldn't remember. When he'd been on the street he used to drink cheap wine and worse, whatever was going in fact, but not lager. Maybe he'd drunk around four pints once with Janet, when they first met, but he couldn't be sure. Sometimes he made up stories like that because it made him sound cool.

Ralph, though, he could drink five or six pints any time of the day or night. If he really went for it, he could probably stand at a bar all night, go through ten or fifteen pints and not even blink. Jesus, he'd been a sailor. On ships.

'I'd never sue Sam,' Geordie said. 'Sam's the best bloke I met in my life. It wasn't for him, I'd still be walking the streets. Me an' Barney both. I'd never've met Janet, that was through him as well, and Echo'd never been heard of.' He supped a couple of inches off the top of the glass.

'All right,' Ralph said. 'Keep your hair on. I'm not telling you to sue the guy. I'm just saying he's got a nice set-up. I'm making a remark, something to talk about.'

'Go on, then.'

'That house he lives in,' said Ralph. 'That's his own house, right? He owns it?'

'Was Dora's house,' Geordie said. 'Before she died. Sam, he inherited it.'

'Y'know how much that house's worth?'

'Dunno. It's a big house.'

'Right. It's a big house, and it's planted in the middle of York. I reckon it'd fetch a hundred and fifty grand, maybe two.'

'No,' said Geordie. 'Sam's gonna give it away. He's just gotta decide who to give it to.'

'Why'n't he give it to you?'

'No, he'll give it to a charity,' Geordie said. 'Some organization that'll use it right. Homeless people or kids, something like that.'

Ralph looked at the table. Geordie had set the balls up to play another game, but he hadn't cued off. He picked up his glass and drank all but the last couple of inches. 'Listen,' he said. 'If you told him you wanted to start a charity for homeless types, would he give you the house?'

Geordie laughed. 'I don't wanna start a charity, Ralph. I'm in the detective business. Me and Sam work together.'

'I know you don't wanna start a charity,' Ralph said. 'But if you changed your mind about detectives and wanted to start a charity, would he give you the house?'

'I don't wanna . . .'

'I know you don't wanna do it,' said Ralph with a sudden edge to his voice. 'What I'm saying is, *if* you did? If? OK? Would the guy give you the house?'

Geordie picked up his cue and examined the tip. 'Sam would know I couldn't do it,' he said. 'Run a charity, something like that. I wouldn't know where to start.'

'OK,' said Ralph. 'So you'd have a manager. Someone who knows how to handle money, someone what could give you advice, show you the ropes. Kind of administrator.'

'Like Celia?'

'Yeah, you could say like Celia. But I was thinking of a guy. Would he give you the house?'

'Yeah, I expect he would,' Geordie said. 'Sam likes me. If I wanted something and he could help, he'd do it. That's how he is. An' I'd do the same for him.'

It was as if Ralph couldn't help it. Slowly a big smile lit up his face. 'Y'know what I'm gonna do?' he said.

Geordie shook his head.

'I'm gonna buy my little brother another pint of lager.'

'OK, what about this question?' said Ralph. Geordie watched him hit the white ball and send it round the table. It didn't connect with any of the reds, but glanced off the green and went into one of the baulk pockets. 'Fuckin' stupid game.'

Geordie took the white out of the pocket and placed it in the D. 'Four to me,' he said. 'What question?'

'I was on this ship, once, and we had a guy who fell into the hold. He was normal as you and me when he went down, but when they brought him up he was a cabbage.'

'Poor guy.'

'Yeah, poor guy. And you know what happened to him? He went out on the streets begging, that's what. There was this charity, there. This was in Portsmouth, and there was this charity there that specialized in head cases, guys falling off ships or cranes, and into holds like this guy had done. But they was full up.

169

The charity was sitting there, and could've cured the man, but they couldn't take him because they was full up. So he went begging. Last I heard he was dead. That was Christmas, couple of years back.'

'This is life,' said Geordie, coming over philosophical. Barney was peering out at him from under the table.

'But it doesn't have to be like that,' said Ralph. 'If someone wants to do something about it, really do something. That could save a lot of misery in the world. If I had a place, I could do it.'

'You?'

'Yeah,' said Ralph defensively. 'Something wrong with that?'

'You really mean it?' Geordie asked. 'You're not putting me on?'

'Hey, Geordie. I'm your brother, right? I'm not likely to set you up with a cock-and-bull story. Today I've had a few beers, and I'm not so hot on explaining myself. But if this mate of yours is so keen to give his house to a charity, then I'll be happy to help any way I can.'

'You want me to talk to Sam about it?'

'Hold it there for a couple of days, bro. Don't let's go tearing away at it without thinking it through. We'll talk round it for a while, just the two of us, see what it looks like when it's matured.'

'OK, time to go,' Ralph said. He downed the rest of his pint and swept his cue through the balls remaining on the table. Geordie rubbed his hand over the long chalk mark on the cloth, glanced around guiltily, as though it was he who had done it rather than his brother.

'Where to now?' he asked. 'I'd better be getting home. Janet'll wonder where I am.'

'Museum Gardens,' said Ralph. 'Get a piece of that waitress action.'

'Not me,' Geordie told him. 'That's your date.'

'Come on. She'll have a friend, they always do. Or we'll take turns.'

Geordie shook his head. He got down on his hands and knees to put Barney's leash on. 'Janet's really gonna love that, isn't she? I go out and get pissed in the afternoon's one thing. Come home falling over all the furniture. But she's not gonna get over some

170

waitress in the park. We'd end up, she'd kick me out and get a divorce and take Echo to Australia or somewhere I couldn't see her.' He tugged Barney out from under the table and started in the direction of home. 'Besides which,' he said, 'I don't wanna meet no waitress in the park, even if she does wear her underwear on top. What d'you think I am, Ralph, a philanderer?'

Ralph shook his head and held out his arms. 'Philanderer?' he said. 'I dunno what you are. Christ, Geordie, I just offered to share a bit of nooky with you, you start talking Greek. How's Janet gonna know about it? I'm not gonna tell her.'

'It won't make any difference if she knows or not,' Geordie said. 'I'll know, won't I? And I'll have to live with it, knowing that I've been a creep.'

'Fuck me,' said Ralph.

'Yeah, fuck you,' said Geordie. 'You're my brother, Ralph, and there's lots of ways you're a good guy. But you shouldn't've done that with the cue, marking up the cloth like that. And this thing with the waitress, you're way out of line with that.'

'What've I done?' said Ralph. 'A bit of chalk on the table. It'll brush off. You don't wanna get your end away before supper, that's fine, but I've got a real boner just thinking about it.'

Geordie knelt down to tickle Barney's throat. He looked up at Ralph. 'D'you know what ethics are?' he asked.

Ralph shook his head. 'I ain't got a clue, Geordie. I only know it's not gonna stop me shagging that waitress.'

'Uh-oh,' Janet said when he walked in the kitchen. She was at the table with a paring knife and a bowl of potatoes. Geordie dropped Barney's leash, and Janet put the knife down and took the leash from Barney's collar.

'I need a piss,' Geordie said. He went towards the bathroom.

'I'll hold the fort,' Janet told him.

He pissed into the bowl, resting his forehead against the tiles. As soon as he'd finished he needed a shit, so he dropped his pants and waited while his back plumbing evacuated a small lake of sewage, fast. It was somehow under control. He couldn't have stopped it – paused, say, and then gone back to finish it off. It wasn't that much under control. But he was sitting on the pan. That was something to smile about. As long as the pan didn't overflow, he'd be all right.

171

When everything that was going to come had arrived, his stomach began heaving. He'd got rid of the egg and bacon and mushrooms and tomatoes and a good quantity of the chips by the normal route, but the hash browns, sausage, beans, the rest of the chips and lager all wanted to come out the way they'd gone in.

Geordie slipped to the floor and rested his chin on the lip of the bowl. His forehead was dripping with sweat. He glanced at his watch. Four o'clock in the afternoon. He retched and a stream of digested vegetable matter ripped through his throat and hit the pan. He looked at it, just managed to catch sight of several vital organs before they disappeared under the water. One of them was his heart.

He didn't hear Janet open the door and come into the bathroom. She placed something over his shoulders, felt like a blanket, stopped his teeth from chattering.

'When you've finished here,' she said, 'go upstairs. Get your head down for a bit. I'll call you when the stew's ready.'

THIRTY-TWO

The note read:

> five grand and I'll go away. Get the
> cash and wait. Or you are dead.

The letters and phrases had been cut out of a magazine and stuck to the page with Sellotape.

'What d'you make of it?' Sam asked. He was at his desk in the office. Celia, JD and Marie were standing behind him.

'Weird,' said JD. 'It's like something out of a book.'

Celia was shaking her head. 'How did he expect her to read it?'

'Yeah,' said Marie, looking at JD. 'The guy's seen too many movies.'

Sam had been wearing a smile of disbelief since he'd first seen the note. 'In a horror movie it'd be written in blood,' he said. 'What I don't understand is why someone would go to this much trouble, when he could've contacted her by phone.'

'She might know him,' said Celia. 'Recognize his voice.'

'Yeah,' said Sam. 'Maybe. It's fairly easy to disguise a voice on the phone.'

'You use a hanky,' JD said with a wink. 'Bogie always did anyway. Muffles the voice. Wasn't there a film where the bad guy used a tape recorder and slowed it down, then played it through the telephone?'

'What we're saying,' Sam said, 'if we'd been trying this on, we'd all have done it better?'

'Anyone'd do it better,' said Marie. 'If it has to be a note, it'd be better to write it on plain paper in capitals. Pen and paper from Woolies, virtually untraceable. But this –' she indicated the note on Sam's desk – 'imagine what a forensic scientist is going to make of it.'

'The name of the magazine for a start,' said Sam. 'That'll narrow it down.'

'And the Sellotape'll have all kinds of bits and pieces attached,' said JD. 'They'll probably be able to describe his front room.'

'Fingerprints?' said Celia.

Sam nodded. 'That might be too much to hope for. But the guy seems stupid enough to've left some.'

'Even DNA,' JD pointed out. 'He hasn't used scissors on the tape, probably bitten it off the roll.'

'Are you going to give it to the police, Sam?' Celia asked.

'Yes, see what they make of it. I've got a few good photocopies. Marie, how d'you feel about finding the source of the letters? The magazine they came from?'

'I'll go down to Smiths,' she said. 'Been meaning to catch up on some reading.'

'Have a word with Sly Beaumont at the *Evening Press*. We don't want anything published yet, but show him the letters, he's a bit of an expert on typography. Probably won't know where they're from, but at least he'll point you in the right direction.'

'I'm on the case,' she said, reaching for her coat. 'I'll ring you at home later.'

'Yeah,' said Sam. 'One other thing. There's a connection between Angeles and ice skating. It's probably nothing, but keep it in mind.'

'How d'you mean?'

'We were talking about sport. She was telling me how she does horse riding and skiing, all these physical activities, and I happened to mention ice skating. She reacted strangely. The words stopped her.'

Marie shrugged and left and JD excused himself and followed her down the stairs, said he'd be back in a minute.

Celia sighed deeply, connected with Sam's eyes and shook her head.

'He's still got it bad?' said Sam.

'And it's going to lead absolutely nowhere. Marie's quite certain they're not going to be anything but friends.'

'He'll get over it,' said Sam. 'Sometimes takes a while.'

'It's been more than a year already.'

'Yeah, about the same time Dora died, wasn't it? Seems like yesterday.'

'Do you miss her, Sam?'

He shook his head, his body wanting to deny any dependence or vulnerability. He said, 'I miss her at night. That's the worst time, when I wake up in the middle of the night and she's not there.'

Celia reached down and patted his good hand.

The truth was he missed her during the day as well. He missed her when he was hungry and when he wanted a drink. He missed her when there was a gap between cases and when he woke up in the morning and made coffee for one.

It would pass, he knew that, just as JD's infatuation with Marie would pass. And he wanted it to pass, to go away and leave him free. Not that he'd ever forget her. But he wanted to remember her on his own terms, not as someone else who had been wrenched away from him. He wanted to remember someone he'd shared a life with, someone who had been so close that they'd dared to make plans.

And it would come in time, an anaesthetized memory, something like those wedding photographs you see in studio windows: soft-focus jobs, the couple fading into the background on the very day they've made their vows. The couple, the background, the day itself being dimmed down to make room for the future.

The telephone rang and Celia went to her desk to answer it. JD came back up the stairs, his mouth set but his eyes alive and twinkling behind his thick spectacles. 'How are we going to make sure she's safe, Sam? The guy obviously knows she's living at your place.'

Sam shrugged. 'We can only watch her. I've told her not to answer the door unless she knows who's on the other side. When she goes to work they pick her up in a car and bring her back the same way. If we don't get this guy soon, we might have to think about moving her somewhere else.'

'Going backwards and forwards to work isn't a good idea. Does she have to?'

'Yeah,' said Sam. 'She has to. She doesn't want the guy to turn her into a prisoner.'

175

'What strikes me about this,' JD said. 'All of a sudden we're talking about this guy as if he's a nerd. But before the note we were thinking he was intelligent.'

'What're you saying?'

'Well, the killing of Isabel left us without a clue. This is someone who can get hold of veterinary drugs, knows how much to use in a syringe. He could keep a watch on the two sisters but never be seen himself. He's a clever guy. At least he's shrewd. But then he comes up with a dork note like that thing on your desk.'

'It's true,' said Sam. 'I'd never've thought the guy was after money. Seemed like we were dealing with a psycho.'

'Dual personality, then?' asked JD. 'Is that possible?'

'Yeah, it's possible, but remote. Takes us back to the realms of fiction.'

'How about two guys? A clever one and a dork. The clever one's a nutter, into some kind of obsession, and his mate's trying to make a buck out of the situation. Could even be brothers, which is why the clever one got fixated on two sisters.'

Sam was leaning with an elbow on the desk. With his thumb and forefinger he got hold of his top lip and pulled it out and away from his face like a deformity. 'Dunno,' he said, still holding the lip. Then he let it go and sat back in his chair. 'Some moments in life have too many possibilities in them to live all at once. You have to take the time and work your way through them. One man, two men, clever or stupid, hell, for all we know this note could be a sick hoax.'

'Whatever,' JD said. 'It's certainly made the thing more complicated.'

'Murder's never simple,' Sam said. 'Not when you get down to it. Usually it's the last resort, and by that time it's a burning passion. Sometimes it's not the last resort at all, it's the first response to a situation. But that doesn't make it simple, the kind of mind that arrives at murder as a first response is as twisted as the stuff in a breaker's yard.'

'Not something we can leave to Mr Plod, then?'

Sam grinned. 'Last I heard,' he said, 'they were gonna try to pin it on me. The police don't solve cases, JD; you know that as well as I do. Sometimes they get lucky and find the perpetrator on the job, catch him red-handed, as they say. Other times they get a tip-off, somebody who wants to get rid of the competition. Or the guy's girlfriend gives him up for the reward money. But most of the time they're feeling their way around in the dark.'

'Your favourite people, the fuzz, aren't they, Sam?'

'By a long way. They blow the competition right out of the water.'

He reached for the phone and dialled the number of the local cop shop, waited for the operator to put him through. He could use four fingers of his right hand, the thumb was still hidden in the folds of bandage.

'Rossiter?' he asked.

There was a pause. He could see the guy at the other end weighing up his reaction. Dark hair with a touch of premature grey at the temples. Sharp, needle-point eyes. A flare to his nostrils that could've won him an Oscar if he'd been in the movies. He'd have to work out if the call was from one of his superiors or a nobody. Sam had a silent bet with himself that the guy'd play safe.

'Detective Superintendent Rossiter speaking. How may I help you?'

Sam smiled into the mouthpiece. He said: 'Sam Turner. Listen, Angeles Falco's received a note you might be interested in. Asking for five grand.'

'Turner,' said the youngest detective superintendent in the country. He spoke Sam's surname as though it was a fresh turd. 'When was this received?'

'Couple of hours.'

'Careful how you handle it. It might be a vital piece of evidence. Have you opened it?'

Sam didn't reply. He left the question where it hung, waited for the cop to answer it himself.

'I expect it'll have your prints all over it,' Rossiter said.

'It was opened by an associate,' Sam said. 'Janet Black. You've got her prints on file. She's the only one who's touched it.'

'Where is it?'

'My office.'

'I'll come and collect.'

'Do that,' said Sam. He looked at his watch. 'We close in twenty-four minutes.' He put the phone down. The police would get little from the note. It was a fair bet that there would be no usable prints on it.

He nursed his right hand. It was cold and the nerve endings were singing, leaving a nagging ache, extending from just above the wrist into the length of his thumb. Forensic science was a useful tool, but too often it could only give the police a list of possibilities. Psychological and criminal profiling on the other hand were the stuff of fiction. The press loved it, the whole idea that each criminal left behind a signature, which, in the right hands, would identify him or her beyond any doubt. The results in crime novels and in film and television portrayals of clinical psychologists at work were always successful, but in the real world the overall results were pitiful.

It was true that psychological profilers added something new to the task of investigating crime, but it would be a long time before their methodology was reliable. One of the biggest hurdles for the profession was that the police resented them, regarded them as interlopers and meddlers and usually disregarded their suggestions.

Sam glanced at the note again. 'Get the cash and wait.' What was the guy's next move gonna be? Another note? A phone call?

Angeles had said she'd get the cash if Sam thought it would help. But she didn't want to pay someone off who had killed her sister.

He picked up the note with a pair of tweezers, folded it with the aid of a paper-knife, and inserted it in the original envelope.

'I'm going,' he called through to Celia. 'The cops'll be here in a minute to pick up the evidence. Tell Rossiter I was heartbroken to miss him. Give him my love.'

THIRTY-THREE

'I'd have liked to see the original,' Sly Beaumont told Marie. 'But I would guess that all the letters come from the same magazine.' Sly was the crime editor at the *Yorkshire Evening Press*, and he was speaking in his office looking out over Walmgate. He was a grizzled old bear of a man with creases in his leathery face that defied access to his razor. His suit looked as though it was still hanging in his wardrobe, draped from his coat-hanger shoulders but not touching any other part of his anatomy. A suit that shone with age and that spoke quietly of a time before its owner's body had begun to shrink.

'You can't say which mag?' asked Marie.

He shook his head. 'The headings are in Hermes, but they've used Times for the body.' He made a face at the copy. 'Arial condensed, which might be from a different mag, or for a special section within the same one. Something modern, probably aimed at a young audience. Professionally printed, but designed by someone without much imagination. That's as close as I can get.' He handed the photocopy of the note back to Marie. 'How's Sam doing? Never calls in to see me any more. Tell him he owes me a visit.'

'I will. And thanks for the help with the note. It'll narrow down my search.'

'Any time.' He gave her a smile that resembled a deflated football, then had another thought. 'He still grieving over Dora?'

'I don't think so,' Marie said. 'He took it hard, but you know Sam: "life's for the living," all that practical philosophy he carries around with him.'

179

'He got himself a woman?' Sly asked.

Marie shook her head. 'There are signs that he's beginning to think about it. Seems keen on our current client.'

'A man needs a woman,' Sly said. 'You don't have a woman, you end up looking like me.'

Marie laughed with him. 'Is that something you want me to tell him?'

'It's a warning. Sam's the kind of guy needs all the advice he can get. He never listens, but that's no reason to stop telling him.'

'I'm writing this down,' said Marie. 'He'll get every word of it.'

El Piano for coffee and a piece of carrot cake to fill the gap caused by a missed lunch. Quiet at this time of day, just Marie and a thin man playing around with the chords of 'Love for Sale'; humming the melody, his voice and the ivories clambering around each other like a wild red rose on a cross.

She watched him for a moment, saw pain in his hunched shoulders, understood for the space of a breath that he could sing no other song. His profile was a line of genius; she wanted to reach out and trace it with the tip of her finger. The slope of the brow, the slight loop of nose, and its echo there again in the chin. He was young, early or middle twenties, and the blues had found a deep gash in his soul and come to rest there for a while. Undeniably queer and undeniably a god.

Sam had always been a friend and never a lover and that was the best way round. He was constant as a friend. If they'd ever overstepped the mark and hopped into bed, turned friendship into a sexual affair, they might have gained the moment but the loss would have been incalculable.

Marie sometimes wondered if the world saw her as a Miss Moneypenny, spending her life waiting for the odd glimpse of James Bond. She couldn't see herself and Sam Turner as an emotional item, and the things you couldn't see were not meant to be.

The Greek god left the piano and paid Maggie at the bar for his coffee. They both watched him turn a corner in Swinegate and disappear into the silent and lonely world of the truly beautiful.

'Who was that?' Marie asked.

Maggie raised her eyebrows, looked over at the freshly deserted piano, and slowly wiped down the counter. 'I'm not sure he really happened.'

Smiths. The shelves lined with magazines of every description. Music, Women's, Pets, Lifestyle, Computers. All of them tempting the passing trade in a variety of voices, commanding attention with whispers and fluttering eyelashes or glass jewellery and hysterical screams. Each one held out a promise: objects to furnish the home or objectivity, nudity or the bare facts, a free gift or personal freedom. She half-closed her eyes, walked past the women's section, picked up magazines at random and checked out the typefaces. *Aviary Birds, The Spectator, Bodybuilding, Time Out, Punch, The Internet*, each had a tale to tell, but none of them had the feel of the letters that made up the blackmail note.

'Something aimed at a young audience,' Sly Beaumont had said. She watched the customers for a while. Girls gravitated towards the women's section, thumbed through copies of *New Woman*, *Cosmopolitan* and *Tatler*. Young men tended to make their way to the computing section, or gazed wistfully at scantily clad models in the lad mags. Both sexes sniffed around the music section in equal parts.

Marie's brain began clicking into PI mode. A middle-aged man wearing a blazer picked up a copy of the *Radio Times* and she didn't need to look at it to know that it wasn't the source of the note. Whoever had written the blackmail note was unlikely to have been a woman. You could never be completely sure; as time marched on Western culture seemed to throw up more crimes of violence that had the woman's touch. There had been reports of gangs of young females recently perfecting the art of mugging. But this one smelled like a man.

She moved over to the section with the men's glossies and read the titles: *Men's Health, Esquire, Loaded, Bizarre*. Escapist mags, offering tales of sexual prowess, soft-porn photographs of implanted breasts and tanned thighs, the latest casual fashions and reviews of videos and films. All of them aimed at low achievers, the kind of guys who were already convinced they were descended from kings. Young men who were the victims of their own egos, ripe fodder for the siren cry of the pornographer. Marie had been avoiding them all her life.

She remembered a well-known occult phenomenon, according to her boyfriend, David Styles, who knew about such things. If you put in all the effort you could in the early stages, the angels came along to help you out when the going got rough. Marie preferred to think she just got lucky, but there was an extra bonus in sharing a bed with someone who believed in angels.

Stuff didn't ring any bells, *Later* and *GQ* both felt wrong, but *Loaded* had headings and intros in that distinctive Hermes font. As she thumbed through a copy she came across the phrase 'five grand' in a sub-heading the same size and density as the phrase in the note. 'Gotcha,' she said, and the guy next to her with his head in a copy of *Bizarre* quickly put it down and left the shop.

Sam laughed when she told him. 'So we're looking for a young guy with a hard-on?' he said over the phone.

'Yeah, I guess,' she said. 'And I thought I'd moved on from there.'

This remark elicited another Sam Turner chuckle, followed by a line of angst. 'Sex and death, Marie. It keeps on coming back.'

'If it's not obvious, you know it's always there, hidden deep in the kernel of every case.'

'Yeah.'

'You don't sound convinced.'

'No, I'm convinced,' he said. 'I was thinking about Isabel. There was no sexual interference. No obvious signs of sexual violence. She was drugged and her back was broken. None of her clothes were removed.'

'I see where you're going,' Marie said. 'We're looking for someone who keeps a more or less constant watch on two sisters, obsessive, he kills, he's into soft-porn mags and chastity.'

'And there's the thing about ice skating, been in the back of my mind all day. You think anything about that?'

'No, Sam. I'd forgotten all about it. The missing piece. Maybe it was just one of the words that got to her. "Ice" or "skating"? What about the accident that killed her parents? Black ice on the road? It doesn't have to be connected with the case.'

'I know,' he said. 'It's probably nothing. But it makes me itch.'

'I know what you mean,' she said. 'The case doesn't hold together. Every time we get a new piece of info we lose some cohesion. I still don't have a handle on the guy who's calling the shots.'

'It makes sense if you think about there being two of them,' Sam said. 'Two guys from different ends of the street.'

'Working together?'

'Dunno,' he said. 'Too early to say. Maybe they're working together, that would account for the different signals we're getting. But it could be they're in competition, a couple of psychopaths working the same patch.'

'You mean they don't know each other? What's going to happen when they come face to face?'

'Interesting,' said Sam, leaning heavily on the word. 'I don't suppose it's covered in the textbooks. Makes me think about a couple of express trains heading towards each other on the same track.'

'Nasty.'

'Yeah, specially for the folks who just happen to be in the neighbourhood.'

THIRTY-FOUR

There was a woman once, back in the days Sam first landed in York, made a profession out of green fingers. Must've been one of the first organic gardeners in the world. Betty? Yeah, Betty Carter, could dig a twenty-metre plot before breakfast, cook up ham steaks with eggs and mushrooms and around a gallon of coffee, then go back outside and lift half a ton of carrots while dinner stewed gently in the oven.

Betty thought good sex, good home-cooking, hard work and the smells of the earth would work miracles on Sam Turner. And she was right in a way. He got fit and tanned and lean living with her. Spent every penny he had on booze, and when he'd emptied his pockets he'd reach for Betty's purse. Didn't matter where she hid it. Found it once buried under the compost heap. A man gets to know a woman's ways.

When he'd taken her to the verge of bankruptcy, and there was no more money for him to drink, he'd started chasing other women. Sam could always summon a charming smile if it was paving the road to a bottle. And he didn't understand at all when Betty showed him the door. Called it betrayal. He stood on one side of the door and Betty stood on the other, and for the length of a long black night he howled chaos as grey worms invaded his brain and his thick, beached tongue sponged industrial alcohol from a gallon can.

Must've been Betty who rang for the ambulance, but she didn't visit him in the hospital, and when he was discharged she'd changed all the locks, put shutters up at the windows.

'Fuck 'em,' he'd said at the time. He'd turned around and

changed direction but kept on going down the same old rutted track of self-deception, perpetrating mindless violence on himself and everyone who came into contact with him.

'I must've been a real prize in those days,' he said to himself. When it didn't matter how much he drank; when whiskey was equal to blood and he saw the world through a combination of them both. And there were still women prepared to take him on. Young and old, women whose self-esteem had fallen so low that the only redemption was through the resurrection of another. Women who would only be able to face themselves if they could wrench Sam Turner from the jaws of Hell.

'Betty,' he said. 'Where are you now?'

Sam knew where she was. Not exactly, but last he'd heard she was digging up a patch in the south of France. She wasn't a lost love, a ghost who haunted his dreams like Dora, or Donna, his first wife. She was someone else he'd abused and who held a place in his conscience. He would never look her up; knowing there would be nothing he could say or do to repair his violence. He'd have liked to offer her a chunk of her life back.

One thing Betty had left with Sam. When he was sober she'd take him round her garden and she'd show him the plants. She'd talk to them herself; he'd sometimes find her there, squatting down by the tomatoes pouring out her heart. But when they were together, she'd point out the different characteristics of the plants, say why she was adding bonemeal around the roots of one, wood ash to another. And she'd be able to see when one of the plants, or sometimes a group of them, needed water. She'd see that several hours before they began to wilt.

'How d'you know?' Sam'd ask. 'I can't see that. They all look the same to me.'

'You're not looking at them right,' she'd say. 'You look at them and you see stems and leaves, a collection of plants.'

'Well, yeah, Betty. You think there's something else there?'

'A whole lot more. In a way there's everything there. Everything that "is" in the universe is a reflection of the whole. If you look for it, you'll find it.'

Wise women, there's one round every corner.

'So how can I tell the cucumber wants water twelve hours before it starts gasping?'

'Oh, that's easy,' Betty said. 'Look at its expression.'

And it was exactly the same with Geordie. You could tell when he wanted something by his expression. Before he got through the door, maybe an hour or two before he got around to saying what it was.

Geordie had a poker face. He blinked infrequently and he kept his head angled downward so you couldn't always see his eyes. It was a mysterious face; the nose and chin prominent but the mouth small, with a hint of femininity in the bow of the lips. It was as if he deliberately sent out mixed signals.

But when he wanted something, which in Geordie's case was usually the answer to one of the riddles of the universe, he made his eyes available and the ambiguity of his features was replaced with a kind of light.

'You thought any more about moving out of here?' he asked in a voice as casual as a pit helmet.

Sam watched him. Geordie looked back, his eyes wide open and popping, as if there was some kind of pressure behind them.

'Moving out?'

'Yeah. You said you was thinking of moving out, handing the place over to homeless people, something like that.'

'Haven't thought much about it,' Sam said. 'Been waiting for inspiration.'

'JD says that's bollocks,' said Geordie. 'Waiting for inspiration. JD says if he waited for inspiration, he'd never write anything. He's written five, six books and he didn't have inspiration for any of them. Just went ahead and wrote them without the inspiration.'

'Some of them, it shows,' said Sam.

'You reckon? I thought you liked them.'

'Yeah. Mostly I like them. I was being facetious.'

'Anyway, he didn't write them without inspiration, he just started them without it. He reckons once you get started, the inspiration comes along anyway. But only if you don't wait for it.'

'Where're you going with this?' Sam asked.

'Well, this house. If you're waiting for inspiration, you might never do anything about it. You could spend the rest of your life here, the whole building falling down around you, the bricks crumbling, ants eating away at the foundations, dry rot, cracked windows. There's homeless people queuing up outside, praying that you're gonna get some inspiration so they can get off the streets. You see what I'm saying?'

Sam nodded. 'I should just wake up in the morning and make a decision, put all my kit in a cardboard box and move out the same day.'

'That's not what I thought,' said Geordie. 'But it'd be better than not doing anything at all. Might mean that you start to get on with the rest of your life, and all the people who could live in this place get a chance to have a life of their own, which they can't do at the moment because you're taking up too much space.'

Sam scratched the top of his head. 'Geordie, d'you wanna tell me what this is all about?'

'You wanna unload this house, right? Because it's too big for you?'

'In theory, yes. I'm not in a hurry. I've got Angeles staying here at the moment. The place's got a function. It's working for me.'

'What about,' Geordie said. 'This's just an example, OK? It's not a true story. But what about if there was a sailor who fell into a hold on his ship and cracked his head open, smashed his brains around. The guy comes out of the hold and he's having to hold his brains in with his hands, real mangled up.'

'Don't get carried away. I've got a picture of a sailor with brain damage.'

'Yeah,' Geordie agreed. 'Brain damage. There's this place can cure it, like a charity, but they're full up with other brain-damaged sailors. Would you give the house to that charity so they could help the guy with the brain . . .?'

'. . . Damage. Brain damage.'

'Yeah, so they could help the guy with the brain damage. That's what I said.'

'You said the guy with the brain.'

'Fuck, Sam, you know what I mean.'

'Yeah, I might give it to some charity. I don't know, I'd have to think about it. And it'd have to be after we've sorted this case. I'd need a place to stay, and Angeles can't go back to her house until we've found the guy who killed her sister.' He pulled Sheryl Crow's *Globe Sessions* album from its sleeve and put the CD into the player, hit the start button.

Geordie struck a listening pose, head cocked to one side. 'I don't know this.'

187

'Angeles brought it. Morning music; get-me-out-of-here-I'm-being-hassled music.'

Geordie did the shrugged shoulders trick. 'I'm only asking a question.'

'A couple of things remain to be sorted out of this bizarre exchange which you call asking a question.'

'What's that?' said Geordie. He'd picked up the CD sleeve and was squinting at the small print, no longer giving Sam his full attention.

'What are those,' said Sam.

Geordie looked up at him over the CD cover. 'Eh?'

'What are those,' said Sam. 'Not: What's that. If I say there's a couple of things to be sorted, you can't say, "What's that?" A couple of things is plural.'

'What are *those*, boss?'

'First thing is, you can't cure brain damage.'

'How d'you know?'

'I've heard you can't cure it, I've read it somewhere. And it stands to reason, if the brain gets physically damaged, you can't really mend it. Ever hear of a brain transplant?'

'What you'll probably find,' said Geordie, 'some brain damages you can mend, others you can't. This sailor guy had the kind you could mend, but the charity was too full, busy mending other brains. You ever hear of brain surgery?'

'You said it wasn't true,' Sam pointed out. 'You said he wasn't a real sailor, that it was just an example.'

Geordie sighed. 'Yeah, it is an example, but that doesn't mean there isn't some truth in it. What's the other thing?'

'I still don't know why you're asking me about the house. We've established that I'd give it to a charity, in theory, under certain circumstances. But why d'you want to know that?'

'Because Ralph and me's thinking of starting a charity for handicaps.'

Sam went for a trek round the room.

'You've still got the limp,' Geordie said. 'Look like a pimp. And we're gonna need some place to do it. Me and Ralph.'

'Ralph,' said Sam.

'Yeah, me and Ralph.'

'I was putting the sailor connection together.' Sam couldn't get a handle on what Geordie meant by handicapped people. Was it OK to call them handicapped? What kind of handicaps did they have? 'You mean you wanna stop working with me and start a home for "handicapped" people with your brother?'

'No, I still wanna be a detective. It's Ralph who wants to do the home, but we'd be like partners. And it'd mean Ralph could move out of our house, and me and Janet'd be by ourselves again, with Echo. And then we'd just see him on Sundays when he came to dinner.'

'And he's had some experience with "handicapped" people, has he?'

'He knew the sailor I was telling you about. But mainly it's like an ambition. Something he's been thinking about for ages.'

'I bet he has,' said Sam.

'And if your house was available, it'd make everything come true.'

'Oh, I can see that, Geordie. I can see that real clear. It'd be like a fairy story.'

THIRTY-FIVE

atch therefore; for ye know not what hour your Lord doth come.

W I was standing by the window watching the street. Sexy Sadie walked by the house three times, dressed to kill, hobbling on a pair of stilettos. She was wearing black-and-white striped tights and a lace-trimmed skirt no bigger than a handkerchief.

I found myself thinking about the original architectural model of this estate, which I have never seen. But I imagined it with its varnished blocks of houses, and the roads with a few trees scattered around. No people or cars or the dirt that populates the finished project.

There are groups of cells in the body called phagocytes which work together as part of the immune system. Their function is to watch. They just sit there watching. They are policemen, of a kind; they help maintain law and order in a semi-closed environment. If something happens to disturb the balance of the organism, sickness occurs and chaos ensues which could result in death or dissolution. The phagocytes act to ward off disease or corruption entering the organism. They sit and watch, but if necessary they cease watching and go into action as an army. They form the first line of defence against that which would overcome the body.

Watching is my profession, my life and my destiny.

For watching to be successful, the watcher has to be hidden, in the shadows, out of sight or disguised in some way.

It follows, therefore, that the good watcher has to feel at home there.

190

The phagocyte doesn't have much choice; it only knows the environment in which it exists. But the owl, sitting on the branch of a tree at midnight, has chosen the branch for a number of reasons. It might have decided to watch from the gable of a barn instead. It is limited only by its lack of imagination.

I watch the blind woman. I watch myself watching her. When she is not around or out of my sight I conjure her up.

And God watches all of us, all of the time. We are never out of His sight. He cannot do other than behold us.

Though I say it myself, my research is impeccable. It is a skill one acquires, not a talent with which one is born. As a young student I learned my lessons well. There were only two of us with a first in my year. The other one was a female and a swot and a professional virgin. I lived then, as now, a more rounded existence. I was a member of the Union, the University Ornithological and Ecumenical societies. Rather dry tastes for a young man, but I was still finding my way in the world. My interests now have matured into something a little more hedonistic.

Research. Yes. Sam Turner calls himself a private detective but he is little more than a local rogue. Many low achievers I have encountered professionally would not want to associate with him. He has a criminal conviction and has served time in prison. He is known as a drinker and there are numerous counts of drunk and disorderly against him, disturbing the peace, and several of vagrancy, though none in recent years.

He was once known as something of a rake but by the look of him, those days are now long past.

The blind woman has moved into his house. But, even taking into account her inability to see, I find it difficult to imagine her forming a romantic attachment to him. Their relationship, therefore, is professional. Ergo, she has hired the man to protect her against me.

Incredible. He's nothing. A nobody.

In the mornings she is picked up from his house by a chauffeur in a black Daimler. He leads her to the car and takes her to her office on the Haxby Road. In the middle of the afternoon he brings her back.

I'm dialling the number of her secretary at Falco's soft-drinks factory. This will be the third time we have spoken. I listen to the phone ringing at the other end.

'Mr Packard? Good morning, Hayes here, ringing in reply to your letter.'

'Oh, yes, Mr Hayes. Ms Falco's back at her desk now. You wanted to see her about your application to the Falco Trust. Let's see, I don't have it in front of me at the moment. Children, wasn't it?'

'Yes, partially sighted.'

'And did we suggest a time?'

'Yes, 4.30 on Thursday. I'm ringing to confirm it.'

'We'll expect to see you then. Thanks for ringing.'

I'm putting the phone back into the receiver. For the first time in my life I feel like dancing.

I have several photographs of my father, but only one in his uniform. Strange, because in my memory of him he wears uniform all the time. He arrives home from work at different times of the day and night and the first thing he does is come to see me. If it is daytime, he lifts me up from the floor or the chair and holds me high in the air so that I look down at him. If it is night, he comes to my room and gazes down at me. I may be half-awake, but I feign sleep. I know he is there and all is well with the world. I am held by his gaze, the centre of his universe, as he is the centre of mine.

I retain these images but they are not accompanied by sound. They are silent films. I imagine my father coming into the house at the end of his day and shouting my name. Perhaps he began calling for me when he was in the street or on the garden path. And when he lifted me into the air it was not a soundless event. It was something joyful and there would have been accompanying laughter punctuated by his pet names for me and my own screams of delight.

The sound-track has been eliminated. Somehow in the confusion of death and grief and time it has been lost or stolen.

I used to think it was retrievable, that one day I would turn a corner of memory and discover it waiting for me. In my mind's eye there was a parcel wrapped in brown paper, slightly dusty on the outside, but when I unwrapped it the contents were as clean and shiny as the first leaf of spring.

192

Four reels of audiotape. The old kind, before cassettes were invented. You put the reel on to the machine and threaded it through the magnetic head, hooked it to an empty reel on the other side. I would be able to synchronize the silent pictures in my head with the sound on the tapes. And the result would be like real life. It would be almost the same as having him back again.

But why four reels?

I still don't know. When that particular vision visited me there were always four reels of tape. I delved into the mystery of numerology, but never came up with a definitive answer. Symbolically the number four represents containment and regularity, as in the square.

This is one of the reasons for my voice-activated recorder. I don't want to lose the sound-track again. Another reason: when I transcribe an event I want to work from an accurate record.

Miriam is not stimulated by speculations of this kind. She is young and excited by dreams of untold wealth and physical passion and pain.

I have built a rack for us. It's a rickety kind of thing but does the job. Miriam or myself can be strapped into it (with a little adjustment to take account of our different sizes) by means of leather cuffs with Velcro fastenings. It's a strange and exciting sensation to be spread-eagled and at the mercy of another human being. Especially when you know she's cruel and she loves you.

Today I have been working on a simple mechanism that will enable me to administer electric shocks to my love's labia.

And on Thursday I have an appointment with the blind woman.

THIRTY-SIX

The countryside was not Sam's favourite place. His natural habitat was the city. He could take long desolate beaches, a coastline of any description. From time to time he'd found himself living in a smallish market town and that hadn't been the end of the world. But open countryside and tiny villages made him think of incurable diseases.

He was on the A64 when it started to snow. The steady stream of traffic kept the road clear but when he turned off on to the country lanes he had to slow down and think about getting a new set of tyres. People imagine running a detective agency is all profit, like there's no overheads involved. But by the time the landlord's had his slice and the insurance company's had its, and you've paid out the wages and the accountant and the tax man and the various kinds of parasites that live off car ownership, you're lucky if you can afford a chicken sandwich for lunch.

Still, it was better than working. You worked for the man and most times the chicken sandwich problem disappeared, but so did your freedom and your soul and your integrity and your hope for the future and your faith in humanity and your balls shrivelled up and died. Take a tip from one who's tried.

The heavens tilted and tipped all the snow they had on to the North Riding of Yorkshire. There was powdery stuff mixed in with crystals, and the angels added hallucinations to the brew, so that huge glistening chandeliers threatened to crash through the windscreen. The spears and javelins of long-dead warriors whizzed past the car in all directions, and as the edges of the road disappeared, Sam fancied he heard drums drumming and somewhere directly above him a brass band began the introduction to a funeral dirge.

As suddenly as the storm had arrived it passed away again, leaving behind a wonderworld composed of ecclesiastical vestments.

The fields lay around the remains of the road like a bleached desert, the hedges absorbed and reduced by the dazzling landscape. A man alone in an ancient Montego, though he be invincible in the panorama of a city, could start to feel groundless out here in the sticks. Keep your eye on the target, Sam said to himself. Don't think about balding tyres or a clutch beginning to slip. And who needs a heating system, anyway? It'd cost more than the old tub's worth.

The final rise up to Skewsby almost broke the heart of the car. Fifty metres before the top Sam got the engine racing along in first gear and sat tight while the rear wheels slewed from one side of the road to the other. His mind never entertained the idea that the thing would actually stall and slide down the hill backwards. His bowels were not so optimistic but managed to stop short of disgracing him.

A private nurse, a woman who looked as though she spent most of her life in the shower, admitted Sam to the house. 'I'm Rosemary,' she said.

And freshly picked this morning, Sam thought. Couldn't help sniffing when she turned her back, check if she smelled like a herb. All that reached him was an aroma of starch and lemon soap. Might even be considered exotic in this neck of the woods.

He followed her into a reception room off the main hall where she offered him a seat and closed the door. She sat pertly on a high-backed chair, her knees screaming for attention through the stuff of her black tights. 'I don't want him upset,' she said.

Thirty-seven, he thought; maybe thirty-eight. She's got two kids at home, both in their teens, and a husband who doesn't see her any more although he still lives in the same house. She got married and raised a family. That was all right in those days, no one sneered at you for it.

'I'm not here to upset him. He rang me.'

'As long as you understand that he has lost his wife and suffered a fairly disabling stroke.'

Her blonde hair was cut short, in a style that had been briefly popular in the late eighties, but she had allowed it to dry out into a spare and frizzy mop. 'Are you trying to prepare me for a shock?' Sam asked.

She shook her head. 'Mr Reeves is considerably reduced. His friends and neighbours were surprised by his condition. Some of the village children have been unkind. He's rather sensitive, understandably so. It's going to take a little time to get him back to normal.'

Sam put his cards on the table. 'I've only met him once,' he said. 'And I didn't like him. He was arrogant and overbearing, the kind of guy I'd walk around the block to avoid. I can't imagine any change he's gone through that would've improved him.'

Rosemary produced her first smile. 'I work with all kinds,' she said. 'But Mr Reeves is one of the nicest patients I've had in a long time. Only two problems: he can get frustrated, especially when his body or his mind won't do what he wants them to.'

'I'm like that myself,' Sam confessed. 'And the other one?'

'The other what?'

'You said there were two problems.'

'Oh, yes, his hands.'

'He can't keep them to himself?'

'No kidding,' she said. 'The man's an octopus.'

Quintin Reeves was almost unrecognizable. Although his facial characteristics had been left relatively unchanged by the ravages of the stroke, the inner man had undergone a metamorphosis.

When Rosemary showed Sam into the living room Reeves was sitting in a Windsor chair by the window. He turned and recognized the detective immediately. He got to his feet and walked forward with a strange Chaplinesque motion. His right leg was paralysed but he managed to throw it out and forward and follow through with his good one. This action had the effect of unbalancing him and he used his left arm to right himself, swinging it around at shoulder height like a boom.

Sam was impressed. The guy had been as rosy as a freshly turned bed the last time they met. Here they were again, less than a month later, and the same man could've given Quasimodo a run for his money. But he had a smile on his face as wide as a bay window, something his former self would never've managed.

'Come in, come in,' he shouted, his voice rising and falling a full octave within the span of the two syllables. 'Have a seat. Sit down.' The arm waving around, seemingly unable to remain motionless. 'Thanks for coming. Beautiful day. How did you get up the . . .?'

Sam waited, watching the man struggling for the word. But it wouldn't come.

'How did you get up the . . . up there –' He pointed out of the window. 'Thing that goes up and down?'

'Hill,' said Sam.

Reeves laughed. 'Hill, yes. Can't always find the words. That's why I've got a nurse.'

'You're doing fine, Mr Reeves,' said Rosemary. She moved forward quickly and plumped the cushion on his chair before he sat in it.

'Thanks to you, my dear.' Rosemary side-stepped briskly as his wild hand came close to her behind. Sam wasn't sure if he'd consciously intended to slap her bottom or if the hand had a mind of its own. Reeves turned back to Sam. 'How did you manage the hill?'

'It was touch and go,' Sam told him. He glanced at Rosemary, but she was concentrating on keeping her distance.

'You asked me to come out here,' Sam said. 'How can I help you?' He noticed that Reeves had been freshly shaved but several clumps of beard had been missed. He had a single-sided wispy moustache and a small red patch of whiskers on his lower cheek.

Reeves looked at him. He'd brought his arm under control and was holding it down on his lap. 'I want you to find who killed my wife, Mr Turner.'

'I'm already retained by your sister-in-law,' Sam reminded him.

'That's all right. There's no law says you can't work for me as well. On the same . . .'

'Case?' said Rosemary.

'Dammit, yes. The same case.'

Sam shook his head.

'What're you worried about? There's no conflict of interest. I'm offering cash up front.'

'I don't understand your motives,' Sam told him. 'I'm already working on the case for Angeles. I have to find Isabel's killer, get him off the street so Angeles is safe.'

'I want to help,' Reeves said. 'The police are so damn slow. They never tell me anything. I thought if you had more money, resources; well, it's not going to work against you, is it? I'm stuck in the house here, I want to be more . . . more . . .'

'Useful?' Sam said.

Reeves exhaled. 'Yes, I want to be useful.'

He was wearing a tie, of course, striped in blue and gold, and the yolk of an egg had dribbled down it for five centimetres before solidifying. The zip at the front of his trousers had stuck half-way and he gave it a polite tug from time to time but it didn't move.

Sam said, 'I've got everyone I know involved on the case. Even part-timers. Doesn't really matter how much you pay me, I'm still gonna have the same number of people.'

'I want to help, Turner. There must be some way.'

'How about you solve a little problem for me?' Sam said. 'You know anything about ice skating? Something connected with Angeles?'

Reeves looked blank. 'Ice skating. It's one thing I've never done.'

'What about Isabel?'

'Isabel? Oh, no. Isabel had a thing about ice altogether. Avoided it like the plague. She'd never've gone skating.'

'A thing about ice?' Sam said. 'What does that mean? She had a phobia about ice?'

'I wouldn't put it that strongly,' said Reeves. 'She was frightened of it. Irrational, really. Something happened when she was a child. Some kind of accident.'

'You don't know exactly?'

'Can't say I do,' said Reeves. 'She mentioned it a couple of times. The village pond, I think it was. All fall down.'

'Angeles as well?'

Quintin Reeves sat shaking his head. He didn't know any more. 'I think so, yes. Childhood trauma. What about it, Turner? Are you going to let me help? I've got money.'

All answers, if they were answers worth having, were vague. The answers that weren't vague were the ones to worry about. When you asked a question and the answer came back with no margin of doubt, then it was time to start worrying. Maybe this ice-skating thing would lead nowhere. Even if there was someone who was there at the time, could explain Angeles' reticence and Isabel's phobia, it still might not be relevant to the case. Difficult to see how it could be, really. Ice skating, an accident on the village pond, two little girls in pigtails; not the kind of scenario that leads to murder. Not usually, but then again, murder wasn't a usual occurrence.

'Tell you what,' Sam said. 'I'll take the case. I'm gonna charge you exactly the same as I'm charging your sister-in-law. We'll double everybody's wages, kind of Christmas bonus.'

Quintin squealed. He did the happiest face Sam had seen since Echo was born. Didn't seem to matter that the guy had done up the wrong buttons on his shirt. 'Do you want me to get cash?' Reeves asked. 'I could go to the bank.'

Sam glanced out of the triple-glazed window. Deep and crisp and even. 'Hell, no,' he said. 'I'll send you a bill.'

On the way back to York the snowstorm returned and Sam ploughed his way through it. A blizzard was how Angeles described what she saw at night, shadows in a blizzard. There were times he thought he could empathize with her and then the time would pass away and he'd feel only pity. She'd hate that, being pitied, because it was less than she deserved. It was less than love; pity was an emotion that could never be productive. Sam would throw it out, dig deep for the more complex empathy again; but when he wasn't looking the pity began creeping back in.

Hitting the A64, leaving those country roads behind, was like landing back on earth after a trip to another planet. He drove and watched the lights of oncoming traffic swimming towards him like huge shoals of fish.

THIRTY-SEVEN

Celia sighed inwardly when Lorna George entered the office. Lorna was one of those women who come from so low down the social scale that it is immoral to dislike them. You know all the liberal arguments which prove that Lorna's unfortunate personality is not her fault – she's the product of a broken home, sexually abused by her father and brothers, teenage pregnancy and a long history of failed relationships – and you want to run a mile when you see her on the street.

'Bloody freezing out there, Celia.' Still a trace of a South African accent after all these years. She placed a well-used cardboard file on the reception counter and blew into her cupped hands. She'd found the time to fix her false nails before facing the world this morning: two centimetres long, flecked with gold. 'Ooh, I love your hair.'

Pass the bucket, Celia thought, watching her long-held Christian principles wither away. And she gave Lorna a smile which, fuelled by guilt, went gushing over the top.

Lorna was a hack, the kind of journalist you find if you turn over a large stone. She edited a local free magazine but doubled as a freelance whenever she got a whiff of the unsavoury or the rotten. Police and local government leaks were all funnelled through Lorna George. Occasionally she got her dirty little fingers into national scandals.

She was in her mid-forties now, wearing a grey suit with a knee-length skirt, fashioned from a cloth that contained a minimum amount of cotton. There were wrinkles in the material around her hips and thighs. She wore black tights and high-heeled shoes and

200

her hair was dyed an unnatural shade of black and pinned up in a bun.

She shook a long chocolate-coloured cigarette out of a pack and put it between her lips. 'D'you mind, Celia?' She raised the pencil lines which had replaced her eyebrows.

Celia shook her head. 'You'll have to wait, I'm afraid. We're all ex-smokers here, fanatics. The office's a smoke-free zone.'

Lorna shook her head and put the cigarette back in the pack. It wasn't clear why she was shaking her head. Could have been because of the no-smoking rule or simply that Lorna didn't understand why anyone would want to give up smoking, or why anyone would want to give up anything. Especially if it was in the area of sex or drugs or money. 'Is the great detective in?'

'I'm afraid not; it's difficult to catch him without an appointment.'

'Didn't use to be like that, though. Know what I mean?' Lorna said. 'After a couple of drinks you could net him with a wink in the old days.'

Celia didn't reply. She kept a deadpan face and held Lorna's eyes, daring her to go on. That was a mistake.

'He'd booze all your money away, shag you stupid and dump you for the next broad with a bottle or a jingle in her purse. He was a knight of the round table, chivalry dribbling down his trouser leg.'

'Is there something I can help you with, Lorna?'

'Now he's got his office and his big house and it costs an arm and a leg to speak to him. But he's still the same guy underneath. People don't change. Not that much, anyway. And men don't change at all. Isn't that the truth, Celia?'

Celia put both hands on the counter. 'Lorna, if there's something you want, I'll do my best to help. But if you're here to run Sam down, it would be better if you left.'

The journalist smiled. 'Loyalty. How touching. I heard a rumour about a note that was sent to Angeles Falco. D'you want to tell me what it said?'

Ah. That's why she was here. 'I don't know anything about it,' Celia said. 'Sam's handling the case personally. You'll have to talk to him.'

'But you're not denying that there was a note?'

'I'm not denying or confirming anything,' said Celia. 'I don't know if what you say is true or not.'

'Because,' Lorna said, opening the cardboard file, 'I just happen to have a photocopy of the note here. What d'you say about it now?'

Lorna George left the great detective's office and crossed over the square to Betty's. She waited for a window table so she'd see Sam when he returned from his jaunt. The irony of watching the detective while the detective was watching over his client was not lost on her. Lorna was good at watching people, watching situations, that's what being a journalist was about. Keeping your eyes skinned, being able to see the moment when a story starts to break. Under different circumstances, Lorna always said, she would have made an excellent spy.

What Lorna liked least about the situation was having to spend time in Betty's, paying Betty's prices for the sake of a cup of coffee. So waitress service costs more to provide? Who cares? Get rid of the waitresses, bring the prices down.

That Celia was a silly old cow. She knew as much about the note as her boss did, just as she knew where Angeles Falco was hiding out. What was it about Sam Turner that his women were so loyal, even the ones he wasn't poking? At least she didn't think he'd be poking Celia. You could never tell, though; the dirty bastards were capable of screwing rubber dolls. Guys who'd do that were capable of anything. And they all did it.

He came around the corner into the square and made for the entrance to the office building. He was wearing grey cords with highly polished shoes and a bomber jacket to show off his tight little bum. He walked with a pronounced limp, no doubt introduced artificially to elicit sympathy. Lorna left her file and scarf on the table and went across to intercept him before he got to Celia.

He turned when she called his name but he didn't see her immediately. She watched him scan the square, looking for something younger and sexier, and when he finally focused on her his face closed down like a vegetarian who'd found a venison steak on his plate. He was good, though, managed to resurrect a smile as colourful as a Kalahari sunset.

'Lorna,' he said. He gave her the once over. 'Shouldn't you be wearing a coat?'

'It's in Betty's,' she said. 'I was having a coffee. You want to join me?'

Hesitation. For a moment there, a dithering detective. 'Is this business?' he asked.

'Could be pleasure as well, Sam. Depends how you want to play it.' She watched his breath on the icy air.

He glanced at his watch. 'A few minutes?'

'I'm offering you coffee,' she said. 'Not a package holiday.'

The waitress brought Sam a coffee and set it down in front of him. He sipped from the cup and put it back on the saucer. He waited.

Some minor showbiz personality was at the table by the piano, probably in town to open a new hotel, and the local fans were out in force. The waitresses tripped back and forth in their black and whites, offering professional smiles to their customers. On the other side of the plate-glass window a juggler, his face as misshapen as a used condom, threw a spray of fire-clubs up into the frozen air.

Sam was staring off into the old days.

'Angeles Falco,' Lorna said. 'A note demanding money or her life.'

'Why ask me? You've got your own sources.'

'I want it from the horse's mouth.'

Slight curl to his lips. 'I'm always happy to be called that end of a horse.'

Lorna took the photocopy of the note from her file and handed it over the table. 'Two questions,' she said. 'Is it kosher?'

'What are you going to do with it?'

'I'm a journalist. What do you think I'm going to do with it?'

'It won't help catch the guy,' Sam told her. 'If you publish now, we'll never hear from him again.'

Lorna shrugged. 'You just answered the first question. Number two: Ms Falco is not at home. Is there anything to the rumour that she's living at your house?'

His eyes reflected red. You could see the violence building up inside him.

Lorna smiled. 'Or is she more than a house guest?'

Sam finished his coffee and put the cup down. 'I don't suppose there's any point in asking you to keep this under wraps?'

'None at all, darling. It'll be in the paper tomorrow.'

Sam got to his feet. 'You're not a journalist, Lorna. You're a fuckin' menace.'

She let the malice boil out through her pores, didn't mind at all that it disfigured her. 'And you don't have to rely on good looks alone, Sam. You've got the blarney and you're gracious too.'

THIRTY-EIGHT

She watched Geordie come down the stairs with his hair uncombed, sleep still clinging to him. Barney got out of his basket, shook himself and went over to lick Geordie's hand. Venus and Orchid both ignored him. He came over and put his arm around her shoulder and nuzzled into her neck.

'Echo's still sleeping,' he said. 'Did you feed her?'

'Yes, I think so. I seemed to be feeding her all night. Every time I woke up she was rooting for more.'

'It's a design flaw,' Geordie said, 'that blokes can't feed them as well. It'd be easier if we could take it in turns. One day on mum's milk, next day on dad's.'

'It'd take some of the pressure off me,' Janet agreed. 'As it is I'm gonna have to think about giving her a supplement.'

'You said breast was best,' Geordie said. 'The classes we went to, everybody said it was.'

'I'm not changing my mind, Geordie. But I don't have enough milk. That's why she's hungry all the time. We'll have to do something.'

He scooped muesli into a bowl and mixed in the milk. He'd started off saying he'd never use skimmed milk if he lived to be a hundred, and there he was, still in his twenties. Now, if Janet got a pint of whole-milk from the supermarket, he'd refuse to use it. Said it felt like raw fat in his mouth.

'The best thing,' he said with a mouthful of cereal, 'would be if everybody had tits and everybody could feed babies on demand. Then Celia or Sam could have a go as well; she'd get more milk than she needed.'

205

Janet laughed at the thought of Sam Turner suckling Echo. She had a mental picture of him lifting his shirt and finding the nipple, slipping it between the baby's lips and settling back with a contented smile on his face. 'I think she'd get more than she needed with you and me, Geordie.'

'Yeah, I suppose we should keep it in the family; just you and me and Ralph.'

'Not Ralph,' Janet said. She turned away from Geordie. She opened the knife drawer and shut it again without taking anything out.

'Me and you,' Geordie said. 'Not Ralph. It'd be great if I could feed her.'

'I wouldn't let Ralph feed her a bottle,' Janet said. 'I don't want him touching her.'

Geordie took a mouthful of muesli. He glanced across at Janet a couple of times, but she didn't want to meet his eyes. She could feel her heart pounding away, the blood rushing around her brain. She didn't want to say or do anything she might regret, but her self-control was tenuous.

'Where is Uncle Ralph?' Geordie said, trying to sound casual.

'Where do you think? He never gets out of bed before midday.'

'Yeah.' Geordie took his bowl to the sink and rinsed it, stood it upside-down on the draining board. 'Why don't you have a lay down,' he said. 'Catch up a bit while Echo's asleep.'

'Because I don't bloody want to. I want to do something for myself.'

He fell quiet again. She wanted to shut him up. She wanted him to take the huff and stalk out of the house, go and talk to Sam or Marie or one of his other mates. If he stayed with her, continued to be sympathetic, accommodating, she'd spill it all, tell him about his precious brother trying to get into her pants.

Geordie came over to her again, reached out to touch her arm, but she shrugged him off. His frustration and lack of understanding filtered into the room like mist. 'What are you going to do?' he said.

Echo woke up then, as if she'd heard her cue. She opened her eyes and shouted. It wasn't an angry or a hungry cry, just a sound to let the world know she was approaching consciousness. Janet went to her. She took her from the cot and changed her nappy in the bathroom. Then she brought her downstairs.

Geordie was kneeling in front of Venus' basket, putting one of her kittens back in there. He got up and looked at the shattered pane of glass in the top panel of the front door. He'd covered it with a sheet of plywood a few days before, but now he'd removed the covering. 'The glazier's coming this morning,' he said. 'You know what I don't understand? If somebody'd thrown a stone at it, then the stone'd still be around. I reckon one of us broke it slamming the door.'

'It'd be you, then,' Janet said. 'You're the clumsy one.'

'It wasn't me,' Geordie told her. 'I'd've known if I'd done it. And it wasn't you. So it must've been Ralph.'

'Oh, come on, Geordie. Perfect Uncle Ralph wouldn't do a thing like that.'

'Not on purpose,' Geordie said. 'I reckon it was an accident. But he doesn't want to admit it 'cause he's frightened what we think of him.'

Janet put Echo in her pram, grabbed a coat and manoeuvred the pram around Geordie and out of the door.

'What'd I say?' Geordie shouted after her. 'Where you going?'

'I'll get hold of myself in a minute,' Janet said. 'Are you working? I should have rung.' She dabbed at her eyes with a tiny handkerchief. She wasn't really crying. There was moisture there, but no tears.

'Yes, I was working,' said Angeles. 'But I've stopped now. I don't want to work. I want to talk to you. I want to know why you're upset.'

'Oh, Christ. I knew I should've rung. I didn't want to interrupt something.'

'End of conversation,' said Angeles. 'I'm going to switch the computer off and put the kettle on.'

Janet followed her to the kitchen. She said, 'I don't want to be the one who makes it impossible for Ralph to stay.'

'You aren't the one,' Angeles said. 'If Ralph's making a play for you, he's the one making it impossible.'

'I know, but I mean in Geordie's eyes. If I wasn't there. If there was just the two of them, they'd make a go of it. I know they would. There aren't any other relatives, apart from their mother, and nobody knows where she is.'

'Is it getting worse?'

Janet nodded. 'He came on to me yesterday, said we could go upstairs for a quick fuck while Echo was sleeping. The guy's really obnoxious. But it was talking to Geordie that got me upset today. Talk about being blind . . . Oh, I'm sorry.'

'Don't worry.' Angeles put her hand on Janet's arm. 'Would it help if someone had a word with Ralph?'

'No. At least not yet. I don't want to involve anyone else until I've tried everything.'

'I don't see what else you can do,' Angeles said. 'Not without telling Geordie that his brother's no good.'

'I'm just going to watch him closely,' Janet said. 'Play him at his own game. Because that's what he does. He watches people, and he keeps his eyes open for any passing chance. Me, Sam's house, anything he thinks he might be able to get his hands on.'

'He's an opportunist.'

'Exactly,' said Janet. 'He's a petty crook. I reckon if I keep my eyes on him, he'll incriminate himself.'

'So long as he doesn't wreck your family in the meantime.'

Janet sighed. 'That's a chance I'm going to have to take. But I think me and Geordie are strong enough to take a few blows.'

'And Echo?'

'Oh, yes, Echo as well. No doubt about that.'

The glazier arrived at eleven o'clock and by half-past he'd replaced the pane of glass in the front door. Geordie paid him and watched while he got in his van and drove off down the street.

The lavatory flushed in the bathroom and Ralph appeared wearing only a pair of jeans. No shirt, no socks. 'What's all the fucking banging about?' he said.

'Glazier was here,' Geordie said, 'We've been fixing the door.'

'Where's the missis?'

'I'm not sure. She went out with Echo.'

Ralph farted and took eggs and bacon out of the fridge. He cut a knob of butter and tossed it into the frying pan. 'I'm starving, Geordie. Cut some bread and stick it in the toaster, will you? D'you want some of this?'

'I'm worried about Janet, Ralph. She's acting strange. She's tired out, but she won't rest, even when she's got the chance.'

Ralph put six rashers of bacon into the pan; pushed them up close together so there'd still be room for the eggs. 'It's normal,' he said. 'Specially after they've had a sprog. Fucking hormones go crazy.'

'I dunno,' Geordie said. 'It's like she's pushing me away. And she's got a downer on you as well.'

'That proves it, then. Neither of us've done anything. It's irrational, Geordie. In Italy, places like that, they know about these things. There was this woman in Naples, killed her husband and all her kids and the judge let her off with a warning.'

'It's not funny, Ralph.'

'Who said funny? I'm just giving you the facts, here. In them countries, round the Med, they understand what happens with the hormones, all that stuff. So they don't blame the woman, the individual woman, 'cause they know that they're all like that, once they've had a kid. It traumates their bodies.' He flipped a slice of bacon and began cracking the eggs. 'They just go batty, man. Plus they've got the sun.'

THIRTY-NINE

I tried out the Gallamine on Miriam with startling results.

Veterinarians have provided the world with these neuromuscular blocking agents, powerful chemicals, designed to make my task easier. They have been used for some time to immobilize wild animals and reptiles. These drugs are not anaesthetic; they work by paralysing the muscles. I could find nothing in the literature that mentioned their effects on blind women, so I assume that my efforts all fall under the general heading of research. There are more modern drugs available, but the neuromusculars fell into my hands from an untraceable source.

Gallamine comes in small ampoules and I injected the required dose during one of our sessions, when I had Miriam bound hand and foot. I didn't tell her what it was and this caused me some concern. If I'd told her that there was a chance of respiratory collapse she might have objected and that would have left me with uncertainties I didn't want to deal with. Anyway, Miriam doesn't need to know about my involvement with the blind woman. What happens between Ms Falco and me is private. It began a long time before Miriam and does not concern her.

These considerations left me little option. I could hardly tell her that I was giving her a drug that was normally used to sedate crocodiles in the wild. She doesn't like reptiles. The thought of them makes her squirm.

So I stuck it in her tail and she squealed and asked me what it was. I turned her over to watch her and she asked me again. 'What was that? Was it a hypodermic?' I didn't answer. She searched my face for a moment, then said, 'What was it? What have you st—' And she finished the word there, didn't get to the vowel. I was put off my stride by that abrupt end to the word and I tried to work out what it might have been, working away at it mentally, like a crossword puzzle. It didn't immediately strike me that her failure to finish the word was part of the effect of the Gallamine.

By the time I realized what was happening her facial muscles had stopped functioning. Her eyes were staring with fright. I saw the muscles in her neck go and was quick enough to feel her shoulders and arms as they relaxed. Within moments she was a dead weight, incapable of resistance of any kind. The whole process took little more than a minute.

I untied her and carried her to our bedroom, wrapped her in the quilt to keep her warm. Her breathing was shallow and her body utterly still and I was taken by her resemblance to a wax model. She looked unreal. A nude of Miriam wrapped in a quilt, which would not have been out of place in the stillness of Madame Tussaud's exhibition.

I was sent a vision, then, during those next few minutes, while Miriam was lying there like some cherry-lipped maiden awaiting the kiss of a frog prince. There was a blinding snowstorm – this is in the vision – and an overnight freeze. In the morning the snow has stopped falling and the boys are creating long slides in the street. There is the stillness of frozen weather, like an echo of the stillness of Miriam in our bed. But in the vision Miriam is transformed into the blind woman. Strangely, this does not disturb me.

She stirs, the blind woman, she opens her eyes and sits up. The director of the dream makes a cut here, as if one camera has finished its work and another one, placed at a different angle is taking over. Only the second camera doesn't show its subject clearly. There is a period of darkness before a hazy image appears. All I could be certain of is that there is movement.

I was reminded of a western. The cowboys have captured a wild palomino mare. There are three lariat loops around her long golden neck and the men are surrounding the horse in a circle, each of them pulling tightly on the rope. She cannot go left or right, back or forth of her own volition. She can only go where the men lead her.

211

Through the mist the forms emerge. What I thought was a pony is the blind woman. The ropes do not bind her; they are around her neck but they are the strings of a puppet-master. I tug at the black thread in my hand and as I do so the blind woman takes a step forward. Another tug and I watch her step on to the ice that covers her swimming pool. She walks forward and with each step the ice crackles and strains; I see the clefts and fissures rupturing the surface of the pool, and the whole is echoed again and again as her smooth features are broken and distorted with fear and recollection.

As the ice breaks up the camera zooms in, pierces through to the black and suffocating depths.

Miriam didn't stir for twenty minutes. I tried a variety of ways to make her react to stimulus during that time, but the Gallamine had her in its power. I was careful not to do anything that would be too painful as these drugs are not analgesic and there have been cases of myocardial damage. It was possible for me, even with a badly damaged thumb, to pick her up by her ankles and swing her back and forth like a trussed chicken. Her mouth was gaping, she was breathless and she was salivating copiously but did not appear frightened.

As the effects of the drug wore off, Miriam seemed depressed. Her blood pressure was abnormally high and her heart was pumping so hard I could see it through her ribcage. She continued salivating and entered a period of acute nervous tension which went on for more than an hour. She insisted that she was all right but it was obvious that the Gallamine had provided a severe shock to her system.

I shall use the other drug, Suxamethonium, on the blind woman. Suxamethonium has a quicker action and, like her sister, she will feel the effects within about fifteen seconds. As a preparation I have hidden it, together with a supply of syringes and a spare voice-activated recorder in her garden, close to the swimming pool. Everything is ready. Except the weather.

I'd been telling Miriam about risk society theory, how there is no big Other in our lives any more, like tradition or nature or religion. We no longer have a guide. Right and wrong have disappeared and what we are left with is an infinite number of choices.

'What it was like in the old days,' she said, 'what I imagine is that there was something or someone watching over us.'

'Like an angel?'

'Could be,' she said. 'You could say that.'

Miriam is not stupid. She is highly intelligent, just a little short on language.

When I first met her she was already a *Rule Girl*. I'm a practising psychologist and I didn't even know what that was. I do now, of course, and it is exactly what Miriam said it was. *Rule Girls* are heterosexual women who follow precise rules about how they will allow themselves to be seduced. They'll go on a date, but only if they're asked three days in advance. They won't sleep with you on the first or second date. You get the idea? The rules correspond to customs that used to regulate the behaviour of previous generations. They emulate the prudish behaviour of old-fashioned women. These women feel the need to impose the rules because the customs that used to do the job are no longer functioning. Women like Miriam are not returning to conservative values; they are freely choosing their own rules. Or they believe they are. In the past there was no choice. Now there seems as though there might be one.

It is the same with the master/slave relationship we have allowed to develop between us. Either of us can be master or slave, depending on the whim of the moment. It is as valid for Miriam to nail my penis to the workbench as it is for me to administer electric shocks to the tissue of her labia.

To those of my colleagues who insist that this kind of behaviour is a direct identification with the aggressive male, or that it is a parody of patriarchal domination, I can only point to the deep libidinal satisfaction experienced by both parties. Miriam and I are equally intent on experimenting with our lives, our bodies, our feelings and emotions.

Someone who keeps his eyes open, who watches what is going on, is in a unique position in the world. He sees everything that is enacted. He sees the same things as everyone else, but he sees beyond the surface illusion into the meaning of the events.

213

When the blind woman was released from hospital she moved into the house of the private detective. This must have been his idea. A better way for him to keep his (private) eye on her. I don't know if there were other considerations, if, for example, he is seeking sexual congress with the lady. Whether or not they are sharing a bed is of no concern to me.

But I watched the house.

And a weird thing happened, though to me it did not seem strange at the time. A man walked along the street. My attention was caught because of his body language. He hesitated outside the detective's house then walked on by. As he did so he had a good look at the house, scanned the upper windows. A few moments later he was back again, but this time he went up to the front door and posted a letter through the flap. When he walked back the way he had come he glanced behind him a couple of times, as if to make sure that he was not being followed or observed.

I didn't pay this happening too much attention. I am concerned only with the fate of the blind woman. I thought maybe the man was some kind of snitch delivering hush-hush information. I speculated that perhaps he was another private eye acting in a manner typical of the profession. Or, finally, that the man was somewhat unhinged and spent his life glancing back at imaginary pursuers.

Whatever, I concluded the man was nothing to do with me.

But I was wrong.

The newspaper article gives the text of the letter, which turns out to be a demand for money in exchange for the life of Angeles Falco. There is speculation in the newspaper about the identity of the sender, and the journalist, Lorna George, assumes that 'the killer of Isabel Reeves, the thug who put Angeles Falco in hospital, and the writer of the letter are one and the same person'.

I can control my emotions. I am actually experiencing anger at this moment but I don't let it show on the page. If you were here with me, face to face, you would not guess that I was outraged, or even annoyed.

But I am furious.

There are no material considerations at work here. Neither gold nor piety can influence the death of the blind woman. Her life is *owed* to me. It is a debt that can only be settled by her death.

This man, this idiot who delivered the letter, has blackened my name.

I thought of writing to the newspaper, denying all responsibility for the letter. But I stopped myself. It would be mad to expose myself in that way before Ms Falco has breathed her last. But I shall have the letter-writer. I have a picture of him in my mind. I have seen him; and when I see him again . . .

FORTY

During the interview something happened. Angeles wasn't sure what it was. The man they were talking to, Mr Hayes, didn't ring true.

It had been a busy day in the office and she had been distracted from the problems in her personal life. The soft-drinks industry is always at full-stretch in the weeks and days coming up to Christmas, and this year was no different. For once she hadn't thought about the death of her sister, and the more or less constant feeling of being observed had been absent.

The last job of the day was to interview Mr Hayes together with her PA, Steven Packard. Hayes had applied for money from the Falco Trust to provide a holiday for a group of partially sighted children. They were to be taken by coach to a holiday camp in the south of Italy.

'Our organization uses the camp regularly,' he said. 'We have taken several groups of children there in the past, and it's always been successful. This would be the first time that we take children who are partially sighted. In the past there have been children with leukaemia, we have taken groups of orphans, and a tiny group of Down's Syndrome kids.'

He spoke the right words. It wasn't anything that he said. There was rather something hidden behind the words. But Angeles felt increasingly claustrophobic listening to him.

It was as if he was reading from a script and the script was only engaging a fraction of his attention. She felt that she was the object of his attention, as if he was observing her with a lascivious leer.

When he'd finished presenting his case she left it to Steven Packard to reply. 'Thank you, Mr Hayes,' he said. 'We might be able to help. We'll put your proposals to the trustees at their next meeting.'

There was a further exchange between them. Hayes wanted to know when the next meeting would be and Steven said something about not being able to promise anything. The value of the pound, contracts already entered into, but that the trustees would certainly feel sympathetic to the proposal.

She didn't listen. She stayed in the chair and wished for the man to get out of her office. All through the drone of their conversation she felt his eyes on her.

When the meeting was drawn to a close Hayes and Steven shook hands. Then Hayes came to her desk and she felt and heard him extend his hand to her. His breathing was controlled; he measured each inhalation and exhalation. Slowly, as if he were counting. It seemed as though the whole meeting had been designed for this moment. The moment of contact. She took a breath and gave him her hand. His hand was large. He was a tall man with an athletic build and he held on to her hand for a fraction too long. Angeles withdrew it, a little too quickly for the proprieties of social convention.

She stuttered, covering her embarrassment with a peremptory dismissal: 'Thank you Mr Hayes, we'll be in touch soon.'

She remained seated at her desk while Steven Packard showed the man out. She felt her right hand where she had come into contact with him. He'd worn a waterproof plaster on his right thumb.

'What do we know about him?' she asked Steven Packard when he returned.

'Not a lot. Lives on the Wetherby Road.'

'Check the address, will you, Steven? Go round there and make sure he's who he says he is?'

'You didn't like him, did you?'

'He made my flesh creep.'

On the way back to Sam's place she asked the chauffeur to stop at Sainsbury's. She wanted to get a couple of salmon steaks for the evening meal. But there was something wrong. Was he there? Hayes, or whatever he called himself, at the fish counter?

There was something. No one spoke and there was no contact, but she could feel his presence, hear his breath slowly inhaling and exhaling.

She got the salmon steaks and put them in her basket, her hands trembling so much that she could barely control her fingers.

'Look back,' she said to the chauffeur as they walked away towards the checkout. 'The man at the fish counter, what does he look like?'

'There's no one there,' the chauffeur told her.

'When I was buying the fish. There was a man behind me, over to the right. Did you see him?'

'I can't be sure,' he said. 'But if there was someone, I didn't take him in I'm afraid.'

'You couldn't describe him?'

'No, ma'am, sorry.'

Steven Packard was on the phone a few minutes after she got in the house. 'Really strange,' he said. 'The house on the Wetherby Road, the address Hayes gave? It's an empty building. No one lives there.'

She put the phone down and thought it all through again. She remembered biting down on the man's thumb, but couldn't remember if it was his right or his left. She knew she had bitten deep, though. It wouldn't have healed yet. He'd be sure to have a dressing on it.

She went back to the door and checked she'd locked it after her. Her fingers were shaking with fear as she imagined the man outside the house. Or was he inside? Her limbs felt feeble and puny as she sat in the chair by the telephone. She dialled Sam's office number and waited for him to answer.

FORTY-ONE

Sam asked Marie to check out the Mr Hayes incident. Steven Packard could give a detailed description of him, distinctive blond hair and all. Someone must have seen him arriving at the Falco offices and there was a chance they could tie him to a model of car, if he'd arrived in one.

Angeles had been shaky when he arrived home but she quietened down after he'd checked the house. By the next day she was almost back to herself. Of course it was only a mask, inside she must have been close to screaming point.

She'd moved the food and crockery in the kitchen, swapped them around. Sam couldn't understand why. Plus she'd bought in packets of pulses, tubes of Tartex, sugar-free jams and a large carton of soya milk. Other stuff, he didn't know what it was. From the look of it you might feed it to birds in the garden, but he suspected it had some dangerously high nutrition count. Kind of stuff serious joggers ate.

He hadn't said anything about the furniture being moved, or how his clothes were now confined to the far left of the coat rack. But the dried pulses and the bird food being the first thing you grabbed when you went to the cupboard for a mug: that seemed to indicate a moving on, the entering of a new phase.

'Hey, everything's been changed around,' he said. He used the nonchalant tone, kind of tone Jack Hawkins or Kenneth Moore might have used in one of those old POW movies. The ones where they're on the escape committee and they don't want the stoolie to know he's been sussed.

'D'you like it?' she asked. 'It started off as a cleaning job, but then I found I couldn't get all the food in the side it was supposed to go, so I swapped it around.'

'They're the same size,' Sam said. 'Both sides of the cupboard are identical. They're mirror images of each other.'

'I know. The way you had it before, it was organized as if you were left-handed.'

'Is that right?'

'You want the crockery on the left side of the cupboard because you open the door with your left hand and get things out with your right, which is the strongest if you're right-handed.'

'And the food on the right side,' Sam said, 'because you open that door with your right hand and get the jam out with your left hand, which is the weakest hand. It's not so bad to drop the jam?'

'It's cheaper,' Angeles said. 'A jar of jam comes cheaper than a new plate.'

'Not if you bought it in a Shelter shop. I could replace the lot for less than a fiver.'

'You want me to put it back the way it was?'

'No, it's OK,' he told her. 'I'll get used to it.'

'After a while you'll think it's better.'

He locked the bathroom door and got a good lather going with the shaving gel. Pants and tights, hand-washed and hanging to dry over the bath. Towels side by side on the rack there, blue and pink. How does she know which is the pink one? Don't even ask. Matching face cloths hanging on cup hooks from the underside of the shelf. Now these hooks were being used, he remembered, vaguely, a long time ago, screwing them in. He didn't remember using them, though, not until now. Took someone who was blind to show him where they were.

Music. He strained his ears. She was playing a Clarence Carter song, something else he hadn't heard since the Berlin Wall came down. Another little gem from her eclectic collection of blind musicians. They'd already had Riley Pucket and Jeff Healey this morning, and he'd woken up to Sonny Terry's 'I'm a Burnt Child and I'm Afraid of Fire', with old Brownie there belting it out in the background. The kind of song makes you want to hit the day running.

She must've explored every inch of the room with her fingertips, maybe the entire house? Reaching out in the dark, tagging markers and consigning landmarks to memory. Sam didn't watch her any more when she was in the house. She walked from room to room, up and down the stairs, as if she were sighted. Within a few days she had grasped the spaces inside the old house and like an experienced colonist was rapidly making them her own. Her scent, which had quickly established itself in her bedroom, now pervaded the whole house. Rochas Tocade it said on the small bottle, no price tag, no list of ingredients, not even a sell-by date. Different times of day and night it subtly changed its suggestions: rose, bergamot, cedar. Was there occasionally a hint of geranium?

There was often a hint of whiskey. He'd looked everywhere except her room and not discovered any bottles. What she did with the empties was a mystery. He'd told her she could go to an AA meeting with him, but she didn't think she had a problem. Maybe she was right. Some people got by on a few shots a day. She was rich and she didn't have dependants. So who was Sam Turner to get on a moral high horse about her drinking? Nobody. But he didn't see that as a reason to give up. Living with a soak seemed like it ought to be a problem.

The pants. His arm outstretched as if to deny the connection between self and hand, he took the thin rim of lace between finger and thumb. *What're you gonna do next?* he asked himself. *Eat them? Wear them? Steal them? Whatever floats your boats.*

It occurred to him that he might be enacting an ancient rite, something similar to the way an animal scents its territory. Was he also putting down a marker in the fondling of the lace? Would she know he'd been there; smell or perhaps feel where his fingers had lingered for the space of a breath?

The front doorbell rang and he heard Angeles show Ralph through to the sitting room. Her voice coming to him stronger when he cracked open the bathroom door: 'Sam will be down in a minute. He's expecting you.'

And I just love being stiffed, Sam thought.

The spirit on Ralph's breath was sour. He had a smile on his face but his eyes were as thin as paint.

'You wanted to see me?' Sam said.

'Yeah, about the house. Geordie said you wanna give it to a charity?' He was sitting on the sofa with one leg bent under him. The other leg was jigging up and down at a fair rate of knots,

221

looked as though it wanted to do a dance by itself. In many ways he was the antithesis of Geordie. Brothers are supposed to be similar, Sam thought. They shared the same parents, the same social milieu back in Sunderland, the same crappy education, and yet each of them came with a separate agenda. Sam always held that distant relatives were the best kind.

'And you're looking for somewhere to house a charity?'

'That's right, yeah. Somewhere for people who haven't anywhere else.' He was wearing a black-and-white striped jumper under his donkey jacket and the collar was turned in on itself. Looked like his mother had been in a rush getting him ready to go out.

'Homeless people?'

'Yeah, like that. And for people've had accidents. They can't manage to live properly.'

'When did this Samaritan influence first show itself?'

'Come again?'

'Your last ship; it was the *Bootham*, right. Registered in Thailand?'

Ralph looked down at his hands and shook his head. 'I've bin on lots of ships. On and off I've bin at sea for ten years. But I came to talk about the house.'

'You've given up the sea?'

'Yeah, finished with all that.' He hooked his thumbs together, index fingers touching, palms outwards, and extended his arms as if to contain the oceans of the world and shove them out of the way. 'I wanna live for other people now. Dedicate my life.'

Sam made eye contact, watched for a blink or something shifting below the surface of the pupil, but the guy was as steady as the murder rate. Sam sighed. It doesn't matter what you do, he thought. Summer will have its flies. 'Only I talked to the agent for the *Bootham*, guy called Phillips. You remember him?'

'Phillips?' said Ralph. 'No, the name isn't ringing any bells.'

'He remembers you,' Sam said. 'He told me he'll never forget you. Could've talked about you all day.'

'I was popular on the ship,' Ralph said. 'Lots of good mates.'

'Now Mr Phillips didn't exactly express it like that,' Sam said. 'He told me that you ripped off two of your shipmates. Took nigh on a grand from the two of them together.'

'That was a lie,' Ralph said. He shuffled around like a fart in a trouser leg. 'Phillips accused me of doing that, but it wasn't me.'

'So you do remember Phillips.'

'There was no proof. If he was so sure it was me, why didn't he call the fuzz?'

'Because you'd covered your tracks too well. As you say, there wasn't enough to prove the case in court. But there was enough for the agent to get you off the ship and blacklist you.'

'The bastard, taking a bloke's livelihood.'

'And for the union to make sure you never get a ship again. They know all about you as well, they reckon you've ripped off fellow sailors in every port you've sailed from.'

Ralph looked up and out of the window, refusing to respond.

'What I also learned,' Sam continued, 'is that you're wanted by the Child Support Agency. They're looking for you to help support your wife and three children.'

'I'm not married.'

Sam waited a moment. 'I wouldn't call it a marriage, either,' he said. 'But it was a legal ceremony you went through three years back. Does Geordie know he's got a nephew and two nieces? A sister-in-law?'

'This is all allegations,' Ralph said. 'There's no proof for it, any of it. Look, if you don't wanna give me the house, OK. I'll look around for something else.'

Sam got to his feet and took a couple of steps over to where Ralph was sitting. 'You'd better find that something else fairly soon,' he said. 'I don't like you, Ralph, and I'm prepared to make your life miserable. You're sponging off Geordie and Janet at the moment, looking around for a way to make your life easier, but that's gonna end quick. Either get a job and pay them for your keep or move out.'

'You can't tell me what to do. What happens between me and Geordie's private.'

'You've got a couple of days,' Sam told him. 'Then I tell Geordie everything I know about you.'

Ralph walked to the door, a grin on his face. 'You're bluffing,' he said. 'You know if it comes to a showdown, Geordie'll stick to family. If he has to make a decision between you and me, he'll tell you to go fuck yourself.'

'You just remember this,' Sam told him. 'You're the kind of guy can get both feet in your mouth at the same time. That's OK, just makes you look stupid. But imagine what it'd be like to have both of my feet in there as well.'

FORTY-TWO

Janet sometimes wondered if she'd got it wrong. In the beginning she'd had a couple of cats, mainly for company. Not that they'd been much good at it. Venus was never there anyway, except for food; and Orchid was always in the house but not at all sociable. They were icons of independence.

Then Geordie came along. He was kind, it was true, and fun to be with. A real love in fact, but he took some looking after. Plus he brought Barney along, a dog into a house full of cats. Life got fuller, but it also got more complicated. All the time she used to have to herself faded away.

By the time Echo was born there weren't enough hours on the clock to get through the day. The first couple of months had been a walking nightmare and Janet had felt her world imploding. Constant fatigue, the need to give more of herself than she possessed, and the numbing suspicion that she was alone with it all toyed with the fragile perimeter of her sanity.

Ralph was almost the last straw. If he had been the perfect house guest it would have been bad enough, but he was a slimeball who was forever sniffing around, making lewd suggestions, dragging Geordie out on afternoon drinking sessions and eating them out of house and home.

Some people might capitulate to the kind of pressure and stress which had entered her life, turn to migraine, or the bottle, or Agatha Christie. But tension and adversity had a galvanizing effect on Janet's consciousness. She was energized, inspired to rise above it, and whereas before Ralph's arrival she had been tired and listless, she was now fired with the passion of a mission.

'Cook us some eggs, darlin',' Ralph said when he came down. He brought a strong odour of stale sweat with him. It was mid-morning and Geordie and Echo were sleeping, trying to catch up on the hours they'd missed in the night.

'Cook 'em yourself,' she said. 'I'm not here to wait on you.'

'OK. I can cook. What about a little kiss, then?'

'Fuck off.'

'Oh, mucky language over the breakfast pots. Trying to make Ralph randy?' He licked his lips, made a face with staring eyes. His long curly hair was so short of vitality it clung to the side of his face for support.

'You're disgusting,' she told him.

'That's what they like,' he said. 'Women.'

She snorted. 'And you're the man to give it to us? Jesus, Ralph, I'm so thrilled. How long've you had this effect on women?'

'Sarky, but you're more interested than you let on. Geordie's always tired these days. He walks round like a zombie all day.'

'Leave Geordie out of it.'

'Yeah, OK, darlin', if that's how you want it. I won't mention him if you don't. Not while we're together.'

'How much longer are you gonna be here?' she asked.

'Come and sit on my knee and I'll whisper it in your ear.'

'You know, Ralph, getting splashed with shit while you're minding your own business is kind of unfortunate. But there's a real insanity about jumping in the septic tank.'

He thought about that for a moment, his brow clouded over, as if he'd been hit with a full row of big words. Then he shook his head and smiled his toothy grin. 'There you go, again,' he said. 'Talking dirty words.'

Janet said, 'Ralph, if I opened my legs for you, would you promise to go away for ever? Walk off down the street and go ruin someone else's life?'

He smiled. 'Here we go,' he said. 'Now we're getting round to it. I knew you was interested.'

'Would you? Go away?'

'Maybe you'd want me to stick around, after you've had a sample.'

'I'd want you to go away. That's the whole idea.'

He leaned back in the chair, stretched his legs out in front of

226

him. 'I'm sure we can come to some arrangement, darlin'. When was you thinking? Only I'm fairly busy today.'

'Don't worry,' she told him, 'it probably won't take long.' She watched him turn it over in his mind, but in the end he let it go. It sailed on past him. Ralph was all kinds of things, but he wasn't an intellectual heavyweight.

She'd do it, too. If she thought for one moment that she could trust him, she'd do just about anything to get her life back to normal. But Ralph would promise anything if he thought he'd get something out of it. After she'd done the deed with him he'd still be around, and he'd be expecting more.

When she came back to it a second time, the thought of him fumbling his way around her body brought the taste of vomit into her mouth. She wondered if she'd ever be able to wash him off her skin, if for the rest of her life she would have recurring visions of the time she screwed Geordie's brother to get him out of their lives. And she knew there must be another way. And she knew that she'd known that all along, only she still didn't know what it was.

Watch him, she thought. That's all you can do. Track him. Dog his every footstep. Make sure there's no area of his life that he can call his own.

The trouble with keeping Ralph under surveillance was that he didn't do anything. He collected his social security, he sat in various pubs, trying his luck with the barmaids; did a round of low-life cafés where he worked on the waitresses or any lone females who happened along. Sometimes he got lucky and was invited to a girl's flat, the two of them with their arms wrapped around each other, their brains addled with vodka. Once he spent the afternoon in the Museum Gardens with a couple of truants, girls of no more than thirteen. He split a bottle with them before taking them into a derelict building down by the river.

It was that day, when he was with the two truants, that Janet noticed the other guy. She'd been aware of him for some time, out of the corner of her eye, but had not completely registered him. When she'd followed Ralph into the park the guy had stationed himself outside the doors of the museum, the huge neo-classical façade of the building rendering him almost invisible.

Later, she remembered seeing him sitting on a bench quite close to Ralph and the two girls when they were getting into the bottle of vodka. He was reading a book, raising his eyes occasionally to check they were still there. A rent-a-drool expression on his face.

Another day he appeared again, this time in Whip-ma-Whop-ma-Gate. The street was named after the activity of whipping petty criminals in the Middle Ages, and Janet thought it was somehow right that she should be watching Geordie's brother here. Ralph had been drinking heavily that day and had come to a stop by the cycle park. He was checking his way through the bikes, seeing if there were any easy pickings. The other guy came out of St Saviourgate and stood by the telephone box with his hands in his pockets. He watched Ralph and Janet saw him shake his head from side to side.

Ralph's life was like his chat-up lines: sad and boring and getting him nowhere. But what Janet did discover while she followed him around was that she was not the only one on his tail. Someone else was watching Ralph.

The man was tall with fair hair, looked like a sportsman. Obviously fit but not muscular, the kind who would play cricket rather than football or rugby. The strange thing about him was that he looked perfectly respectable. His hair was short and neatly cropped and he wore a fresh shirt and tie under a two-piece suit. His overcoat looked like a Crombie or a good copy. Janet couldn't understand it. If someone was watching Ralph, she would have thought it was because Ralph had ripped him off – a guy from the same side of the tracks as Ralph, petty criminal, or someone with gang connections. Maybe Ralph's sticky fingers had upset some kind of drug syndicate and they were looking for revenge.

Only the guy didn't look like that at all. If she'd seen him in any other context, she'd have thought he was a doctor or a teacher. Someone with a profession. It didn't make sense that a man like that was watching Ralph, the slimeball in her life.

She wondered, could the guy be a cop? And she gave up the thought almost immediately. The clothes were wrong. Even when they're working undercover, there's something about the bearing of a cop that they can't hide. They get away with it sometimes, but only when they're working with dopers or criminals who have more brawn than brain.

So perhaps the guy was a private eye? Employed by someone

Ralph had victimized or exploited. Whatever, Janet found it strange to imagine herself as a single link in a chain of surveillance. There was Ralph at the cutting edge, watching the world for anything it might put in his path, then there was the blond guy watching him doing it. And Janet was standing behind them, watching the two of them, watching the blond guy watching Ralph and Ralph obviously not watching his back. She wondered if there might be someone else, Geordie, say, who was watching her in turn. And further back still, another Other? Makes for a creepy feeling down your spine when you start to think like that. Find yourself looking around, scrutinizing the old lady with a shopping trolley, checking out the unshaved youth in the long gabardine.

She thought: the blond guy is some kind of private detective. He's watching Ralph on behalf of someone else with a grievance. OK, let's assume that Ralph is on the run from someone or something in his previous life. If that's true, then that's exactly what she needed as a lever to pry him out of her life. Next time she saw the blond guy she'd go up to him and say, Hi, my name's Janet. Have you got anything on Ralph that I can use? Just lay it on him like that. See what happens.

But the next day the blond guy wasn't around. She kept her eyes skinned for someone else, the blond guy's replacement or partner, but didn't find anyone obvious. It was a cold day and Ralph got himself settled in the bar of the Lowther on King's Staith. Janet had Echo with her, in the pram; she hung around for half an hour and felt her feet go numb and then decided to call it a day and go home.

His room was a tip. There was a Gustav Klimt poster on the wall, *Garden with Sunflowers*, which she'd put up the day he arrived, but it was the only bright thing in there. His clothes, shoes, dirty socks and underwear were all mixed together on the floor. Not an inch of carpet showed itself. Janet had put a waste bin in the room but he hadn't used it. Instead he had three or four plastic carriers filled to the brim and overflowing with cigarette packets, betting slips, racing papers, sweet and chocolate wrappers, old envelopes and bits and pieces of household items that he'd systematically taken apart. The drawers in the chest were almost empty. A pair of jeans in one and a jacket with holes in the elbows in another. The top left drawer was locked and there was no key. There was an alarm clock that Janet had had in her flat, before she met Geordie, but it was now separated into its component parts. Several pens, similarly broken, the casings split apart and abandoned. There were a couple of patterned mugs in there as well, both stuffed with decaying food, apple cores and the remains of a sandwich, might once have been Coronation chicken. The mugs Janet had bought in the market only a fortnight ago. Another two carrier bags contained hard-core porn mags, stuff you couldn't ignore: magazine called *Cum Shots*, and another one which promised Black Hard-fucking Amateur Babes.

There was nothing else in there. No birth certificate, no National Insurance card, not even a letter from the taxman. There were no personal photographs. The poverty was so overwhelming that Janet sank down on her knees in the entrance to the room. Nobody lived in this room. Mr Nobody.

She took the two mugs – green-and-yellow abstract design with a chain of daisies on the inside – downstairs and emptied the decaying food into the dustbin. She washed the mugs and left them on the draining board.

There was a time when Geordie could have gone the same way as Ralph. There was a time when Janet might have taken the same path. She'd even begun on it: regular shoplifting trips and a casual relationship with prostitution. The only thing that made the difference was that she'd found Geordie and he'd found her. There'd been Sam as well, of course, and Celia, the small handful of people who had seen the best in them rather than the worst. All of those things were missing in Ralph's life. He didn't only have nothing; he had no one.

But, apart from Geordie, who would offer him love? He was so damaged that he couldn't recognize value. He saw love as a form of weakness, something to be exploited. The closest he got to it was in his *Euroslut* mags.

Janet wondered if she should go softer on him. Take a back seat and let Geordie's brotherly affection and concern do its work. She could cook and clean and do the washing and be an all-round toe-rag in the house.

Could she?

Yes, she could, and she'd do it too if she thought that it would make a difference. But all that would happen is that Geordie would slowly be disillusioned and she and Echo would be exploited. Ralph would gain more power out of the situation than any of them could handle. And he'd abuse it; he'd abuse it on a daily basis.

Is there anything I can do? she asked herself. Are there any actions available to me that will bring this whole thing to an end? She sat down at the table and put her head in her hands and thought hard.

There were a number of things, of course. But there was not one single thing that Janet could think of that wouldn't involve a series of risks to her family. Risks that, on balance, she was not prepared to take. She didn't believe she had the authority to take those risks without consulting Geordie. And that was out of the question.

After mulling it over for forty minutes she was left with one option. One thing she could do, and it didn't really amount to much. She could clean his room.

She took everything out of there and left it in piles in the hall. She hoovered the room and went to work on a couple of coffee stains with carpet shampoo. Next she tried to decide which of his clothes were clean. She made two piles, taking one of them downstairs to the washing basket and folding the others neatly and placing them in drawers and on shelves. The skin mags she left in their plastic bags and put them under his bed.

When everything was done she looked at the room. She hadn't touched the bed, for reasons she didn't want to think about. But it was crazy to leave everything else clean. She stripped the cover off the duvet and picked up the pillow. A pair of scissors was there: green plastic handles, exactly like the ones in her sewing basket. She took them downstairs and checked. Yes, they were hers. She returned to Ralph's room, thankful that she had found them in time. Another day and he'd have taken them apart.

Janet changed the sheet and the pillowcase and realized what was missing. She brought up a vase of dried flowers from the kitchen and set it on the dressing table. Pleased with herself now, for having thought of the extra thing. The thing that makes the difference. She wasn't doing it for Ralph, she was doing it for Janet.

She stood at the door and smiled when she saw what she'd done. It looked really pleasant in there, a nice place to be. She took a step back and was about to leave and close the door when she changed her mind.

She took three steps forward, towards the bed. She lifted the top corner of the mattress and saw the roll of Sellotape. She hadn't known or consciously thought that she would find anything at all. It was as if some invisible force had drawn her there. She lifted the mattress a little higher and withdrew the magazine.

It was called *Loaded*, and when she flicked through it several pages had had sections cut out of them. The cut-out sections were not of naked women, which is what one would have expected of Ralph. They were cut-out sections of text.

FORTY-THREE

Ralph had seen the redhead and done nothing about it. Nearly nothing. He'd given her a look down the length of the bar. Then he'd ordered a pint and waited.

Fourth bar, fifth lager. He'd had two in the Lowther, one in the King's Arms, another in the Robin Hood, and now this one. Posh pub, but every place had its barflies. She came over when he'd taken the top off his pint. Tight little ass and a short leopard-skin coat with smooth hair on it like a real cat.

'Got a light?'

One of those extra-longs hanging from her bottom lip. He flicked his lighter and lit up her face. The tiny cracks in her rouged lips caught his eye, the elasticity as she rearranged the cigarette between them. She sucked in and the flame bent towards her, her eyelids fluttered and she held his gaze for a moment before blowing out the smoke and enshrouding them both in a halo of sweet nicotine.

'Ta,' she said, pulling out the vowel, holding his eyes.

'What you called?' he asked.

'Ramona.'

'You on your own?'

She nodded. 'Want some company?'

He asked her how much it was going to cost and she reeled off a price list. Ralph didn't take it in, having no intention of paying. He liked the look of the goods, though. 'Sounds about right,' he said.

'I don't do rough stuff,' she told him. 'If you want that, I've got a friend.'

'No. You'll do nicely.'

He went with her to a flat in Walmgate, feeling good all the way. She linked her arm in his and laughed at his jokes. Ralph was into simple pleasures; it didn't take a lot to make him happy. If the day was going well, that suited him fine. And today was running on schedule.

He could imagine this tart was Janet. About the same size, tight little body and good legs. He'd have to ignore the red hair, the Birmingham accent. Close his eyes, filter out the bits he didn't want, filter in the fantasy.

'The cash up front,' she said.

Ralph laughed. He took her forcibly on the narrow divan. When he pinned her arms behind her back she began to protest but he gave her the look and she shut it. When he'd finished he was still hard and he flipped her over on to her face and went in the other way.

'I don't do that,' she said, twisting her head around, trying to wriggle away from him. Ralph put the pillow over her head and pushed down with both hands, thrusting with his hips.

'Jesus, Janet,' he said as he juddered to a climax, his back arched like a performing seal.

'You bastard,' said Ramona, emerging from under the pillow. Her make-up was streaked and her hair and face were dripping with sweat. 'You could've suffocated me.'

'I still might,' he said, pulling himself out of her and rolling over on to his back. 'If you don't keep quiet.'

'You owe me,' she said.

Ralph ignored her, reached for his jacket and lit up a fag.

Ramona got to her feet and went through to the bathroom. He put one arm behind his head and smoked and listened to the shower cascading against the tiles. Why pay? he thought. What's she gonna do about it?

He stubbed out the cigarette and dressed. He was stepping out of the room when Ramona came back. 'Where's my money?' she said.

Ralph smiled, showing the gap where his teeth used to be. 'Sue me,' he said. He stepped through the door and closed it behind him. He walked down the short staircase, the smile in place, glad the day was still working for him.

When he reached the front door it was locked. He turned quickly, sensing something behind him and was faced by two men. The first was small with narrow eyes and carefully coiffed dark hair, couldn't have been more than twenty years old and around fifty kilos. No problemo. But the other one was different. He wore a double-breasted striped suit that could only have been bought at High & Mighty. He had lost all the hair off the top of his head and was left with a cropped border like a monk. There was nothing pious about him, his main feature being a scar of tissue where he must once have had an eye. He had a cricket bat cradled in his arms, but he didn't look the sporting type.

There was a movement at the top of the stairs and they all looked up at Ramona as she came to the banister. She wore a black silk slip and fluffy mules on her feet.

'How was it, babe?' the little guy asked.

'He doesn't wanna pay,' she said. 'And he fucking hurt me.'

'No problem,' Ralph said, pulling his wallet from his back pocket. 'Nothing we can't sort out, fellers.' He tried to smile but his top lip seemed to have a mind of its own and he couldn't get it lined up.

The young guy plucked the wallet out of his hand and threw it into a corner of the hall, then the two of them rushed him. He saw the cricket bat coming for the side of his head and ducked, but while he was going down he realized he'd misjudged. It caught him on the ear and the jaw at the same time and he went deaf and watched an arc of blood explode and leave his body. Perfect really, he thought, as he rolled over on to his back. Just one blow and all the fight was knocked out of him.

They frisked him, found the twenty in the top pocket of his jacket and another one in his shoe. He watched everything they did. He couldn't move; if they'd started to eat him he wouldn't have been able to fight. He was nauseous and a riff from a song kept going through his head, maybe it was a hymn or a carol, something about a blackbird.

They took his feet and dragged him through to a backyard. The one with the cricket bat spat on the concrete and looked up at the sky. Ralph thought he must've been built by the same firm that did Stonehenge. Didn't tell him, though; no point upsetting the guy.

Ralph must've passed out for a while, then, because when he

opened his eyes he wasn't in the backyard any more. He was in a long alleyway on his knees. The little guy had said something and the big one-eyed one was walking away, the bat swinging easily by his side. 'Just don't kill him,' he said.

Which was good news, the best Ralph had heard all day.

The little guy kicked him, must've been twenty times. A rib went, and something in his back but he couldn't help feeling glad it wasn't the big guy doing the kicking. A boot in the ear sent his consciousness reeling and when he came back to his senses he was alone, shivering with cold. He crawled out of the alley and over the pavement to the kerb.

A couple of university students on their way to the Spread Eagle found him and rang an ambulance. Ralph had hated students all his life but those two were OK. One of them had a thick woollen overcoat and he took it off and wrapped it around Ralph's body, kept him warm until the ambulance arrived.

Janet had got Echo off to sleep and Geordie was telling her about his conversation with JD. 'He reckons we're genetically programmed to recognize beauty. Men like women with big eyes and lips and boobs.'

'Fascinating.'

'And women like tall handsome guys who put it around.'

'Not necessarily, Geordie. There's someone for everybody.'

'Yeah, I know, but what we think is beautiful, the things we think are beautiful, JD reckons that's the same for everybody. Things like good skin, small lower face, and the way the face is proportioned.'

'Theories like that worry me,' Janet said. 'They seem to leave so many people out.'

Geordie opened the door of the stove and put another log in. He almost stood on Barney, who was stretched out on the rug, and the dog opened one eye for a moment, lifted his tail clear of the floor and held it there.

'He told me about this guy who lost his memory for faces. Student, was in a car crash, and he had these head injuries. So the medics put all the pieces back together again and the guy was good as new, except he couldn't recognize faces. He lived a more or less normal life, got married and had a bunch of kids, held down a job. But he couldn't recognize his wife or kids or any of the people he worked with. He never recognized anyone by their face. He'd look at people and it would be like a light show, but a different light show every time. There'd be no clue to who it was. Can you imagine that?'

'Barely. Poor guy.'

'Anyway, the point I'm getting at,' Geordie continued, 'he still knew who was attractive and who wasn't.'

'What's considered attractive is a matter of fashion,' Janet said. 'It changes from generation to generation. There's no such thing as universal beauty.'

'Yeah, JD said the same about fashion, but he reckons there are a few basic proportions and lines that our genes respond to, and those things don't change.' He laughed. 'Have you noticed how Echo stares at you?' he said. 'She just lies in your arms and looks up into your face as if you're the best thing she's ever seen.'

'Well, she hasn't seen that much yet.'

'Even if she had, it'd still be the same,' Geordie told her. 'You're the best thing I've seen.'

'You're not too bad yourself,' she said. 'Tall, anyway.'

'You give me the silver tongue like that, it makes me wonder what you're after.'

'Cup of tea'd be nice,' she said. 'If you fancy making one.'

'OK,' he said. 'Then I'll have to take Barney for a walk.'

The telephone rang while Geordie was in the kitchen. Janet picked it up. She registered the message, replaced the handset and waited for Geordie with her hands folded together in her lap.

He came through with two mugs of tea, placed one of them on the low table next to her chair and took his own over to the couch. 'Who was that?'

'The hospital,' she said. 'Ralph's been in some kind of accident.'

Geordie was back on his feet again. 'Jesus,' he said. 'Is he OK? Where is he? I'd better go.'

'He's not dead or dying, Geordie. They want to keep him in overnight.'

Her tone must have got through to him because he sat on the couch. His face was a series of question marks. 'What's going on, Janet?'

'Will you come up to his room with me?'

'Yeah.' He followed her up the stairs. 'What kind of accident? Did they say?'

'He was in a fight. He's gonna be OK.'

She lifted the mattress in Ralph's room and showed Geordie the evidence. Geordie's thinking was a transparent process; you could see the physical workings of his brain reflected on his face. He took the copy of *Loaded* and flicked through it, stopping at a page which had had some text cut out. He read the text, his lips moving as his eyes scanned the line. When he came to the missing words he filled them in, using his memory of the blackmail note as an aid. He picked up the roll of Sellotape and looked at Janet. 'Jesus,' he said. 'Ralph?'

'The scissors were up here, too,' she said. 'I took them downstairs.'

'I don't know what to do, Janet.'

She touched his hand and he spread his fingers and let her take it. 'That's not everything, Geordie. Ralph's been coming on to me since he arrived. Trying to get me into bed.'

She watched him shake his head from side to side. Suddenly there were tears behind her eyes and one of them got away, slid down her cheek. Geordie looked up at her and wiped it away with his finger. 'You should've told me.'

She nodded her agreement.

'What d'you want to do now?'

'I don't want him in the house,' she said.

'No. I'll tell him he's got to go. And I'll talk to Sam about the blackmail note.'

'Tomorrow,' she said. 'The hospital said he's sleeping now, they don't want him disturbed.'

They were still sitting on the floor next to Ralph's bed an hour later when Echo woke for her feed. Geordie went downstairs to check on the stove and the kittens and take Barney for his walk. Janet felt peace descend on the house like a physical presence. It was similar to the time she had the fever as a child. When it was at its height, she remembered, a cool hand had passed over her brow.

There was an old git in the bed on his right who would have been

238

better off dead. The other side was a guy whose face was swathed in bandages and he had some kind of metal contraption, looked like it was designed to keep the guy's head on. The nurses were all ugly, 'cept for one who gave Ralph a bone every time she walked through the ward. Looked like she went to a gym and ate healthy. Maybe she needed a personal trainer?

They wouldn't give him breakfast until the doctor had been round, so he watched the rest of them tucking into bacon and egg and cornflakes, toast and jam. 'More coffee, Mr Smithson?' The old git packing it away like he had something to live for.

Ralph sipped at a glass of lukewarm water.

The doctor said he could go home. He'd have to take it easy for a while. He had a cracked rib but the other injuries were superficial. 'You have someone who can look after you for a while?'

'Yeah, my brother's wife. I live with them.'

'Lucky man. Light exercise. Nothing strenuous.'

No change there, then.

A nurse with a face like a robber's dog told him he could get dressed but he wouldn't be able to leave until his medicine came up from the pharmacy. 'And there's someone here to see you,' she said.

Sam Turner, not Geordie or the sexy sister-in-law. Warning bells went off in Ralph's head, but there was nowhere to run.

'We found the magazine, everything you used to write the blackmail note.'

Just like that. Straight into it. No question of asking a guy how he felt after being half-kicked to death by a fucking psychotic pimp. 'You been going through my room?'

'Yeah. I'm thinking of turning it over to the police.'

'What for? A joke? It was just a laugh.'

'And all the harassing of Janet? Was that just a laugh?'

'Harassing? What's she been telling you?'

Turner didn't raise his voice. He took a slim wad of twenties from his pocket, put it down on the cover of the bed. 'It's all over for you here, Ralph. Janet wants you out of the house and I want you out of the town.'

'What's Geordie got to say about this? It's Geordie's house just as much as Janet's. I bet he doesn't want me to go.'

The detective raised his eyebrows. 'You mess about with somebody else's woman, how do you think the guy's gonna feel? There's two hundred quid there,' Turner said, fingering the wad. 'Enough to get you wherever you want to go, keep you in a bed and breakfast for a few days. If you're still around tomorrow, I'll pass the evidence of the note over to the fuzz.'

Ralph watched him go. He walked to the door of the ward and saw Turner's broad back disappearing along the corridor. He walked back to the bed and picked up the twenties, slipped them into the back pocket of his jeans.

They gave him some dinner at midday and the little nurse with the body told him his brother and sister-in-law were here to see him.

'What do they want?' Ralph asked.

She smiled. 'To see how you are, I should think. They've got a bag with them.'

'Tell them to leave the bag,' he said. 'I don't wanna see them.' The reproachful looks from young Geordie he could live without. And Janet would be on her high horse, strutting about as if she'd got something left in. To hell with them, he'd managed OK without them all his life, now it would just go on as normal. Ralph thought he'd probably go back to his wife and family, somewhere to crash until he came up with some new ideas.

A couple of hours later they gave him a cup of tea and then his medicine arrived on the ward at four o'clock. Pain-killers and some swabs for the cuts on his face. 'Is this it?' he asked. 'I've been waiting all day for this?'

The nurse shrugged. 'You can go now, Mr Black.'

No offer of a lift to the station. A cracked rib, aches and pains all over, and there you go, Mr Black, on your own, Mr Black. Only a couple of miles to the station. He picked up the bag and walked outside. Dark already and a sharp frost in the air. He could manage the bag but the weight caused a pain in his chest. He kept swapping it from hand to hand.

He cut through Bridge Lane and across the grounds of Bootham Park. Some of the nurses' flats were lit but most were dark. As Ralph put the bag down for a minute, give himself a rest, a tall guy overtook him, striding along in the same direction. The man looked back and stopped. 'Are you all right?' he asked. Ralph gave him the once over. It wasn't really necessary though; the guy's voice gave him away. A doctor, maybe, something like that. At least a social worker or a teacher, but this being the hospital grounds, he'd be a doctor. You could bet on it. And look at the state of him, his bearing, the blond hair, the suit, the overcoat. Could be a consultant.

'Yeah,' Ralph told him. 'Just having a rest.' He winced to show the guy his chest hurt. 'Cracked rib.'

'You shouldn't be carrying that, then.' The guy walked back along the path and bent to pick up Ralph's bag. 'I'll give you a hand. Going far?'

'The station.'

'No probs.'

'I'm not sure, really,' Ralph said. 'I was going to the station, but I could go to my brother's place.'

'There's a café in Gillygate. You could have a coffee and take the time to decide.'

'Yeah,' Ralph said. 'Good idea. Specially if the café's a pub.'

On the corner of Union Terrace the doctor said, 'This is really very heavy.' He changed hands and walked alongside Ralph until they got to the Wagon and Horses.

'Thanks,' Ralph said. 'You're a real gent.' He took his bag back and went into the pub. He got himself a pint of lager and felt better even before he took the head off.

He didn't make a decision about what to do. He spent the evening in the pub and drank at the expense of Sam Turner. Funny how the lager always tasted better when somebody else was paying for it. Towards the end of the evening he had a few whiskey chasers. Why the fuck not?

But now, at this time of night, there was no way he could go to the station and buy a train ticket. He ordered a taxi and when it came he told the guy to take him to Geordie's house. There'd be plenty of time to sort his life out tomorrow. And, anyway, there was his passport, all his official papers locked in the drawer of his room.

Ralph paid the taxi off and picked up his bag. There was a sharp pain like a sliver of glass in his chest, so he dropped it back to the pavement. He tried to lift it again, this time with his other hand, but the pain was just as bad.

'Still giving you some trouble, is it?' said a voice he recognized. It took him a few moments to put the voice and the face together, though. The doctor, whatever he was, who'd carried his bag to the pub. Must be a doctor. What the hell was he doing here?

The guy came up close. He looked at Ralph and squinted. 'You know that dressing's coming off your forehead.' He shifted Ralph's bag with his foot. 'Let me fix it.'

Ralph bent to allow him to stick the dressing back in place and as he did so he felt a sharp pain in the side of his neck. Could've been a bee sting, something like that, except you don't get bee stings in the dark in the middle of winter. Must be one of those goofy nurses'd left a pin in his shirt collar.

As he drew back something flashed in the doctor's hand. Ralph focused on it for what seemed like an age before he saw that it was a syringe. He wanted to protest, tell the guy he didn't need no injection, and still time went by until he realized there was no point in saying anything: the guy had already given him it.

Then he fell over. Thought the guy must've pushed him. Hell, no, not another kicking. But it wasn't the guy pushed him over, his legs had refused to hold him. He couldn't move his arms, either. His head was at an awkward angle, his neck twisted to one side, but he couldn't do anything about it. It was as if he was paralysed.

The doctor dragged him through Geordie's gate and down the side of the house into the back garden. Then he disappeared for a while and came back with the bag.

The guy was kneeling by him now. Ralph wanted to ask for help. He wanted to say, Come on, you're a doctor, you can help with this. I don't want to be paralysed for the rest of my life.

The guy had the syringe. Ralph couldn't tell if it had anything in it. Leant low over Ralph, put his mouth next to Ralph's ear. He said, 'You shouldn't have sent the note.'

Ralph felt the needle go in again. He would have flinched if he could have moved at all. Whatever it was, he felt it enter his bloodstream as the guy depressed the plunger on the syringe.

Then he was gone.

Ralph realized he was completely alone. He couldn't shout for help and he couldn't move. Where he lay, just off the path, it was dark and cold. He thought he might have to lie there all night, but then his heart missed a beat, and another one. It started up again, but he couldn't get his breath. His mouth filled with saliva and the saliva ran down his throat.

The next thing he knew the man was hauling him to his feet. Ralph couldn't stand, none of his muscles would respond. The doctor hitched him over his shoulder in a fireman's lift and carried him to a tree next to the shed. Ralph was half-placed and half-flung against the trunk. The skin on the back of his head split open as it cracked against the rough bark. The pain set up a throbbing in his temples. The drug had killed his ability to move or protest but it in no way affected his ability to experience pain.

The doctor appeared from behind him. He smiled at Ralph. He produced a couple of six-inch nails and a hammer. 'This won't take long,' he said, stretching Ralph's arms out as though he was on a cross. 'We don't want you falling down, now, do we?'

The few stars that Ralph could see in the early evening sky seemed suddenly much closer than he had ever imagined. Off the Great Barrier Reef, he remembered, the stars had seemed huge, but never as close as this.

He'd been a sailor, that was his last thought before the agony began; and *sailor* the last word, only the silent screaming that ran through his body had obliterated the last syllable. I was a *sail* . . .

I watched him go with the prostitute and he looked perky enough then. I presume her pimp gave him the beating. The prostitute was a small, even frail woman, and I cannot imagine her inflicting those injuries on him even if he begged her. He was the kind of man who would not appreciate the joy of pain; he would only understand its role in the acquisition of power.

The master/slave relationship is probably as old as prostitution and each of them would be poorer without the fertilization of the other. If it ever comes to it, Miriam will make a fine whore. She understands the theory and practice of libido with her body. I have always discounted Lawrence's musings in *Fantasia of the Unconscious*, preferring the more obviously flawed reasoning of Freud. But since meeting Miriam I have had to reassess Lawrence's opinion. The physical body is an older and deeper mechanism than the human mind and it contains a primal knowledge that is equal to the sum total of our experience.

Miriam finds enjoyment and fulfilment in pain because it is more real than pleasure. What we euphemistically call pleasure is a fleeting emotion. It is something that barely touches us. But pain is far-reaching. It lasts much longer, sometimes for ever.

Drugs are wonderful things. And Viagra is one of the best. When I took it (for Miriam, of course) the result was a dark, cruising sexuality, which lasted, quite literally, for hours. It was not particularly good or bad, it was interesting. Now we know what it is and what it can achieve, we won't bother with it again.

In my profession there has been a predictably mixed reception for the drug. Most of them think it's wonderful. They point to the benefits that it will bring to the impotent. I do not subscribe to that view. What we have in Viagra is a drug that acts by forcing a chemical reaction in the body. It does not act on the mind.

It is a sex drug. And having taken it, you are expected to have sex. You are expected to have lots of sex. Great sex. If you take Viagra and refuse to have sex, or decide that the drug isn't working for you, you are, clearly, a failure.

Who would do that, anyway? Who would take a dose of Viagra and then turn round and say, 'No, I don't feel like it tonight'? The only person who would say that is a wimp. Someone who looks around him and sees the expectations of the world and immediately begins to crumble. That man would probably be impotent.

This is how we are organized. We take a man who can't manage an erection because of a psychological problem, we give him a chemical stimulant and tell him, 'There, now you can easily get an erection, go and use it, you sexual beast.' If he doesn't use it, he'll feel guilty, which in turn will enhance his original psychological problem.

This is our world. This is how we do things. We live in a surrealist universe.

I took the impostor. He was no problem. As is usually the case, the world had prepared him for me. I live close to my feelings and I listen and respond to the subtle messages of my body and am at one with the world. When I fixed on that man, or perhaps as early as when he fixed on me by using my name, our personal ecologies became intertwined. That spiritual, etheric, astral world by which

244

my life is surrounded sent out messengers, like invisible fingers, to search out the spiritual, etheric, astral world which surrounded him. Our worlds became united, like the worlds of lovers or of the hunter and the hunted, the master and the slave.

We were, for a time, inextricably one.

The tape is wonderful. The sound of the nails driving home. The words he spoke and tried to speak as the drug overcame him are poignant. They will live with me for ever.

Now I am alone again, except for Miriam, my handmaiden; and my enemy, the blind woman.

FORTY-FOUR

For once Echo was sleeping. Janet had fallen asleep with her arms wrapped around Geordie and it had felt good while she was still awake, the way the contours of her body used every inch of his back. But now she was sleeping he felt confined by her nearness.

He managed to struggle free without waking her and crept down the stairs to talk to Venus and her kittens. He found a can of Caffreys in the fridge and popped it, sitting on the base of his spine next to the cat's basket. Venus kept all of the kittens close to her, occasionally eyeing Geordie with a look that could've killed.

He hoped Ralph would get in touch again. Not straight away, there'd have to be a gap, let things settle down. He pictured him back home with his family in Bristol, a wife and three kids according to Sam. Nice for the kids, that, getting their dad back for Christmas.

I hope it works out for you, he thought, that you all live together and don't split up again. And then when we meet it'll be like it should've been this time. Ralph with his family and Geordie with Janet and Echo. They could swap houses in the summer, stay in a different town for a couple of weeks. And Echo'd have real cousins . . .

Geordie took another swallow from the Caffreys can. No point in going back upstairs yet. He was tired as hell but nowhere near ready to sleep. He got a blanket and stretched out on the sofa and listened to one of Janet's CDs. Dinah Washington, *Mad about the Boy*. Made you forget who you were, fooled you into thinking everything was all right and the world was benign.

Before Echo was born Geordie had been learning a new word every week. What you did, you got the word, out of a book, say, or off Celia or JD. And every day for that week you found a way of using the word in the right place. Benign had been one of those words, and, hey, look at that, it'd stuck.

Except the world wasn't benign.

Which was one of the reasons you had to pretend it was from time to time.

Geordie couldn't work out if he'd been thinking about the world being benign or if he'd been dreaming about it. The CD had finished and the blanket had slipped off the sofa and there was a knocking sound coming from somewhere. Sounded like one of the neighbours was doing a spot of DIY in the middle of the night.

They'd had a mad neighbour once who got up and played the piano before dawn. He couldn't remember her name now, but she'd had a tumour in her head.

The banging stopped. It had sounded like someone knocking nails into a piece of wood. But the night plays tricks and as soon as the noise had gone Geordie couldn't be sure he'd heard it at all. If Echo'd woken up, then he could've been sure, maybe even done something about it. But there wasn't a peep out of Echo.

Oh, hell, there it was again. And not far away. He got off the couch and moved over to the window. He pulled back the curtain and watched a shaft of light dart along the length of the garden. There was one more bang, as if the light had been enough to warn off whoever was out there. A single hammer blow, the one that confirms the head of the nail is fully embedded.

Geordie was ready to sleep now, but there was a possibility that someone was trying to break into a neighbour's house. He put on a pair of shoes and a coat and found the torch that Janet kept in the kitchen. It was still outside and bitterly cold, the ground covered with a glittering layer of frost. Geordie played the beam of the torch over the fence and on to the façade of his neighbour's house. The windows were tightly curtained and the door was closed and unmarked.

He walked down the garden, shining the beam a couple of feet in front of him. He stopped when he discovered the step-ladder by the side of the shed. 'Oh, Jesus,' he said as he saw that the shed door had been forced. There you go, worrying about the neighbours and all the time there's somebody breaking into your own shed.

He folded the step-ladder and put it back in the shed. He closed the door as far as it would go and walked back towards the house. They'd probably taken all his tools.

He turned around and looked back at the shed, wondering for a moment if the burglars were still there, watching him from the shadows. They'd probably have the steps away as soon as he got into the house. But there was nothing he could do about it now, not without waking everyone in the street.

As he opened the door and stepped inside the house he heard the long wail that Echo gave when she woke up and wanted to be fed.

FORTY-FIVE

JD turned the gas fire up as far as it would go. It threw out heat in a six-foot semi-circle and he and Sam pulled their chairs into the confines of the space. This meant burning your shins but JD preferred that to shivering and he knew that Sam had a similar value system to himself, at least in respect to body temperature.

'I love this room in the summer,' JD said. 'In the winter I'm always making plans to move. But I'm slow, so by the time I've got around to doing something about it, the winter's over and spring reminds me what a great room it is in summer.'

'Me too,' said Sam. 'As soon as this case's over I'm gonna unload Dora's house. It's more than I want to carry.'

'If it wasn't so big, you wouldn't have Angeles living with you.'

'I didn't say it was totally negative,' Sam said with a wink. 'If there were no benefits, I'd've gotten rid of it years ago.'

'Like a peacock's tail,' JD told him.

Sam looked at the wall, seemed like he deliberately wasn't going to ask JD to explain himself.

'It's to do with evolution,' JD said. 'The peacock's tail is mostly useless, it uses up energy that the bird should be spending on survival. But instead it grows this massive and beautiful tail that's only useful for sexual display. Everything is about sex anyway, so the peacock actually knows what it's doing. We do the same when we go out shopping for designer clothes; the more we pay the greater the pulling power, or so we're led to believe.'

'It doesn't work,' Sam said. 'I've been doing that for years and it only got me in trouble. Women who fall for that are messed up, so you end up attracting them, and then they mess you up in turn.'

'But it's how nature works,' JD said. 'You go buy a Porsche or some Bang & Olfsen equipment and what does it mean? It means you're rich, for one thing, you've got taste. It sends signals out into the world about you. Delineates you. You look better than the next guy already, unless he's got a yacht.'

'Every move I make is a sexual signal?' Sam asked.

'Yeah, if you're a smart monkey and you want to evolve into a human, you have to learn to transform the raw materials of nature into status displays. If you don't manage that one, you and your offspring'll be swinging around in the jungle for millennia.'

'On balance,' Sam said, 'I'd choose the jungle. The alternative is madness. According to you, there's millions of us here all putting out sexual signals. The world is jammed up with synthetic peacock's tails, and most of 'em get lost. There's guys out there splashing fortunes on new Porsches, Hugo Boss suits, Leica cameras, and they don't even get a blow-job for it.'

'What Darwin discovered was really simple stuff, Sam. He saw that if peahens fall for peacocks with tails that are gaudier and longer than average, then it stands to reason that the tails are always going to get gaudier and longer. The only way that peacock genes are going to make it into the next generation is if they are carried in bodies with long and gaudy tails.'

Sam tried to interrupt but JD carried on talking, getting into it now. 'Where Darwin went wrong was that he thought evolution was driven by the survival of the fittest, but it isn't, it's driven by the reproduction of the sexiest.'

'OK,' Sam said. 'I'm getting there. This's why the advertisers never tell us anything about the stuff they're trying to flog; they just put a pretty girl next to it, or a guy with a cheesy grin?'

'Exactly. Everyone's given up trying to sell their wares on product features; they go for image, just like the peacock. If you want to sell coffee, you have to show it as a consensual object of desire. If the advertiser gets it right, we all come to believe that his or her brand of coffee will automatically lead to a romantic liaison with someone wonderful.'

'This's awful,' Sam said. 'I dunno if I want to hear any more. It'll put me off sex.'

'You're all right,' JD told him. 'You have the right mixture of cynicism and poverty to bypass these things. You've still got a sense of humour. Guys like you can get away with hitching up your pants and breathing down your nose. You use real signals. But most people are brainwashed into responding to virtual signals. They watch television all night, save up their pennies to buy the right T or the latest trainers.'

'Oh, cheers, JD. That your way of saying I've got no style or finesse? I attract women through some base animal signalling technique, like not changing my socks?'

'Don't make it personal. What I'm saying is that each product, if it's going to be successful, the advertisers have to create an independent sexual signalling niche for it. OK?'

'I'm listening.'

'And that creates problems. People watch the ads, they see that the guy who buys the product gets the girl. And they then spend more time and energy displaying virtual signals, using these products, than they spend displaying real, biologically validated signals, like humour or gentleness or creativity.'

'So they lose,' said Sam. 'They get frustrated, maybe buy more or different products. Deodorants, aftershave, frilly knickers. Rather than improve their personalities, they buy something else that the Man tells them will work wonders.'

'Yeah,' said JD. 'They go out looking for more sexual signalling systems.'

'But they just end up with more products.'

'This is alienation, Sam. Welcome to the millennium.'

The psychoanalyst in JD's novel was a professional watcher. A deconstructionist heavily influenced by Derrida and Lacan, he daily focused his trained gaze on the stream of patients visiting his clinical practice. JD was torn about labelling the character with bisexuality. He preferred to keep his murderers well within the confines of the white heterosexual community, practising a kind of literary positive discrimination. But he had been unable to resist the echoes of a post-modern killer's bisexuality. A character who spends his time questioning the traditional boundaries between the categories that we assume to be distinct could not be enslaved within those boundaries. The critics would complain that JD was politically incorrect again, but he didn't write for them.

A secondary problem with the character was technical. JD

wanted his psychoanalyst to be understood in human terms. He didn't want the reader to write him off as a monster. The murders had to be seen, of course, as the brutal and destructive acts they were, but JD was concerned that the entire blame for the violence didn't fall on the individual. He wanted to show the substantial contribution of the environment in which the individual lived and worked. JD was a political animal and he didn't want to write a novel in which the individual's failure was condemned while the institutionalized violence of the state was ignored.

Most fictional murderers were presented in stereotypical terms, described as having the puffy eyes and absorbent skin of a boozer, perhaps, or as a burned-out schizophrenic with shaking and trembling hands. They smoked cigarettes continually. When JD described his psychoanalyst's thin, grey, Presbyterian conscience, his instinct was to cut the two adjectives. He highlighted them in the text and pushed the delete key, watched the computer do its magic.

He shook his head, read the sentence over and over again. Finally he reached for the undo key and pressed it quickly. As the two adjectives reappeared JD felt the ghost of a First World War ambulance driver move closer to his right shoulder.

He was at that stage in the writing of the novel where it would be good if he could bring in a man with a gun. He could introduce another murder, but it seemed facile, somehow, upping the body count just to keep a reader's eyes glued to the page. He felt something for all of his characters in different ways, sympathized with their individual plights and could not justify bumping one of them off without a good reason. The only reason that would suffice would be if the death somehow furthered the development of the plot.

But the idea of furthering the development of the plot brought a smile to JD's lips. There was little or no plot to the novel anyway, only a main theme supported by tributaries and echoes, by humour and ideas and dialogue. His novel, like the case of Isabel and Angeles Falco, was at an impasse. All the groundwork and the research had been done, the usual suspects had been identified and the witnesses primed. Now the miracle had to happen. JD waited; and someone on the street outside rang the doorbell.

Pancake make-up. Huge virtual eyes. The gap between jacket and skirt and the flash of silver and quartz from a navel ring. Christine Moxey had gone blonde since the last time he saw her but the make-up and schmuck with which she adorned her body couldn't hide the underlying brash vulnerability.

'Come in,' he said. 'You must be freezing.'

'Thought you'd never ask.' She brushed past him and marched down the hall and up the three steps to JD's workroom. He followed, trying to put together the monstrous Reeboks, which reminded him of Minnie Mouse, and the skirt that was so short he could see right up to the maker's name.

'I've seen my bike,' she said.

He could have kissed her. JD took a moment out to consider if he'd rather have heard her say anything else. But he couldn't think of a thing. It was as if she'd lived out her fifteen years with only this one utterance as the objective.

'Tell me,' he said. She was blue, goose pimples colonizing her midriff. He wanted to gather her up in his arms, wrap her in a blanket of warmth.

'It's at work. This café on Pavement. I work there weekends. All the girls leave their bikes in the back.'

'It was there?' said JD, dismayed. 'You'd left it there. Forgot about it?'

'Not me,' she said. 'I told you, it was stolen. But it turned up again this morning, back of the café. One of the other girls must've left it there.'

'You don't know who?'

'You're the detective, not me. But it's my bike. Green Raleigh and CAM on the saddle. Christine Annabelle Moxey. There can't be two bikes like that.'

'So what did you do?'

'What I wanted to do, I wanted to ask who'd brought it and scratch her eyes out. But I controlled myself. I told the boss I'd got period pains and came round here damn quick to collect the reward.'

'Reward?'

'Yeah, you told me if I found out who stole it, you'd give me a hundred quid.'

JD didn't remember making that promise. He took out his wallet and extracted two twenties, passed them over to her. 'All

I've got at the moment. When we get the guy you'll get the other sixty.'

'It's not a guy,' Christine said. 'There's no guys work at the café. We're all girls.'

'OK,' JD said. 'It was a girl rode the bike to work, but there's a guy behind her.'

'So what do we do now?'

'You go back to work. Tell the boss you're feeling better and keep your eye on the bike. Don't ask any questions but at closing time make sure you see who takes the bike. I'll be outside, and whoever it is, I'll follow her, find out where she lives.'

'What if you lose her? It'll be dark.'

'I won't lose her. But if I do, you'll already know who it is, so we can trace her.'

'This is exciting,' she said.

JD did a double-take. For a moment or two he went with the fantasy, then reality came back to claim him. 'Just routine,' he said. 'All in a day's work.'

FORTY-SIX

When he left the AA meeting Sam saw himself as one of hundreds of thousands of people who were leaving similar meetings all over the world. Most of them had seen death close up. Some of them had been talking but the majority had been listening, seeking for that extra ounce of strength that can only be supplied by another.

JD was waiting on the corner of Friargate. Sam detached himself from his sponsor, Max, and walked over to join JD. He'd never seen him on a bike before and the man and machine somehow didn't fit. Without each other the bike and the man had, respectively, style and dignity. But together they excited only a comedic pathos.

The meeting had gone well and Sam was convinced he'd never drink again. A danger sign in itself for an alcoholic. In a culture that reaches for ethanol whenever it feels a celebration coming on, any feelings of elation are to be watched with caution. One drink sounds innocuous, even tame, and it is for most people. But there's a fairly sizeable tribe of others in the world for whom that one drink is a virtual death sentence.

'This's never happened to me before,' Sam said. 'I come out of an AA meeting and there's a guy on a bike waiting for me. Is it symbolic?'

'I didn't want to miss you.' JD told him about Christine Moxey's visit and how the missing bicycle had turned up at the café.

Sam grinned. 'So she'll be coming out around six o'clock. JD, you go there now, for half an hour or so. I'll get Marie to relieve you. Then we'll meet up at five and follow the girl home together.'

All heiresses are beautiful. Angeles Falco was no exception. She had a face that could come back and haunt you. She was wearing a faded red cotton shirt, the top two buttons unfastened. Red lips and a faint blush to her cheeks, could've been painted on or it could've been natural. If he'd been forced to guess, Sam'd guess it didn't really matter. Heavy cord strides, looked like they were three sizes too big for her, and abb socks in hand-spun, undyed wool.

She looked like she was glad to see him. 'Where've you been? I thought it was your day off.'

'It is,' he said. 'I was with JD, talking philosophy, we solved a few global problems then I went to an AA meeting.'

'Philosophy,' she said, managing a satirical spin on the word.

'You disapprove.'

'No. It's just that much of philosophy seems to cloak medium-sized ideas in large words.'

He laughed. 'You're a jacket job, you know that?'

Angeles shook her head. 'What's that?'

'A jacket job. Something that drives you mad.'

'Oh. Thank you kindly. Men think all women are jacket jobs, don't they?'

'I don't know what other men think.'

'But you know what you think.'

Jesus, he thought. We're flirting. This's not just me flirting with her. She's coming back at me. He wondered briefly if it had just started, or had it been going on for a few days without him noticing? 'Concerning women,' he said. 'It was different when I was younger. But now I have to approach them on the strength of my beautiful nature and my wealth and fame rather than count on dazzling the eye.'

'You seem quite proficient at that. And I'm sure you could dazzle a girl's eye as well, if she had one.'

'It's low animal cunning,' he told her. 'Usually gets me where I want to be.'

She was quiet for a couple of beats, long enough to make him wonder if he'd gone wrong. 'There's been a lot of women, hasn't there?'

'I've been round the block at least twice.'

He looked around the room for a seduction-sized couch. But it was his room and the furniture hadn't been properly thought through. He took a step towards her and she stepped back into the corner, voluntarily trapped between the door and a huge oak cabinet that had been in the house longer than Sam.

He came close enough to hear and feel her breath on his face. She reached up and placed her hands on his chest. He lifted her face and brushed her lips with his own and felt her arms go around his back. She had her eyes closed, which was something to think about some other time.

The feel of her body moving under his touch was an invitation to a sweet and tumultuous chaos that sent his mind swimming. He bore down on her mouth with a gentle force that she returned with short, sharp, seemingly uncontrolled movements. She took his lower lip between her teeth and pulled it down and out, releasing it only a moment before pleasure turned to pain.

He lifted his head to give her space to breathe, to allow her to reconsider, but she reached for him greedily. She growled.

A moment later the telephone rang. Sam and Angeles were by now committed to follow their emotions to the inevitable end and neither of them intended to answer the call. After four rings the answer-machine kicked in and Janet's voice came down the line.

'Sam,' she said. 'Sam, if you're there, pick up the phone. The police are here. Ralph's been killed. I need some help with Geordie.'

Sam took a step back and left Angeles on the wall. 'Sorry,' he said. He picked up the handset. 'Janet, you still there?' He paused. 'Save it,' he said. 'Gimme ten minutes. I'm leaving now.'

Angeles had let her shoulders slump but her head was high, pressed against the wall, her eyes closed, her arms by her sides.

'I'll be back later,' he said.

She straightened. 'No, wait, I'll come too. Janet'll need someone.'

Sam looked at her. She was a champ.

Angeles opened the side window and let a stream of icy air into the car. She felt it carve a shallow bowl out of her waxen features. Sam drove fast, grim and tight beside her; she had to brace her body each time he took a corner. The high-pitched whine of protest from the tyres was barely audible, treading only on the fringes of the human ear's capability.

257

When they arrived Sam described the scene to her in clipped sentences, like a parody of one of the guides who showed tourists round the town. 'Police car outside, badly parked. Young copper standing by. Janet at the window, coming to the door now.'

Angeles had her hand on his shoulder. She'd never been here before and all of her senses were on alert. She'd set up a grid inside her head and was busy placing herself inside it, noting the objects, the barriers and the pathways around her. She'd felt the heat from the bonnet of the police car as they passed it; and she'd been expecting some kind of gate or an outer approach to the house, but there didn't seem to be one. A house door opened a couple of metres in front of them and she heard Janet's voice.

'Sam, thanks for coming.'

Sam's shoulder raised as he embraced her, and Angeles felt Janet's hand squeeze her own at the same time.

'How is he?' Sam asked.

'Not too good. He's just staring at the wall.'

Sam moved away and Angeles felt Janet lean forward and kiss her on the cheek. There was the scent of the mother about her; that soft fleshiness to her lips and cheeks, the heavy pull of her breasts. It seemed to Angeles that Janet's entire being was an enticement. In close proximity she was suddenly reminded of the awesome power of sexuality. That's twice in one day, she thought. Which is pushing up the average for a girl who spends most of her time in bed with an audiotape.

Inside it felt dark and oppressive, like the House of Usher. Angeles could have walked straight to the spot where Geordie sat, so strong was the emanation of his disbelief and his grief. He was like a cold, raw diamond that occupied the centre of the house, and a low mist of despondency and woe issued from him. His breathing was four-four time, largo.

From the mumbled voices she discerned two policemen in the room and one woman apart from herself and Janet. One of the policemen was extremely tall and there was an embarrassed catch to his voice, as if he would easily bubble over into laughter. All of them hugged the room's periphery, anxious not to be contaminated by Geordie's despair. Only Sam had moved in there with him and he must have wrapped his arms around Geordie because there was the rocking sound echoed in the cushions on the couch.

Sam's voice whispering, *Geordie*, over and over like a mantra, *Geordie, Geordie.*

She felt a hot flush of tears behind her eyes as the bloody pity of it all touched her.

'Can we go outside?' she whispered, and Janet led her through the kitchen. The remains of last night's meal lingered in the air: olive oil, garlic, tomato. A door led them into the garden, where frosty fingers made them both shiver.

'Maybe this is not such a good idea?' Angeles said.

'We'll be all right for a few minutes. I can hardly bear to be near Geordie when he's like that.'

'Does anyone know what happened?'

'Ralph was crucified against a tree in the garden. The man next door found him and came round to tell us. Geordie heard it happening last night.'

'Crucified?'

'His hands were nailed into the trunk,' said Janet. 'It was horrible. We couldn't get him down. Geordie started to fade when he saw him. I was frightened. I thought he might disappear.'

Angeles reached for her and Janet took a step forward into her arms. They clasped each other for a full minute. Angeles hummed a Klezmer chant, something she had heard on one of her outings with Felix and which suddenly seemed apt for the occasion. Janet stiffened and then relaxed, let the music seep into her. 'What is it?' she asked.

'I don't know,' Angeles said. 'In the West people sing when they're happy, but Jews and Slavs sing when they're unhappy.'

'It's so beautiful,' Janet said.

Angeles didn't answer. But, yes, she thought. If you have a soul and you hear music like that, you can only be moved.

FORTY-SEVEN

Sam had taken Geordie to the morgue, waited while he identified the body as his brother, Ralph, then he had driven him back home, picked up Angeles and taken her back to his own house. 'What a day,' he said. 'I'm supposed to be meeting JD at five.'

Angeles felt the protruding digits on her wristwatch. 'You'll be late,' she said.

'I'm going on the bike.' He threw the car keys on to the table.

'You'll be even later, then. Why the bike?'

'JD's got a lead. I'll tell you when I get back.' He dragged his bike out of the garden shed and pedalled into the centre of town.

Something else she'd said on the ride back from Geordie and Janet's house. 'He watches people but he doesn't see them.'

'How d'you mean?'

'He watches me, but it's like he's looking at a picture. He doesn't see the me that I see me as. He sees something static, something that he's brought with him. It's the same with Isabel and Ralph; he couldn't have killed them if he'd seen them. You can only destroy people if you're blind to their hopes and aspirations and weaknesses. A successful murderer is someone who can't see. He looks but he misses the point.'

'Yeah. Guys like this are obsessed with themselves. They see others, but they only see them as distinct from themselves. They don't invest us with human characteristics. They see objects.'

JD was leaning against a brick wall behind Pavement, his bike parked on the kerb. He was smoking a small J, the whiff of weed almost visible in the frozen atmosphere. 'You're late,' he said.

'You're stoned,' Sam replied.

'Yeah, I'm stoned, but at least I'm here.'

'I got involved,' Sam said. 'They found Ralph's body nailed to a tree in Geordie's garden. They think he'd been pumped full of something they use to cull elephants.'

JD whistled. 'He was a big lad,' he said. 'But not that big.' He took another toke on the J and his eyes shone in the frozen evening air.

'You gonna be OK if we run into trouble?'

'I'm a little stoned, Sam. All I've got to do is ride my bike, find out where the girl lives. I'm not gonna get into trouble. If trouble happens, I run away, you know that.'

'You get stoned,' Sam told him, 'you sometimes run the wrong way.'

'Don't be a Puritan, it doesn't suit you.'

'I take it nothing's happened here? The girls haven't started coming out yet?'

'Two separate questions,' said JD. 'No, the girls haven't started coming out yet. But that doesn't mean nothing's happened. I had a long conversation with the lovely Marie. I think she's starting to break down. She really fancies me, you know.'

'You're out of your skull,' Sam said. 'How many of those things have you smoked?'

'First of the day,' JD said, grinding the roach under his heel. 'If I'm high, it's with life's possibilities.'

Sam shook his head as the back door to the café opened, sending a shaft of light across the road. Two girls emerged with bicycles: a blonde with a red racer and a small brunette with a green Raleigh mountain bike. The second girl had a protruding jaw and small eyes and her bike had a Mickey Mouse bell.

'This's us,' Sam said. 'Don't lose her.'

JD pushed away from the kerb and wobbled over the road in pursuit of the girls. Sam rode behind him, carefully keeping his eye on the rider of the green Raleigh. Watching Geordie at the morgue, he had been struck by the fact that he could only see his friend from one point. Every observer was limited to a view from a single point but they themselves were observed from all possible angles.

The killer of Isabel, the one who was almost certainly

responsible for the death of Ralph, was an observer. If he could see his victims from another point of view, would he decide to draw back? If he could see Angeles from Sam's point of view as well as his own, would he still be a threat to her life? And the people who observed him, the people he lived and worked with, this girl on the bike, perhaps, did any of them see him as a killer?

The girls made a right turn on to the Stonebow, where the traffic was tailed back and cars and buses were at a standstill. The cyclists wove in and out of stationary vehicles and a slight mist came down. When they separated the blonde carried on along Peasholme Green towards Foss Bank, while the quarry took a left into Aldwark and then a right again into one of the closed courtyards.

Sam drew level with JD and they dismounted. 'Stay with the bikes,' Sam told him. 'I'll take a look. If you hear a scream, come and save me.' The mist was swirling now and when Sam looked back JD and the bicycles were already swallowed up.

It was clear in the courtyard, however, and the girl with the green Raleigh only gave him a cursory glance as he came through the gate. She was wheeling the bike into a garage. Sam stood at someone's front door and pretended to ring the bell.

When she disappeared inside he made a note of the house number and spent the next half-hour trying to look inconspicuous as several residents arrived home from work. Finally a blue Mazda pulled through the gates and drew up to the same garage that the girl had used. Sam felt himself stiffen as soon as the driver got out of his seat. There was a shift in tension as he realized that this could be the man who attacked Angeles. Sam had not seen his face that night but he had gained an impression of his bulk and height, and the figure who was now opening the garage door fitted the bill.

Sam kept to the shadows, watched and waited until the man let himself into the same flat as the girl, then he returned to JD.

'So?' JD said.

'We've got the girl with the bike and a guy with blond hair about the same shape and size as the guy I saw in Angeles' garden. We know where they live, next we have to find out who they are.'

'So we follow him?'

'Bright and early tomorrow morning.'

Sam was on his bike now, but JD was kneeling at the front of his, fiddling with the dynamo. Sam waited.

JD stood and looked at the bike then he walked around it, passing it from one hand to the other. The saddlebag was leaning over to the left and he adjusted the right strap to get it back in line. He became aware of Sam watching him and looked up, smiling.

'All set?' Sam asked.

JD swung his leg over the crossbar. 'You know something, Sam? I never cared who was the president of the US after Kennedy was killed. Bobby, that is.' He stood on the pedal and pushed away from the kerb.

Sam followed. He said, 'JD, don't let anybody ever tell you different: you are a fountain of wisdom.'

FORTY-EIGHT

Geordie had gone to look at plots in the old York cemetery; Janet's idea. Something to keep him moving, get him out of the house. Plus, it was a practical job which needed doing. The cemetery was a quiet place, a haven for wildlife, and Geordie would be able to collect his thoughts there, maybe remember that he had a wife and child as well as a dead brother.

Janet called on Angeles at Sam's house, but she'd gone to work and there was nobody home. At the office she found Marie. 'Where is everyone?' she asked. 'It's like a grave in here.'

'Celia's gone to the bank. Sam and JD are on a stake-out. They think they've found the guy.'

'Hope so. Who is it?'

'That's what they're working on. He lives in Aldwark with a girlfriend who's a waitress.'

'Waitresses always end up with shit,' Janet said. 'I hated it. The worst job in the world.'

'Worse than nursing?'

'Dunno. Probably about the same. Whenever I stopped working in a café or a restaurant I'd throw all my clothes away. They'd stink. All the fat and whatever it was they cooked in the place, it'd get into the weave. You could wash a shirt five, six times and it'd still smell of rotten food.'

Marie looked up from her desk. 'How's Geordie?' she said.

'He's gone to the cemetery, look for somewhere to plant Ralph. I don't wanna talk about that. How's your love life?'

Marie raised her eyebrows and kissed the air.

'That good? What's he called, Davy?'

'David. David Styles.'

'Are we talking lurve, here?'

'Yes. I'm in love with him and he's in love with his children. At the school, his class.'

'And not with you?'

'Oh, he likes me,' Marie said. 'He's attentive. But if we were in a sinking ship, he'd get the kids out first.'

'D'you mind?'

Marie nodded. 'Yes, I do,' she said. 'I want him to be mad about me. I want him to feel like I do, to wake up in the morning and be thinking about me rather than the lesson he's got to teach.'

'That's like JD,' Janet said. 'He wakes up in the morning thinking about you and then he goes through the day thinking about you, and you don't even want to see him.'

'Yes, he's as loyal as a Dobermann pinscher.'

'And it's not enough.'

A smile passed over Marie's face. 'Crazy world, isn't it, Janet? The sex is better than I thought sex could be. It's like the kind of sex you dream about when you're not getting it. But I'm looking for something else. Sex can give you a sense of self-discovery and fulfilment, but it's just as likely to leave you overwhelmed by loneliness.'

They turned towards the door as Celia's footsteps sounded on the stairs. She was wearing knee-length boots with a Russian coat and a round fur hat. 'Oh, girls' party,' she said. 'The men still out hunting?'

'Presume so,' said Marie. 'We haven't heard anything.'

Celia slipped her paying-in book into the top drawer of her desk. 'I hope they're watching this chap,' she said. 'Only there was a blond in the bank giving me the once over. I hope it wasn't him.'

'Who?' said Janet. 'What blond in the bank?'

'The guy Sam and JD are tailing,' Marie explained. 'He's a blond.'

'Oh, my God,' said Janet. 'Of course he is.'

'Explain,' said Celia, coming around her desk.

'I was following Ralph,' Janet said. 'For a few days before he was killed. But I wasn't the only one. There was a blond guy watching him as well. I didn't think about it before, what with Ralph's death and the state of Geordie. It must be the same man. Rent-a-drool face?'

'Sam said six foot three or four, but slim, long legs.'

'It's him,' said Janet.

'Would you be able to pick him out of a line-up?' asked Marie.

'No problem. I've seen him two or three times. If it's the same guy, I'll recognize him.'

The girl left the house early, just after eight. She didn't take the bike this time, walked in the direction of the café. An hour later the man came out and walked off in the same direction.

Sam said, 'I'm going inside. Cover me.'

They were sitting in the Montego and it was so cold that they had lost feeling in their toes. JD's breath steamed his window. 'I thought we were going to follow him.'

'Change of plan. I wanna see what he lives like.'

'Don't be long, Sam. I'm feeling more like Cap'n Scott every minute.'

There was a window with a small screw lock on the inside. Sam cracked it, removed the lock, opened the window and was through it within five minutes.

In someone else's space now. He stood quite still for a full minute. He closed his eyes and listened to their silence. There was a yearning in the hush, something similar to the quiet of his own house, but there was taciturnity as well. It was as if the house was trying to tell him something and he could detect the sounds of the vowels and the consonants but was incapable of hearing the words.

He walked through the rooms. The guy was tidy, his clothes hung up or neatly folded on shelves or a chair. On his side of the bed the book was placed squarely on the bedside table. *The Undermining of Psychological Principles*. There was nothing of his that was on the floor. She was the opposite; instead of a book there was a Walkman and a mess of tapes and magazines by her bed. On the wall were pop singers wearing skimpy and transparent clothes, an abundance of glossy lipstick. Her clothes left a train between bed and bathroom, her underwear drawer was half-open and had slips and pants hanging out of it as if they were trying to escape.

The obsessive and the trollop.

A corner of the bedroom was given over to a personal torture chamber. There was a home-made rack there and some kind of electric-shock machine, handcuffs, gags, blindfolds, leather belts and restraints and a selection of instruments with which to pierce or cut or bruise.

In the sitting room there was a bookcase with hundreds of textbooks on psychological practice and theory. They were not for show either, they were well thumbed and many of them had bookmarks and scribbled notes in the margins.

By the door on a chair was a worn leather satchel. It had a brass fastener with a keyhole and it was locked. Sam carried it back into the bedroom and prised open the lock with an implement that looked as though it was designed to remove stones from horses' hooves.

He tipped the contents of the satchel on to the bed. Syringes and needles and a small bottle with no label containing a tiny amount of colourless liquid. Must be the stuff that Ralph had been injected with, a drug for sedating animals in the wild.

'This'll wrap it up,' Sam said aloud to himself. His voice was out of place in the room, not simply because there was no one there to hear it but because the room was predominantly a place of silence, of emptiness. He left everything where it was and walked back through to the sitting room, looking for a telephone. But before he picked it up there was a knock on the outer door. Must be JD telling him the guy was on his way back.

Sam lifted the latch to let himself out, expecting to see JD on the step. But it wasn't JD. The blond guy was standing there, the yale key in his hand and an expression of complete surprise on his face. 'You,' he said.

He recovered fast and pushed Sam into the house, sending the detective staggering back towards the bedroom. Sam stopped himself falling but before he had recovered the bigger man had pushed him again. Sam bounced off the edge of the bedroom door and went down on all-fours. Immediately the blond had him in a lock, the man's forearm wrapped around Sam's neck while with the other hand he pushed Sam's right arm into a tight half-nelson. The man was sweating, his skin suddenly slick as his pores oozed an oily combination of adrenalin and fear and absolute conviction.

Sam felt himself being lifted clear of the floor and saw the bedroom wall coming at his head, fast. He tried to struggle free but was not quick enough to avoid the impact. The room reeled around him. White painted walls with a couple of Bruegel prints and a smear of red blood freshly squeezed from his own forehead. Once again the blond ran him head-first into the wall, then dropped him on his back over the wooden foot of the bed.

In the dream Sam was a character in a soap opera. It felt as though the budget had been cut and the director was getting ready to write him out. There were three angels playing horns, all too tired to sing; and there was a disembodied refrain coming from concealed speakers. He couldn't make out the words, something about ice and fire, raging against absolutely everything.

He was aware of his body being dragged along the floor, could feel the carpet trapped beneath him. Then he was hoisted aloft, his body swinging into open space, an astronaut now, something else to add to the long list of jobs on his CV.

The smell of stale sweat was the first sense to kick in. An ache in his back. But the dream was mixed in there as well, that voice going round and round, 'Don't fall apart on me tonight.'

Sam was lying full-length on the rack. It was his own voice he had heard. He was muttering away to himself, chanting, rhythmical, on the point of song. One of his hands was handcuffed to the side of the rack and the guy was about to lock his other hand in a leather cuff. 'What're you doing?' Sam said.

He looked up briefly, engaged with Sam's eyes. 'I've got a drug you might find interesting. It'll keep you awake while I take your eyes out.' The blond hair was sticking up in clumps but the eyes were dead, pale blue, almost transparent. The eyes were windows on to a deserted landscape. There was nothing behind them. They concealed nothing.

Sam didn't think. He sat up and nutted the blond with all his might, bringing his forehead down on the bridge of the guy's nose. There was a crack and the man's blood shot down the front of his shirt and sprayed Sam's face. Sam leapt from the rack, dragging it after him with his handcuffed hand. With his free hand he reached for the wooden handle of an implement of torture which was decorated with fish-hooks and lead-weights. He lashed the man across the face with it, feeling it stop for a moment as the hooks dug into the flesh of his cheeks. But the velocity of the blow carried it through and the flesh was gouged out in a bloody wake.

The blond reeled backwards. He turned around on the spot and touched his fingers to the congealed blood on his face. He picked up the duvet and wiped some of the blood away, but as quickly as he mopped it up his body produced more. He screamed like an animal, without restraint of any kind and hurled himself across the room towards the detective. Sam stayed cool, let his breath come easily, knowing that he had the measure of the guy now. He waited until the man was within striking distance and then let go with his right foot, bringing it up between the guy's legs with the force of a sledgehammer. The blond stopped. All of his systems seemed to close down simultaneously. Sam watched the breath leave him, saw the colour drain from his torn and ravaged face.

Sam was ready to lash out again, he still held the fish-hook implement and if necessary he would have taken the man's head off. But the guy had had enough. He went down on his knees and slowly brought his head on to the blood-stained carpet. Sam allowed himself a tiny smile that hurt every muscle in his face. He said, 'I don't take drugs. I'm not even an athlete.'

They were still in the same positions a few minutes later when the police arrived.

Sam had lit a fire in the large grate and Angeles could feel the heat on her face and legs, hear the wood cracking and splintering as the flames consumed it. She fingered the rug and turned to Sam as he stacked logs into the wicker basket standing in the corner. 'They actually locked him up?'

'Yeah. Don't worry. They won't let him go. There's the evidence of the syringes and Janet can identify him. They arrived and arrested the guy. They took him away. They had him in cuffs.'

'You saw him?'

'Yeah, we were there. The police have got him. He's out of circulation. Stop worrying.'

'I need a drink,' she said. She went upstairs and poured a half-tumbler of Scotch. She got a chunk of ice from the fridge and brought the drink back into the room where Sam was waiting. 'You don't like this, do you?'

'I don't mind people drinking,' he said. 'As long as they're in control.'

'But you think I'm an alcoholic?'

'Doesn't matter what I think. I know I'm an alcoholic; only you can say if you are.'

'Maybe I'm a little bit?' she said.

He laughed to register the irony. 'Doesn't work like that,' he said. 'Either you are or you aren't. If you can manage it, you aren't an alcoholic. If you repeatedly drink more than you intend to, you probably are.'

'And if I come to one of your AA meetings, will there be someone there to make a diagnosis?'

He shook his head. 'It's not like that. You have to make your own diagnosis.'

'Then I'm not,' she said. She sniffed at her glass and took a sip. 'I like a drink and I can't remember the last time I fell down.'

'OK. So you're doing good.'

Angeles turned towards him, tried to imagine the expression on his face. 'Then what happened? After they arrested him?'

'Hardwicke arrived with a van-load of guys. They combed the house, took away armfuls of documents, different devices. He had a home-made torture chamber in there.'

'And his girlfriend. What about her?'

'They picked her up from the café. Took her down the station.'

'What kind of torture?'

'Heavy. He had something to cause electric shocks. There was leather gear and knives.'

She tried to imagine being cut or electrocuted and enjoying it. She shook her head from side to side. 'So he's a random killer? He's a sadist who fixated on Isabel and me? Is that what we're saying?'

'I don't think so. The guy himself's not saying anything. But it looks and feels like something personal to me. Plus he's a psychologist, you'd expect him to have a reason.'

Her sensitive fingers found the edge of the brass fender and she traced the floral patterning. 'I don't know any psychologists and I'm certain that Isabel didn't. How old is he?'

'About your age, maybe a couple of years older.'

'What's he called?'

'Jenkins. Rod Jenkins.'

She shook her head. 'Why me, Sam? Why Isabel and me? There's got to be a reason.'

270

'D'you want to tell me about the accident at the pond?'

She whirled around on him. 'Why? How can that have anything to do with it?'

'I don't know. Everything else comes up blank. It might lead somewhere, give us a clue.'

She sat upright on the rug, crossed her legs. She'd found the fire-fork and as she spoke she rocked it backward and forward on the stone hearth. It set up a tapping rhythm, somehow comforting, as she recollected the events of a day far in the past.

'I was tiny,' she said. 'Five years old, Isabel would be about three. It was a Sunday morning. Daddy was going to take us out in the car that afternoon. Mummy was baking a cake in the kitchen, making sandwiches. We would be sledding and then have a picnic in the car.

'I said I'd look after Isabel, we'd play around in the paddock outside the house. And Mummy wanted us out from under her feet. "Not on the road." She always said that.

'I don't know how we got to the pond. I suppose we just wandered. You know what it's like in the countryside after the snow has fallen, the landscape was magical. Everything was glistening and new and I remember showing Isabel that there were no footprints in the snow, and then looking back and seeing our own footprints, like the only footprints in the whole world.

'It was a big pond, not very deep. In the summer, the rest of the year, there were ducks. Sometimes you could walk around the edge and disturb frogs and they'd jump in, almost too late, so you'd nearly stand on them.

'That morning it was frozen over. I remember throwing stones on to the ice and watching them bounce around. It was while I was throwing stones that Isabel went on to the ice. She didn't walk on to it; she fell on to it, rolled down the bank and landed on the ice. She didn't cry, just sat there beaming up at me as though she'd done something special. She was a beautiful child, always smiling.

'I picked my way down the bank and on to the ice, but as soon as I got there my feet slid away under me and then we were both sitting there. It felt as though the pond was frozen right through. It was completely hard, like concrete.

'I ran into the middle and Isabel came wobbling after me. We

271

were dancing, singing and dancing on the ice, slipping and sliding and falling over. We must have been making a racket because someone rang the fire brigade.

'When my foot went through the ice it only added to the fun. There was no sense of danger with us. We carried on dancing and jumping around. At some point I remember hearing the ice cracking. It was as if the earth was splitting apart. It was loud, the kind of noise that you stop and listen to. We couldn't see anything but we could hear the run of the fissures and breaks as the surface cracked up around us.

'I didn't understand what was happening but a sixth sense took over and I made Isabel sit down with me. I put my arms around her and told her to keep still. She looked frightened and I told her to listen for a bird. The ice was no longer dry. Where we were sitting on the ice the water was slowly rising. Isabel said there was water in her wellie, but I wouldn't let her take it off.

'The fire engine came. We saw it pulling up at the edge of the pond. A huge monster with the mechanical ladder on the top. Red in the white landscape. Red, to match our wellies. And then we were gripped by panic.

'The men jumped down from the fire engine and started running around, shouting out to us. I couldn't make out what they were saying and I don't think it would have made much difference if I could. I was paralysed. Isabel began crying and everything suddenly seemed hopeless.

'They pushed a ladder out towards us and one of the men crawled along it. He pulled and pushed me until I was on the ladder. But when I got on to the ladder the ice cracked again, sharply, as if it had snapped and I turned and saw Isabel topple over sideways and disappear.

'I screamed. I suppose you'd call it a scream. But it was something else. I've been in a couple of scary situations since then, situations where I've screamed. But the scream that came out of me that day, when Isabel went under the ice, well, I've never been able to reproduce it. It wasn't confined to my throat, to my vocal cords.'

She picked up the fire-fork for a moment and held it in two hands. Then she placed it back down again, partly missing the hearth. She knew it was half on the hearth and half on the rug but she didn't care. She didn't look at him.

'I was five years old, Sam. A scrap of a girl. I didn't know I had a being until that moment.'

He put a hand on her shoulder, squeezed it lightly. She reached up and brushed his fingers. Sam's voice was husky. He said, 'Go on, what happened next?'

'The fireman went in after her. He plunged in and disappeared, just like Isabel. There was only me left. The water was as black as oil. There were a few pieces of broken ice floating on the top, but I couldn't see anything beyond the surface. And it was still, there was no movement, nothing to betray the fact that my sister and the fireman were under there. It was as if they had been swallowed by a void.

'I expected that I would be sucked in next. I sat there on the ladder and waited for it to happen, something like a huge vacuum cleaner to pop up out of the blackness and suck me into it. It may have been only a second or two but in my memory it was a space beyond time. It was as if everything had stopped. I didn't expect to hear sound again or see anything move or feel warmth. It was as if I was suspended there, as if the world had stopped at that moment and nothing would ever happen again. That that would be the end, that suspension. I imagined my parents at home, similarly suspended: Mummy over a baking tray and Daddy about to strike a Swan Vesta to light his pipe.

'And it was all broken up by bubbles. Huge bubbles coming to the surface of the black water and bursting. Isabel came out of the hole like a rocket. She only had one wellie on and the fireman's arms were holding her clear of the icy water. He plonked her down on the ladder next to me. I saw his face and it was blue. I mean really blue, not just a faint blueness about the gills. His face was dark blue, violet-blue. He shouted something and the men on the other end started pulling the ladder in to the bank.

'Isabel was still. She wasn't crying any more. I didn't touch her. I held tightly to the ladder and waited until they got us back to dry land.

'They bundled us both into an ambulance and took us to the hospital. Isabel had nearly drowned, of course, and they were worried she'd die. And we were both in shock. At the end of the day Isabel rallied around better than me and we were allowed to go home together after a few days.'

She looked over her shoulder as if she could see. 'And that's it,' she said. 'I've never been on ice since without having some kind of panic attack. Isabel and me, we didn't talk about it much, but she was the same. Ice skating was never a possibility; I'd rather go hang-gliding.'

'Thanks,' he said.

'Any clues in there? You think it'll help us find out why a psychologist wants to kill me?'

'I don't know,' Sam said. 'He could decide to talk. They usually do. If he doesn't, you might have to reconcile yourself to not knowing the answer.'

'I can live with that if I have to,' she said. 'The search for certainty is a kind of mental cowardice, an avoidance of reality.'

Sam whistled through his teeth. 'I like you a little more each day,' he said. 'But reality is when two or more people are pretending the same thing.'

'Like us,' she said, reaching for his face.

'Could be.' He slipped down on to the rug beside her and they fumbled with each other's clothing.

'Shhhhh,' she said. 'We've got lots of time.'

Sam closed his eyes and kept them shut, even up the score a little. They made love quietly in the empty house, as though someone was listening.

FORTY-NINE

Felt like it was the end of another case to JD. It'd been good to be close to Marie again, for as long as it lasted. One of the things that had finished it for them, put the final nail in the coffin, so to speak, was when she found and read his journal. Specifically when she read what he'd written about her.

Everyone was in JD's journal. Sam Turner, Geordie and Janet, Marie and Celia. All of JD's friends and neighbours and acquaintances. No one escaped. He watched them because character was his stock-in-trade. He stole bits of them, a mannerism from Sam, a phrase from Celia, the peculiar stoop of the man who cut his hair, and he combined them within the confines of a novel. JD laughed when people sneered at fiction, said they preferred biography or documentary, wanted to deal with the real world rather than something from a writer's imagination. Picasso had said it more than once: 'Art is a lie that makes us realize the truth.'

Guilt? Should he feel guilt for getting his friends and neighbours down on paper? For watching them, for spying, for being an observer of human nature? JD didn't think so. The supreme watcher was not the writer but the reader. It was the reader who greedily gobbled up the end product. The reader who looked into the souls of all the characters in the book, and who, ultimately, tried to discern the movement of the mind of the writer.

He didn't store people away in a computer. His object was to discover, to retain and enhance the humanity of his stolen characters. He didn't reduce them to data. His stock-in-trade was art, language. He didn't digitize people, wasn't concerned with the jargon of cyberspace.

He'd tried all of those arguments on Marie, but she didn't like any of them.

FIFTY

What would've happened if he hadn't told Ralph to get out of the house? If he hadn't delivered his brother's things to the hospital? Geordie had asked himself these questions over and over again, and he knew the answers. Ralph would still be alive, that's what would have happened.

Ralph would still be alive because Geordie or Janet or someone would have arrived at the hospital to bring him home. He wouldn't've been left there to hobble across town on his own. Injured, after being beaten up, unable to defend himself.

It was as if everything had conspired to set Ralph up for the chop. The psychiatrist, whatever he was, the fucking murderer must've thought it was his birthday when he saw Ralph on his own.

OK, so Ralph was no angel. Geordie knew that, just like everybody else. He was a chancer, but that didn't mean he was gonna be a chancer all his life. Their mother had been a chancer and so had Geordie for most of his life. Their mother had taken her chance and run off with the landlord, somebody with money. She'd had the chance to change her life and she'd grabbed at it with both hands, took it by the throat.

Geordie had seen his own chance the day Sam Turner came up to him in that shop doorway and offered him a job, and Geordie had done the same as their mother. He'd taken the chance and everything that'd happened since that day had led to his present position as a husband and a father. It'd meant he had a group of friends he could rely on.

And the same thing could've happened to Ralph. If Ralph

could've seen that Geordie and Janet and Sam were willing to be there for him. If he could have understood that they weren't just there to be taken, then he'd've had a chance too.

But instead of those things happening he'd gone and got himself killed. Inside his head Geordie called his brother a stupid bastard. He wanted to go down the morgue and get hold of the body and shake it. Everything could've come up roses if Ralph'd only opened his eyes for a few minutes, let himself see that the whole world didn't have to be painted the colours of Hell.

He remembered Ralph when he was a young boy, when they were both living together with their mother in a Sunderland sham. Ralph had been the breadwinner then, the one member of the family who gave a degree of hope to the others. He'd always been a big lad, forever hungry, and Geordie loved it when he strolled into the house, a grin on his face and somebody's television set or stereo equipment under his arm.

There were other times, too, that Geordie's memory threw up. When he couldn't sleep at night for bad dreams or when he woke up with his sheets soaked in pee. Their mother's bedroom was off limits because there'd usually be some guy in there with her, and Geordie would go over to Ralph's bed and shake him awake.

'Not again, bro,' he would say. 'You're gonna have to grow up soon.' But he would help Geordie out of his stinking pyjamas and dry him off with a towel. Then they'd cuddle up together in Ralph's bed. 'You piss yourself in here and I'll fucking kill you,' Ralph would say. But Geordie never did. There was no reason to do it when you were cuddled up with someone else.

All of his memories were confined to that house in Sunderland. Four rooms and an outside bog, and it was the size of a mansion in his mind. Every other house he'd known was nothing compared to the one in Jeddy Road. It was true, the house you were born in was the most interesting house in the world.

Janet was worried about him. She tried not to show it, smothered her feelings in a brash display of efficiency. She dressed Echo in half the time it normally took and she had the evening meal on the table an hour before they were going to sit down. Geordie told her he needed to sit and think, that he would be all right in a few days, but she wasn't convinced. Her face was drawn and there was a shrill note in her voice.

Celia came and sat with him for a while. Before she left she said, 'Geordie, it's all right to sit here the rest of the day, but tomorrow you should do something else.'

He nodded, grunted agreement.

She said, 'It is an extreme evil to depart from the company of the living before you die.'

Shakespeare maybe. One of her literary heroes. Geordie didn't think he'd departed from the company of the living. He was still there. Maybe he'd become a little more shadowy, but he hadn't gone anywhere.

JD quoted Ezra Pound. 'For most people,' he said, 'life slips by like a field mouse not shaking the grass.'

'I feel like shit,' Geordie told him.

'A guy feeling like shit,' JD said. 'That's a condition that has changed the world more than once. Not always for the better.'

Geordie had tried to read Ezra Pound once, all those *Cantos* things, but he didn't have the right kind of brain. Celia had told him that Pound ended up in Venice in the early seventies, a madman feeding the city's stray cats.

Marie arrived only half an hour after JD had left, which would piss JD off if he found out. If he'd known Marie was coming, he'd have hung on and left with her and tried to make her fall in love with him.

'What's happening inside your head?' she asked.

'I dunno. It's like a whirlpool.'

'It's important to pin it down,' she told him. 'What we can name and understand we can begin to heal.'

'I wanna remember my brother,' Geordie said. 'I wanna remember him when he was good.'

Marie smiled. 'You're half-way home,' she said.

Sam came late at night. 'I saw the light,' he said. Janet and Echo were upstairs, sleeping. He fussed with Barney for a while. 'You want me to take Barney for a run?'

Geordie shrugged.

'You and me, Barney,' Sam said.

They returned an hour later. 'Dead of night,' Sam said, 'and not one fuckin' killer on the streets.'

They sat together through the small hours. Sam didn't speak again and Geordie let his mind tumble around inside his head. It was good to have Sam there; even better that he was quiet. When dawn cracked Sam got to his feet, did a stretch almost as good as one of Barney's. 'Got things to do,' he said. 'People to see. I'll catch you later.'

Geordie nodded.

Sam stood by the door for a couple of seconds. Then he took a step back into the room. He said, 'It's all right to look back, but you mustn't stare.'

FIFTY-ONE

Silence frightens people. The age in which we live is so ear-shatteringly noisy that when they are faced by muteness they become uneasy, as if part of their anatomy has been removed.

I am their silence.

The Trappists renounce speech as a mark of religious observance, preferring to commune in silence with the order of the universe. Traditionally we mark the death of someone special with a period of silence. And death itself, of course, is not renowned for kicking up a fuss.

When all is quiet, folk seem to think that a storm is brewing.

I have only spoken three words since they came for me. There was a remote possibility that they would have given me bail if I had spoken more, denied the charges they levelled against me. But I deny nothing; and neither do I admit that they are right. They are small people, the police, the prison authorities. They have no right to judge me.

Neither do they have the ability, the qualifications to judge acts of a higher nature. Their minds are ideally suited to the everyday, the domestic, the functioning of the PTA and the Highway Code.

They do not understand consequences, that one thing inevitably leads to another. They can never understand that, that one act becomes another.

Kant is Sade. That is what I told them. I ran the words into each other so it came out as three syllables: *Kantisade*. They brought in a senior police officer and asked me to repeat it. He shook his head and left the room. One of the brighter ones decided it was a foreign language and they brought in someone from the linguistics department of the university. He went away to confer with his colleagues.

Kantisade.

I have heard nothing from Miriam. They asked me about her, wanted to know if she was involved. I didn't answer. In my own mind I blamed her at first, for taking the bike. But it was my own fault. I shouldn't have kept it. She was late for work and thought it would be all right to use it.

They threatened me repeatedly and one of them took a swing at me in the cells. I didn't flinch. Took another full-bodied punch in the eye and stood there feeling it puff up as the blood raced towards the damaged tissue. I am not afraid of them. They are little men. They cannot touch me.

In the *Critique of Practical Reason* Kant said:

> Suppose that someone says his lust is irresistible when the desired object and opportunity are present. Ask him whether he would not control his passions if, in front of the house where he has this opportunity, a gallows were erected on which he would be hanged immediately after gratifying his lust. We do not have to guess very long what his answer may be.

This is seen as Kant externalizing the voice of conscience. But what he failed to take into account is the emergence of individuals who can only fully commit themselves to a night of passion and find joy there if they are threatened by some form of 'gallows'. I am not the only man and Miriam is not the only woman who needs to violate society's prohibitions in order to achieve sexual fulfilment.

Donatien Alphonse François Sade, known as the Marquis de Sade, showed us how, but it was Kant himself who set the ball rolling. In his definition of marriage, Kant describes it as 'the contract between two adults of the opposite sex about the mutual use of each other's sexual organs'.

An interesting phrase, is it not? And one that has been pored over for many hours in the universities of the Western world. Interesting because if we didn't know already that it was written by Kant, we might be persuaded that Sade penned it.

Kant is Sade because the two of them together allowed us, no, demanded, that we reduce the sexual partner to an object, and not only an object but a *partial* object. Sexual pleasure and gratification is dispensed via a bodily organ, not by a whole human person. Kant said so, and Sade said so. And Kant is Sade.

Together they are our heritage.

The temperature today is well below zero. The windows are encrusted with ice crystals. In the garden hoarfrost is nipping the leaves of the plants and a deep ground frost has turned the grass verges as white as an old man's beard. Even the pebbles on the drive are clinging together for warmth.

The inmates and the screws are suffering. They button up tightly. One of the inmates is called Jack the Shepherd because he is a pimp. This morning I watched him blow his nail. Later he handed me a sliver of glass. A simple tool which will allow me access to the fair blind maiden at the heart of my story.

FIFTY-TWO

S he came down the stairs with a small suitcase. Sam had already put her other bags in the boot of the Montego. He'd given up trying to convince her to stay. What was the point? A woman wants to stay, she'll stay. He didn't want to listen to all the bullshit about how she had a life, a job, commitments. Who wants to hear that stuff?

Oh, sure, he was glad about her having a life. Whaddaya think, he wants to put her in a cage, a museum, suffocate her with love? No, just leave it as it is. Her with her job and her commitments, walking out of the house as an independent being. Going back to big business and blind politics and designer clothes.

And his injured hand was playing up again. Numb this morning, no feeling in it. The hand standing in for the whole man.

'It's been good, Sam.'

'Yeah, yeah.'

'Really. I've enjoyed being here.'

I'm not about to argue. 'Sure.' And there's that smile on his face, designed to win Oscars.

Dressed for the weather: a three-button mohair coat with the collar up and underneath she's wearing a tube of a dress in blue silk that creates illusions about the length of her neck. There's a fur hat at one end and opaque tights at the other, sensible shoes.

She's standing close enough now and he has a quick whiff, trying to decide how much of it is her and how much the perfume. It's like trying to separate the toast from the marmalade once you've chewed them up. They go so well together you wouldn't do it if you could.

'We're going to keep in touch, aren't we?'

'Try and keep me away,' Sam said, hitting the right note, pacing it like a virtuoso. Competing with rich friends, middle-class sentiments, middle-of-the-road-mystical politics. He'd had a couple of stabs at it when he was young. Now it felt like a strain. Except it was her.

And there was no doubt about it: he needed a woman.

He took her bag and led her out to the car.

He unloaded at the other end but didn't stay. He put the bags and cases inside her bedroom door, to the left, along the wall, so she wouldn't trip over them. He headed off for a new case, just routine, but it needed organizing.

She held out her arms and their lips brushed against each other's cheek. 'I'll catch you later,' he said, backing away, not looking at her in case he saw what he'd done.

The Montego took him to JD's house without thinking about it. He rang the bell four times and was half-way down the path, leaving, when JD answered.

'I'm disturbing you,' Sam said.

'Too true. I'm trying to write a book here.'

'I'll come back later.'

'No, come in, it's not great literature.'

They sat and looked at each other. JD was wearing a ragged hand-knitted jumper that came down to his knees. 'You came to see me,' he said. 'So it's your turn to talk.'

'I just took Angeles home,' Sam said. 'So I thought I'd call in.'

'Angeles lives on the other side of town. You can't use that line. You weren't in the neighbourhood.'

'I was feeling low, my hand's playing up and I wanted to talk to somebody who hates the middle classes more than I do.'

'You're not going soon, then?'

'Going?'

'Leaving me alone to write my novel.'

'If you want, I'll go,' Sam said.

'It was a joke. Anyway I'm writing a chapter with deep emotional connotations. Lost love and betrayal. I need inspiration.'

'What d'you think about a grown woman who calls her parents Mummy and Daddy?'

JD laughed. 'Yeah. It puts you off. This Angeles?'

'Could be.'

'Signifies emotional immaturity.'

'Or could it be a cultural thing? Like that's the way they do it in their social group?'

JD scratched his head. 'Yeah. Could also be that the group itself is emotionally immature. Might be genetic. For example, there are certain crimes the middle class can't understand, like rage, say, or the way some people just love fighting, or they go straight for the jugular, can't wait to get in there and mix it. The middle classes think these things are inexplicable, or they're mental disorders, or the result of drugs. They can't understand that some people have violent personalities. They're blind to it. You can explain it to them, show them examples, but they still don't understand. D'you like her a lot?'

'Maybe.'

'What d'you look for in a woman?'

'One thing?'

'Yeah, just one.'

'Someone who can get through to me, someone who doesn't give a damn.'

'That's two.'

'I'm a fussy guy; minimum requirements.'

'And she fits the bill?'

'I want her to.'

'She's been asking around, wants to know what your face is like.'

'What did you tell her?'

'I said you look like a fucking turkey.'

Back home he stood in front of the mirror in the bathroom and remembered the thing he'd heard about Austrian girls. The mirror was cracked and the face in it was cracked as well. A cracked person. Someone with a flaw.

'C'mon,' he said. 'Show me someone without a flaw and I'll show you someone dangerous.'

But there's a mean somewhere. No flaws at all is way off, but how many flaws do you have to have before you go rolling down the opposite side of the hill?

He couldn't answer that one. Left it hanging in the air and went to use the phone. She picked up on the third ring. Said, 'Hello, Angeles Falco.' It was a pretty good sentence really. Didn't waste words and got the message across. Didn't leave any room for doubt.

'Hello?' She said it again. It was taking Sam a while to get his own words out because they had to come all the way up from his socks.

'I was out of order this morning,' he said.

'You don't have to apologize.'

'Tomorrow night?' he said. 'If you're free, we could talk. Maybe listen to some music?'

'Sounds good. I'm free.'

'Austrian girls,' he told her. 'Traditionally, in the country areas, they put apple slices in their armpits when they go dancing, and at the end of the evening they present them to the boy they like best.'

'Ugh,' she said down the line. 'That's disgusting.'

Sam laughed. 'Have I blown it?' he asked.

'No,' she said. 'But I don't suppose it will stop you trying.'

'Another thing,' he said. 'People tell me you've been asking what I look like.'

'A girl needs to know what she's getting herself into.'

'And now you think you know?'

'I know more than I did. Being blind makes me more focused.'

He put the phone back on the hook and returned to the cracked face in the cracked mirror. A distinct change had taken place; he looked as rampant as a billy-goat.

FIFTY-THREE

A ngeles was walking into things all morning. It was good to be back home, to have all her things around her, though it was quiet after Sam's house. She rubbed her shin and remembered that the stool was there for a purpose. A short time away and she had already forgotten the layout of her own house.

She missed his touch. When you're blind and you live with someone else they touch you all the time. And touch means so much more when you live in the dark. It undermines loneliness.

She switched the computer on and pushed an old Feliciano album into the CD slot. It opened with the acoustic guitar intro to 'California Dreaming', magically hustling Mamma Cass's wistful song into a soulful lament. Something to play for Sam, she thought, in return for 'Tomorrow is a Long Time', which he'd whispered to her in the dark that night by the fire.

The phone rang but when she picked it up there was no one there. At least there was no sound. Someone listening to her voice, to her breath? She put the handset back into its cradle and held it down with both hands. Surely they weren't giving him access to a phone. The man was in custody. They wouldn't let him have an outside line, wouldn't let him harass her. Would they?

A couple of days before they'd heard that he made a suicide attempt, slashed his wrists. So he wasn't in prison any more, he was in a hospital somewhere. But he'd be under guard.

She took the phone off the hook but put it back again. Don't let him panic you, she thought. He's been taken now, removed from the scene, don't let him reach over the divide and dictate your movements.

It couldn't be him, anyway. She was letting herself be spooked over nothing. There are other explanations. A hoax call? Some fault on the line? A crossed wire? If it had been him, he would have said something. He would have made it plain that he was still around.

Couldn't be him.

She watched the phone, expecting it to ring again at any moment. And then what would she do?

She took the CD out of the player and put it back in its case. The music wasn't working.

She remembered the time in the garden, when he'd been there, just before he attacked her. It had felt like this, the same sense of foreboding. The silence of the house seemed to deepen and the tiny sounds that are usually buried in the everyday took on a new significance. The ticking of a clock, the cracks and creaks of expansion and contraction, the movements of water draining through the heating system, all gave cause for concern.

Was there a footfall on the path outside or was it something else? Could her mind be playing tricks? She walked around the house, checking each door and window, locking herself away. She rang Sam at home but he didn't answer and she was about to try his office or the police when the ringing of the front doorbell rocked the house.

The sound seemed to take hold of the fabric of the building, to undermine the walls and the floors and penetrate through her feet and fingers up into her heart.

Angeles felt herself sway. For a moment it was as if she could see herself objectively, look down at her own body standing in the middle of her living room. There were two of her: the blind woman standing, terrified, with her mouth open, and another being equipped with seeing eyes and who lived at some higher vantage point, way above floor level.

The bell rang again, longer this time, causing the two aspects of Angeles to collide and merge back together. She took a step, wiped her brow, relieved that she was no longer split, fragmented. She recollected Aristotle's doctrine of courage as the right mean between cowardice and temerity.

She put her face close to the door and spoke. 'Who is it?'

Silence.

She asked again, louder this time, so there could be no doubt that whoever rang the bell would hear her. 'Yes, who is it?'

There was no reply. Angeles let out a long breath and strained to hear any sound or movement from the other side of the panelled door.

There was a rapping sound, knuckles on glass, but some way off. She thought it might be at a neighbour's house. Whoever had rung her bell was now checking next door.

But no, it couldn't be that far away. The sound was coming from her own house. It was coming from the rear of the house. And she'd been right first time, it was the sound of knuckles on glass. Knuckles on the glass of her patio door.

Angeles had no intention of going to answer it. She had no intention of going back to her sitting room. The memory of the man coming through that patio door, his hands on her throat, were too close, too vivid. She let her weight sink against the front door but kept her legs rigid, making sure she didn't slip down to the floor. It was far too tempting to adopt a foetal position.

The rapping came again, but this time there was an accompanying sound, not unlike the wail of a cat. Something grabbed hold of Angeles' consciousness and twisted its focus. The cry was not a cat but a human sound.

It was a baby.

Echo.

She rushed through to the sitting room and over to the window. 'Echo?' she said through the glass. 'Janet, is it you?'

'Open up, it's freezing out here.' Janet's voice was faint through the triple-glazing. Indistinct and yet undoubtedly friendly.

Angeles scrabbled at the lock and pulled open the door. She brushed away a hot flush of unwanted tears from her face. 'Oh, Jesus,' she said. 'Janet, come in, I'm so glad to see you.'

'Has something happened?' Janet asked.

'No, nothing. I'm being hysterical.'

Janet pushed Echo's pram through the patio door and closed it behind her. 'I'll make you a cup of tea,' she said. 'And I'm not leaving here until you tell me to.'

Angeles went upstairs to the lavatory. When she'd finished she flushed it and listened to the gulp as it consumed the water. She smiled; it was as if all of her portentous imaginings had been sucked into the plumbing.

Janet answered the second knock on the door and showed Detective Superintendent Rossiter and Detective Sergeant Hardwicke through to the sitting room.

'He's free, isn't he?' Angeles said, not giving the police time to speak. 'You've let him go.'

'We'll catch him,' Rossiter said. 'It's only a matter of time.'

Angeles took a deep breath. 'Janet, will you ring Sam and ask him to come and get me.'

'I'd prefer it if we took you into protective custody, Ms Falco,' Rossiter said. 'Just for a few hours. We have a safe house and you'd be under the protection of DS Hardwicke.'

Angeles imagined Hardwicke's professional demeanour.

Janet said: 'Sam's not in the office, I'm trying him at home.'

'I can't believe you let him go,' Angeles said.

'He slashed his wrist,' Hardwicke explained. 'They took him to hospital and he broke away from the guards taking him back to the prison, put one of them in hospital with a fractured skull.'

'I want to go to Sam's house,' Angeles said to the detectives. 'I'll be safe there.'

Rossiter shook his head. 'I'll leave an officer at your front door. When you're ready to move to Turner's house he'll accompany you and stay with you there as well.'

When they got to the door, Rossiter turned. 'This is not the course of action I would have recommended,' he said.

'You've already made that clear,' Angeles told him.

FIFTY-FOUR

Sam was up all night, drinking coffee, playing half-remembered songs from a dozen different albums. He didn't find the one he wanted, got waylaid in a street full of memories. By the time the frozen dawn threw up some light he'd had time to think about it for a while. Played some old Sonny Terry tracks, the volume turned down low, let the blind man take him into a new day.

Slept in a chair for five hours and woke with a crick in his neck and a sluggish consciousness. There was a lassitude about him that he used to call depression. Outside the light was poor, as though the day couldn't be bothered to make the effort.

He browned some toast, thought about going round to Geordie and Janet's house, play the uncle to Echo, try to recover slivers of his soul from the fragmented night. But that wouldn't work, he wasn't the best company with the wind of the old days blowing through his hair.

He set off towards the office on foot, walking through a world composed of silvery frost crystals, long pale shadows cast by a frigid sun. The people of the city had found scarves and gloves and shiny noses, their faces framed in woollen hats. Sam tried to pick out the drinkers, isolate the lonely, separate the rich from the poor, but most of them had perfect masks. These days you had to dig deep for identity. Sometimes you tunnelled right through to the other side without finding anyone. Bodies without egos. Victims of millennium culture; game-show consciousness.

At the office door he turned around and walked back along Parliament Street, past Betty's and Debenhams, past Laura Ashley and the new façades of the banks, the stalls set out for the tourist trade. He bought a copy of the street paper off a middle-aged man with an unfortunate sales technique – *Big Issue*, sir; *Big Issue*, madam. *Big Issue*, sir; *Big Issue*, madam – and gave it away to another seller on the other side of the street. He'd abandoned reading them years back. Beggars were hustling for the prime sites, their penny whistles and mouth organs only partially effective shields against police harassment.

The world wasn't constructed with consciousness, it was fashioned out of fear and greed, and all of its inhabitants were in hiding. They were there on the street, in open view, but each of them was purblind to the predicament of the others. Their buzzword was 'communication' but the signals they gave out semaphored only their paralysis of choice. We're all puppets, he thought, our strings being jerked this way and that by genetic and social patterning. The result was a race of fools, men and women who believed they could manipulate Satan.

He cut through to Coney Street and walked back towards the library. Upstairs in the reference section he began ploughing through microfiches for the year which marked Angeles Falco's fifth birthday.

Headlines activated memories – '*Nixon Denies All Knowledge of Watergate*'; '*Guildford Pub Bombings*'; '*Arab-Israeli War*' – tales of treachery and revenge, intrigue and inhumanity in the name of wealth and power. It was one of the years in which Sam Turner had obliterated himself with alcohol, a time in which he had stopped reacting to everything but crises. And more than once a crisis had gone past without him being aware of it.

The trouble with microfiche is that it's not a database, you can't search for a word or a date or anything else. All you can do is plough through page after page of mainly trivial local detail. There was the occasional murder or embezzlement, a couple of mysterious disappearances and a hint of a sexual scandal involving one of the local councillors. There was an almost unbelievable report about an apotemnophiliac – someone who can only achieve sexual satisfaction or fulfilment through the amputation of a limb – who had lost faith in conventional medicine, laid his leg across a railway line and waited for a train to come. The guy had drunk himself unconscious while he waited and when he woke he was a new-born amputee with a hard-on.

Sam let the breath come out between his teeth. Wondered what genuine amputees thought about a guy like that.

Genuine? Who's sitting in the judge's chair?

He took one fiche out and replaced it with another, rubbed his eyes, and there it was, the article he'd come here to find.

Tragedy of Local Lifesaver Hero

A fireman was killed today, but only after he had saved the lives of two small girls on a village pond.

Angeles and Isabel Falco, both of them under five years old, had strayed on to the ice-covered pond in the tiny village of Whenington.

As the ice began to break up the local fire service went into action and fireman Alan Jenkins crawled out to the girls on a ladder.

He successfully plucked one of the children to safety but the second girl fell into the freezing water.

Fireman Jenkins did not hesitate, he plunged into the water after her and eyewitnesses reported an agonizing wait until he returned to the surface with the child held aloft.

Unfortunately, the fireman did not have enough strength to save himself and immediately after placing the girl on the safe haven of the ladder, he sank into the depths and drowned.

The two girls were taken to the local hospital, where they will be detained overnight.

Fireman Alan Jenkins leaves a wife and a young son of six years.

Sam made a note of the date and set off for the *Evening Press* offices in Walmgate in the dark. While he'd been trekking through microfiches the night had tumbled in on the town. His friend Sly Beaumont, the oldest serving journalist in the north, would remember the case and be able to fill in the background. Sly, with a face as creased and worn as an old glove and the memory of an elephant.

'You wrapped up another one, then, Sam,' he said.

'We got the guy out of circulation, but there's still a couple of loose ends to tie up.'

'Like why he did it?'

'You don't think that's important?'

'Not as much as you do, Sam. The most important thing was to get him off the street. Anything else is a bonus.'

'Life gets miserable without the occasional bonus.'

'So how can I help?'

'You remember the Falco sisters being in a pond accident when they were small?'

'Should I?'

'Yeah. You wrote a piece in the press about it. Village pond in winter? A fireman was drowned.'

Sly scratched his head. 'Jenkins,' he said. 'Alan Jenkins, local hero. Yeah, I do remember now, two little kids, I hadn't put it together that they were the Falcos. And, oh my god, Rod Jenkins is his son?'

'You're getting there,' Sam said. 'What do you remember about the case?'

'It was tragic. The fireman, Alan Jenkins; everybody knew him. The year before he'd saved a young colleague after the guy collapsed in a warehouse fire. He got some kind of medal for that. Went to the palace, was on television, in the papers. Good-looking guy, mop of blond hair, strong as an ox, he was. They reckoned he got cramp in the cold water, the muscles in his limbs just stopped working. It must've been bitter in there.'

'What I don't understand,' Sam said, 'Angeles Falco told me the story just like it happened, but she didn't mention the guy drowning.'

'They didn't tell the kids,' Sly said. 'The parents thought they'd had enough trauma with the accident.'

'And what about Jenkins' son?' Sam asked. 'He must've grown up nursing a revenge fantasy. He killed Isabel and if we hadn't ferreted him out, he'd have found a way to get to Angeles.'

'I remember him vaguely,' Sly said. 'Not after his father was killed; his mother kept him out of the way after that. But we interviewed Alan Jenkins when he got the medal and the lad was there then. Rod; was he called Rod? Beaming, he was, his eyes shining like his father was Superman. Beautiful young kid, the two of them together looking like a couple of generations of Norse gods.'

'And just as tragic,' said Sam.

'Yeah. But you wouldn't have guessed it then. They looked like they ruled the world. And when Jenkins showed us the medal, I've never seen a kid look more proud.'

Sam got to his feet, ready to go. Sly walked around his desk but the telephone rang and he picked it up without thinking. 'Sly Beaumont.'

'I'm off,' Sam said. 'Thanks for the info.'

Sly covered the mouthpiece with his hand. 'It's a pleasure, Sam. Any time.'

'See you.' Sam left the office, walked down the stairs and out into the street. He turned back towards the town and hadn't gone more than a hundred metres when he heard Sly Beaumont calling after him.

He waited for the old reporter to catch up with him. 'Going my way, Sly?'

'No.' Beaumont was breathing hard. 'I'm not going anywhere at all.'

FIFTY-FIVE

Scopophilia. The art of deriving sexual stimulation by watching. Voyeurism to you. Except that the voyeur is someone who watches without participation. I am an active player.

There are two women in the house. The blind one and a young woman with a baby. At the front door there is a uniformed policeman. This is a complication. I don't want complications. I want to finish it now. I shall have to be strong.

The first thing I do is retrieve the roll of syringes and Suxamethonium from its hiding place by the swimming pool. I fit the microphone of my voice-activated recorder to the lapel of my jacket; the recorder itself goes in my shirt pocket. I notice the hard crust of ice which has covered the surface of the pool. I touch it with two fingers to test its strength and I see a vision of a saint floating in the dark water below.

I put emotion and feelings to one side. For the task ahead I need to be cool and calm and collected.

The next job is to cut the telephone connection, to isolate the occupants of the house. I move stealthily, like a cat.

In the garden shed I find a piece of hacksaw blade and put it in my pocket. There is also a lump hammer, a crowbar, a long Phillips drive and several metres of old rope smelling of tar. I take these objects back to the shadow of the house. I carry the lawn-mower in my head.

The telephone wire enters the house via a conduit along the outside wall. By following it I find a break where the engineer had to run the cable around a corner. I saw through it, making sure that the ends of the wires are not touching.

I fill two of the syringes with enough Suxamethonium to pacify a bask of crocodiles. The moon is high and it has a face just like it did when I was a child. I review the plan in my mind, double-check to make sure I've reduced the element of chance to a minimum. My toes are numb with cold; my fingers stiff. I have been too busy to notice the cold.

I climb the fence into the next-door garden. I walk down by the side of the house and when I draw level with the policeman on the blind woman's doorstep I stop and say good evening.

He nods his head, fingers the collar of his coat.

I ask him if something is wrong, ambling across the driveway towards him. 'Because I thought I heard something round the back.'

He moves towards me, reaching for the radio on his belt. 'You'd better show me, sir,' he says.

I let him go ahead of me and push the syringe into the fleshy spot behind his right ear. He turns. The radio is in his hand; he holds it there while I watch his eyes go dead. Then he drops to his knees and I take the radio away from him an instant before he falls on his face. I drag him to the rear of the house, bind and gag him and lay him on the floor of the garden shed.

Now I am ready. I reason that the best way to get into the house is to knock on the front door. Whichever of them opens it I simply have to rush them. I have surprise on my side. If they refuse to open the door, they will be trapped inside. They cannot telephone out. I shall have ample time to go around the back and throw the lawn-mower through the sitting room window.

If I don't win with my first strategy, I still can't lose.

This is a nice neighbourhood. Professional people who keep themselves to themselves. Socio-economic class 1–1.2. They don't go prying into each other's business. The likelihood of someone calling round to borrow a cup of sugar is remote.

With real estate of this value the boundaries are strictly observed. High hedges mark off each householder's title and these people are so rich that they aren't actually interested in their neighbours' activities. To acquire and maintain great wealth the ego must be constantly tumescent.

As I tap lightly on the front door I am in a state of high excitement. The blood is rushing through my veins like a swollen river. I can feel the pressure as it passes my temples on its way to oxygenate the brain. There is movement inside the house and I have to keep telling myself to breathe as my ears strain to hear the approaching footsteps. It is not Angeles Falco's voice that I hear: 'Someone at the door. I'll get it.'

The latch is lifted and like something out of the storybooks we had as children, I am bathed in the soft light from the hallway. The woman looks at me and smiles and in the same instant she recognizes me. Angeles Falco's voice comes floating down the stairs: 'No, don't answer it.' There is despair in her voice.

As the woman who has opened the door is rearranging her facial expression – from a happy smile of welcome to something between revulsion and sheer terror – I move in. I go for her throat but the needle actually enters the side of her neck. I shoot a dose of the drug into her and she pulls away. For a moment I wonder if I have injected any of the substance into her, but I don't have to wonder for long.

'What have you done?' she asks. She's looking at the syringe in my hand. She raises her hand to her neck and looks at it. But already I can see the drug going to work. She totters for a moment, then falls into the pile of the carpet.

I have a back-up syringe but I'm not going to need it. The one I am carrying is still more than half-full.

Soft footsteps on the stairs. 'Janet, who is it? Is there someone there?' I stand by the fallen body and hold my breath. She comes around the corner, into the hallway and stops dead. Her feet are bare. She cannot see anything. She feels that something is wrong but she doesn't know what it is. 'Janet?' She speaks the woman's name quietly. She knows I have come for her and she doesn't want me to hear.

She is so close to me that I can see the network of small creases around her eyes. I can hear the way her respiration has become jerky and unreliable. Her lips are trembling and I can smell whiskey. If I stretch out my arm towards her, still holding my breath, the point of the syringe is only half a metre from her neck. She takes an involuntary step backwards, her blind eyes staring, her nostrils flaring. She is like a thoroughbred filly spooked by a wolf.

To fight or take flight. This is the age-old formula with which she is faced. All animals display the same characteristics when they are trapped. But most animals know what it is that they have to fight, and they know from what they have to flee. This woman knows nothing. Except, perhaps, that she cannot win. That whatever she does will lead to the same result.

She takes another step backwards and moves her right arm towards the phone. She picks it up and holds it to her ear. Another flash of panic crosses her face. She depresses the hook-switch and listens again. The silence gags her, it sends a tremor of certainty through her body.

'I've come to collect,' I tell her.

She drops the telephone, lets it slip out of her hand, but she doesn't move. Her hand remains where it was, near her face, as if she was still holding the instrument. 'Who are you? Where's Janet?'

I don't reply. She knows who I am. I take a step towards her and she reaches for the wall. 'Where's Janet? What have you done with her?'

'Take three steps forward,' I tell her. 'Short ones, or you'll stand on her.'

She hesitates. She moves forward by feeling the area in front of her with her toes. It is as if I had directed her through a maze or an area of open country littered with animal traps. She is fearful that a set of iron claws will snap around her legs. She takes the third step and nudges the inert body with her foot. She comes with a tiny cry and falls to her knees. Her hands are on the woman's face. She cradles her head, relieved that Janet is still alive, that she can feel her breathing, however lightly.

'What have you done to her?' she asks. 'What do you want of me?'

I can reach her easily now. I push the point of the syringe into the back of her neck and depress the plunger. 'You bastard,' she says. 'Leave us alone.'

She goes down like a tree. Within a few seconds there is a mound of unconscious female flesh in front of me.

I open the front door and bring in the lump hammer, the crowbar, the screwdriver and the rope. I drop the latch and lock the door with the mortise lock as well; good-quality stuff, several levers to impede the most determined thief.

They are like dead lovers, these women. A tangle of arms and legs. I separate them and even within their paralyses they seem to cling to each other. Their mouths are gaping and their bodies are convulsed by uncoordinated muscular contractions. The blind woman is salivating copiously, sputum discharging on to the carpet.

I truss Janet like a turkey, her hands and legs bound together behind her back. With a sharp knife from the kitchen I cut a strip from her skirt and use it to gag her. The finished result is somehow fashionable, everything neatly complementing each other. I don't mind for myself, but I know women are keen to appear at their best even in the most extreme situations. Miriam, if she were here with us now, would be very happy with the work I have done on Janet. If there are photographs in the newspapers, it could even catch on. One of the top fashion designers will wrap it up as a revival of *bondage chic*.

Using the rope between her hands and feet I lug her through to a small alcove in the sitting room where her baby is sleeping in a pram. They can be together there, out of the way.

The blind woman I secure less rigorously. Her hands behind her back and her legs tied together at ankles and knees. There is no need for a gag. I lift her on to a couch.

I found Doncaster prison interesting from a professional point of view. It was, of course, a flagship prison when it was opened. The idea of a privately run prison had not been discussed in the community and was introduced by a government that was already rife with corruption. It was soon, and rightly, christened Donca-traz.

The initial teething problems are over now but the place is overcrowded and there have been at least ten suicides of inmates within the last five years. I saw much blood there and many of the prisoners looked little more than children.

I look at the policeman's radio. It crackles occasionally and coded messages are passed back and forth. There is no mention of this road or the Falco name. I know it is only a matter of time, but I have to wait for the blind woman to come round.

I slashed my wrist as the prison officer approached my cell. He

301

was very good, didn't panic at all. He removed his tie and used it as a tourniquet. Not only did he save my life; I didn't actually lose much blood. It was messy, of course, the blood spurting out with every beat of my heart. But it was not as bad as it looked.

I feigned unconsciousness while they rushed me to the hospital. The same guard accompanied me all the way, stayed with me while they hooked me up to the transfusion equipment. I remember watching him in the chair with his sodden tie rolled up in his hands. I slept for several hours. A peaceful, dreamless sleep.

No one stopped me. You don't stand in the way of destiny.

I walk over to the window and part the curtains so that I can see the street. All is quiet out there. My moment is approaching. I place my worries out of reach.

I found Wells' *The Country of the Blind* in the prison library and read it for the first time in my life. Perhaps I should have given fiction more of a chance, but I always preferred to read scientific, factual texts, or religion, or philosophy.

The Country of the Blind is a satirical story about a man who accidentally falls into a secluded valley. The people who live there have all lost their sight and been blind for the last fifteen generations. As a result they have developed their own religion and creation myths and have lost all of the words for sight. They sleep by day and work by night.

The central character, who can see, is called Nunez, and he expects that he will have an advantage over the people of the valley, that he will be their king. But every attempt on his part to show his superiority is met with failure. The blind people regard him as clumsy and insensitive and when he falls in love with one of their women they are reluctant to allow the marriage in case it corrupts their race.

The solution, of course, is that he agrees to allow the blind surgeons to remove his eyes. If he goes ahead with the operation, everything will be his. His life in the valley will be a fulfilled and fulfilling experience because the valley is a kind of paradise containing 'all that the heart of man could desire'.

But rather than conform to that society by giving up his eyes, Nunez decides to attempt an impossible escape by scaling the sheer mountain walls. He chooses to die in a small cleft of rock almost a mile high, content and with a smile on his face. The human spirit soars away from the pain of conformity and acceptance, though the cost may be physical extinction.

I read the story at a sitting, then I read it again. I put the book down and thought about what I had read and wondered at the workings of destiny. What had brought me to Doncatraz where the book was waiting? I read *The Country of the Blind* a third time.

I check the street through the curtains again. Then I bring some water in a glass tumbler and sprinkle it on the blind woman's face. She doesn't move. I check the back garden through the window of the patio door. All is dark and frozen. The swimming pool is a village pond.

There was an altercation between the prison guard and the hospital authorities. The doctors wanted to keep me in the hospital for another day, but the prison guards wanted me back in Doncatraz. They put me on a trolley and wheeled me down the long corridor to the waiting van that would take me back to my cell. The original guard, the one who saved my life, was still with us. He had a new tie on, there was no trace of my blood on him, but it was the same man. I insisted on standing when we got to the hospital exit. The guard came to help me and I lifted him off his feet and rushed him into the wall. He was on his back on the floor, trying to get to his feet. I grabbed the trolley and rammed it at him, crushing his head between the wall and the heavy metal wheels.

I turned to take on the hospital porters, but they didn't want any trouble. Not one of them made a move towards me.

The blind woman moans and stirs on the couch. I wait until she is fully conscious, then I drag her into a sitting position. There is a feral odour to her and I imagine some kind of vaginal discharge has occurred.

'He should have left you in the dark under the ice,' I tell her.

'I don't want to die.'

'He should have left you there.'

'Who? What are you talking about?'

I laugh. 'You know exactly who and what,' I tell her. 'My father gave his life for you.'

'This is a mistake. No one gave his life. If something happened to your father, I'm sorry. But it has nothing to do with me.'

I want to cause her pain. I want to go to her and take different parts of her body and crush them. I want to hear her screaming.

'Be careful what you say,' I tell her. 'I'm on a knife-edge.'

'Start again,' she says, placatory now. 'I'll try to understand.'

'You and the other one,' I say. 'You're on the ice.'

She looks genuinely puzzled. Shakes her head from side to side. 'We were children,' she says eventually. 'You mean on the pond, when we were children?'

'He comes on a ladder.'

'Yes, the fireman came on a ladder. He saved our lives.'

'You go under the ice and he dives in after you. He pulls you out of the water but he stays behind. He sinks to the bottom. It was your grave and he died in it.'

'He didn't die,' she says. 'This's a mistake. The fireman didn't die. No one died.'

'The fireman was my father,' I tell her. 'He never came home again. He died that you might live.' Somehow I am falling apart. My personality is fragmenting. I have to use all my energy, all my willpower to maintain my identity and my purpose.

'No one told me,' she says. She has been quiet for a while and now, when she speaks, it is in a whisper. 'But it fits. They wouldn't have told us. We were too young.'

I leave her words there. I let them echo. I do not say that I was too young as well, but that no one could hide it from me.

'I'm sorry,' she says. 'I'm truly sorry.'

'In the country of the blind,' I tell her, 'the one-eyed man is king.'

'Oh,' she says, as if she has never heard it before.

'If you had been a good woman,' I tell her, 'it would have been all right. I would have accepted it. But your life has been useless.'

'I can make it up,' she says. 'I didn't know he'd died. I can try to make it up to you.'

'It would have been better for the world if he had lived and you had died. I'm here to put that right.'

'What are you going to do?'

I laugh a wild uncontrolled laugh. It is something that I'm not surprised to find inside me, although I never knew it was there. 'We're going skating,' I tell her. 'Ice skating.'

FIFTY-SIX

Geordie was sitting alone in the house when the police came looking for Rod Jenkins, the guy who had killed Ralph. He talked to them on the doorstep. 'Keep your doors locked,' said the auburn-haired WDS Hardwicke. 'He killed your brother so he might have something against you as well.'

'Right.' Geordie closed the door. Locked it.

He went back to the chair.

He wished Janet was there with him. That they were locked in the house together. He got to his feet suddenly, pulled out of the chair by the thought that it was Janet who had identified Jenkins.

He was pulling on his leather jacket. He got his sheepskin-lined boots out of the cupboard under the stairs and hit the road. The policewoman in the car outside watched him go, shaking her head in disbelief. Geordie didn't stop to explain. If this guy was on the street, he'd be looking to finish Angeles Falco, and Janet and his daughter Echo were with the blind woman . . .

Geordie went around the back of the house and over the wall. He could see clearly in the moonlight. There were lights on in the bedroom and in what appeared to be a ground-floor kitchen. Thick drapes were closed around a patio door. He strained to hear but there was only silence.

He moved slowly from tree to tree, past the frozen swimming pool, intending to get close enough to the house to put his ear against the wall. It would be Echo's feeding time soon and if she was in there, she'd broadcast it to the world.

When he reached the ash tree he paused. In front of the patio

305

door was a paved area and he didn't want to take the chance of making audible footfalls. If Janet and Echo were being held in the house, the last thing he wanted was to warn their captor that he was here.

He felt rather than heard a movement behind him. As he turned he was pinned to the tree by powerful arms and a gloved hand smothered any sound that might have come from his lips. With his face up against the dark bark of the tree he could see the movement of a small insect draped in the red and black colours of anarchy. Sam's voice in his ear whispered, 'Don't suppose you thought to bring coffee.'

'Nearly shit myself,' Geordie whispered when Sam released him. He followed Sam back up the garden, away from the house. Looked like Sam was going to sit on the stone bench next to the swimming pool. Maybe break through the ice and have a moonlight swim. He stopped at the pool and tested the ice with one foot. It looked solid but Geordie felt his hair rise from his scalp when Sam stepped off the side of the pool and moved on to the crystallized surface. It creaked and groaned but held his weight.

He left the ice and went down on all-fours at the side of the bench, disappearing under a bush. Geordie went after him and found himself in a small clearing with enough room for the two of them to sit cross-legged like a couple of Buddhas. Sam had found a plank of wood somewhere and put it on the earth to insulate them from the ground-frost.

'Nice,' Geordie said. 'This your den?'

He began to scramble out again but Sam stopped him. 'Wait.'

'No,' Geordie said. 'Janet and Echo're in there with the guy who killed Ralph.'

'And you're gonna bring 'em out?'

'You bet.'

'Listen, Geordie. If we try to break in, he's gonna hear us. It's not possible to get in quick enough to save them. We're better off waiting until he makes his move.'

Geordie shook his head. 'I don't know if I can do that, Sam. What about we get a ladder and go in through the bedroom window?'

'We have to wait,' Sam said. 'The guy's interested in Angeles.

306

He'll be bringing her out here. When he does that you can go around him and get Janet and Echo out the front door.'

Geordie thought about it. He didn't know the exact numbers but he reckoned if they counted how many times Sam had been right and how many times Geordie had been right, Sam'd come out tops. The guy seemed to have an instinct for these situations. Geordie just wanted to go in there, all guns blazing. Except he didn't have a gun. Sam was different. He was sure. He could sit on a plank and wait, all night if necessary. The guy better come out soon, though; the two of them would be ice-statues by the morning.

'What's with walking on the ice?' he asked. 'You gonna take up skating?'

'An informed hunch,' Sam said. 'The swimming pool is one of the reasons we're here. The main reason that Rod Jenkins is here.'

'Save it,' Geordie said. 'I just want my family back.'

The moon walked the night sky and Geordie watched. There was a moment when the orb seemed to become blood and he reared up involuntarily in the bushes. Sam pulled him down again and he felt the older man's arm around his shoulders. He watched their breath turn to ice as it mingled together, listened to the call of an owl and the tiny far-off shriek of something caught in a beak.

'If anything happens to them,' he said, 'I'll never get over it.'

Sam pulled him closer. There had been tight spots in the past, and they'd managed to come through. But back then it had been Sam and Geordie who were facing danger and the danger was an acceptable risk because that was their job. It was what they did for a living. Janet and Echo didn't deserve to be held like this. They were innocents. They shouldn't have been here at all, in this house with Angeles.

Geordie wondered if he should go to the house and explain to the guy. Tell him to let Janet and Echo go, take him instead. Take anyone else in the whole world, but don't hurt Echo, for the love of God don't do anything to Janet and Echo.

It became a chant for him. He felt himself swaying as he silently intoned the words, *Jan-et, Ech-o, Jan-et, Ech-o*. Geordie had once been to a Sufi *dhikr*, years back, when he was on the street. Someone invited him and he went along because they said there'd be food. After every prayer the Sufis did a mime of washing their hands and faces. He remembered them sitting around in a circle, the men with hats, the women with scarves covering their heads, together chanting the name of God: *All-ah, All-ah, All-ah* . . . They said it brought Him closer.

Sam touched his arm and the chanting in his head stopped, became one with the silence of the frozen night. He followed Sam's eyes and peered through the gloom at the house. The curtains that had covered the glass of the patio door had been drawn back. Inside the house was the tall blond man, Rod Jenkins. He was kneeling at the feet of Angeles. Geordie shifted his position slightly to get a better look, but Sam told him to be still.

Geordie could see that Angeles had her arms tied behind her back and that Jenkins was untying a rope from around her ankles. The blind woman was frail and unsure of her balance. Even from this distance it was clear that her lips were trembling.

Jenkins removed the rope from her ankles and tied it around her neck. He led her to the patio door and there was a crack as he unlocked it and slid it open. As the house became accessible Geordie wanted to rush over there and find his wife and daughter. Sam's grip of him hardened. 'Sit it out, kid,' he said softly. 'He'll come to us. The longer we can keep shtoom, the better our chances'll be.'

The man led Angeles across the garden. As they approached the swimming pool it was clear that Angeles was murmuring softly to herself. Geordie couldn't make out if she was uttering some kind of prayer or if the sounds coming from her throat were incoherent ramblings. She stumbled and almost fell, but Jenkins tugged at the rope around her neck and pulled her upright.

The guy's eyes were staring. He wasn't observing what was going on around him. He could see Angeles and he could see where he was leading her, his intentions for her. But he was blind to the possibilities of anything interfering with his plans.

He had the rope in his right hand, Angeles tethered to the end of it; and he carried a heavy crowbar in the same hand. In the crook of his left arm was a small bundle. Geordie wished he had some kind of weapon, but it was too late now. If he was to get past the guy, he'd have to be able to dodge the crowbar. One good crack with that would split a skull like a coconut; it'd fertilize the winter soil with cerebral spinal fluid.

Geordie's eyes kept being drawn back to the open patio door. Were Janet and Echo in there? Maybe he'd been wrong and they'd gone somewhere else instead. Janet had a couple of friends on the other side of town, Margaret and Trudy, and she'd been talking recently about taking Echo to see them.

Then he heard Echo's cry. It wasn't a cry of distress, just the noise she made when she wanted attention. The problem with the cry was that it didn't come from the house at all. The sound hadn't travelled from the patio door; it was much closer than that. Echo was wrapped in the bundle of clothes under the guy's arm. She was a joint hostage with Angeles, and the two of them together were being taken to the frozen swimming pool. Above them the stars were pressing down out of the night sky.

'Shhhhh,' Sam said, maintaining his grip of Geordie. 'Wait.'

Where was Janet, then? Geordie looked back at the house but there was no movement or sound to suggest that she was there. If Janet was conscious, she'd be screaming at the top of her voice. If she was tied to a bed or a wardrobe she'd find the strength to drag the thing after her. Janet wouldn't let anyone take Echo away from her.

In the back of his mind was a dark pebble that suggested Janet was lying dead in the house. He knew that if he gave that thought any credence, the pebble would metamorphose into a rock large enough to crush him. That's not happened, he told himself. She might be in the house or she might be somewhere else, but wherever she was she was safe. Still safe, waiting for him to come for her.

The blond guy led Angeles to the edge of the ice-covered swimming pool. He stood behind her while the tremor of her lips unfurled into her face and spread along her limbs until she was shaking from head to foot. Geordie felt Sam easing himself into a springing position beside him. He moved slowly, careful not to disturb the undergrowth or draw attention to himself in any way. The guy adjusted his hold of Echo and she made an appreciative sound that almost ripped Geordie's heart out.

The three of them were ten metres away, but the ground between them was shrubbed and uneven. It would not be an easy task to get to them before the guy could shove Angeles or Echo on to the ice.

Rod Jenkins said something that Geordie didn't catch and it seemed that Angeles didn't hear him either. He repeated it: 'Take a step forward.'

She shook her head.

'It's you or the kid.'

'No, stop,' Angeles said. She put a foot forward and then withdrew it. She took control of her body, the shaking stopped and she stepped forward on to the ice.

'Further,' Jenkins said.

Angeles took another step and the ice groaned under her weight. The scream that came from her lips was like a bandsaw.

Jenkins swung the crowbar and it caught her on the shoulder. She tottered for a moment then went down, face-forward on the ice. Jenkins dropped Echo and the child rolled into the grass verge, only really complaining when she had come to a stop.

The tall blond man was berserk now. He strode around the swimming pool hacking away at the ice with the crowbar. He was shouting at Angeles, telling her how it would be when the black water sucked her under. His voice was competing with the cries of Angeles and the baby and the fracturing of the ice as his crowbar chopped away at it.

'Go,' Sam said, and he and Geordie reared up in the bushes and leapt out into the open. Geordie went straight for Echo, retrieved her and held her close to him. He turned to watch as Sam hurled himself at Rod Jenkins. The blond turned in time to see him and he raised the crowbar over his head. But Sam's velocity carried him forward with the momentum of an express train. His foot connected with Jenkins' chest and the guy was hurled backwards on to the ice. The crowbar spun away from his grip and was lost in the night.

'OK,' Sam said to Angeles. 'Don't worry. We'll get you out of there.' He went on to the ice and stepped gingerly towards her. He reached out to her and she plunged towards his hand as though she could actually see it.

Although the impact of Sam's boot and his fall to the ice had stunned Jenkins, he still wasn't out of the equation. He pulled himself to his feet and searched in the undergrowth for the crowbar. When he couldn't find it he turned back to the swimming pool and ran towards it. He jumped high in the air like Geordie used to do when he was a lad in Sunderland, pulling up his legs and wrapping his arms around them, ready to bomb the water. As he landed the already weakened ice cracked apart like a shattered windscreen that has been punched through.

Jenkins disappeared immediately. He didn't make a sound, the dark water sucked him below the surface and he was gone. Geordie looked towards the patio door and took a few steps in the direction of the house. But his attention was drawn back towards the swimming pool.

The combined weight of Sam and Angeles at the other end of the pool capsized the now broken ice. The free end of the plate of ice rose up in a jagged silhouette and both Sam and Angeles called out as they toppled into the black water.

Geordie was torn between running to the house to find Janet and staying to see if Sam and the blind woman could be saved. His mind was working at a hundred miles an hour and getting nowhere.

He put Echo down on the frozen grass and told her to wait. He raced back to the pool and ran around to the spot where Angeles and Sam had disappeared. There was no sign of them for a moment and then suddenly the surface was broken by the appearance of Angeles' head. She reached out and Geordie grabbed her and began dragging her out of the water. Sam's head appeared behind her and Geordie could see that he was pushing her as Geordie was pulling. The water was so cold that Geordie lost all feeling in his fingers after only a few seconds contact.

He hauled her up and out of the water and she lay coughing and spluttering on the side of the pool. Geordie turned back to Sam and was barely in time to see the older man's head disappearing below the surface again. Sam's eyes were dead. Geordie watched his boss going down, but there was no returning glance from Sam. He was not going to come up again.

Geordie stopped thinking. He took the rope that was around Angeles' neck and tied it around his wrist. The other end he tied around the wrist of the blind woman. 'I'm going after Sam,' he said. 'When you feel me tug, pull us up.'

And he jumped in.

311

Jesus Christ. The water was like a vice. He was completely blind down there. It was like being immersed in pitch. He could not see his own hands and was rapidly losing all feeling in them. His lungs were bursting and the surface of his body was like a fire.

He crawled along the bottom and found an object. Something heavy. He made out clothing, the leg of a pair of trousers, a shoe. He tugged on the rope and felt his body being pulled back to the surface. He hung on to Sam's leg.

'There's a ladder,' Angeles said. 'Over here, in the corner.' She dragged on the rope and Geordie let himself be led. He listened to the sound of police sirens in the distance.

Together they pulled Sam's inert body out of the water. His face and lips were livid. A fine froth lay around his mouth and nostrils. Geordie went to work on him like he'd learned in the classes. He opened Sam's mouth and looked inside for obstructions. He gave mouth-to-mouth resuscitation, alternating external heart compressions with the heel of his hand. After a few moments Sam coughed and spat water from his mouth.

The police arrived but Geordie carried on working until a pair of paramedics took over. He watched while Sam and Angeles were both loaded on to stretchers and taken away. Then he found Echo and took her into the house. A policeman had just finished untying Janet and taken the gag from her mouth. She was sitting on the floor rubbing her wrists, a piece of her skirt had been cut away but she didn't look as though she was injured.

She reached out her arms for Echo, and Geordie handed his daughter over. He crouched down beside them and put his arms around them and he would have cried if he could have stayed conscious for long enough. As it was all he could remember later was that everything, the whole world, slewed over to the left and his mind went racing down a helter-skelter of incomprehension. He didn't mind, though; he knew at the end of it he'd still have his family.

FIFTY-SEVEN

Sam was blind. Images tumbled over in his mind like the garments in a washing machine. Voices belonging to forgotten and forbidden memories played at the edge of consciousness. He could hear his daughter, Bronte, and his first wife, Donna, strangely freed from the hit-and-run that had taken their lives so many years before. Gus, his old partner, not talking but laughing, like he'd just heard the joke of the century.

There was the clinking of glasses and bottles as all the booze he'd ever poured down his throat was lined up on a mahogany bar for another round.

In the far distance the princely voices of childhood friends came and went, and all the women were there, barefoot, silently watching.

There was nothing substantial. All was ethereal. Pieces of moonlight.

She was there when he opened his eyes, sitting quietly by the bed. He didn't speak or move but she knew he'd come back. She lifted her head and smiled and reached for his hand, came to sit on the edge of the bed.

'How're you doing?' he asked.

'I'm fine,' she said. 'We've been worried about you.' She reached for his face and traced the bruises there with the tips of her fingers. He didn't want her to stop; it felt good, like she was getting to know him all over again.

'I didn't want to drown in someone else's wine,' he said. It just came out of him, and he liked the sound of it, kind of poetic, fitting for the darkened ward and the way they were close to each other.

She smiled self-consciously. 'Are you looking at me?' she asked.

'What d'you think?'

'It makes me feel good.'

'Touché.'

He didn't speak for some time, drifted away into unconsciousness. When he opened his eyes she was still there. A real nice surprise.

'Thought you'd've gone,' he said.

'No,' she whispered. 'I'll watch you through the night.'